ONE IN A MILLION

ONE IN A MILLION

TONY FAGGIOLI

For my father...who gave so much for one little boy. And who was always happiest when that boy was writing.

CHAPTER 1

STANDING IN THE BATHROOM of his hotel room, the sweat of lust glistening on his chest in the mirror before him, Kyle Fasano realized he had done a terrible thing. Her lipstick was smeared on his neck. He could still feel her hands on both his temples, pulling at his hair, urging him on, silently begging for something far more than the deed itself could ever provide.

He heard her stirring in the bed. He'd waited until she'd fallen asleep, her breathing soft and level, before he slid her arm from his chest and snuck to the bathroom. He still couldn't believe he'd done it. A twenty-three-year-old, the most ogled girl at the company the last two months, and he landed her. Or more likely, she landed him. He knew his intentions, but really, this had always hinged on hers. Even when they decided to get a room a few hours earlier, the look in her eye, the hesitation, and yet... a faint smile betrayed a subtle hint of determination.

What had he done? It was all a mess. He could keep getting laid, screw up his whole life for a kid who would grow weary of him soon enough, or he could stop it all now and risk ending up in Richard or Jerry's office on Monday with a stack of sexual harassment paperwork to square up.

He wiped his face with a hand towel and took a leak, aiming for the inside of the bowl. He didn't want to wake her. If he did, she might want to go again, and he would.

There was no stopping it now, this lust that had sparked the first time he'd laid eyes on her and inflamed over drinks after everyone else bailed at the end of happy hour. That was right before the jokes about getting a room started. Just kidding around, just a little joke.

He looked in the mirror again, seeing the punch line.

He couldn't breathe. It were as if the lust was a living thing, sucking up the air in his lungs and suffocating his heart.

He remembered his grandmother when he was all of fourteen, lecturing him on the Bible while she chopped vegetables for dinner, telling him in her stern Catholic voice that all sins were forgivable save one: adultery. She told him that her best friend once died on the operating table and had been brought back to life, and she'd claimed to see, to her horror, that hell was filled with adulterers. "That is one sin you don't get past, Kyle. Remember that."

How absurd. He was only fourteen. How in the world did he have any idea what adultery was, or marriage for that matter, in any real sense? Now, as an adult, he wished he'd been old enough to ask the obvious questions that day, the ones that might've gotten him slapped upside the head. Exactly how did your friend know all this if she hadn't done that very deed herself? Was it some sort of whorish act of infidelity with the butcher in the deli just after closing, or had she simply fulfilled a cliché and been seduced by the mailman, turning to her rosary just after her orgasm in a sense of shame that would haunt her the rest of her life?

What was it, Grandma? And by the way, it wasn't you, was it, Grandma?

His conscience was beginning to dig and bite at him like a cornered rat. He was starting to care again, just a bit, just enough to make it feel wrong, and the feeling was incomplete, as if there was more guilt to come, a ton of it actually, but just not right now.

God, what have I done? I'm so sorry.

The irony of the prayer, lonely and brief as it was, was not lost on him. As if any God, Almighty or otherwise, was interested in bailing out a thirty-eight-year-old man who had just broken his marriage vows, tossed the security of his children to the wind, and, oh yeah, in many ways just taken advantage of somebody's loving daughter.

The gears in his mind turned and rang like a cash register tabulating the price that would have to be paid for this night. He chuckled. He hated being in sales; everything came down to the math: the commissions, the residuals, the losses.

After turning on the cold water, he splashed his face, trying to wash her smell off his lips, that sweet smell of sin and victory that comes from getting a girl to do something against her better judgment, after she's done pretending that she doesn't want it too. His shoulders felt tight. Standing naked on the marble floor made the cold air around him seem more intense and he began to shiver, causing the shadows cast by the lights over the mirrors to move across his body in eerie patterns.

He thought of his wife, Tamara, and as swiftly as her face came to mind he banished it. No. Not here. Not now. Not with the smell of another woman's perfume all over him and that deep red lipstick still smeared there on his neck like blood from the marriage he'd just murdered.

Tamara was never anyone's fool and never would be. She would never tolerate this. Not even to protect the kids. Well... maybe. That would be the only card left

3

to play. But what did it matter? He didn't care anymore, right? That's right. Who cares? Screw it.

Perfect word. You screwed her and now you've screwed yourself, all in a few short hours of your life. Great job, champ.

He had to leave. The urge to get out of the hotel room struck him as surely as the urge that had gotten him into it. His breathing became even more labored as his lust morphed into anxiety, and he mocked himself for probably being on the edge of a heart attack.

That's what you get for banging a kid nearly half your age. She had so much energy. You could barely keep up, and now, well, how about a big laugh at the idiot who goes into cardiac arrest in a hotel room with another woman on the night of his wife's thirty-sixth birthday?

He forced himself to concentrate. Deep breaths in, deeper breaths out—but even then they were barely more than puffs. He remembered football in high school, the game against Mater Dei when the wind was knocked out of him. Coach Pete standing over him like a stone golem, screaming at him to breathe, because he had cost them a time out. Coach Pete was the biggest bastard he ever knew, and sure enough here he was again, all these years later, a mirage on the bathroom wall, screaming at him again, "Kyle, you little priss, don't you black out on me! Breathe, dammit!"

He did, barely, clawing air down his throat in desperate gulps.

Again, it hit him: he'd really done this. He had. Worse still it was dawning on him that, like it or not, he *did* care. He did. Hearts would be broken by this, and lives, all for a college-style lay.

He thought of his daughter, Janie, ten years old, and her soft brown hair, and what it would feel like to read her bedtime stories only on every-other-weekend visits.

Nausea stirred his stomach, and he grabbed a towel. First he couldn't get air in, and now he could feel vomit trying to come out. He willed the urge away and scrambled toward the bedroom. He would get his clothes, quietly, and like a low life piece of shit, he'd sneak out of here before she woke up. Later it was going to be bad, when he'd have to see her again at work, but now, this moment, was more than he could take.

As he stepped from the half-light of the bathroom back into the bedroom, he heard her before he could see her. It was an odd sound, half-murmur and half-whisper. His lack of vision as his eyes adjusted to the darkness seemed to heighten his sense of hearing. He could barely see her outline; she was sitting at the foot of the bed, slightly hunched over.

"I've done what you want, what you want, done what you want, want…"

He froze. Was she on her phone? Had this whole thing been some sort of setup? How? Why?

Her voice was changing, the words now gone, and then she began a soft chant of some kind. He felt hairs across his entire body rustle to some sort of primal attention, as if an unknown danger had just joined them in the room. But that was ridiculous.

He stood there for a good fifteen seconds, naked and exposed, trying to get his head around what was happening.

Adrenaline poured into his bloodstream. The breathing problems? Subsiding rapidly. The nausea? Gone.

Jesus! What do I do?

Something was very wrong here, in a very bad way. Something told him that he would be the stupidest man alive to make a sound, to yell at her or try to snap her out of it—whatever "it" was that she was doing. What the hell? Was she a head case? She had never seemed like one. Was she on drugs? Possibly.

But if the explanation was as simple as some bad X, then why was there an irrational command from somewhere deep in his mind telling him to consider every move he made next very, very carefully? It was as if he was being introduced to an instinct he never knew he had and it was telling him, point blank, not only to avoid disturbing her but to run, naked, right out of the room.

The whispered chant, intonations from deep in her chest, continued as he willed himself to move forwards, to the chair where his shirt was tossed. He did so slowly, to avoid making any sound on the carpet.

Shirt in hand, he grabbed his shoes and looked for his socks.

As he moved to the side of the bed, closer to her now, her chant subsided, and again she began to speak. "I know, I know, I know, I know, I know." The two words were like rocks skipping across a lake, slippery and fast, plunking between each pause. She shook and her hands fidgeted in her lap, the fingers strumming one another uncontrollably.

Screw the socks. He could do without his jacket too. Then his stomach dropped.

His pants lay on the floor, opposite the corner of the bed where she sat but still far too close to her for comfort.

He actually decided to go without the pants, as crazy as that sounded, before realizing that his cash and keys were in the pockets.

Shit. She's probably got Tourette's or something, Kyle. Just let it go. Snap your fingers and she'll come around.

As if in response to this thought, the girl he knew as Caitlyn went completely silent.

Are you kidding me?

Not a word. Not a sound. And the silence was far worse than the chant.

He dropped to one knee and half-scooted to the pants. The bed was a nice big California king. She was a little thing, easy to bounce around, and oh what fun that had been a hundred years ago, before this moment. But still… at five foot four or so, her at one corner and he at the other, she couldn't possibly reach him.

Yes. That's the good salesman. Do the math.

But that same new instinct was telling him that she wasn't human anymore.

That's ridiculous! She's hopped up on speed or something. That's it. She's just tripping.

He was losing it. Barely able to stifle the panic in his body, he edged closer to his pants, realizing that he would have to take his eyes off her for just a second to reach down below the bed, sacrificing his line of vision.

He grabbed the pants and immediately looked up. She was staring directly at him, her chin out and her head tilted at an odd angle.

The room, his heart, time, and the heavenly host above, all stopped. Frozen.

"You weren't supposed to see, supposed to see, supposed to see…" she said. Her words, deep and guttural, were nowhere near as chilling as her eyes. They were now pure black orbs.

Again, he pleaded. *Oh God, please, get me out of here.*

She stood, but even this movement, from sitting to standing, was jilted and inhuman, a cross between a mime and a puppet, the joints in her knees popping loudly.

It was time to go. Period.

He moved toward the door, and she smiled.

7

Here he was in this horribly unreal situation, in a hotel room with a woman who was not his wife, and a part of him was still clinging desperately to the notion that he could get out of this clean somehow. But her smile proved how pathetic that idea was and how desperate he had become; it was the same level of warped desperation that makes an animal stuck in a trap believe that it can still get away if it just chews a little flesh off its leg, right around the edges, just a little at a time, then just a little bit more.

"Was I good, Kyle?" she asked, and the words came out with a half-click at the back of her throat. She moved towards him, bringing her arms out at her sides like a gunslinger, her fingers splayed as though she was in some sort of primal attack mode.

He couldn't speak.

She *wasn't* human. It was obvious now. She wasn't. It made no sense, and deep down inside, way deep down, he hoped that he was the one who was tripping, some weird brain convulsion caused by too much rum and the Viagra he'd snuck earlier at the bar.

Yes. This whole thing had been very much premeditated, hadn't it? Right down to the pill he'd taken to bang her better. He was no innocent husband seduced by the office harlot. He had planned it all out, very carefully. Like a suicide.

"What do I do, do I do, do I do?" she asked, speaking to the floor now, caught in a conversation with someone or something else, momentarily distracted.

He saw his moment and took it. In three quick strides he sidestepped to the door and opened it so he could escape. He didn't take his eyes off her for a moment, his hand still on the door handle, his peripheral vision guiding him.

She looked up. "Kill him." She said it matter-of-factly, as if she were ordering a scoop of ice cream, before those horrible black eyes went wide with rage and those fingers with their French-tip nails came forwards to stab and claw the soul right out of him.

She charged the door with a scream as he stepped out into the hall and slammed it shut behind him. He heard her thud against it loudly on the other side. That too was abnormal. A human being would've slowed down upon seeing the door being closed in their face, but like a feral cat or a rabid dog she had charged directly into it.

He fled down the hall, nearly naked and with clothes in hand, closing the thirty feet to the elevator.

She banged and screamed from inside the room as if she couldn't get out, the sounds echoing down the hall, and he realized that she might not be able to, that the difficulty of using those claws to open that door might be the only thing saving him right now.

But still, what *was* human in her, if anything, might figure it out any second now. Then she would be out and after him.

He had no time to waste. Making it to the elevator he pushed the call button, and to his relief the doors opened immediately. There was no one inside. Finally: a moment of luck in this whole mess.

He jumped in and punched the "close" button repeatedly. He held his breath as the doors shut agonizingly slowly, certain that she would appear in the opening before they fully closed.

When the doors finally came together and the elevator began its descent, he exhaled deeply, still in a state of shock.

Oh God. What just happened? God, please, just help me. Get me out of this.

He had twenty-two floors to get himself dressed and he managed it, but just barely, and only because there were no stops along the way. The elevator opened and he was out into the lobby at a quick clip. Passing the front desk, he nodded curtly at the smartly dressed employee on duty, thankful it was a man for some reason.

When the front doors of the hotel opened and the crisp night air outside spilled over him, he began to reason with himself. This was all a bad dream. Yes. He was brilliant enough to have had an affair with a closet crack addict who was up there in that room right now in some sort of drug induced hallucination. That's all it was. He just had to get to his car and—

"Kyle Fasano?"

The voice was deep, authoritative, and came from some-where to his right.

This *had* been a setup. He *was* going to get scammed somehow.

He turned to face a tall man with a gray face, who was in a gray suit and wore a gray hat that sat evenly over his white hair.

"This is not a scam, Kyle," the man said, his face full of pity.

Had this guy just replied to his thoughts? No. That was impossible.

I must've spoken aloud without realizing it.

"No, you didn't," The Gray Man said.

Kyle hadn't buttoned his shirt up all the way, and the cold air bit at his chest as the night came to a standstill.

"What is this?" Kyle finally asked.

"You've been asking for God's help, haven't you?"

"What?"

"Yes, a number of times, actually, in the last few minutes."

"What are you talking about?"

"You know, Kyle, I actually feel a bit sorry for you, I'll admit it," The Gray Man said.

"Why?"

"Because God has heard you. But I'm not sure you're going to like His answer."

CHAPTER 2

HER THOUGHTS AS HEAVY as her heart, Tamara Fasano turned north on McClendon Street on her way to the freeway, which would take her home to Janie and Seth.

It wasn't supposed be like this, but they had made their choices, she and her husband, for a nicer home and fancier vacations. Somewhere on that path their priorities shifted. The time she wanted to spend with the children was sacrificed to sixty-hour workweeks and nights like tonight.

Janie had taken it the hardest, not understanding why the cake she and her little brother Seth made after school with Juanita would have to wait until tomorrow. Tamara explained, but really, how could a ten-year-old understand the notion of working to past 9:00 p.m. on your birthday?

She sighed heavily. At seven, Seth had probably understood even less.

Kyle had actually taken it worse, though, but that wasn't a surprise; things were strained between them and only getting worse. Ever since their romance began in college seventeen years ago, he'd sent her mixed colored roses on her birthday. Today none had come, and tonight, intent on going to some stupid office party, he'd bluntly hung up in her ear when she'd asked him to get home early because she had to work late.

That was a first, and once her fury subsided she'd taken refuge in her spreadsheets, determined to talk to him in the morning after things cooled off. Ripping his head off when she got home would do no good, especially since he willingly moved to the couch these days anyway.

A Prius cut into her lane at the on-ramp, forcing her to hit the brakes and momentarily lose her train of thought. She heard the crunch of gravel beneath the tires of her SUV as she hit an uneven patch of road. The Prius sped off on to the freeway ahead of her as she held back the urge to lay on the horn.

The night bloomed full around her, a swath of stars like paint specks off to her left, a waning moon directly overhead. She took a deep breath and turned on the radio, channel surfing until she came across a Dave Matthews song, yet another reminder of her college days, and settled in for the ride home.

Trying not to think about Seth, she stared through the windshield at the sporadic red maze of taillights ahead of her across all four lanes, everyone jockeying for position even though there was no real traffic to speak of at this hour. Habits die hard. What was that quote? *Habit is a second nature which prevents us from knowing the first?* Something like that. Working late, always hurrying, and treating traffic like mortal combat: they were all habits. Everyone had them, and little Seth was no exception. In fact, his whole world was still about routine, like Mommy reading him a book after his shower, both of which she had missed tonight.

Radiohead flooded the speakers next. She thought of changing the station but didn't really care enough to follow through. Drained, the road ahead no longer seemed to have an end, as if the home she was headed to was getting further away instead of closer. It was an odd thought.

She didn't like it, so she tried to ignore it.

She pulled her hair back and rubbed her neck.

The meeting for the east coast project had extended well past dessert. Tim and Ben tried their best to hold the line on support and implementation strategies, but the German client was relentless, wanting drill downs on almost every issue. How many assembly plants could the sales center support? How many employees could be squeezed into part-time slots? It didn't help that he'd also had an instant eye for Tamara, who was the lead on the project. Evidently, in some perverted male way, being a female leader made her something to conquer as much as any price point or contract nuance.

Since many of their contracts were with EU firms she was used to the European male approach to business, so this didn't bother her too much at first. At least he wasn't Italian. They were the worst. She tolerated it, and yes, even used a little innocent flirtation to get what she wanted from time to time. In a man's world it was a woman's prerogative, and she wasn't going to apologize for it.

Tonight though, with thoughts of her daughter's pleas to come home and her birthday cake waiting, she was in no mood. The meeting didn't go badly, but it wasn't a home run either, making the sacrifices of the evening only harder to accept.

She dazed out, awake but mostly on autopilot, vaguely hearing Blind Melon come and go, then Bowie. The songs kept coming and her eyelids kept trying to shut. The last thing she needed to do was crash the damned car, so she lowered the windows and resolved to think about something that would keep her awake.

Like something that would piss her off.

What was it that Kyle said to her earlier? "If you don't care enough anymore to be home, what's the point?" She started to ask him what the hell that meant just before he hung up on her.

The point of what? Life? Their marriage? Or was she just being dramatic? Maybe he had just been referring to her birthday. Whatever.

She yawned. This wasn't working.

How about the German client? That might work. Mr. Holger was twenty years her elder but still convinced he was just as virile as a man half his age, like Ben. Tamara worked all the time with Ben. She knew he had a crush on her, but she ignored it for both of their sakes.

Tonight things had been different though, with some silly rivalry between the two men injecting itself into the meeting. Who could tell the better joke? Who could sound the most knowledgeable? Mr. Holger, as the client, had all the leverage before the water glasses even hit the table, but Ben was too young and stubborn to accept this. Worse still, he was barely able to hide a subtle hint of jealousy every time Mr. Holger got chatty with her. Holger's reference to how much Tamara looked like Vera Farmiga—as if she'd never heard that one before—started their little male digression, and it lasted until the end of the meal.

That's what botched the meeting. Not her. Not her concern over a birthday cake (*"With sprinkles, Mom!"*) that the kids made just for her with those little hands working the blender and bowls, their nanny at their sides, where Tamara herself should've been standing.

That did the trick. She was wide-awake now.

She promised herself that she wouldn't take this out on Juanita when she got home. It wasn't her fault that she was asked to—no, paid to—play Mommy.

The freeway opened up and she pushed on the gas pedal, eager to end the night. When her off-ramp was in sight, the lights of a highway patrol car lit up behind her.

She banged the steering wheel with the base of her palm in frustration. "Give me a break!" she yelled in the empty car.

She exited the freeway while shaking her head, preparing for the ticket to come, having no idea that after tonight the police were going to be a regular part of her life for quite a while.

At least until they were finally convinced that Kyle was dead.

* * *

He knew football season was just around the corner, but in spite of this fact, Napoleon Villa, Detective Third Grade, with the Los Angeles Police Department's Central Station, couldn't get excited. He attributed his lack of interest to the fact that he was fighting off a cold and lacking a girlfriend to make him some *sopa de pollo.*

Being a tough-guy homicide detective was hard when you felt like you had a fever and your nose was stuffy. He would never admit it to anyone but himself, but he needed a little babying right now.

It was almost 10:00 p.m. and he wished he could just go home and crawl into bed. Instead, he took another swig of his green tea and got back to the file on his desk.

The police report and photos strewn there told the story of a very simple robbery gone terribly wrong.

One of the last places you wanted to mess up these days was in Koreatown. The kid from Cuatro Flats, one Hymie Villarosa, had been outside of his safe zone, probably earning jump points of some kind with his gang, when he walked into the liquor store at Sixth and Commonwealth and stuck a gun in the owner's face.

Hymie was too young to know that Koreans, be they from the north or south, don't give up in a war, much less in a robbery. The owner was a veteran of that war and after playing nice to get the kid to lower his guard he pulled a Gold Cup .45 from behind the counter and began shooting. Being in his mid-eighties, that meant he shot in just about every direction, missing Hymie entirely, clipping one customer in the leg and blowing a large bag of Doritos out of the hands of another.

Hymie, of course, returned fire. And after surviving two years of a bloody war that, officially, still wasn't over, Woo-Jin Kim had a nine-millimeter bullet shot through his chest by a kid younger than some of his grandchildren.

Hymie then fled the store and promptly found himself face-to-face with two members of a Korean gang who had been across the street changing the tire on their ride, which unfortunately for Hymie meant that he was in exactly the wrong place at exactly the wrong time.

Hymie was shot five times and would never live to have any children, much less any grandchildren.

Napoleon, on nothing stronger than two herbal cold pills every four hours for the past two days, had been left to sort through the facts and clues with a sore throat and Echinacea-fogged mind as he tried to identify the two Korean gang members who, like ice, had melted into the background of Sixth and Commonwealth right after the shooting.

The car? Stolen, of course. Gotta love thieves who are willing to change a tire.

His tea was cold. He drank it anyway.

"Yo, Nap!" The voice came from a young detective named Parker, who was new to the precinct.

"Whatup, rook?" Napoleon replied.

"Nothing. Except a dead girl who took a header right outta the twenty-third floor of the Hilton about an hour ago."

Shit. Sometimes the bodies just kept coming. It was beyond frustrating.

Folding the file in front of him, he put the two murderers from Koreatown on hold and moved on to the next case.

"So what're the facts?" Napoleon asked. "And be ready to take notes."

Parker smiled. All the rookies did.

At this point in his career, Napoleon was fairly well known as the guy who worked the Robbery-Homicide Division for over twenty years and as the detective who was "street" once, long ago, with the tats to prove it. He never had a record of any kind, nor any arrests, nor any proven gang affiliation, and back in the '80s they were a little more flexible at the LAPD with their enrollment guidelines. So in snuck Napoleon to police the very streets he once roamed.

Parker scratched his head and began. "The girl was twenty-one. Blond. Blue eyes, I think. The uniforms that just called it in say her face is kinda like pudding now, she's a mess, and the way they described—"

"Cut the shit, Parker." Napoleon sighed.

"Okay, okay. They found her driver's license in the room. Caitlyn Hall. From Pasadena. Found an expired UCLA student ID too."

"And?"

"Based on a business card they found in her purse in the room, she worked nearby."

"Where?"

"Dynavac Industries. She was a sales rep."

"She check in with anyone?"

"Desk clerk says a guy was with her. Kinda handsome. Brown hair. Built like a baseball player, whatever the hell that means."

"Probably means he was fit, dumb shit."

"Well, yeah, but so are football players and hockey players and lacrosse players."

"So?"

"So what exactly makes a person fit *like* a baseball player?"

Napoleon's head hurt, and it wasn't only from his nasal congestion. He counted to ten. A dead body on the docket and diaper boy here was obsessed with fitness types. He knew he was getting old, but truly, the city was in a ton of hurt if he didn't get Parker trained up right.

"Did the desk clerk see the guy leave?" Napoleon asked.

"Yeah. But, like, almost a half-hour before the body took the tumble."

"How do we know that?"

"Well... the body wasn't found until then," Parker replied, sounding nervous.

"That doesn't mean she didn't take the tumble before then, maybe with lover boy's help."

"With all due respect, I got that."

"So then you think she had help?"

"Yeah. Most likely. No doubt."

"Never rule out doubt, Parker." Napoleon had learned this the hard way, more than once.

"Well, if she didn't have help, then the theory would be that she jumped, and to do that she musta had wings," Parker said with a shrug.

Napoleon blinked, not sure if he'd heard him right. "What?"

"Wings. There's no other way she could've jumped."

"And you have 'detectivized' your way to this idea how, exactly?"

"The hole in the window."

"What about it?"

"They're telling me it's clean, a solid hole with most of the window still intact."

"That's possible. It's a hotel window. It's thick. It's not supposed to just shatter. I'm actually surprised it even gave way," Napoleon countered.

"Maybe. Sure. But it's a big-ass window. Twelve feet. The hole is almost at the ceiling, like, eleven feet up. So she musta had a flying start. Ya know, wings."

"Dude looks like a baseball player." Napoleon shrugged. "He's probably six foot plus. With a body lifted over his head, that's nine foot plus. He throws her with some elevation, eleven is doable, especially if he's trippin.'"

"Yeah. I thought of all that too," Parker said with a smirk.

Napoleon sneezed. He was beyond annoyed now. "So what are you leaving out, shithead?"

"The hole?"

"Yeah?"

"The glass was melted, all the way around."

"Melted? Was she on fire or something?"

Parker's smirk grew bigger. "Nope."

"What the hell then?"

"They're saying we gotta see this for ourselves, man."

But Napoleon was already past him, his jacket in one hand and a throat lozenge in the other. If you want something done right, do it yourself. He wasn't sure what the kid heard wrong when the call came in, but this didn't add up.

Twenty minutes later in Room 2303 of the Los Angeles Hilton and standing in front of the window in question, Napoleon shook his head.

The hole in the window was about six foot by three foot. It looked like some odd work of art, melted glass with black rounded tips where the shatter points were and a brown film that spread out around the entire circumference of the hole in a smoky outline.

The heat that would've had to have been generated to do this to glass would've left some sort of residue or burn marks elsewhere, on the drapes perhaps, or the ceiling. But there were none. Napoleon took in the crime scene the way he'd been trained, from top to bottom, around the room in sections. The room was clean.

The crime scene guys were down below looking over the body, but they'd already radioed up that from their preliminary review of the remains there was no evident sign that the victim had been on fire.

Already shit wasn't adding up.

"Remember when I told you last week that I'd seen it all, Parker?" Napoleon asked with a sigh.

"Yeah," Parker replied.

"I shoulda known better."

CHAPTER 3

"I T GOES LIKE THIS…" The Gray Man began. They were seated at a coffee shop some fifteen miles from the hotel, a distance covered not with Kyle's car but by some sort of teleportation that still had his head spinning, a process of white light and warm heat that pressed in on every inch of his body the entire way here.

"I don't want to hear how it—" Kyle objected.

"Nor did you want to come here, did you? Or speak to me at all? And yet here we are, nonetheless."

"Why?"

"Because you just don't get it yet, and, to be fair, it's too soon for you *to* get, which is why I'm trying to explain it to you."

The waitress arrived with their order, which The Gray Man had made when they were seated: two cups of coffee and a blueberry scone.

"Here you go, gentlemen." Her name badge said "Tammy." She was on the skinny side and had red hair and an orchid tattoo on her left wrist. After sliding their coffees to them, she gave The Gray Man a big smile and presented the scone to him as if it were on a platter.

"Many thanks to you, my dear," The Gray Man said with a nod. "The older I get, the more I enjoy the simplest of things."

"No problem. Let me know if you need anything else," she chirped. Kyle caught her sideways glance at The Gray Man as she walked away though; her curiosity at his shade was obvious, as if maybe he were some sort of albino or leper.

Their privacy now intact, The Gray Man continued, "You've made a mistake, Kyle, a grave one, and you know it."

"I didn't mean to. I've never done it before. I just lost myself there for a bit."

"Yes, you did mean to, and never having done it before in no way lightens the punishment for having done it at all… because you've lost more than your self, my boy." He paused to sip his coffee, and looking over the rim of his cup and directly into Kyle's eyes, he added, "You've now lost your soul."

"What?" Kyle said, feeling his face twist in perplexity as he struggled with what he was hearing.

"Give yourself time," The Gray Man replied, turning his attention to his scone. He ignored his fork and simply picked it up and chomped into it, a slight grunt of pleasure escaping his otherwise heavy demeanor.

"This is…" was all Kyle could manage. His brain was on overload. He knew this wasn't a dream, but in less than an hour he'd just fled from a psychotic lover in a hotel, ran directly into a man who could read his thoughts, and then been teleported in an instant from the front of that same hotel to this coffee shop in the middle of nowhere. All the rules of logic and physics were like rowboats being tossed about in a hurricane, and now, somehow, he was supposed to understand and accept the condemning words of someone he'd just met.

Seconds passed. Kyle managed a sip of his coffee but his stomach protested immediately. The Gray Man meanwhile seemed to be barely containing his joy with the coffee and the scone. "So warm," he muttered after another bite.

Finally, Kyle couldn't take it any longer. "What's going on then?"

Holding up a hand in protest as he finished chewing, The Gray Man shook his head at Kyle and then finally cleared his throat. "Well. First off, you're a millionth."

"A millionth? A millionth what?"

"A millionth is a principle, a person, a light of hope for the nine hundred and ninety-nine thousand, nine hundred and ninety-nine souls that have preceded him."

"Preceded him in what?"

Folding his hands in front of him, The Gray Man replied, "Preceded him in the same sin."

Kyle blinked. "This is fucking crazy."

"No, it's not." The Gray Man shook his head, then sighed. "You're just like all the rest, Kyle."

"All the rest of what?"

"Of humanity."

The words sounded like flat notes played on a broken piano.

Looking up to meet The Gray Man's eyes, Kyle decided to ask the obvious. "Humanity? You say that as if you were talking about a separate species. So what the hell are *you*?"

Something in The Gray Man's eyes flickered brightly and Kyle sensed a power, a frightening power, in them. "Hell has nothing to do with *me,* my boy."

Swallowing hard, Kyle forced himself to go on. "So, what then? Are you saying you're an angel?"

The Gray Man simply smiled. "It doesn't matter what I am. You should be more worried about what you are."

"Which is?"

"I've already told you. You're a millionth."

"Fine. I'll bite. Okay, then. I've joined a club of sinners, right? Great. What's my prize?"

The Gray Man choked on a sip of his coffee and laughed softly. After another sip he managed to speak again. "You've won no prize, that's for sure. A burden? Yes. A mission? Absolutely. But I doubt anyone would call it a prize."

Kyle downed his coffee. Screw his stomach. He needed the caffeine to jolt alive whatever brain cells he had left to reason his way out of this.

"Reason is a crutch, Kyle."

Startled at having his mind read again, Kyle blurted, "Dammit!"

For the first time, Kyle saw The Gray Man's demeanor change. He almost winced at the word. "Please. If you would. Enough of the language."

Kyle laughed. "You've got to be kidding me! You tell me I've lost my soul and now you want me to watch my potty mouth?"

A burly man at the counter in a tan jacket and wearing a John Deere hat glanced at them.

"We all have our vices. Swearing was one of mine once. Easy not to say words you don't hear, so for me, please refrain."

"Fuck this." Kyle replied defiantly. Suddenly, the coffee cup in his hand was pulled free. Kyle watched in stunned amazement as it slid away from him across the length of the table, levitating a good inch above the brown glossy laminate, until it came to rest alongside the napkin dispenser by the window.

The Gray Man's eyes had turned from light to dark blue. "Please, Kyle. I've asked nicely. Twice now."

Kyle nodded and swallowed over the knot jammed against his Adam's apple. There was no sense in arguing about it anymore; he was into something deep. And yet, oddly, something inside him twitched with excitement. This was all unsettling, but if it was real, then it was an affirmation of things he'd always believed.

The Gray Man spoke, his eyes blurring back to light blue. "You *all* believe it, Kyle."

Startled again, Kyle couldn't take it anymore. "We have to make a deal. You have to stop that. I'll do my best with the f-bombs, but you have to stop with the mind reading thing. I can't take it. It's freaking me out!"

To his surprise, The Gray Man chuckled softly and nodded. "Deal."

"Good. Okay. We all believe *what* then?" Kyle asked, nervously rubbing his forehead.

"In good. In evil. In your role between the two. From the very moment you begin to sense them."

"You mean understand them?"

The Gray Man smiled. "Ah. Understanding. Yes. The beginning of reason. Genesis. Chapter Four. 'The serpent was subtle.' You know the story, right?"

"Yes," Kyle replied with a look of disbelief. "I went to Sunday school."

"I know you did. So you can imagine how *sensing* good and evil is a much simpler thing than trying to *understand* them, right?"

Kyle shrugged. He didn't like where this was going.

"In the former, my boy, you accept them for what they are; you gravitate to the one and avoid the other. It's simple. It's only when you begin to trivialize the instinct, or rationalize it and determine to understand it… only then do you take the very first step towards *playing* God instead of *worshipping* Him."

"That's not true."

"But it is."

"Please, how can one 'sense' evil?"

"Kyle. Come now. Let's see. How about an example? You knew it when you were eight. The way the grocery bagger looked at you in the market. You remember right? His eyes were full of an unnatural lust. It's why you clung to your mother's skirt. After a while you even dreaded going to the market at all. You even volunteered to do yard chores with your dad to spare yourself any more trips there."

The diner grew eerily silent. Kyle thought maybe his ears were playing tricks on him, but if so his eyes were in on the same gag; the room grew darker, as a room can do midday when swift-moving clouds blot out the sun. But it was evening now, with no such sun in the sky.

"All of you sense it, Kyle, from time to time. You come home late one night and something in your home feels off, as if someone is there. You chuckle about ghosts and turn on the lights as quickly as you can, but you don't really sleep well that night until the memory of it goes away. A woman can feel it in the way a certain type of man looks at her, as if she senses that he's not in control of his wants and desires, as most men are, and therefore he is more likely to violate her space, or violate her."

Kyle shifted in his seat. The Gray Man continued.

"But if we talk of demons then it's like silly child's play, right? Yes… no… because you've seen it when you've watched the evening news, right? Perhaps it's a crazed leader in the bowels of Africa who allows a million people to starve to death beneath a hot desert sun. It is beyond comprehension, but you know… only something evil could do that. Just as you know that only evil could crawl through a bedroom window at night and carve out the eyes of an elderly couple with a spoon. They caught that particular demon, didn't they, Kyle? Then one night you bump into a person on the corner who looks at you with eyes absent a soul and your gut drops, because something tells you that you're in trouble. You wait for the light to change so you can cross the street as soon as possible and get away. You count the seconds, Kyle, and deep down you know that evil thing next to you is doing the same. Counting. One. Two. Three…"

Breaking eye contact, The Gray Man looked out the window to the parking lot beyond. "Later, when you've gotten home safely, you're thankful for a few minutes before another part of you will try to reason it all away, blame that whole feeling on a horror movie you recently saw. But that first part of you knows better, the part of you that sensed it."

"I still don't get it."

"It's God-given, Kyle. That *sense* of evil? It's knitted into you before birth, woven into the very fabric of your being. And *reason*, Kyle? Reason is a biting moth."

For the first time Kyle really studied The Gray Man. There was a stillness that seemed to emanate from him, to the point that Kyle seemed enclosed within his aura. They were in the diner, yes, but they also weren't. Tammy the waitress and the other patrons were real and present, but somehow separate, like double images in a photograph.

Kyle sighed. "I didn't know this would happen."

"Don't, Kyle. No lies. Not to me. I'm here to help you. If I can."

"No. I mean it…"

"You planned the whole thing for months. You were on the hunt for this misery the first day you saw her. Let's just cut to the truth here, okay? We don't have time—"

"That's not true. It isn't," Kyle argued.

"You spent hours imagining how she would look in lingerie, Kyle, of the things you would do to her when you got her alone…"

"Hey."

"You knew it was wrong. You sensed it, didn't you, Kyle? Ah. But then reason set in and the excuses came like snowfall: your wife wasn't satisfying you anymore, or she was barely trying to, she didn't love you the same anymore, no one had to know, it would be fun, everyone does it, most wives almost expect their husbands to do it sooner or later, and so on until the snowfall began to pile up and bury you."

"I didn't… It wasn't… Shit, I dunno what was wrong with me." Kyle felt tears welling up in his eyes and his hands were trembling.

"Yes you did, yes it was, and yes you do." The words cracked like dry wood on a fire.

"Fine," Kyle replied, growing defensive. "So be it. I screwed up. What about forgiveness?"

"You've asked and it's been granted, Kyle. That's how it works. But in a sense, you *are* forgiveness now, if you succeed. It's what makes you a millionth."

"I can't take this… this whole… What does that mean exactly?"

"It means that those who came before you have lost their souls too. But, unlike you, they have not repented. And God's reply is to choose one person amongst their million to serve as a possible catalyst for their repentance."

"That's crazy! Whatever happened to free will?"

The Gray Man sighed and closed his eyes and whispered, as if in prayer, "You never told me he was going to be this difficult." He stayed silent a few moments before opening his eyes again. "If you succeed, you will be a simple *glimmer* in the periphery of their consciousness, and that tiny spark of hope that they can be forgiven can trigger them to freely choose their salvation. It's still their choice."

"Why me?"

"Because you are capable."

Rubbing his hand over his mouth and chin, Kyle felt a boiling dismay provoking his frustration. "How did this happen to me?"

"You defiled your vows."

"That's between me and my wife."

"Oh, no." The Gray Man shook his head firmly. "No it's not, Kyle. When you make a vow of love, even if you leave the word 'God' out of it, you make a vow to that very force that created you, because God *is* love Kyle. And tonight you betrayed Him, too."

Kyle was speechless. His legs felt weak, and a childlike sense of abandonment came over him like it used to when his parents would leave him at daycare and he would be afraid that they'd never come back to get him.

"But God *has* come back for you, Kyle."

Kyle glared at him.

"Sorry," The Gray Man offered. "Force of habit. You owe me a few anyway."

The waitress looked over at The Gray Man when he motioned for the check.

"How has He come back for me?"

"Through the mission you will be given."

"How is that fair to the other nine hundred thousand-plus people who don't even know me?"

"Because given the choice, they themselves would gladly choose you. None of them, Kyle, are strong enough to do this. Only you are. You're one in a million."

"Jesus." Kyle began to weep softly. Burying his hands in his face, he spoke in a muffled voice. "Please, man, you gotta help me. This is crazy. Say something on my behalf. Get me out this. I can't do it…"

"Save the pleas of forgiveness for the only one who can do anything about them, Kyle. When you do, please don't forget her."

"Who?"

"The girl who was the object of all your lust earlier tonight, the one who slipped up too, a long time ago, before you, and chose the other side as it were."

Like a splash of cold water this seemed to shock Kyle back into the moment. He wiped his eyes. "Are you talking about Caitlyn?"

"Yes. She'd taken up company with evil and then, I surmise, something went wrong."

"What do you mean?"

"You weren't supposed to see her like that, the way you saw her in the end. She broke character; something in her couldn't quite do it, I guess. Maybe the misery in her life, her anger at God, was sufficient for a time. But in the end she hesitated, and her punishment… That poor girl."

To Kyle's astonishment, there were tears in The Gray Man's eyes now. Putting his hat back on, he said, "We should pray for her."

"She tried to kill me and you want me to *pray* for her?" Kyle asked.

The Gray Man looked at Kyle with disappointment. "You would have me pray for your forgiveness, but you refuse to pray for hers?"

Kyle avoided his question and looked around. "Where's the waitress with the check?"

"She won't be coming back," The Gray Man said, finishing his coffee. "By the time we leave she will have completely forgotten that we were even here. And we have to leave now. They'll be looking for you soon."

"What? Who?"

"All of them. But our immediate concern is the police."

Kyle felt his hands go cold. "The police? Why would—"

"As we were traveling here, Kyle, the girl you knew as Caitlyn was thrown out the window of your hotel room by the forces she failed."

Kyle's jaw dropped.

"She's dead, Kyle, and by tomorrow morning you'll be wanted for her murder."

The air around Kyle grew thick and his vision tunneled.

The Gray Man stood to leave. "You have to get it all in your head first, Kyle."

"But... my kids..." Kyle finally managed.

The Gray Man put a hand on his shoulder. "I'm sorry, my boy, but the life that you knew? It's over."

A bright light engulfed Kyle and he felt as if his body were somehow being tightly wrapped in something before he was transported away.

But where to next?

CHAPTER 4

"**I** TRIED TO KEEP THEM up for you, but they're already asleep," Juanita said with a faint smile.

They stood in the kitchen, the dim light of the oven range casting shadows across the tile floor. It was just past 10:00 p.m.

Tamara shrugged. "I figured. It's okay. I'll catch them in the morning."

A pot of albondigas soup was on one of the burners, still simmering. "I saved you some. It'll help you sleep," Juanita said.

"Thanks so much, Juanita" Tamara replied before asking the question they were both waiting for: "And the cake?"

Juanita gave a tiny grimace. "I put it in the refrigerator."

Tamara exhaled and put her purse on the counter. "What a bummer."

"I know. It's okay, though. I explained to them that sometimes these things happen." She was wearing jeans and a faded blue shirt with her hair pulled back into a ponytail as she fumbled with a dish towel.

Tamara suppressed the urge to tell Juanita that child counseling was not part of her job description, but then she realized it actually was. It had been Juanita's resume, filled with previous clients who sang her praises for just such a gift, that had made Tamara hire her in the first place.

"Thanks, Juanita."

Juanita hesitated and then continued. "It's okay. I was actually more worried that they would hear Mr. Fasano's call."

"What call?"

"It's on the message machine. I didn't get to the phone in time, but I heard it. Janie had her headphones on and, thankfully, the little one was in his room…"

"What did he say?"

Juanita wouldn't look her in the eye; instead she looked down at her hands as she folded and unfolded the dish towel. "That he wouldn't be coming home tonight."

"What?"

Juanita shrugged. "He said something about staying with a friend who was having some sort of problem."

Tamara felt her jaw stiffen. Juanita was looking at her with a sense of pity. A slightly jaded look that seemed to say, "Hey, we're both girls here, I mean, seriously, a *friend*?"

To her surprise, Tamara's growing rage gave way to embarrassment. A message from a husband spending the night somewhere else to help a buddy for the night was not an immediate cause for suspicion in a normal household. But this wasn't a normal household anymore, and even Juanita had picked up on this now.

Tamara lowered her head, removed her heels and crossed the kitchen, the coolness of the travertine floor bleeding into her feet as she got to the answering machine—a relic from a bygone era that Kyle refused to let go of, citing the annoyance at the dialing-in process of normal voice-mail. A red number one flashed on the analog display. She pressed play.

Kyle sounded like he always sounded when he was lying: way too smooth. That, and Tamara could tell he was drunk. She knew her husband well. One too many drinks and he immediately sounded like a frat boy again. Mr. Happy-Go-Lucky. Tossing a few with a "friend in need," is what the message said, "who was way too drunk to get home now." Kyle was going to get them home to this... "Tim's" house... to sleep it off. That was the worst of it. Tamara knew all of Kyle's friends, and none of them were named Tim. Most of her didn't believe that Kyle would ever hurt her. But a small part of her was taking note of the past three months, his impatience with her and, worse still, his indifference towards her.

Now this. On her birthday.

She could hear Juanita behind her, pulling out a bowl and spoon for the soup.

"Well, it looks like you had to carry the whole load tonight, Juanita. Sorry about that."

"That's okay. I'm sorry you missed your cake, but they will be so happy to see you in the morning."

"Yep," Tamara said vacantly. She was playing the message over in her head. He had cared enough to lie, but only barely. Tamara was bound not to buy it, and maybe that was the point. She felt tears welling in her eyes.

"Thanks for everything tonight, Juanita. You can go home now," Tamara said, keeping her back to her.

Silence for a few seconds, then, "Are you sure?"

Tamara nodded curtly and made her way into the family room, her back still to Juanita as she took off her suit jacket and tossed it onto the couch. "Absolutely. Thanks so much for the soup."

"Okay then. Have a good night."

She heard Juanita gather her keys and bag, walk to the door and leave. The loud click of the door lock snapping into place betrayed Juanita's efforts to close the door softly.

The rest of the house was quiet, save for the low hum of the refrigerator. Tamara looked at the mantle over the fireplace where a collage of framed photos was arrayed to show happier times: their wedding photo, a picture of Janie in her first soccer uniform, a Christmas photo at their favorite cabin in Big Bear. There was also that great shot of Kyle from his famed sushi-making class; he survived one lesson and decided it was far easier to buy and eat it than it was to make it.

The years had come and gone so fast. But always, in those photos, they were together. First she and Kyle, then the dogs, then the addition of each child as their family grew.

The pictures overwhelmed her with loneliness.

And now God only knew where Kyle really was.

* * *

They were in the manager's office just off the front desk at the Hilton Hotel in Los Angeles. It was a sparse room containing a single desk with a leather chair and two guest chairs jammed up against a wall opposite the door. Napoleon and Parker stood while Paul, the night manager, sat at his desk, the sweat on his forehead glistening under the fluorescent light fixtures in the ceiling.

"So what do we have here on the surveillance tape, Paul?"

"I'm sorry, Detective Napoleon, but—"

"It's Villa, Paul. Napoleon is my first name."

"I apologize. I'm still waiting for my supervisor to call me. I mean, I don't know the legalities of releasing the tape to anyone just yet."

Napoleon rolled his eyes to the ceiling in an "Are you shitting me?" gesture to the universe. He wanted Paul to feel so ridiculously stupid that he would surrender his objections and get the hell out of their way. It seemed to have an effect.

"Here we go, Parker," Napoleon said as he wiped his sleeve across his runny nose. "Another one who has watched too many episodes of *Law and Order* or *CS-fuck-me-up-the-ass-I*."

Standing to Paul's left, Parker leaned against the wall and shook his head.

Obviously rattled, Paul cleared his throat. Napoleon had sized him up for gay the moment he'd met him, so the anal visual had been intentional. Everything Napoleon did had intentionality to it, at least on the job. Off the job he was as unintentional about as many things as he could be.

"Detective, I—"

"First off, Paul, we aren't taking the tape right now so you aren't 'releasing' anything. Second, we need to view it as soon as possible so we can glean any evidence off it we can. And lastly, while your supervisor is sleeping with his ass up in the air and dreaming about dolphins and sunshiny days, we have a dead girl going into rigor right now on your property and on *your* damn watch."

The ass-in-the-air comment was, again, intentional and meant to give off the appropriate homophobic vibes that unsettled most gay men and that was anything but appropriate in real life. In truth, Napoleon didn't care who anyone slept with, as long as they didn't steal from or murder each other in the process. As for the use of the word "rigor"? It was a hip little term that would feed into Paul's CSI vernacular. Always let someone feel like they're in the know when they don't know shit but have something that you need.

Be it the gay comments or the TV lingo, it worked. Paul cracked. He straightened the edges of his desk calendar, thought for a moment and then, nodding, he said, "Okay, gentlemen. I see your point, Detective. Back through this door is the security room. It's at the end of the hall and to the left. At this hour only Ralph is on duty, and last time I checked, he was out front trying to keep any guests from getting in the way of everything. I'll take you down there and let you in myself."

Napoleon gave Paul a little two-handed Buddha bow in mock thanks. Paul seemed to deem it sincere. Whatever.

A few minutes later they entered a small, dimly lit security room. Opposite the door there were two black desks against the wall, with twenty-eight monitors above them: one showing the main entrance, another the rear, one the utility entrance near the kitchen, another outside over the parking lot, and one each for the hotel's twenty-four elevator entrances on each floor.

After being shown in, they received a brief explanation of how the equipment worked, which wasn't all that complicated really. Then Napoleon gave Paul a dead-eyed stare. "We've got it from here. You probably want to get back to the front desk in case things start getting out of hand with the guests."

Paul hesitated briefly, but then he nodded curtly and left.

Napoleon and Parker began rolling the recordings back one by one, keying on the lobby camera first, which most everyone had to pass when checking in.

After rewinding them, they let the cameras tell the story in chronological order. First they focused their attention on the parking lot camera. It was mounted above the parking booth, which had been unmanned with the gates up and lights out.

On the tape Napoleon watched a blue BMW 323i pull up and park.

It was the same car the night bellhop had seen Caitlyn Hall arrive in earlier in the evening with "some guy." Parker had already canvassed the parking lot earlier, found this very vehicle and run the plates. The car was registered to a Mr. Kyle Fasano of La Canada, California.

On the tape, a man, presumably Mr. Fasano, exited the vehicle on the driver's side and began making his way around the back to the passenger's side, evidently to let his lover or lay or whatever she was out of the car.

But then Napoleon noticed that Mr. Fasano did something interesting: he hesitated.

At the back of the car Fasano stopped and just stood for a moment, his left hand on the trunk.

"What's he doing?" Parker asked.

But to Napoleon it was obvious by the perplexed and doubtful look on Fasano's face.

You're married, aren't you? You were deciding, one last time, weren't you, Mr. Fasano? About whether or not you really wanted to do this. "He's thinking," Napoleon replied.

"With a firm piece of ass in the car?" Parker chuckled. "What a dipshit."

Napoleon sneezed and kept watching the tape as, evidently, the last domino of Mr. Fasano's conscience fell; he was around the car and opening the door for his princess.

Caitlyn Hall got out of the car and kissed him, long and hard, and began pulling him towards the hotel.

"Vroom, vroom," Parker snorted.

"Shut the fuck up, will ya?" Napoleon snapped.

As they entered the hotel the main lobby camera caught them both, clear and up close.

This was always the oddest part of a homicide for Napoleon: seeing someone so alive not so very long ago who was now simply dead. Mr. Fasano's motivation was now obvious. Ms. Hall was beautiful, in a blue dress and red heels. She had long blond hair and a Pilates body that some young girls seem to have without actually doing the Pilates.

Seeing their likely suspect clearly for the first time, Napoleon noted that Kyle Fasano was, indeed, built like a baseball player. Tall and broad shouldered, he arrived with perfectly combed hair, his jacket cut to fit and open, his tie loose and hanging below the confident smile of a man who had just hit the jackpot with the twenty-something little spinner who was hanging all over him.

As they checked in, Napoleon noted that it was Caitlyn who used her credit card for the room. She was smiling and laughing, the camera catching her perfect white teeth, which were now scattered like Chiclets across the parking lot outside.

From the front desk the two made their way to the elevator and up to their room, the camera in elevator bay three showing them kissing heavily on the ride up. Then the camera on the twenty-third floor caught them exiting and hurrying to their room number.

The room door closed and then whatever happened, happened.

There was no sign of them as Parker fast-forwarded at four times the speed through nearly the next two hours of footage, then suddenly Fasano emerged from the hotel room, half naked and in a panicked state. Charging the elevator, he looked over his shoulder ever few steps before cramming himself through the elevator doors when they finally opened.

Up to this point Napoleon had seen a happy, confident man on camera. But now Fasano was a man seemingly afraid for his life. He frantically pressed the down button until the doors closed, then dressed hurriedly in the elevator, emerging into the lobby looking as if he'd been dressed by a blind man, his shirt tucked in on one side in the front and the other in the back, no jacket, no tie, his hair in all directions and his face drawn.

"Someone looks like he messed up," Parker commented.

"Yeah." But Napoleon said it because he was tired of training right now and just as tired of talking. In truth, Napoleon wasn't so sure. Something was off. But these were "for later thoughts," which is what Napoleon liked to call thoughts he would hash through in the wee hours of the morning when a case wouldn't let him go and he couldn't sleep. He could already tell that this was going to be one of those cases.

Parker reached across the console, nearly spilling a half-empty bottle of Gatorade in the process, and switched the view to the exterior entrance camera. There, outside the lobby doors and just off-camera to the right of the bellhop stand, was Fasano again. Just standing there.

"What's he doing?" Parker asked.

"He stopped and turned around, as if something caught his attention off-camera."

"Hm."

They watched Fasano stand there for a few seconds more.

Then, he disappeared.

"What the hell?" Napoleon said.

Parker leaned into the monitor and tapped the glass. "Did something block the lens?"

"I dunno. I don't think so," Napoleon replied.

"Well people don't just disappear. Everything else is still there: the stand, the planter, the—"

"Yeah, yeah. I get it Parker."

"The video just tweaked or something."

"Like I said, I dunno. But right now that's less important to me than the obvious."

Parker looked at him with genuine curiosity.

"He's not acting like a man who just tossed a girl out of a window, a girl who should be splattered about seventy-five yards from where he's standing when last we saw him in the video. Yet he doesn't even look in that direction when he comes out."

"You ask me, he was scared shitless and guilty as sin coming out of there."

Napoleon sniffed and stared hard at the monitor.

"Yeah. Sure. But maybe not of murder."

CHAPTER 5

THEY STOOD JUST OFF Artesia Boulevard in Torrance, near the on-ramp of the 91 Freeway. *Fifty-plus miles,* Kyle thought. They had just traversed that distance in the blink of an eye. *Incredible.*

"So it begins," The Gray Man said, as if he had done this many times before.

"What begins?" Kyle asked with some effort, his lungs expanding, as if he'd held his breath for the entire ride. His hands were sweaty and his neck damp.

"Do you remember this place?"

Kyle hesitated. "Sort of... I mean, my dad lived just down the street."

"Yes. But what else?"

A mild Santa Ana wind blew in from the east, shifting Kyle's pant cuffs and warming him even further. "I'm not getting you."

"Over there," The Gray Man said, pointing at a 76 station across the street.

Still confused, Kyle took note of the gas station. It seemed new and shiny at first. Then his mind began to reassemble all the surrounding buildings and yards, fence posts and businesses, the bus stops and benches, until he had most of the details he needed for his memory to be properly jogged. As if by some odd sort of time travel, the 76 station was replaced by...

"A Pizza Hut. There used to be a Pizza Hut here."

"Yes. Good," The Gray Man said.

"But I don't get it. I mean, I think I only came here a few times…"

"Once. You came here one time."

Still stuck, it took a few seconds to click, and then she came to Kyle's mind like a Post-it note from the past. "Victoria?"

The Gray Man nodded.

"What does she have to do with any of this?"

The Gray Man sighed. "You broke her heart that night, Kyle."

Up beyond the ramp, the traffic on the freeway was heavy. The sound of tires moving at high speed along the road mixed with a crosswalk button chirping in the distance. Kyle shook his head and shrugged. "We were kids, man."

The Gray Man nodded in a way that reminded Kyle of the only time he'd ever taken golf lessons, when the instructor had barely suppressed his impatience as Kyle repeatedly whiffed at the ball.

"I mean, what, we were seventeen or eighteen. Our whole lives were ahead of us."

"Life is never really ahead of us, Kyle, or behind. Such thoughts are tricks played on us, or that we play on ourselves."

"What?"

"The present is all that counts, Kyle. The present moment. On that night you traded what you had for what you might have. For you it was all about the road ahead. For her, sadly, it was a detour. And a bad one."

Kyle thought of Victoria, of her long light-brown hair and dark eyes, of her slender body and firm breasts, of her thin lips that rarely surrendered a smile due to her shy and reserved personality that had always made her seem just out of reach. He'd pined over her in junior high and all the way through his senior year of high school, when he'd finally managed to get her attention in—of all places—their Econ Honors class.

"She noticed you that day, didn't she?"

The wind picked up. An odd smell of pollen and motor oil began to blow into Kyle's face. The asphalt near them changed from green to red beneath the matching traffic light above.

"Yeah, she did."

"How?"

"I don't remember."

The Gray Man reached up to adjust his hat. "Quit lying," he said softly.

Kyle shrugged in frustration. "I was drawing, I think, on my notebook."

"Go on."

"What? I mean…" Kyle let the words dangle. He felt silly, but it was no use. This guy could read his mind anyway. "It was a road. On a beige notebook. Whatever."

"We're wasting time, Kyle."

"Okay. Fine. Screw it. It was a road, disappearing into the distance. I used a black pen. At the end of the road there were clouds. I did a fade out around the edges with a No. 2 pencil. The lecture was killing me and I was bored. That's all."

"She was sitting next to you, right?"

"Yes. From day one. I couldn't believe my luck. My fantasy girl since we were in seventh grade was right there at the desk next to me. It's a miracle I didn't fail that class."

"She noticed you drawing, didn't she?"

"Yeah. It caught her eye for some reason."

"No, Kyle. She noticed *you*. You drawing."

"Whatever."

"For all her shyness and reservation, yours was far worse. You were locked up in your sketches and short stories until you joined the football team, right?"

"Yes. The damned football team. Hooray."

The Gray Man laughed. "You went from poet to warrior-poet, Kyle. That's a tough combo for a girl to pass up."

Kyle shrugged again. To their right a homeless man was making his way into a parking lot near the opposite corner, passing a teenager who was sitting on his bike.

"Still, to this day, you will not accept that she noticed you instead of the drawing."

"She noticed both then—how's that?"

"You still haven't described that sketch fully, have you?"

"Oh, man. Are you kidding me?" Kyle sighed, pretending to try to remember what he could still, for some odd reason, remember in the greatest of detail, even to this day.

"I wrote some weird words at the bottom, like it was an album cover or something."

"It was the words she commented on. Those 'weird' words, right?"

"Yes."

"What did they say?"

"Traversing the fields," Kyle replied, laughing uneasily as he recalled the block letters he'd drawn with fading shadows.

The Gray Man nodded. "Yes. 'Traversing the fields.' Sort of like you've been doing tonight. With me."

Kyle noticed that the boy on the bike hadn't moved, and he seemed to be staring at them, though it was impossible to tell for sure in the dark. He was leaning on the handlebars, and his head was facing in their direction. It was nearly midnight; kind of late for a kid to be out riding his bike.

"Yeah. I guess. So what?"

"We are rarely better at living in the present than we are when we're young," The Gray Man answered. "As such, we're never in a better position to appreciate what's yet to come."

"Okaaaaay? So you're saying that when I was seventeen I drew a picture—"

"—of today. Yes. That's exactly what I'm saying."

Kyle shook his head. "This just keeps getting nuttier and nuttier."

The sound of the traffic slowed and Kyle noticed something strange... The traffic light was stuck on yellow. Looking around, he was stunned to see that the traffic was moving in slow motion, both on the street and the freeway beyond. Even the homeless man, inside the parking lot now, looked like a television replay on super-slow.

But not the boy on the bike; he was riding in circle eight's at normal speed. Head down one moment, looking over at them the next.

"What's happening?"

"Never mind that now. Just focus. Victoria. The drawing. The words. She noticed."

"Yes. F—" Kyle caught himself and looked at The Gray Man. Despite the wind, not a hair on his head moved, nor did his clothing.

"Once you captured her attention it wasn't long before you captured her, and what a wounded bird she was, right, Kyle? Lost her virginity in seventh grade and watched that boy brag about it the next day to the whole school. You remember because that was the first day you ever noticed her. She'd been at her locker, crying just a little bit."

"That guy was a pot-smoking asshole."

"Yes. But he was the cool kid, and you were a nerd: new to the school by three weeks, hair in your face, still reading books at recess, at fourteen years old. After that guy came a few more surfer-types, and more assaults on her heart until, finally, she decided to give the nerdy guy a shot for once."

Thoughts of Victoria flooded Kyle's mind. He remembered her face when they first kissed, her slender fingers entwined in his, and how he stopped feeling like a boy the minute he held her close, smelled her hair and listened as she shared her dreams.

"She was beautiful," Kyle whispered.

"Yes, she was."

"We were just kids, man."

"And what did you do?"

"It just didn't work out."

"You dumped her over a cheap dinner, Kyle, at the Pizza Hut that stood right here. It was three days before you went off to college."

"I thought it would be best for both of us."

"No. You wanted to get laid as much as possible on your way to your bachelor's degree, Kyle."

The lighted signs of the stores around them lost their contrast, their colors bleeding together in a blur of letters and symbols, warping somehow into false facades.

The boy on the bike was off the curb now and fixed in their direction.

The Gray Man continued, "To make matters worse, you just disregarded her pain. You shut her off. Ignored her messages. Didn't call her back. You got the beauty and then realized all your own ugliness, and so you fled, leaving her behind."

"You grow up. You move on," Kyle said, his voice flat.

"Not always."

"What's this kid—" Kyle held up his hand, trying to call The Gray Man's attention to the boy on the bike.

"Focus, Kyle. Never mind him. We're almost there."

"Okay. Fine. I messed up. That's part of being a teenager. You screw up."

"No, no, no… No hiding behind the masses, Kyle."

"I don't know what you—"

"What did you *do*!"

"I hurt her."

"Yes. You changed her life, forever. She never quite recovered. It would never be about love again, with any relationship she had going forwards. She was done with it. You made her believe, once and for all, that love was a lie. Even after her marriage and having kids."

"Kids?"

The boy was bearing down on the pedals, the swift hum of the spokes on his wheels growing louder as he grew nearer.

"Oh, yes, Kyle, life goes on. Indeed. She's still alive. She has a family, and for what it's worth, she's still quite beautiful."

"What're you saying? That this is all about *Victoria*?"

"It's about a lot of things, Kyle," The Gray Man answered, and then grimly motioned over his shoulder with his thumb at the boy on the bike. "But first, it's about him."

Then The Gray Man disappeared.

The boy on the bike was only ten yards away, on a crash course with Kyle.

"Hey!" Kyle yelled.

Even now, close up, beneath the streetlights, Kyle couldn't see the boy's face beneath the hoodie. It was only when the boy stomped hard on the brakes of the bike and launched himself over the handlebars like a hooded missile that Kyle realized he wasn't human. Nothing human could move into flight that quickly from such an abrupt stop.

Stumbling backwards, Kyle tried to get away, but it was too late. The… thing… tackled him, clutching at his throat as the momentum toppled them both to the sidewalk. Kyle was barely able to turn his body enough to partially roll with the impact, the side of his head scraping across the sidewalk instead of bouncing, helping him to avoid a concussion in the process.

Bestial in ferocity and strength, the boy-thing began to overwhelm him. Kyle pushed at it, trying to put space between them and gain some leverage on the ground, like his father had taught him: when in a fight and facing any opponent stronger or larger than you, take the fight to the ground. Everything was more equal on the ground.

But this was just a boy, maybe in his teens, and yet he was still too strong for him, and a leathery hand was now punching at Kyle's face.

As they fought, his assailant's hoodie fell backwards, revealing a face of twisted raw meat, gouged cheeks and teeth like slivers of bones. His eyes were the worst: glistening red orbs that filled his sockets. Then, to Kyle's horror, it spoke in a gargled sound, as if its throat was filled with liquid. "You can't have her, maggot. You won't."

It had breath like the smell of the dead. Sweet. Sickly. Rotting flesh.

Kyle's adrenaline tripled, and he shoved at the creature with all his might, catching it off balance. It fell backwards and rolled over. Kyle heard scraping and realized that it was the creature's claws gouging for traction on the sidewalk in order to regain balance and launch another attack. Kyle stood and looked around for a weapon, a piece of wood or metal. But there was nothing.

This can't be happening. But it was. He believed it now. He had no choice but to.

The creature advanced on him and unleashed a series of punches and kicks, first to Kyle's face and chest, then to his stomach. It was no use. Kyle's mind shifted from fight to flight. He spun and grabbed at a nearby stop sign, using it to pull away from the creature, and took off at a full bolt, his right shoe slipping on a McDonald's wrapper briefly before gaining traction again.

He made it maybe ten feet before the thing jumped on his back and wrapped its legs around his waist and its forearms over his face and mouth. Kyle spun, first in one direction, then the next, trying to shake it loose. It was no use. He couldn't breathe. He could barely see.

His legs growing weak, Kyle was about to try one last time to flip the creature off of him when he saw The Gray Man reappear directly in front of them and reach up, his hands now glowing in white flame as he grabbed the creature by the head and pulled it off Kyle as though it were a child's toy.

The creature screamed and tried to push away, but The Gray Man held it firm, the white flame enveloping it from the head down and smothering its screams as its feet kicked in all directions, the predator now the prey.

The Gray Man looked at Kyle. "Do you realize now what you're up against?"

Still gasping for air, Kyle struggled to reply, managing only one word: "Yes."

The Gray Man forced the creature to the ground as he continued to speak. "Understand two things: you can see them, and they can see you. But you need to avoid them at all costs."

"No arguments," Kyle managed, his face frozen in shock.

The Gray Man's gaze fell on Kyle. "Do you know now what you need to do next?"

Kyle hesitated. "I need to find Victoria?"

"Yes."

"Seriously? You want me to go find Victoria? Why?"

"Because she's about to make the same mistake you have."

Stunned, Kyle looked warily at the creature scrambling madly in The Gray Man's grip and could only manage a weak nod.

The Gray Man nodded back. "I'll get you started, but the rest is up to you. See you soon."

Then he and the creature disappeared.

Kyle stood, stunned for a moment, before the energy that had originally transported him returned, now as a white orb that began at his feet and then expanded until it was like a cocoon of light, enveloping him and then transporting him, to where he didn't know. Panic and confusion pushed in on him as the world dissolved into blurring colors, like a melted box of crayons.

He realized that he would have to call Tamara. To tell her what he'd done. That would be bad enough. But to then tell her that he was off now to find his first love?

There was no way in heaven or hell that this was going to turn out well. He knew that much for sure.

CHAPTER 6

WITH JUANITA GONE AND the kids asleep, Tamara tried calling Kyle twice, but each time his phone went straight to voicemail. Evidently this would have to be dealt with tomorrow, but her frustrations were rising and sleep was not going to be an easy commodity to come by. Something was wrong. She could feel it.

But she was just being silly. "Best to just go to bed and end this day," she whispered.

After turning out the lights in the kitchen, she went and checked on both kids one more time. Seeing that they were sleeping peacefully, she turned out the hall light, in the process noticing more family pictures, neatly arranged on the wall, with a lingering sense of sadness.

While undressing in her bedroom, she took note of her body. The Zumba classes were working. Her arms and shoulders were becoming leaner. She had never been heavy, but the baby weight had been the hardest to purge. It had taken carrot juice in place of two meals a day, the Zumba classes and a three-month boot camp to get her to this point. Her abs weren't ripped, not like when she'd been on the volleyball team back in college, but they were firm now.

Age was most evident in her eyes and in the crow's feet that had been planted there, one line at a time, over the years. But her body was still good.

Based on the meeting tonight, she still had "it," and that made her feel good. She'd had an old buck and young buck circling her, and she was embarrassed to admit it, but it felt good. But why be embarrassed? She hadn't been with anyone but Kyle for over seventeen years now.

Besides, what was wrong with thinking about... Ben.

He was a baby, but she could teach him things.

Shaking her head she turned away from the mirror, as if it were the cause of these odd inner reflections, showing her not just the lines around her eyes but the lines that were forming inside her now too, delineating her.

While walking to the bathroom, she noticed the quiet of the house. After putting her hair up, she removed her makeup and washed her face before finishing the ritual by rubbing Oil of Olay into her cheeks and around her eyes. She felt like crying again but instead brushed her teeth, noticing that a glob of toothpaste had fallen into the sink. She didn't care in the least.

Her thoughts were calmed, as if the bathroom were some sort of cave immune to the wavelengths that she'd been fighting off a moment ago. But as soon as she stepped back onto the soft carpet in the bedroom, her thoughts turned once again to Ben.

He was not her subordinate so much as a junior cow-orker. Still, she had learned back in college, when she had waitressed at Red Lobster and made out with the prep-cook, that work was a place to best avoid messing around.

But Ben's broad shoulders reminded her of one of the swim team boys she'd dated, the only other man she'd slept with besides Kyle, and the way he kissed her and almost enveloped her when they made love, making her vision blur every time they finished.

She laid in bed in the dark and tried to fight the memories off, but they were like ghosts reclined in the sheets next to her, a whispering audience demanding more and more attention.

And maybe a little self-satisfaction.

No. She shouldn't do this. It wasn't right.

She and Kyle had just had a fight, that was all.

But Ben was young, and he wasn't tired of her like Kyle. He still thought she was beautiful, and he still listened when she talked. He was almost like a sweet puppy the way he panted after her. But unleashed, given his moment to conquer her, he would take charge, she could sense it.

She closed her eyes and was just about to surrender to the fantasy when for some reason she thought of Kyle dead somewhere, broken and bleeding in some idiot friend's car, one or the other of them having decided to take the wheel that night.

The force of this jarring vision ruined the mood completely.

What if he was dead?

What would she tell the children? Worse, what would she do? Despite everything, the notion that she would never see Kyle again made her sick to her stomach.

She rolled over and buried her face in her pillow. She was just full of terrifyingly crazy and emotional thoughts tonight, wasn't she? Maybe it was just PMS.

Or maybe this was just the worst birthday ever.

** *

Napoleon sat in the passenger seat of the car, the interior lights reflecting off the windshield in contrast to the night sky beyond, while Parker drove to Kyle Fasano's residence in La Cañada. It seemed like a logical place to start because, as far as they knew, Fasano was the one who was still alive. Why he'd left his car behind at the hotel was a mystery that could be figured out later.

Since it was about a half-hour drive and he still felt like crap, Napoleon tried to get in a quick nap, but he couldn't. Despite the ache in his head and the weariness that hung on his bones, there simply was no getting around it: he was fighting *la desesperación* again, too.

The black asphalt of the 5 Freeway stretched out like an endless eel, the headlights from the car casting a dull glow ahead of them. Like a hypnotist's watch, the yellow lane lines ripping alongside the front of the car in rapid succession lulled Napoleon into recollections he would have preferred to avoid.

She said she was leaving because he was a hard man, with or without the booze, drunk or sober. She had been raised in a good Venezuelan home by parents of modest means who were never able to escape the barrio she'd been brought up in, a place not as bad as Napoleon's East LA neighborhood, but not much better either. Countries could be different in all sorts of ways, save poverty; it was a human condition that transcended politics or culture.

Over the years Napoleon had observed that hunger was hunger, be it for lack of food or lack of love, and it could always reduce things back down to the base roles of the human species: men used violence to get what they wanted and women used their bodies. Each gender had a weapon and used it at will. To the men, life became cheap; no less so than the notion of love to the women.

Despite the odds, he and Esperanza had first met by bumping into one another at Union Station in Los Angeles, Napoleon on his way back from a fishing trip in San Diego,

Esperanza on her way to Montebello to live with her aunt after finally getting her green card. He was twenty years younger and thirty pounds lighter then, freshly tanned and returning to work as a beat cop on the streets where he'd grown up.

She was strikingly beautiful and blatantly sexual in her self-confidence. Napoleon had seen this type of *chica* before, many times. Even then, in her mid-twenties, without what was between her legs she was little more than a jaded child. There was one very important difference to Esperanza though: she had figured this out for herself already and was resentful about it. She was determined to become something more than a new position in someone's bed.

Since they were joking and flirting with each other as they exited the building, Napoleon figured he had nothing to lose and asked her if she wanted to get some dinner nearby, on Olvera Street. She asked what, exactly, was Olvera Street, and he laughed and told her that her Spanish sounded funny. She said his did too. Her aunt wasn't expecting her for a while, so she agreed. She was not only hot, but she had the guts to go out with a stranger in a strange city too.

It was later that night, back at his place, as he reached up her skirt and felt the switchblade strapped against her thigh, when he realized why she'd been so bold. She could take care of herself. They screwed the night away, and afterwards she cried, telling him that she felt cheap. He told her that he loved her, words he'd never used before and couldn't believe he was saying, especially to someone he'd just met, and she laughed in his face, her spit and tears mixing on his forehead like a baptism of shame.

It took him weeks and then months to win her over, driving out to Montebello to see her and prove to her that finally, in her life and his, they could both believe that love was more than a fake commodity with a bad exchange rate.

She left him, three years later, two years after they were married, for another man who'd gotten her pregnant. Napoleon would never forget that day; in fact, he still relived it a few times a week. He'd asked her why, and she simply replied: *desesperación.* Desperation.

She was desperate for the love they had first shared, which wore off after Napoleon was promoted to detective and buried himself in those first cases so crucial to a young career. Napoleon didn't believe her, and he told her so. What she was really desperate for was the child that Napoleon wasn't able to give her. After standing by her the whole time they thought she was the problem, she bailed six months after the doctor's test showed *he* was the one who was sterile.

He sighed heavily in the car, hoping that Parker didn't hear. These were never good thoughts. He wanted a drink, but he was eight years sober and not about to go there. Briefly opening his eyes, he noticed the traffic on the freeway was light, even for this hour, before his mind slipped back in time again.

That's what had really unraveled things in the end. His hard life and hard job mixed with hard liquor and, well, what kind of man can't make babies? He hated himself, and he hated her for reminding him every day of what he couldn't do. His mother had been killed in a car accident when he was nine, his father had fled to Mexico never to be seen again, and his grandparents had been forced to raise him on two nickels and their feeble-ass prayers, which everyone in their neighborhood knew were answered one out of every ten times. And after all of that, what had God blessed him with? A broken dick. Thanks. Amen.

He coughed a bit but was able to keep it under control this time. He thought of Caitlyn Hall, dead now, before life could kill her like it was killing everyone else, like it was killing him: slowly.

Esperanza had gone and left behind only one thing, it seemed: *la desesperación*. It was his now, and whenever it came over him, Napoleon had trained himself to think of one thing: his nephew, Efren.

In Napoleon's apartment there was a Batman night-light that Efren had given him "cause you're a good guy, Tio, like Bruce Wayne." Efren was all of ten and one of the few things in this world that Napoleon could say he truly loved.

His older sister, Ana, became a hood rat after their mother was killed. Ana had become pregnant four years later, by some shit *vato* who had gotten "jumped" into Cuatro Flats, a local gang, and a year later, gotten himself jumped right into a coffin after taking two to the head behind a trash dumpster. Life was cheap.

Life was desperate.

Ana found a new thug soon after—this one a member of a different gang, White Fence—who knocked her up with two more kids, the youngest being little Efren. Welfare provided her a base income. Ana sold stolen jeans and blouses from Macy's and Nordstrom's to cover the rest. Not despite the fact that Napoleon was a cop, but *in* spite of it.

When Napoleon graduated from the police academy, she showed up drunk to tell him what a sellout he was. This from a woman who had taken two lovers from two separate gangs, which was practically unheard of. They hadn't spoken much since, save for Christmas and the kids' birthdays. Whenever he did make a brief appearance, he ruined the whole party, filled as they were with gangsters, all of whom knew that he wasn't just a cop but a real cop, one who would jack them up in an instant if given the chance. Ana had kept Napoleon away from her first two kids, but tolerated him now for Efren's sake, because his father was in jail and he adored his uncle. The feeling was mutual.

It was sad there was no love between Napoleon and his sister, but Efren? He would be fine. Napoleon wondered what Ana would think when the day came that Napoleon checked out, killed no doubt by one of the very thugs she partied with, and she found out that it was Efren's name that was on Napoleon's life insurance and pension funds.

He took Efren out every other weekend, to the movies, to the park, to the station. Wherever. Each time it was the same message: get an education, be the smart one, stay away from the gangs. If Napoleon had a say, Efren would be different. Efren would never be desperate.

He and Parker had transitioned from the 5 to the 2 Freeway a while back. The Fasano's lived in La Canada, a nice suburb nestled in the upper foothills of the San Gabriel Valley, on a street called Haven Way, off Angeles Crest Highway. They would be there very soon, but not soon enough.

He had to change the channels in his mind. That's what his therapist used to tell him. When the thoughts got too heavy, you just had to reach into the clicker of your consciousness and change the damned channel.

So he did.

The hole in that hotel window was not man-made.

The thought astonished him. A case was all hard facts, data and a touch of intuition, but above all else, it was always centered in some form of reason. That a pretty blond banged a married man and ended up dead was of little surprise. Love triangles almost always ended badly because one of the corners inevitably couldn't bear the weight. Someone sometimes kills someone else to be with the one who's left, usually to find that the one who's left doesn't want to be with them to begin with.

In his twenty-three years on the force, Napoleon could count on two hands the number of love triangle cases he had dealt with where one of the three parties ended up dead, one way or another, with families, careers and futures left in ruin, all for a few steamy nights and whispered lies in the dark. He didn't get it. Never would.

Napoleon focused, reimagining the crime scene at the hotel. That hole in the window was all wrong. Get her drunk? Okay. Throw her out of the window? Maybe. But there was no balcony, no sliding glass door. The window was thick and the hole simply too high up to make any sense. She says, "I love you and I want you to leave her." He says, "I can't." She says, "Then I'll call your wife and tell her." He throws her out a window? No. Okay. She says, "I will report you to HR for sexually harassing me." He throws her out a window? No. Unless Mr. Fasano was a complete psycho, he doesn't risk everything over a girl who just paid for the room on her *own* credit card. It showed mutual consent. There was a used condom in the room too, and assuming the autopsy came back with no semen in the body or obvious signs of forced entry, then that showed the event was pre-planned by one or both parties as well.

But that credit card move was smart, wasn't it, Mr. Fasano? Having her pay for the room was a smart move. What did you say, I wonder? "I left my wallet in the car?" You were covering your tracks before you made them, weren't you? I haven't met your wife yet, Mr. Fasano, but I bet she handles the finances in your house. You didn't want that on the credit card statement, did you? *"Honey, what's this $275 charge to the Hilton for last month?"*

He coughed, this time onto the back of his hand.

The 2 gave way to the 210 eastbound, where it would be a short jump to the Angeles Crest Highway exit.

Parker finally spoke. "Hope you're covering that damn cough."

"Screw you," Napoleon replied while laying his head against the cool glass of the passenger window to belay his fever, his thoughts still troubled by that hotel window and another image, stubbornly clinging to the edges of his mind.

Of Esperanza, walking down the sidewalk to her lover's car, her gait hurried and determined.

He'd been desperate.

Desperate to stop her. To tell her that he still loved her, no matter what.

Instead he'd let her go.

Because she'd been desperate too.

CHAPTER 7

THEY ARRIVED AT THE Fasano home at just after one in the morning. Napoleon was not surprised to see the lights were out. Perhaps Mrs. Fasano had waited for her husband to get home and then given up. Or maybe things in their marriage were such that Mr. Fasano stayed out late quite frequently. Either way, it was about to get interesting.

As they parked in the driveway, a light came on and there was movement in the kitchen window. The backlit outline of a female with long hair appeared. Over twenty years of being a cop and you learned how to fill in the outline. Odds were that Mrs. Fasano was going to be attractive.

She answered their knock only after making them hold their badges up to the small semi-circle window at the top of the front door, and she did not disappoint. She had dark hair, big eyes and a full chest. That was as far as Napoleon would let his eyes go, and even then only briefly. But the rookie didn't seem to know any better; he was allowing himself a full-body scan, as if he worked at the airport or something. Napoleon cringed. They needed Mrs. Fasano to be receptive to their visit, and the last thing any woman wanted on top of two strange men on her doorstep in the middle of the night was to have one of them leering at her.

As if reading his mind, Mrs. Fasano folded her arms across her chest instantly, and though he could hope that it was only to fend off the cool night air, Napoleon knew better. Parker had already put her on the defensive before their first word had even been uttered. Great.

"Mrs. Fasano?"

"Yes?"

"I'm Detective Villa with the Los Angeles Police Department, and this is my partner, Detective Parker."

The same look Napoleon had seen on hundreds of faces came over Mrs. Fasano now, a blend of concern, fear and disbelief. It was the Holy Trinity of denial. "Uh… yes? How can I help you?"

"Do you mind if we come in?"

"First, I want to know what this is about."

Her voice was firm and self-confident. She was evidently not going to allow an inch of cooperation until she established some sense of control over the situation. Not the usual response to the police. Napoleon was impressed and immediately aware of his cold again. This was not going to be easy. He had hoped, deep down, that it would be. Anything to get home to bed a little sooner would've been nice.

"It's about your husband," Parker piped in, breaking protocol by not following Napoleon's lead. He was going to have to teach the rookie from the ground up, it seemed.

"Kyle?" she said, a little more concern in her voice. "He's not here. What's wrong?"

Napoleon held his hand up slightly towards Parker, a silent signal to put him back in the passenger seat, before continuing, "Well, Mrs. Fasano… there's been an incident."

She blinked. Twice. "My God, what happened?"

"Please. May we come in?"

The shock was now setting in a bit, and they hadn't even begun. Stepping aside, she motioned for them to come in.

It was cruel, but Napoleon let the dozens of horrible thoughts she might have going on inside her head do their work. Early onset panic was good for getting information. You had to stop it before it got too far though, or most people either got hysterical or started babbling like idiots.

"We can sit in the dining room," she said, almost in a whisper. "My children are asleep, so can we please keep this quiet?"

"Sure thing," Napoleon replied.

Parker nodded and, to Napoleon astonishment, walked over to the table and sat down first. *Idiot strikes again.* All the "ladies first" stuff aside, Mrs. Fasano was supposed to be put at ease. It was the little things that mattered, and kicking back at her dining room table before she even pulled out her own chair was just plain stupid.

She sat down slowly, her eyes a little wide. Her face said it clearly; she already thought her husband was dead.

Napoleon immediately moved to counter that notion. "Have you heard from your husband tonight, Ma'am?"

She sighed heavily. "No. Why?"

"We're trying to determine his whereabouts."

"Why?"

"We need to discuss something with him."

"What the hell does that mean?"

"It means we think he may have information important to our investigation. Have you heard from him tonight?"

She blinked some more. "No. I mean… yes. There was a message when I got home from work a little while ago."

"What did it say?"

"That he was going to help a drunk friend get home," she answered, looking from Napoleon to Parker and back again. "Why? What happened?"

Again, Parker chimed in. "Are you and your husband separated?"

Napoleon looked at the floor in frustration. All rookies were green, but this one? He was winter green. No. Worse. Green like deep-water moss. Now questioning her would be a mess.

Mrs. Fasano's back stiffened. "What? No! What kind of question is that?"

Napoleon checked Parker with a glance that said "shut the hell up," which Parker evidently understood because he immediately looked down at the table.

The rookie's eagerness hopefully squashed, Napoleon moved to damage control. "I'm sorry, Mrs. Fasano, it's been a long—"

"Listen, what the hell is going on?" She had one hand on the table now, as if to assert authority in her own home, but Napoleon noticed that her other hand was shaking.

"There's been a fatality, and we think your husband may have some information as to what occurred." The word fatality was intentionally used. The word "death" might've put her even more on the defensive.

"A fatality? Who? Where?"

Napoleon had been holding back a wicked cough since they'd come in the door. He couldn't suppress it any longer, letting loose into the sleeve of his jacket and swallowing the phlegm. He would've killed for a glass of water, but now was obviously not the time to ask.

Mrs. Fasano removed her hand from the table and crossed her arms again, a hard look in her eye. There was no use; her walls were up. He had to remove a few bricks.

"A young lady. At the Hilton downtown."

Silence. Her eyes locked with Napoleon's and they were like mirrors to her thoughts. Reflected in them one moment was indignation at what was being implied, and reflected the next was a very real fear that what was being implied might actually be true.

"Who?"

"Does the name Caitlyn Hall mean anything to you?"

She pressed her lips together in a thin line. Before she even spoke, Napoleon could tell she knew who Caitlyn Hall was.

"She works at my husband's office. She's new." It was a short reply, but Mrs. Fasano's face kept speaking; her eyes pinched slightly shut in a swift squint, and she was shaking her head ever so slightly. Nothing seemed to ring all the bells of human emotion more than betrayal.

"Well, sadly, she's dead."

"Oh my God." Mrs. Fasano's jaw dropping a bit before she recovered and asked, "That's horrible. But what do you think my husband might know about this?"

Napoleon had to hand it to her. She moved very swiftly back to the defensive. Maybe she was a good wife, or maybe she was just protecting her turf; but she seemed smart, which meant she most likely knew what was coming next.

"I'm sorry to tell you this, Mrs. Fasano, but your husband and Ms. Hall checked into the Hilton together."

She looked to the ceiling, locking her gaze there for a few seconds, and then the tears came, perching in the corners of her eyes before she wiped them with the back of her hand so quickly and defiantly that you would've never known they were there. Immediately Napoleon was able to surmise a little more about Kyle Fasano: he was most likely not a weak man, because he had married a strong woman.

Napoleon watched the gears in Mrs. Fasano's head turn before she replied, "So maybe she was the friend he was trying to get to a safe place."

In most instances, denial was a tad pitiful. Not so with Mrs. Fasano. Napoleon almost smiled. *A brilliant observation, my dear Watson. A defense attorney would no doubt raise the same question. But too bad you're the prime suspect's wife, and most likely only half-believe what you're saying to begin with.* Still, it was a chance to chill things out a bit.

"Perhaps, yes."

"So what happened to her?"

Napoleon's response was calculated. "She fell to her death."

"Fell? As in, what, off the balcony?"

"There, uh, was no balcony."

"So how did she fall?"

"That's what we want to ask your husband about."

"How do you know he was there when it happened?"

It was the wrong question to be asking, and Napoleon was glad.

"We have reason to believe he was the last one to see her alive."

She paused for a moment, and then, impressing Napoleon even more, she smoothly redirected her attention to the weak link at the table, asking Parker this time, "What makes you think that?"

"We have footage," Parker replied, glancing nervously at Napoleon.

"What type of footage?"

"Surveillance footage from the hotel," Napoleon cut back in, still relieved she was asking the wrong questions. "But we'd rather not get into all that right now."

"Well, with all due respect, maybe I do."

Napoleon exhaled slowly. Mrs. Fasano was taking control of the conversation, which he would've never let happen if he hadn't been so damned sick, and if he hadn't had the rookie's fumbling to cover for.

"Wait." She paused and held up her hand. The light from the chandelier over the dining room table was bright and cast shadows across her face. She had a few wrinkles here or there. Napoleon had her pegged in her mid-thirties, or a little older.

"You said she fell but..." Mrs. Fasano hesitated, looking confused for a moment before she composed herself and at last asked the right question. "But how is that, if there was no balcony? Did she fall out of the window?"

Shit.

"Ma'am, we really can't get into any details of the investigation—"

Mrs. Fasano pressed. "Did she kill herself?"

If this lady gets an attorney, she's going to be dangerous, Napoleon thought.

"We really need to speak to Mr. Fasano."

"I told you, he only left the one message."

"Can we listen to it?"

"No."

It was one word, and it ushered an awkward silence into the room. This was going nowhere. Napoleon didn't want to do it, but it was time for another low blow.

"Were you aware that your husband and Ms. Hall were having an affair?" Napoleon asked, faking his embarrassment at the question.

Mrs. Fasano's stare bore into Napoleon, and her self-confidence seemed to come back with a full head of steam as she replied, "I think you should leave now."

6 9

Beyond belief, Parker opened his mouth again. "We have footage of that as well, Mrs. Fasano."

Indignantly, she turned her head and glared at Parker. "I said I want you to leave."

Napoleon sneezed and then coughed again. This had all gone to hell, and quickly. He'd never handled an interview so badly before. His cold and fever were killing him, the numb-nuts rookie wouldn't shut the hell up, and the captain would have their asses for this.

He decided it was time to go and was rising from his chair to leave when the phone rang. Mrs. Fasano had a stunned look on her face.

It rang a second time, and now Mrs. Fasano was obviously torn.

She knew as well as they did that it could be her husband calling, and at the worst possible time as far as privacy was concerned. Napoleon guessed she had only three or four rings to pick up the call, so she didn't have enough time to kick them out and answer the phone too.

Sometimes you just got lucky.

So what's it going to be, Mrs. Fasano? Smarts say you hold your ground right now, with these two asshole cops in your home, but love? Love says you gotta answer that phone.

The third ring did her in. She rose quickly and raced to the counter, leaned over it to the phone beyond and answered with an anxious hope coloring her voice. "Hello? Kyle?"

Napoleon smiled, on the inside.

Love won.

She was a good wife.

CHAPTER 8

HEARING HIS WIFE'S VOICE, Kyle exhaled deeply. His heart went flat in his chest, as if it were being pinned down by his throat. This was it. Time to own up to the mess he'd made of things. And what a horrendous mess it was.

"T-Tamara," he managed, swallowing hard.

Her voice sounded scared. "Kyle? Kyle where are you. No... wait—"

He felt the blood draining from his arms and legs. Dammit. There was a distinct chance he was going to cry. What a coward. *You do this, and then you cry?*

"Listen, babe, I..."

But she cut him off. "Kyle." It was his name voiced as a plea. He could tell she was crying, probably still upset about their fight on the phone earlier.

"Tamara, listen... I don't know what's happened, but I've really messed things up, baby."

"No." She spoke sternly this time, one word, a flat command that startled him. It was out of place. How had she gone from crying one second to such a—

"The police are here, Kyle. They want to speak with you."

He sat involuntarily, his legs collapsing beneath him on the dirt gravel next to the wall of a Circle K in Beaury, the small town he'd arrived at when the light cocoon around him had receded, when he'd finally decided to stop and make the call.

No. This wasn't how he wanted her to find out.

"What are you talking about?" he managed, complete denial now flooding both spheres of his brain, his emotions drowning in panic. *This must be what shock feels like. I'm going into shock.*

"They want to know what happened with Caitlyn," Tamara replied, a hint of accusation in her voice.

"Tamara, it's not what you think. I mean, it's—"

"Dammit, Kyle! I don't have time for this! The kids are asleep and there are cops in the house and I don't know what the hell is going on but…" She was crying now. He heard her say something to someone and then the phone was jostled before a new voice came on the line.

"Mr. Fasano? This is Detective Villa with the LAPD."

The world grew dizzy. *Is this really happening? Yes, it is. Oh my God. It is.*

Kyle managed to summon four words, but like some sort of spell, they brought him a little energy. "I didn't do it."

"I have no reason to doubt you, sir, but the fact of the matter is we need you to come home so we can discuss it."

"Discuss what?"

"Whatever it was that happened tonight," the detective replied.

Be it the shock, the numbness, the horror of the moment or whatever, Kyle felt a fleeting sense of panic, and he almost did a crazy thing: he almost laughed. Surely only guilty people laughed in such situations. But wait, he *was* guilty. But not of what they thought he'd done. He imagined that this man on the phone with him, Patton or Attila or whatever the hell his dictator name was again, would be the one to laugh, actually, if Kyle tried to tell him the real story, of Caitlyn, The Gray Man and teleporting to Torrance and wrestling a demon boy on a bicycle.

"You would never believe me," he thought, and then to his dismay realized that he'd actually spoken aloud.

"I'm sure there's a reasonable explanation, Mr. Fasano, but we have to talk, sir."

"I didn't do this!"

"I'm sure you didn't, sir," and he said it so kindly, so smoothly, that Kyle almost missed the tiniest tone of condescension in his voice. It was the same tone Kyle used with the kids from time to time when they didn't finish their dinner or brush their teeth before bedtime.

Anger welled up in him, firing the circuits to his brain. "She wasn't normal," Kyle managed.

"Sir, please, can you just tell us where you are?"

"You have no idea what's going on."

"Nor can we, until we get a chance to talk. I can send someone to pick you up if you need me to. Where are you?"

Kyle's imagination went into overdrive. He saw himself being hauled away in a police cruiser, being questioned and no doubt being jailed. Then he thought of Tamara and the kids, the scrutiny and the humiliation. A second mortgage on the house would be next, no doubt, for bail and to hire a good attorney—if he even got bail.

"You don't understand."

"Mr. Fasano, the situation you're in is serious, and we need you—"

He could hear Tamara, demanding the phone from the detective and telling him to leave the house.

"Ma'am, he needs to listen to us, and so do you."

Kyle felt his panic returning. "You let me speak to my wife, you asshole!"

"Mr. Fasano, you need to come home."

"Give me the phone! Now!" Tamara screamed in the background.

"I'm not coming home," Kyle said. Again, just four words. But these four felt like stitches, sewing him to his fate.

"Sir, I strongly suggest you rethink that."

"I didn't do it."

"Sir…"

"Tell my wife I love her…" Kyle despised himself as he felt his throat catch and the tears came, all while on the phone with another man, and a stranger at that.

"Mr. Fasano, you need to tell her that yourself. Just let us pick you—"

"You tell her that she knows I would never hurt anybody."

There was more screaming and yelling now. A third voice joined the discussion, probably another cop, and he was telling Tamara to calm down.

"Mr. Fasano, let's just talk a bit here…"

Suddenly, all those movies where the cops need a certain amount of time to trace a call came racing to Kyle's mind. He was on his cell phone, and they had GPS these days and…

Oh shit!

Kyle stepped away from the side of the Circle K and smashed his phone to pieces against the wall, leaving gray and white plastic chips like glitter below a sea of graffiti across the red bricks.

My God. Oh my God. What now? They're after me. They're gonna be after me now. What if they already tracked my location?

He felt sick with adrenaline and nervous energy, both coursing through his veins and colliding in his stomach. Wiping the back of his hand across his eyes, he felt hot sweat on his neck as a brief gust of wind raced over the Circle K. He should have looked up Victoria's address before he smashed the phone. He should have done his homework, something, a little scouting for data before cutting off his main avenue of information.

No. No, it was good that I didn't. They would have all that data on their end now too if I had.

They would know where he was going and who he was looking for. Now they didn't. That was his only edge. They knew where he was though, or they would shortly. He had to get moving, no matter what direction.

He reached into his pocket and pulled out its contents: a toothpick, a hundred and eighty-four dollars and his ATM card, which he had pocketed at the bar after paying the tab, too much in a hurry to get going with Caitlyn to worry about putting it back into his wallet. The card would be shut down soon. Or they might wait to use it to trace his movements. He needed to find a bank and get what money he could.

He turned from the wall and looked up. The sky had gone from flat black to the deep black that harkens the true dead of night, the color of time between one and two in the morning, when only insomniacs and grave yard shifters roam the earth.

The buses wouldn't be running for a while. A cab would be too obvious and provide a witness to where he would be dropped off. He wanted to get moving but it was obvious that now was not the time. He was thinking too much.

Stop. Find a bank. You're going to need money. There's a boulevard up ahead, looks like about two miles. Just start walking and hope you get lucky.

So he did, his head swiveling, his eyes trying to pierce the darkness, hoping that between here and the boulevard he didn't hear the whooshing of any bicycle tires.

* * *

Napoleon looked at Parker. "The line went dead."

Mrs. Fasano stood at her kitchen counter in tears, looking both confused and furious. She grabbed the phone from Napoleon, spun and threw it against the couch. "Get out!" she yelled.

A small voice came from the hallway adjacent to the kitchen. "Mommy?" A little girl, about ten or eleven, stood there in the half-light cast from the kitchen.

Napoleon glanced at Parker, who looked like a man who had just crapped in his pants. Being a beat cop and roughing up tweakers was one thing, but this sudden jaunt down the back alleys of domestic bliss turned upside down had obviously thrown Parker for a loop.

That's what you get, dipshit, for staring at her tits on the way in, looking her over, making yourself too much at home, popping off about her marriage. She was hardly going to like us after tonight, but she didn't need to hate us.

Napoleon sighed. When the kids arrived it was time to exit anyway. "Ma'am, I'm gonna leave my card."

Tamara glared at Napoleon before speaking to her daughter. "Janie, go to your room."

"But Mom…"

"Now!"

Tears welled in the little girl's eyes and she hesitated before, much to Napoleon's relief, she retreated back into the hallway. Napoleon's gut told him that she hadn't gone back to her room though, just far enough away to keep listening, and why not? Her mother was crying, and two strange men were in the house.

As if she were a ghost summoned by his thoughts, little Janie reappeared and it was her defiance, not her tears, that broke Napoleon's heart. "I won't go, Mommy. I won't! Who are they? What are they doing here? Where's Daddy?"

Mrs. Fasano put out her arms, and the little girl raced to her side. As he walked towards them, his hand outstretched with his business card, Napoleon noticed that Mrs. Fasano's left hand was under her daughter's chin, cradling it. She used her right hand to wipe the tears from her own eyes before she took Napoleon's card.

"Thank you. I will forward this to our attorney in the morning, and I promise you I will be speaking to your boss at that time as well. How dare you come into this house and act this way towards me?"

Amazingly, Parker opened his mouth again. "We're just trying to get to the bottom of—"

"Oh you will get to the bottom, trust me, I'll see to it," Tamara shouted. "Now get out!"

Napoleon nodded, and he and Parker exited the home with Mrs. Fasano and the child following behind them. She slammed the door at their backs as they made their way off the front porch before Napoleon heard the lock and deadbolt being engaged.

"Great job, Parker," Napoleon seethed as they walked to the car.

"What?" Parker protested.

"To Protect and to Serve," Napoleon added wryly, then sneezed twice.

They got into the car and Napoleon waited until they pulled onto the street before he let Parker have it. "Okay, dumb shit, listen up. The next time you tag along with my ass, you better keep your asshole mouth puckered shut, are we clear?!"

"Hey, man!"

"Don't 'hey, man' me. You're a damn *trainee*! Your job is to learn, not take the lead. You do know that, right?"

"Yeah, but—"

"No 'but' nothing! You jackass, are you trying to impress me? Earn a gold star or something? The captain's gonna have my dick in a vice over this one, all because I couldn't keep some greenhorn in his fucking place!"

"She wasn't cooperating and—"

"She never had a chance to. Everything you did was wrong."

"Look, man, I thought—" Parker again tried to interject.

"There! Right there is problem number one. You thought. Therefore you weren't."

"I wasn't what?" Parker said defiantly.

"You weren't attuned to the attitude or the body language of the interviewee. Had you been, you would've noticed she was ours from the moment we arrived. She was worried. She wanted the same damned answers to the same damned questions we did, you numb-nut."

"Hey, man, I don't appreciate the name calling, dude."

"Dude? ¡*Ay Dios mio!* Él no conoce su cabeza de su culo."

"What's that mean?"

"That you don't know your head from your ass! I ain't your dude, or your pal, or your *Brokeback Mountain* running buddy, you got it?"

"Shit. Okay. Calm down."

They drove down Angeles Crest Highway to the 210 Freeway in silence, Napoleon needing to reload on throat lozenges, one inside each cheek, to offset the extra pain from all the yelling. He was beginning to ramp up for another round of brow beating when his fatigue accelerated from dog-tired to bone-weary.

He looked over at Parker, who sat stiffly with both hands still gripping the wheel. Kid had pride. That might be good someday, when he knew how to use it. He needed help in the smarts department, but what person in their first week at McDonald's didn't screw up, much less as a detective on their first murder case? For a second Napoleon felt a little bad for him.

"She wanted to know where her husband was, Parker."

Parker nodded slowly, chin out.

"What wife doesn't want to know that—heck, to be fair, what husband doesn't—at one o'clock in the morning *before* two cops show up at the door? Had we handled ourselves like proper gentleman, had we been support-ive, acted worried and concerned, had we played up the kid angle properly… you know, like, 'We don't want the children waking up in the morning asking where their father is, right?'… then her mommy instincts would've come out in a healthy way, instead of the momma-bear-snarling-her-fangs-at-us-on-the-way-out-the-door way we just experienced."

"Okay. I hear ya," Parker said, sounding encouraged, taking one hand off the wheel, relaxing a bit now. *You were a jock, weren't you, Parker?* Napoleon thought. *You're going to be all about the whole "coach me up and put me in" approach, aren't you?*

"We're their friends, Parker. Remember that. Perp. Perp's mamma. Perp's priest. I don't give a shit. We're their friends first, until we get what we want, at least. If they help us, then we can be their friends forever. I don't wanna hurt nobody. I got enough enemies."

"What if they don't help us?"

Napoleon sneezed again and wiped his sleeve across his nose. It was starting to get damp with snot, like when you're a little kid and pay the tissue box no mind. "People been killing other people for forever and a day, Parker. People like me and you been trying to catch 'em for just as long."

"So, what about Mrs. Fasano?"

"She gets a pass for now, because we never gave her a chance to be our friend. We never got a read on her. If we had, maybe she would've told him to turn himself in, like we wanted, instead of what just happened."

"What do you mean?" Parker asked, looking at Napoleon.

"You heard it. She stonewalled us. She shut him down on the phone. She doesn't want us to find him. At least not now."

"Why?"

"Because in some cases it goes like this: husband bangs pretty little office girl for a few months, but pretty little office girl is a gold digger who has college tuition to pay off or gets mad when he won't fall in love with her and leave the wife, whatever, and so she starts to fleece him, or maybe she threatens to tell the wife or cost him his job for banging a subordinate. So husband runs to wifey, who loves him, or doesn't really, but doesn't want to lose all she has and go back to square one because of some little home wrecker. Together, the loving couple has a brilliant idea to off the bitch and make it look like a suicide."

"You think that's what happened?"

"I dunno yet. But I doubt it. I think she's just protecting her turf and her man's back right now, until she gets the real scoop from him."

"And when she does?"

"Let's just say I have a feeling she'll come around to our way of thinking."

"Yeah?"

"Yeah. There's that age-old saying, Parker. Can you guess which one?"

Parker mulled it over for a little too long before he finally said, "The one about hell hath no fury?"

Napoleon smiled. "You bet your ass."

CHAPTER 9

EVEN IF HE'S ONLY *slept with this girl, I'm going to want a divorce.*

Tamara looked at the clock on the nightstand in her bedroom: 1:43 a.m.

If he's slept with her and *murdered her…?*

She cut her thoughts short. It was too horrible to even imagine. She ran her fingers through her hair and pulled at the roots, using the pain to keep herself awake. Then she tried calling her best friend Trudy, who was in New York on a business trip. No answer, so Tamara left her a message. It was barely Saturday morning. If Trudy partied with co-workers the night before – which was highly likely – there was no telling what time she'd call back.

Tamara didn't think she was rational enough right now to trust her judgment, but Kyle had sounded guilty. They'd talked so briefly, the conversation unnatural and stiff, but a wife gets to know her husband, inside and out, like dust knows an old book.

He hadn't made a flat proclamation of innocence, which is what she would've expected after all these years together. So was he guilty of the affair, the murder, both or neither? How many pieces of this story was she missing?

She thought of Caitlyn and felt nauseous. Tamara had seen her once, when she'd stopped by Kyle's office to get some paperwork signed for the addition on the house.

Caitlyn fit the MO of the sales reps at Kyle's company: young and pretty. But she dressed a little sluttier than the others, which might've been an omen of sorts. Now she was dead, and the police thought that Kyle had something to do with it and...

She was stunned at the emotions that began to overcome her, a vitriolic mix of rage, sorrow, jealousy and self-loathing on repeat, like a music playlist that she couldn't pause or turn off. She repressed her sobs so as not to wake Janie, who was breathing softly next to her, having refused to go back to her own bed after the police left. She'd seen too much and had too many questions in her little head, which forced Tamara to lie to her to get her to settle down. "The police have mixed up Daddy with someone else, honey. They just need to talk to him to clear things up." Half-truths, yes, but there was no reason for both of them to go through the night without any sleep.

Had Kyle really done this? *Oh my God. This can't be true.* Their community was small and affluent, which meant the gossip might be tinged with just a little bit of glee. Word would spread fast. *What will everyone say? Will I have to pull the kids out of school? Jesus, what do I do?*

She looked around their dimly lit bedroom, everything a water-colored blur through her tears, before her attention rested on Kyle's pillow, right next to her. How many times had she looked upon him in his sleep and thought how lucky she was to have him? It was all ashes now, every bit of it. She kept trying to tell herself that nothing had been proven yet, and that she owed it to her husband to hold the line.

But she couldn't forget Kyle's voice, and worse, she couldn't get the look in that Mexican detective's eyes out of her head either, those dark Saint Bernard eyes with the big bags beneath them. They seemed to be gently telling her that her world was coming undone.

Wiping an arm across her eyes, she tried to pull herself together but couldn't. There was too much to think about. She would have to call off work for Monday, but not right now. Tomorrow she could call Ben and let him relay the message that she wouldn't be in for a few days. That would be better. He would understand if she told him something had come up, and he wouldn't pry, though right now that wouldn't necessarily be an unwelcome thing. At least he'd care. Perhaps a bit too much, but she told herself that maybe she didn't care about that anymore either. All this time while she'd been busy playing the good wife, Kyle was probably having his affair with Caitlyn.

How long has this been going on? I'm such a fool!

Shame came over her, and her mind began going round and round, one detail after another of what might've happened, could've happened and now would happen. Details upon details, like a Google search in her head predicating the answer to one query alone: *What do I do next?*

* * *

From the Circle K, Kyle made his way to the main boulevard. Once there, with the night at its darkest, he found it impossible to get the lay of the land. He had nowhere to go and nothing he could do, at least not yet, and it was getting cold.

Beaury was a small town, and enough behind the times that it still had, to his amazement, a stand-alone telephone booth. He went back and forth in his mind over which was safer, the exposed openness of sitting on the curb, where he could at least escape another attack if something else came after him, or the shelter of the telephone booth, which could leave him hopelessly trapped. Who was he kidding? Without The Gray Man's help the last time around, he would've been killed easily anyway.

After stepping inside the phone booth, he shut its accordion-like door tightly and sat on the corrugated steel floor, where he jammed his feet against the door hinge to give him an added sense of security. It was a little warmer in the booth than it was outside, but not nearly warm enough or comfortable enough to get any sleep. Or so he thought. The next thing he knew he was somehow waking up to the morning sun and the sound of a passing car.

He exited the phone booth groggily and with a splitting headache. The morning shadows were coming to life, casting themselves off trash cans and parked cars, and his eyes, still filled with sleep, were having trouble focusing, so at times it appeared as if the shadows were moving. He wished more cars would come by, to break up the silence. Hours earlier, that silence had been eerie. Now it was just lonely. Neither feeling was a good one.

He heard the coos of wild doves in the brush across the road and felt anything but refreshed. There was a lingering grief hanging on him, heavy, like one of those x-ray smocks filled with lead at the dentist's office. He knew this feeling. He'd felt this way after his dad had died, two years ago. He realized with bitterness that it made sense; he was experiencing *another* death now: the death of the life he once knew. *One night, one mistake and now this. That's all it took.*

Looking around he noticed that Beaury was small but not backwater small. Off to the east was a gas station. He set off towards it, figuring it was a good mile or so away. The road he traveled was wide, with a few bus stops on one side and a row of houses on the other. Taking note of the yards, trees and bushes staggered in front of and between the houses, he opted for safety reasons to stay on the bus stop side, his head and neck tucked into his shoulders against the cold morning air, his eyes scanning the road for signs of any more attackers.

Once at the gas station, he was tempted to go in, but then noticed a Denny's sign further down the road to the north and opted instead to push on. As he got closer he could see that the restaurant was actually part of a mini-mall. There was also a Dickies outlet, a CVS, a tiny post office, "Troutie's Bait and Tackle" and the obligatory yogurt shop.

Once inside the Denny's, he noted that the clock on the wall said 7:45 a.m. and took a seat at the counter and ordered coffee and pancakes from the skinny waitress who came over. He was hungry, mostly from nerves he guessed, because the smell of bacon and eggs in the air made his stomach roll instead of rumble.

The Gray Man promised him that he would be able to see them now, the demons, when they were present. He warily glanced around. There was another waitress on duty, a heavy-set redhead who was cackling in the corner with an old man in a Dodgers jacket. Besides them, a number of early waking truckers were scattered about, laughing and talking between sips of coffee, and a delivery man sat by himself, the word "Lolo's Breads" in blue cursive letters stitched on his shirt, hunched over his newspaper in furtive study of the sports page.

None of them displayed the dark eyes or sneer of the girl he was now going to be accused of murdering. He was thankful for that, but he was more thankful that none of them resembled the boy on the bike, with his gnashing teeth and hate-filled eyes.

When his order came, the skinny waitress lingered, making sure that everything was to his satisfaction. Her nametag said "Jasmine" and it made Kyle think of Tamara, of how it was the name of her favorite perfume. When Jasmine left, between syrup-covered bites of what the menu advertised as "Buttermilk Bliss" pancakes, the wheels began to turn in his head, and he was surprised at how quickly one could go from thinking like a domesticated husband to thinking like a wanted felon, as if all of us have, lying dormant within us, the ability to go rogue if forced to.

The mini-mall probably had all he would need.

The CVS could provide him with scissors, black hair dye and a bandage for the cut on his hand from when he'd smashed his cell phone against the Circle K wall the night before. He had no intention of using either the scissors or the hair dye. It was a bluff. They would hopefully begin to look for a man with short black hair. Whatever. His hair would be neither short nor black.

Kyle had one edge when he didn't want to be recognized: he was a freak when it came to wearing baseball caps. Hardly anybody could recognize him in one, not even his pastor, who one day at The Coffee Bean had stood right next to Kyle while waiting for his latte, not recognizing him until he turned to leave. His pastor had done not a double, but a triple-take before saying hello, and Kyle was used to this. The same thing had happened to him his whole life, at high school parties, in college, even at the gym. People often joked that he could rob the neighborhood bank with a cap on and get away with it.

The CVS would have cameras, a requirement now with all the meth head Sudafed and cough syrup junkies out there. Kyle imagined the cameras would be everywhere, which was fine by him. He would also buy a calling card, and the thought of what he would do with this gave him hope.

It dawned on him that he could also get a greeting card for Tamara there, and the thought of her almost made him lose it. Tears began to creep into the corners of his eyes, but he held them back. *God, I'm a basket case. I've screwed up so bad...* he thought before downing the rest of his coffee in one gulp.

The greeting card might be a bad idea, but he had no other way now of telling Tamara about what had happened, or how sorry he was, without it. Phones were out of the question.

He would get a change of clothes from the Dickies store. He doubted there would be cameras there, but just in case the hat could come later. Again, he wanted them looking for a dark-haired man with short hair, not one in a cap.

He ate a few more bites of pancakes as Jasmine came by to top off his cup, and that's when he noticed them: two truckers who hadn't been there before, sitting at the opposite end of the counter.

One wore a John Deere hat, green with a blazing yellow logo, over greasy blond hair that fell to his shoulders. He was also wearing a denim jacket over a dirty Lynyrd-Sky-nyrd t-shirt. Kyle couldn't see the rest of his outfit, but he imagined jeans and work boots. The man's eyes were a flat blue, and they stared at Kyle with such intensity that Kyle immediately shifted his gaze to the second trucker, who had long brown hair beneath a black beanie and a patchy beard. He was staring directly at Kyle too.

Beanie smiled, ever so slightly, and then inhaled deeply through his nose, like a dog catching a scent. He glanced at Jasmine, who had just arrived in front of them with their waters.

"You in season, honey?" he said to her with a sudden smile that revealed dirty yellow teeth.

Jasmine grimaced at him as if he'd spat on her. "Pig!" she said in protest, but it was a weak protest. Her body language said she didn't know them, and the grimace was soon replaced with a look of insecurity, as if maybe Beanie had been right.

"Oh, baby cakes, don't be so uptight." John Deere chuckled.

As she walked away, the look on her face was one of fear, the same thing Kyle felt when both men returned their gazes to him.

He was so lost in his grand plans of throwing the police off his trail that he hadn't even seen them come in or sit down. They were making no secret of their purpose, and they didn't seem to care one bit that Kyle knew either: they were here for him.

He thought of running, but like an animal that knows instinctively not to turn its back on two predators, Kyle knew that was a bad idea. Instead, he took a deep breath. The Gray Man would certainly come again, right? He just had to wait.

The idea was short-lived.

The Gray Man will not be coming this time. He's preoccupied somewhere. I'm on my own right now. All three thoughts were his, but they came to him like telegrams from a far off part of his mind, a part previously unknown to him.

Kyle glanced down at his pancakes. They were half gone and so was his appetite, but he opted to force some down to buy time. As he did so, Beanie started smacking his lips together like a baby suckling on a bottle. Kyle didn't want to look at them again but felt an unnatural pull to do so. As soon as he looked up, he wished he hadn't.

He was now confronted by a new vision, as if a veil had been pulled from his eyes. Beanie and John Deere still had human bodies, but their heads and faces looked like those of badly burned animals, goats perhaps. They had long, twisted horns that rose above their heads to sharp tips and their eyes were orbs—not black, as Caitlyn's had been, but red, like the boy on the bike's. It was a distinguishing difference that he knew was important but had no time to consider right now. Their animal mouths were pulled back in ghoulish grins that reached from ear to ear and emanated a raw sense of insanity.

Again, a bending sense of reality overcame Kyle, paralyzing him. No animal should ever cast a human-like grin at you.

If these were demons, these horribly mangled things with their sick smiles, what did the devil himself look like?

"You'll find out," the creature that had been Beanie said.

"Like sugar on toast, boy. Yum-yum," John Deere added before he licked his teeth with his little goat tongue and chortled.

Oh Jesus!

"Get this one, will ya? *Now* he's calling on a savior!" Beanie laughed.

John Deere leaned forwards and turned his head sideways at Kyle, mocking him. "Yeahhhhh… why weren't you doin' that when you were doggy-styling that little bitch of yours last night, boy?"

"Shut up," Kyle whispered, unable to turn away now, his gaze fixated on those horrible eyes.

"Nah. Where's the fun in that? Do you wanna know, slug, where she's at right now?"

"No," Kyle managed. His head pounded. He had the sudden sensation that this restaurant was a trap, with doors and windows but still no way out. As if to confirm this fact, he managed with the greatest of effort to use his peripheral vision.

His heart sank.

Everyone in the restaurant was frozen in place, frozen in time.

"What? You don't care no more about your little honey bee? Your little whore?"

"Shut up!" Kyle's heart raced as his words bounced around the restaurant in a muffled echo.

"Oh looooook, buddy." Beanie chuckled, slapping his partner on the shoulder. "He don-wanna know, do he?"

John Deere's eyes flashed like two briquettes peaking on the grill. A wave of hatred and mockery washed over Kyle and stole the breath from his lungs. "She getting it good now, boy. Hundreds of us are just taking turns, gang-banging her something wonderful. Did you know you could still bleed in hell, Kyle-man? She's bleeding too, a lot."

Involuntarily, something shifted inside of Kyle, starting with an odd warmth in his eyes that grew and seemed to melt into his brain. Like hot porridge going slowly down your throat, it burned but also comforted as it went.

It was a power that was neither self-righteous nor self-serving, but indignant in the face of what he'd just heard and the evil he was confronting, and it began to overtake him.

The warmth spilled over his shoulders and down his arms until it pooled like water in his hands. He felt his eyes widen and air pour back into his lungs in a rush, and then, incredibly, his hands started to glow a soft whitish-blue.

Another telegram came to him from that other place, this one encouraging and firm: *You're never alone.*

When Kyle looked back up at the creatures from hell that had come to kill him, he noticed something.

They weren't grinning anymore.

CHAPTER 10

DESPITE HIS PROTESTS, THE captain had sent Napoleon home to combat his cold right after they got back to the station from the Fasano house, assuring him that he wouldn't be pulled from the case. Three additional detectives were assigned the tasks of interviewing witnesses, re-canvasing the crime scene and securing a warrant to pull Kyle Fasano's cell phone data. It was grunt work but it was important, and Napoleon didn't like missing it. Still, he felt beyond horrible, and it was obvious he was no good to anyone right now anyway.

Still. It felt wrong. He might miss something, like he had once before.

He'd managed his way home and to bed just before 3:00 a.m., slipping into the meager, restless sleep that his fever would allow. Somewhere in the early morning, he vaguely recalled getting up to piss and then drinking a cold glass of water, which aggravated his parched throat as much as it alleviated his fever. He tripped over his shoe on his way back to bed, literally falling on to the covers before burying his head under his pillow and passing out again.

He dreamed of his grandmother and those barrio days, with her potions and crooked teeth. She sold herb-induced oils and remedies every week, using one in particular to rub into her own arthritic hands, the same hands she used to hold her rosary every morning in prayer to Jesus and the

Saints. Even as a little boy, Napoleon found this behavior to be a little conflicted, but he didn't dare mention such thoughts to his grandmother for fear of upsetting her. She always worried about him, and fretted over his soul in a *mundo del mal*, a world of evil.

When he awoke six hours later to a blindingly bright morning sun, he could've sworn he could still smell that oil: an odd mix of hemp, fennel and lemongrass. But that was silly. Dreams didn't have smells, did they?

He sat up and stretched weakly. The night held him down and his cold beat on him until dawn, but he could finally feel his immune system beginning to put up a fight. His throat and head hurt a little less, but the congestion in his chest had gotten worse. After making his way to the kitchen, he spat a few rounds of phlegm into the wastebasket and set on a pot of coffee, using his old-school percolator. It had been in the family for decades, cared for and watched over like an Egyptian relic. To Napoleon, Starbucks coffee was a travesty, nuclear hot and overly spiked with caffeine. The real deal got you high and alert the same way it brewed, nice and slow.

His apartment was part of a small building on the corner of Fourth and Boyle, right near the on-ramp to the 5 Freeway. Every morning was like waking up on a manhole cover in the middle of the street, the sound of traffic so thick it felt as if the apartment itself was in the fast lane. The barrio he had just dreamed of was only a few miles away, but it was like a different world now. It had gone from a simple but tough neighborhood to a brutally murderous one, with tennis shoes from twenty different gangs hung on power lines like Christmas ornaments, the neighborhood being claimed at different times, and with varying body counts, by White Fence, Evergreen or Cuatro Flats, to name a few.

It was the East LA version of the Bermuda Triangle; whoever went into it might not come out, and more than a few folks simply disappeared forever.

Before the city temporarily drained the man-made lake at Echo Park, Napoleon had been sure many of these missing souls would be found there, bloated and rotten corpses that laid in silent protest for years beneath the pedal boats filled with romantics who floated around on the surface on all those sunny Saturdays. But that theory proved false. The lake was empty, save for the remains of a few dead animals.

Napoleon wanted to feel relieved, but he hadn't. It simply meant that the bodies were somewhere else, still waiting to be found, the end of their lives still a mystery.

Nothing bothered Napoleon more than things that remained unsolved. As a child it didn't matter if it was a game of Clue, the latest *Encyclopedia Brown* book or a crossword puzzle; it had to be finished and solved. He remembered to this day the time his grandfather, to challenge him, had gotten him a five thousand piece jigsaw puzzle of nothing but M&M's. In his mind, Napoleon could still see them: thousands upon thousands of pieces with the same shapes and colors. It was maddening. He struggled over it for weeks before his grandmother waited until he went to school one day and threw it out. He'd come home later and thrown the biggest fit of his life.

Years later, at the Rose Bowl Swap Meet of all places, he found the same jigsaw puzzle on sale at the table of a little old lady who claimed she'd completed it and now had no use for it. As he relived his childhood trauma, she smiled at his story and then assured him that all the pieces were still in the box, even showing him it was taped shut on all four sides. He bought it, took it home and worked on it for a week before discovering about a dozen pieces were missing. He supposed he should take solace in the other 4,988 pieces he'd managed to fit together, but he didn't.

That old lady was probably in her grave by now, and that was good for her because he was still pissed about it. That damned puzzle had gotten the better of him twice now.

Just like Joaquin Murietta.

He'd gotten the better of Napoleon twice now too.

The very name seemed to darken the room. Napoleon sighed. He wasn't hungry, but since he was in the kitchen he decided to grill some bacon and scramble a few eggs, if for no other reason than to try to forget that name. But then the bowl he had chosen to crack the eggs into was tan, and that reminded him of little Esmeralda's tan skin, and that, in turn, reminded him of the shallow grave, and how you learn the hard way as a rookie cop not to screw up a crime scene; because all the accused needs is a public defender fresh out of law school with a hard-on to make a name for himself, who can take the technicality of soil and grass—many feet removed from the victim's body—to turn the case upside down and put a monster back on the street.

The same monster who looked at Napoleon on the way out of the courtroom with a big smile. A "watch what I do next, homie" smile.

Then the monster disappeared. Until three years later.

Napoleon stood over the bowl of his eggs and gently ran the tongs of his fork up and down against his forehead. *Stop. Stop it. Don't go there.*

He leaned against the counter and wrestled that demon a good number of minutes until he was saved by, of all things, the gentle rumblings of the percolator. He brought himself back from that place one thought at a time, using his usual mental talismans: thoughts of little Efren, then the 1978 Rams starting lineup, then the design of his first tattoo, then... now.

Now was defined by two words, Kyle Fasano, the latest thing to be solved. A person was not unlike a puzzle, with a lot of pieces that fit together to make a picture of who they were and what they'd done. Except with people you didn't start with the corners and work your way in, you started in the center and worked your way out.

He added some butter to the heated skillet, set his fork to the dueling yellow suns of his eggs, poured in some milk and then added the mixture to the skillet. Feeling lazy, he just microwaved the bacon. A few minutes later he was sitting down at his small dining room table, over-looking the freeway and streets beyond, picking at his food and sipping his coffee.

Fasano was out there somewhere, just like Joaquin had once been. The hunt was on, and there was no getting around it. A girl barely out of college was now a corpse at the morgue, and Fasano was likely the last person to see her alive. Napoleon felt the urge to turn it all over in his head again, then decided to hold off for now. He was still only half-awake.

Something wasn't right though, and there was no get-ting around it.

He glanced at himself in the Aztec mirror that hung over his dining table; his face was a wreck, his hair greasy and blotted to his head. His skin was pale, making the tattoo on his right arm stand out even more. It was a tra-ditional tattoo, done all over the world: a pair of praying hands. Usually it was done with the hands clutching a rosary, but Napoleon had gotten it when he was four-teen, the rebellious nature of his teen years already in full swing. As a result, he asked the tattooist to leave out the rosary.

"¿*Por qué, mijo?*" the old man queried with an odd grin as he mixed the ink.

Napoleon answered, "Because when I pray, I don't want nothin' between me and God."

The old man raised his eyebrows and nodded slightly before continuing his work, the two teardrops tattooed beneath his right eye a testament to the fact that he and God had some issues of their own to deal with someday.

The eggs were getting cold.

Outside his apartment a car horn blared, reminding him that he needed to get moving, get back to the station house and back on the case, but Napoleon continued to stare at his tattoo.

Something wasn't right with the Fasano case. But it was way too early to start forming assumptions or opinions. That'd be a rookie move he'd expect out of Parker, not himself.

But the thought stayed anyway, a hunch embedded in his mind that was as stubborn as the ink carved into his arm.

Kyle Fasano wasn't guilty.

* * *

They sat there for what seemed like hours, the three of them just looking at each other in the now frozen world of Denny's. Beanie averted his gaze only once, down to Kyle's hands. At some point Kyle realized that the force moving around inside him and to his hands was also now shielding his mind. They couldn't read his thoughts anymore.

So they sat like three deaf mutes preparing for a rumble. This would've made Kyle laugh on any other day but, to be honest, right about now he was scared shitless. Beanie and John Deere were bad enough, but the blue glow in his hands scared him even worse. It was warm and rhythmic, as if he were attached to a lightning bolt on a controlled current.

What's happening to me? This is crazy.

He had no idea what to do next, and thankfully they hadn't figured this out yet. But they would. Then what?

Beanie shifted his weight and Kyle jumped ever so slightly, but neither one of them seemed to notice. That was good, but this movement seemed to kick-start something in Kyle's mind. He had to play this straight out of Guy Code 101: when in doubt, bluff—and bluff in as macho a way as you can.

When he spoke he couldn't believe his own voice as the words rolled out of his mouth. "You should leave. Now."

John Deere managed a weak smile, but Beanie was no poker player; he looked genuinely worried, well beyond surprised and into the land of confused, and this gave Kyle added confidence to continue.

"I'm not going to tell you again," Kyle said, leaning forwards on the counter.

When John Deere spoke, it was with a primal, hate-filled voice from another world, from hell itself. "Tell your master that he has chosen poorly."

Finding courage in John Deere's taunt, Beanie spoke up too. "You don't have what it takes, Kyle-man," he said with a sneer.

Fear began to well in Kyle's chest, but he held it down. Thank God they couldn't read his thoughts anymore. If they could, he just knew they'd be upon him without hesitation, like wolves on a sheep.

The power pulsed in his hands, swelling against the tips of his fingers.

Without thinking he opened his hands and put them palms down on the counter, and in an instant the blue light shot down the counter's length, violently vibrating the cups and plates before it reached the target it evidently desired; Beanie's left hand, resting on the counter, was enveloped in blue light and vaporized. Screaming, he fell back, holding up the cauterized stump of his arm in horror.

John Deere stood as if to attack, and Kyle, again following school yard logic, did the same; but he was getting very close to the flip side of that same child's logic that warns that—bravado or not—when the bully's coming for you, sometimes it's best to run.

As quickly as that thought came, Beanie and John Deere returned back to human form.

"You shit! Put that under your coat." John Deere shrieked at Beanie, who whimpered softly as he put the handless stump inside the fold of his jacket.

They slowly slid past the booth behind them and then moved quickly to the exit, the view of the world around them warping as they did so. Awe sunk into Kyle's chest. The patrons, the waitresses, the traffic outside, even the sunbeams coming in through the windows, began to move incrementally at first, then a little faster.

John Deere looked at Kyle with bulging eyes as his lips pulled back in a vicious sneer. "We're not finished with you yet," he spat.

Encouraged by their retreat, Kyle couldn't resist a bit of bravado. "You better hope you are."

Beanie and John Deere laughed, and this was worse than any of their smiles or taunts because it was a laughter absent all happiness. It sounded like the blackest and saddest of things. They laughed all the way out of the diner,

John Deere pausing just before he stepped out the door to glare at Kyle one last time. "See you soon, slug," he said.

They disappeared, and almost instantly the world returned to full speed. Kyle exhaled for the first time in what seemed like an hour as the blue in his hands began to fade, gradually at first, before it blipped off all together, as if someone had hit a switch somewhere.

He was shaking so badly he couldn't even pick up his cup of coffee, so he forced himself to sit down and take deep breaths to steady his nerves. Around him the world went about its business: the truckers told another dirty joke that made one laugh so hard he began to choke; the bread man folded his sports page and settled his check; and the fat waitress was reaming out the chef for under cooking someone's hash browns.

Only Jasmine still seemed a bit off.

Standing at the register and sifting through receipts, she seemed confused. She was obviously upset, but it looked like she was unsure as to why, as if she had a bad memory or a premonition of sorts. Kyle watched her glance more than a few times at where Beanie and John Deere had been sitting, but they were gone now, their place settings on the counter undisturbed as if they'd never been there in the first place.

The bread man exited the restaurant, brushing against Kyle by accident as he did so, and in some after-effect of the blue a heightened sense of awareness came over Kyle and he immediately began receiving information about the bread man in small, mental flashes: he was single, he liked pornography, especially girl on girl, and he watched it for hours every night on his computer before going to bed, where he would then abuse himself, never aware of the squatting goblins in his room who always led his eyes to just *one* more video and one more step towards complete disrespect for the women he saw each day.

Lately, one woman in particular had become the object of his obsessions: a girl on his delivery route who'd never outgrown her need to tease, and who would flirt with him one day and then be bitchy to him the next, exacerbating both his passions and his contempt.

Kyle tried to stop the images from flooding into his mind but he couldn't.

The girl had no way of knowing that she was finding her way more and more into the bread man's dark and twisted fantasies, or that he often dreamed of tying her up in his garage and making her watch videos with him. When he was done with her? Well. The bread man would have to make a different kind of delivery, maybe to the ravine off of Highway 14.

Repulsed by the images, Kyle pulled his attention away from the bread man's mind like a man who pulls his gaze away from a dead animal he's seen dismembered on the road.

His hands were shaking worse now, and the fabric of who he was, what reality was, who we all were and what was happening around us, every day, was coming undone again, like pulled threads.

In frustration he reached out to a God he didn't feel he really knew.

"Why have you chosen me for this?" he whispered softly.

As expected, there was no answer.

He knew why, anyway.

Because he deserved it.

CHAPTER 11

Tamara moved the coffee maker to one side of the counter and wiped beneath it. Cleaning was normally a good way to get your mind off of things, but not when your life was falling apart.

No. It *wasn't* falling apart. It just needed to be reorganized, like the salt and pepper shakers cast off haphazardly by Juanita to a lonely island atop the toaster oven when they actually belonged next to the seasonings rack and butter dish near the stove.

She'd already cleaned the microwave and range hood, even getting the filthy fan grill beneath. Her attention now turned to organizing her many cooking oils, infused as they were with garlic or basil, saffron and chili peppers. She had quite the collection, some from the Montrose Farmer's Market and others from the olive oil specialty shop in San Luis Obispo.

She arranged them from tallest to shortest, then changed her mind and went with fullest to emptiest.

Janie was still asleep, though twice in the night she had stirred and cried out for her father. Seth had awoken, made his way to the television and was now watching Saturday morning cartoons, his stuffed horse tucked under one arm as he leaned against the cushions.

She looked at the back of his little head and her heart contracted.

He had no idea how much his life might change now. If this played out the way Tamara feared, with Kyle in jail or out on bail with months of legal hell to endure, there was no way she'd let either of her children be subjected to the tortures of the school, or even the neighborhood, for a while.

She sighed and forced herself to focus.

The oils in order, she now began to organize the pasta containers on the far right counter. The straight pastas were first, fettuccini to angel hair, thickest to thinnest, then the round pastas, rigatoni to penne, again thickest to thinnest. The rice jars came next, by grain size.

She used to love to cook, until she began working so much. Now it was only a weekend exercise, and rare at that, as work often followed her home.

She paused. *How did all this happen?*

She and Kyle hadn't had sex very much the past year.

She had to be honest with herself. All women knew that men needed one thing. Sex was always the elephant in the room. Add kids and overtime to the mix and there simply wasn't enough energy to go around.

This was all her fault.

Bullshit. Quit thinking this way. Quit thinking about all of it.

Her eyes filled with tears before she steadied herself.

She turned and began to clean the refrigerator, the top shelf first so she could knock crumbs and the like down as she went, sadly removing her birthday cake and placing it on the dining room table before she began. She noticed that Juanita had cleaned the refrigerator recently, but no woman can take care of your house like you can.

Though some of them can take better care of your man.

She immediately thought of Caitlyn.

Shut up! Just stop it!

She began to clean the shelves harder and harder, her blue sponge making mad semi-circles as she scrubbed away dried-up liquid drops and bits of celery on the middle shelf, until the weight of her arm collapsed it. Cheese packets, tortillas, a half-empty can of peaches and a plastic container of pesto spilled down her body and across the floor.

She saw the peaches on the floor, and then the world went red. She began to smash at the rest of the shelves, collapsing them one by one, the milk and orange juice cartons tumbling out with heavy thumps, apples and oranges scattering out across the floor like oversized marbles, a cream cheese container and jar of pickles tumbling next. She grabbed at the items that dared not fall, the plastic ketchup and mustard bottles, the ball of fresh mozzarella cheese, a bag of cilantro, a bottle of soy sauce and a can of A&W Root Beer, Kyle's favorite, throwing each of them at the kitchen cabinets she had just wiped down.

Hot tears were burning down her face, and it was like the emotions they carried were reabsorbed into her body, because her chest began to burn too, more intensely with every short breath she could manage.

He's ruined everything. My whole life. The kids' lives. It's all ruined.

But she loved him. She loved him anyway, even now. How could that be?

She collapsed in a heap, right smack dab into a puddle of milk and apple juice, and began to sob uncontrollably. "Nobody's perfect," she whispered, over and over. "Nobody's perfect! Nobody's perfect! Nobody—"

Her children came to her in stereo.

"Mommy?" Janie, from the hallway, her hair in her face, tears in her eyes.

"Mommy?" Seth, from the entryway to the den, his stuffed horse clutched like a shield against his chest, confusion in his face.

Jesus! Could I blow this any more? Hadn't she told herself last night, right after those detectives had left, that the number one thing she had to do was protect the children from all of this?

So much for that idea.

Now she'd failed miserably at that too.

She got to her knees, a hand held up to each child like a traffic cop, trying to stop them from coming to her across the mess on the floor because there was surely broken glass somewhere. But they both ignored her warning and ran into her arms, and the three of them embraced there on the kitchen floor, rocking back and forth in tears, Seth not even knowing why yet, evidently just crying because his mother and sister were.

Just then the sun rose fully in a yellow brilliance, lighting up the kitchen in hues of red and orange, and on any other day Tamara might've seen all those burning colors as beautiful and bright.

Not today.

Today they were the colors of only one thing: hell.

* * *

Napoleon looked at the captain, with his white hair and peeling cheeks, and waited for him to speak.

"I tell you to get some rest and you're back here already?"

"I got some sleep. Feel a little better."

"Bullshit. You're already bird-doggin' this one, aren't you?"

Napoleon shrugged and nodded.

"Okay. Fine. So? We make the husband for this?"

They were seated in the captain's office, near the main area of the second floor of the station house, phones already ringing and people talking in a sea of sound outside. The captain motioned his head towards the door. Napoleon closed it before answering, "Hell if I know. Until we get those lab results, we can't be sure."

"What are the lab results going to tell us that we don't already know? That most likely the last guy in that room was lover boy, who then fled the hotel half-naked? We still got a twenty-something-year-old girl splattered below a hotel room window." He scratched absentmindedly at his face when he talked. Napoleon never had eczema. It looked like a bitch.

"The timeline hasn't been established yet."

"There are no cameras that are going to catch her going out the window, right?"

"No."

The captain picked up the coffee cup on his desk and drank out of it slowly before continuing. "So. What then?"

"I dunno."

"You don't know?" the captain replied, a look of exasperation on his face. He ran his fingers through his hair, his cold blue eyes fixed on a spot in the ceiling. "What *do* you know then?"

"The husband says he didn't do it."

The captain laughed. "Fuck me."

"It's what he said on the phone."

"Yes. I know. As he was refusing to come in, and while, as far as we know, he was fleeing."

"He's the likely suspect, don't get me wrong, I'm not an idiot, I know that."

"So?"

"Something isn't jibing."

The captain rocked forwards in his chair and looked hard at Napoleon. It was a look Napoleon had seen a hundred times in the past two years since this particular captain, who was an asshole, had become his superior. It was a look that portrayed good management skills and masked shitty people skills, an approach that tried to intimidate instead of coaxing agreement.

"I'm glad you got some rest, Nap. But now we're twelve hours out on this thing, and I still can't get a read on where we stand. Murillo came up with jack on the witness statements. A few people at the bar remembered them all cozy. No signs of hostility or jealousy. Still, the last person we have her with when she was alive was Fasano. So just what, at least at this point, isn't jibing?" He added air quotes with his fingers to the last word.

Napoleon sighed and the act brought on his cough, which gave the appearance of weakness. His throat hurt less but he would kill for some cough medicine. But that was an AA no-no. He also didn't think his answer was going to go over very well.

"I don't know yet."

"Well that's just apple-pie-fucking a la mode!" the captain half-shouted. "Did you hear yet who this girl's father is?"

That was never a good question.

"No."

"Assistant DA Hall."

Napoleon felt as if he'd been gut-punched. *Shit.*

"We got two uniforms bringing him and the mother—who's the head of the local chapter of the Red Cross, by the way—in here right after they've been to the damned morgue, where they're gonna see their beloved child by the damn shovelful. And when they finally get in here and ask me what's going on, I'm gonna tell them, what? 'Well, Mr. and Mrs. You Could Screw Me Six Ways to Tuesday, not much, because my lead detective on this thing has got *no jibe on things*,' is that right?"

Napoleon fought the urge to tell him just where he could shove his damn sarcasm. It was an urge he had to stifle often while in the presence of the captain, who was, on his best day, a pretentious prick burned out on his job but too damned stupid to retire.

"Captain, I—"

"You nothing. Fasano's cell phone's dead now too—"

"I figured he was likely to ditch it."

"Well… that's a reasonable act for an innocent man, right? Does that jibe, Nap?"

Napoleon crossed his arms and shook his head.

"I want an APB out on his ass. The press isn't on this yet, but it won't be long. We go with 'person of interest' to cover ourselves legally, but you need to load up on cough drops, get Parker and head out after this clown."

"I take it you already pulled the GPS from his last call?"

"That we did, and there's your starting point—off the 5, a town called Beaury."

Napoleon sighed. "Okay. But one more thing?"

"What?"

"I figure him to call the wife again. I was going to get the tap going first, to get a read on his trajectory from there, east, north, whatever—"

"I'll take care of it."

Napoleon stood and put his hands on his hips. So they were bolting to Beaury with no idea of where the suspect was going to next. It was a pure panic move, so the cap could cover his ass with a grieving ADA, but there was nothing he could do about it. "Fine."

"Nap, I swear… Okay… You been on the job a long time. I wanna hear both sides here."

No you don't, Napoleon thought. He knew he was delaying the inevitable, but he tried anyway. "The hole in the window is a problem. It's too high."

"I agree. Too high for a suicide."

"That's not what I meant."

"But it's what *I* meant. Go ahead."

"Even if we make the husband for a pitch and toss, he would have to be damn near superhuman to pull it off."

"Maybe the guy was high as a kite. Maybe we get the tox report back on the vic and they were both stoned on meth. Maybe they fucked like bunnies plugged into a wall socket and then got into a squabble when he couldn't get it up again."

"Cap—"

"Nap, c'mon now. We've seen drugged-up guys fight off seven, eight uniforms at a time."

"The glass was melted."

"Okay."

"Okay?"

"Look, I've been doing this a long time too, did my time in your job for fifteen years in South Central…"

Oh no, here he goes with the damned credentials.

Napoleon looked at the ground so he wouldn't roll his eyes.

"… some things you just can't explain up front. Time will tell, and all that shit."

"So… what? He turned into a human fireball and threw her out the window?"

"Maybe. How the hell should I know."

"Cap. Seriously?"

"We'll figure it out. Eventually. Right now though I'm trying to understand why any reasonable cop in his right mind would be arguing anything but going after the husband. It's clear as day."

"I'm not saying we shouldn't."

"Yes you are. You're getting ready to tell me your gut is telling you something, or some other Hollywood bullshit."

The captain was actually right on that one, but Napoleon wasn't going to give him the pleasure of admitting it.

For a minute there was silence between them.

"Are you too sick to handle this case?" the captain asked with a hint of suspicion in his voice.

Napoleon looked at him firmly, suppressing another cough by sheer will alone. "No."

Then the killing blow. "You haven't taken any meds or shit that you're not supposed to, have you?"

You piece of shit. You gonna check my locker for NyQuil? See if you can pull my AA card? "Of course not."

"Good. Now that we've established that your judgment is not impaired in any way, I suggest you get your 'jibe' on all the way up to Beaury, rope this bastard and bring him in."

Napoleon stood, dropped his hands to his sides and stuffed them in his pockets. "Sure thing, Cap."

As he left the captain's office, he could feel the smug bastard's eyes on him the whole way out. This is what the job was like now. Work twenty-plus years to have some prick promoted over you who knows you can do his job better than he can, so he sets out to make your life miserable any chance he gets.

Except this time, Napoleon hated to admit it, the jerk-off was right.

Kyle Fasano was a gimme for this one.

Damn near.

Except for that window and that melted glass.

And what about that video out in front of the lobby, when Fasano was there one second and then just gone the next? Just a camera glitch, right? Yeah. Sure.

It didn't jibe.

CHAPTER 12

KYLE STOOD OUTSIDE THE Beaury Public Library. It was an old brick building with tired mint-green trim. A row of hedges, someone's idea of great landscaping at some point, made the building look even more tired, many of the plants dying off and wasting away in varying shades of brown.

He was hoping the library would open early, but that wasn't the case. The Saturday hours on the door were spelled out in white vinyl letters: 10:00 a.m.–6:00 p.m. It was currently ten minutes past ten o'clock. Beaury moved at its own pace, and it seemed the librarian did as well; she was nowhere to be seen.

Before leaving Denny's Kyle had decided that he needed to find a computer, and he almost missed the poster in the lobby that led him here, advertising Beaury Library's "Annual Summer Movie Series," which this year featured the work of Alfred Hitchcock, beginning with *Rear Window* and working up to the *Psycho* finale, with *The Birds* and Kyle's personal favorite, *North by Northwest*, sandwiched in between.

The woman who finally opened the library door another five minutes later appeared to be in her late sixties. She had pure white hair, pudgy hands and wore a floral-print dress with purple flats to match. Her smile was thin but courteous as her eyes sized up Kyle.

This was to be expected. He'd managed to clean up a bit in the Denny's bathroom, but he still looked a bit disheveled: his shirt was a wrinkled mess, his hair needed a good combing and he was in need of a shave. These were probably the things that caught her eye, but Kyle always felt that librarians were a lot like bartenders anyway—they knew the regular clientele and made note of those who weren't. That was fine. His plan allowed for witnesses. It even counted on them.

A half-dozen people filed into the library behind him, two adults and four teenagers, everyone fanning out to separate tables once inside. Kyle didn't need a table, but with the old lady no doubt watching, he made a show of it. He walked calmly over to the periodicals section for a few magazines and the day's paper, which, he was happy to see, said nothing so far about him, at least on the front page.

Using them and his duffle bag to mark his table, he sat down and forced himself to read for a good fifteen minutes, using his peripheral vision to track the librarian as she unlocked the restrooms, shuffled some books between a few carts and turned on a light in the children's reading room. She then cleared her throat and made her way to the front desk, where she sat down facing the lobby, her back to him.

Perfect.

He also took note of his fellow library visitors; none of them appeared the slightest bit interested in him or, more importantly, sported any horns or hooves.

Relieved, he turned his attention to the walls of the library and was saddened. The shelves were not as full as they'd been in the library he'd used as a kid. Books were going out of fashion it seemed, and as if in testimony to this fact he noticed one of the teenage boys approach the island of computers that was situated off to one side of the library and mostly out of view of the front desk. Technology waited for no one. Even Shakespeare was digital now.

Kyle rose quietly and went to the computer nearest the librarian, noting that the teenager was partially obstructed from her view and thankful for it. That would be important when the moment came. He needed some quality private time with Google to track down Victoria, and he wasn't the least bit worried that he would be able to do so. In this day and age, no one could hide.

This being sleepy little Beaury he doubted that he needed a password, but after a few seconds of internal debate he walked up to the librarian anyway.

"Excuse me?"

"Yes?" she politely replied.

"I want to use computer number…" He paused for effect, to make it easier for her to remember the number later, in case the cops came looking for him here. "Four. Do I need a password?"

"No, but if you're planning on checking anything out or doing any printing, you'll have to use your library card—if, that is, you have one?" It was a question couched in an assumption. They both knew full well that Kyle didn't have a library card, but she left him the opening he needed to answer without really answering.

"Oh, okay, well I'm not planning on doing either of those things, but thanks."

She nodded at him curtly then returned to whatever logbook she was filling out.

Back at the computer, Kyle hit the space bar. The screen popped up immediately. He checked the security systems as best he could. The standard firewalls were up, Windows 8 was running and a fairly recent version of Firefox was installed too. He was by no means a master of IT, but he knew enough to erase his search history within the browser but leave it in the control panel for when the time came. They needed breadcrumbs to track him, after all. So he would lay them out accordingly.

He began typing in random websites and doing random things. First, he went to the Bank of America website, where he tried to log in to an account name he made up by using the barcode from a book on the counter next to him. He also threw in a few odd password tries. He was denied and moved on. Then he searched the La Jolla and Coronado areas near San Diego on Google Maps, using one of the stubby pencils and some scrap paper that was provided at each monitor to write down a few addresses. Next was Zillow, where he entered in these addresses one by one, making sure to click on the property details at each page and linger there awhile so it would appear as if he were really researching them.

He wrote down the names of the property owners, Larry Klein and Timothy Reardon, and began Googling them, digging up all he could on each one and even clicking through to their Facebook pages. He had no intention of making this easy for the police, for Caesar, or whatever that detective's name was, by logging in with his own Facebook account. So he quickly created a new account using a name he just made up: Joaquin Murietta.

He had no idea why he chose that name, but he vaguely recalled that he was some sort of Mexican bandit who killed a bunch of ranchers in the old west. Using the name of a murderer might not prove to be the smartest choice if they ever caught him, but he was out of time; the teenager had just stepped away from his monitor, leaving the opening Kyle needed to use the one computer that was out of sight of the librarian and therefore couldn't be cataloged in her memory.

Kyle then pulled down the browser history and deleted everything. He left the cache untouched.

Next, he worked his way calmly around the island, watching as the boy disappeared into the non-fiction section before he went up to the computer he'd been using. Looking at the monitor, Kyle had to smile. The boy hadn't bothered to navigate away from his last web page: the Maxim Top 100 Hotties. Maybe he was doing a term paper on fake breasts and the "mystery" of the female orgasm. In either case, he probably belonged in the fiction section.

Kyle went to Google and paused a moment before he typed in her name. Was he really going to do this? Yes. He was.

His fingers tapped the letters of her name: Victoria Duncan.

It was her maiden name, but he was hoping to get lucky. He didn't. So he took it a step further and added in her middle name, Alisa.

This provided a solid hit half way down on the second search page. It was a public announcement in the *Monterey Herald* of the marriage between Victoria Alisa Duncan and Michael Vincent Brasco. Seven years ago. She waited awhile to get married, evidently. Kyle went back to Google, where he searched for "Victoria Alisa Brasco."

The first page that came up listed a half-dozen links, three of them for the same Victoria, who lived in Monterey, California. The first hit was for a PTA meeting a few months back, the next for a charity function at Pebble Beach from last summer, and the last was, of course, for Facebook.

He clicked the Facebook link, and there she was, clear as day.

A weight settled in his chest at the sight of her profile picture.

She was in a ski jacket and smiling that same slightly sad smile that she always wore, as if she knew something about happiness that the rest of the world didn't, perhaps namely that it was an illusion.

Her profile and photos were private, but her "Likes" were on display. Any remaining doubts he'd had that it was her were now wiped away by three of the five items listed: The Cure, Walt Whitman and Slurpee. It was part of the genius of Facebook. Our cumulative likes identified us almost as well as our photos or even our fingerprints.

How many Cure songs had they listened to together? He took her to see them at the LA Sports Arena for her seventeenth birthday, a present she had been overjoyed by. He wondered if she still had her Whitman collection and that silly blue t-shirt of his portrait she always wore. And as for the Slurpee? How many times had he driven home with that sweet taste of her favorite flavor, cherry, on his lips, lingering there from all their kissing?

He felt himself lost in a daze of nostalgia before the world came back to him. When it did, he switched to Google one last time and typed in her husband's full name, her full name and "Monterey, CA." Their property listing came up multiple times without even the need for a click through: 12546 Genevieve Drive. He wrote this final bit of information down and backed the browser bar up to the Maxim Top 100 list again.

Looking around he noticed that no one else had entered the library and that the librarian hadn't moved. Still, the room felt oddly different, less like a place now and more like a detour. It was. He could feel it. He'd just taken a turn to somewhere, in the world, in his life.

The police were coming. He could feel that too, though he didn't know how. It was just a vibrating sort of "knowing." With this in mind, he grabbed his duffle bag and walked out of the library without a goodbye.

As he left he didn't see The Gray Man, who'd been quietly standing near a stack of books behind the computer island the whole time.

"Once more unto the breach," The Gray Man said to no one in particular as he watched Kyle leave and cross the parking lot outside.

After a moment, The Gray Man walked over to the computer the teenage boy had been using. Kyle shouldn't have returned the web page to where it had been. The Gray Man reached up and typed in a new website. He knew it was most likely an exercise in futility; teenage boys were unbelievably fertile ground for the enemy, but he did it nonetheless, if only to show the boy that there were two sides to every coin.

Then, The Gray Man was on his way, his leaving marked only by a gentle rustling of scrap papers on the computer island.

The library remained quiet, and before long the teenage boy returned to his computer to get one last look at the Asian supermodel in cut-off shorts and a red bikini top, ranked fifteenth on the Maxim list. This was his favorite model, since she reminded him so much of the girl in his math class that he couldn't keep his eyes off. Looking at the screen, though, he squinted with surprise, then let out a soft "what?"

On the screen was a website for the local women's abuse shelter.

CHAPTER 13

TAMARA SAT ON THE couch with the kids. They were watching cartoons and eating macaroni and cheese for lunch while she wondered just what to do next. This wasn't something a wife could plan or prepare for. She was very good at crisis management at work, but this was different. This was forced adaptation. The scenarios that banged and clamored through her head were already numerous and multiplying, leaving the path forwards muddled at best.

The sun cut through the den in patterned formations from the plantation shutters covering the windows. Tamara looked at Seth first, noticing the shape of his head, so much like his father's, and she couldn't imagine how she was going to explain this to him. It wasn't long ago that he'd sat with Kyle out on the patio and put together their first model car. It was an old-fashioned hobby that Kyle had dragged from his childhood into the Wii era, and Tamara had stood at a distance in the dining room watching them with a smile as Seth tried so hard to pretend he was interested. Truth be told, he would crush cans with Kyle all day if it meant they could be together. As father and son they were nearly inseparable.

Tamara shook her head softly. This was all going to devastate his little life forever, and sadness bloomed in her chest with a frightening fierceness. She looked to Janie, her own little shadow. The likeness between them was something that everyone always mentioned, filling Tamara with pride. She watched her daughter now as she lay on the floor playing with a strand of her long brown hair as her feet, in mismatching socks, seesawed behind her. Janie might handle this better in the long run, but there was no telling for sure. She could internalize things so deeply that even Tamara couldn't get in sometimes.

What Janie was thinking or feeling became brutally inconsequential when a news report appeared on the screen, momentarily pushing the cartoons into oblivion.

A brief preview of the noon headlines immediately displayed the Hilton downtown with the words "Woman Dies from Mysterious Fall" in white print on a red banner that ran along the bottom of the screen.

Tamara swallowed hard. *No!*

The reporter was speaking, but Tamara's mind was like melting wax, her thoughts a sticky mess as she struggled with what she was seeing on the screen.

They were avoiding details so far. No mention of Caitlyn, just her age and that she was a graduate of UCLA. Tamara immediately put her bowl down on the side table and began to look desperately for the remote—*It had been right here, right next to the damned pillow!*—and that's when Kyle's face came on the screen.

She felt like she was going to be sick the moment she saw the looks on her children's faces as their father was being described on TV as a "person of interest."

Giving up on the remote, Tamara charged at the TV and turned it off just as a phone number for the LAPD came on the screen with instructions to call if anyone had seen Kyle Fasano in the last twenty-four hours.

They'd used a work ID photo, which meant his job already knew about things. In the photo Kyle was wearing that "I've got everything under control" smile of his, and it was with this image that she attempted to calm her panicked children as they ran to her, peppering her with questions and worries. For the second time in a half-day, she was cradling her babies and trying to soothe them. *Is this how it's going to be from now on: one piece of devastating news after another? He's caught. He's in jail. Sorry, we had to shoot him. What the hell was next?*

She kept telling herself he wasn't guilty of this. He couldn't be.

The house phone began to ring almost immediately.

She was freezing, and yet sweat was beginning to cover her. *So this is what a cold sweat feels like.*

She hadn't turned the answering machine down. It was on, just as it had been the night before when she had listened to Kyle's message with Juanita, before the cops had come and before Kyle himself had called to tell her that their world was now about to be blown apart.

She wanted to get up and turn it off, but the kids were weighing her down like anchors. First came her neighbor's call of concern, then the woman who ran Janie's Girl Scout troop.

It wasn't until Kyle's mom called the house, her voice bleeding pure panic, that Tamara pried the kids off of her and ran to the machine, wanting to smash it to pieces but realizing at the last minute that Kyle could call again.

So she simply pushed the volume dial down to zero, silencing her mother-in-law in the process and upsetting the children even further.

First Daddy was on TV, and now Grandma was calling in a panic, and Mom had already torn the kitchen apart, and now…

She felt all the arrows hitting her at once: pain, denial, fear, guilt, sadness.

No matter how hard she tried, she couldn't take them all, and now the worst arrow of all had managed to get past her and strike her children: the arrow of horror.

"Where's Daddy?!"

"What's going on?"

"Find Daddy!"

"Why can't you call Daddy?"

"Will the police hurt Daddy?"

Mommy help him. Mommy stop them. Mommy. Mommy. Mommy.

The phone kept ringing and it was all so much. Too much.

Her cell phone was on the kitchen counter, and now it too began to ring. The caller ID showed that it was Ben. She needed help. She needed someone, anyone, right now. As she decided to answer it, she thought she saw someone in the kitchen window and, startled, she jumped. Shit. Now she was seeing things.

Her hands were shaking when she grabbed the phone and answered, "Hello? Hello?!" she nearly screamed.

"Tamara, what the hell is going on? I just got back from my run and was watching the news…"

"I know," Tamara replied, her voice trembling.

"I'm coming over, right now."

There was something in his voice that she didn't like, an assertiveness that conveyed that he thought he had a right to come over. He didn't. It was a confidence that they were close enough as coworkers that he would be wanted in the midst of a family crisis. He wasn't.

And still she heard the word come out of her mouth. "Okay."

She hung up the phone in a state of disbelief, and that was a really good word for her entire life right now.

It might be how she lived it from now on.

* * *

Efren called just as Napoleon was heading out of the station, Parker still inside getting note copies from the detectives who had worked the case overnight.

"Tio!" Efren shouted so loud that Napoleon had to pull the phone from his ear.

"¿*Qué pasó, mijo?*" Napoleon replied with a smile.

"I made the team! I did it!"

"¿*Si? ¡O de lay!*"

"You gotta see my uniform. It's awesome! Dodger Blue!"

Napoleon laughed, feeling neither weary nor sick for the first time in days. "That's great, my man! Good job. What position?"

"Shortstop. Coach says maybe third some games."

"Lotta action that side of the infield. You ready for it?"

"Yeah. Mom's worried I'll catch one in the face. She said you did when you were little."

"I had two left hands, *mijo*. And besides, your mom's got a bad memory. I pitched. Comebackers happen."

This time it was Efren laughing.

"When's your first game?"

"Tomorrow. You're gonna be there, right, Tio?"

Napoleon thought of the captain and his damned order to drive to Beaury. Tomorrow was possible, if Kyle Fasano proved an easy catch.

"Probably not, mijo. I'm sorry," Napoleon answered, immediately aware how unlike him this response was. He

124

never missed something important with Efren. Why the hesitation now?

Efren also seemed surprised, and more than a little bit let down. "Oh. Okay. But, ya *gotta* be there, Tio. I'll get a hit, just for you."

Napoleon felt his heart break. "You don't gotta get a hit for me, *mijo*. I'd come just to see you in uniform. You know that."

"Yeah." Efren said it like he believed it.

"It's just that I'm working a big case right now. But I'll be there for the next one, okay?"

"Okay." But his little voice still sounded let down.

Parker had evidently gotten the notes, as he was leaving the station house and walking towards Napoleon, who was leaning on their unmarked car.

"In the meantime, keep practicing and... hey, little man?"

"Yeah?"

"Good job."

"Thanks, Tio. You wait and see. I look gooood in my uni. The ladies will liiike it."

Napoleon chuckled. "Okay... Romeo."

He hated the sound of Efren hanging up. It was the sound of Napoleon getting back to his shit life.

"So what's the deal?" Parker asked with a yawn.

"We're going to Beaury, partner," Napoleon said with a sigh, not knowing if it was Beaury that had caused the sigh or his use of the word partner in referring to Parker.

"What?" Parker replied with a grimace as they got into the car.

"Yep. The hunt is on."

"Don't they got local cops up there they can call?"

"Cap's already on it."

"Yeah. That and the press angle. He's on that too."

Squinting, Napoleon shook his head. "Are you shitting me? He just told me he was happy the press wasn't on it yet."

Parker backed out of the space and pulled through the lot, a line of police cruisers to one side, the maintenance garage to the other. The damaged and broken-down cars in their stalls were a reminder that the whole thing was a façade, that law and order was just as fragile as anything else, and even justice busted a tie rod every now and then.

"With 'yet' being the key word, I guess. They just came in, and he wasn't acting shy, I'll tell ya that. I guess he's starting to get his fifteen minutes of fame. Glory whore, huh?"

Did Parker just call the cap a glory whore? Napoleon thought. It appeared that there might be hope for the rookie yet.

"Balls," Napoleon said with a nod.

"Hey man, we got this murdering bastard's face on TV and a call into local PD up there, and he still wants us to play US marshals?"

"Looks that way."

"Only one reason for that," Parker added.

"What's that?"

"He wants the cameras for himself, *homie*," Parker answered with extra emphasis on the last word.

Napoleon winced. "Maybe, numb-nuts, but save me the damned hood talk. Nothing worse than a white boy trying to talk street."

"Hey man. I've seen some tough times."

"Shit. Toughest times you saw was when your mama said 'no' when the ice cream truck came by."

Parker chuckled and shook his head. "If only that were true."

Napoleon looked at him sideways, remembering something from Parker's file that he'd received prior to the start of his training: Parker was an army vet of both desert wars, which made him a gang member from a different hood of a different kind. "We got an hour north, depending on traffic. So just drive… homie."

It was a classic Los Angeles day, hot but a little cloudier than usual. As they exited the parking lot, uniformed officers came in and out of the station with frequency. It reminded Napoleon of easier times, days of reporting and patrolling, not hunting and searching.

They eased into traffic on Hill Street before jumping on the 5 Freeway, where a stalled mid-80s Honda sat at the side of the on-ramp, jammed with five or six wetbacks. Some people thought they'd seen hard times. Laughable. Hard times were when you had no dinner that night because the car that was supposed to get you to work for your pay-per-day job had broken down. Hard times were what happened when you had to walk home to tell your wife that.

As they made their way through the tight midday traffic, Napoleon noticed that amid the usual mix of hybrids and SUVs there was a big rig a few lanes over with rather unusual mud flaps, each displaying a skull with a tiny halo.

It reminded him of a joke his grandmother used to tell. Something about how being an angel wasn't so easy because, well, you had to die first, and who wanted to do that?

The freeway was like some sort of diseased artery, clogged in places, free flowing in others. This was going to take more than a few hours. Or who knew? They might get lucky and Fasano would get collared by the hick lawmen in Beaury who were eager for a little bit of the spotlight. He'd pay to see the captain's face if that happened.

Parker tapped the radio buttons until he came up with a little classic rock, Kansas, which was fine by Napoleon. *Carry on my wayward son… carry on.*

Maybe it was the mud flaps on the big rig, or maybe it was his regret at not promising Efren he would make that game, but as they made their way north past Cesar Chavez Avenue, Napoleon saw his apartment just off the freeway—and the oddest thought crossed his mind.

He would never see his home again.

CHAPTER 14

KYLE STOOD IN LINE at the CVS and cautiously looked around. There weren't a lot of cameras. The one over the pharmacy counter would never catch him, but the two over the registers and the one over the entrance would. He couldn't believe the way he was thinking, all about cameras and being clever with the cops. It was like he was channeling his teenage years, when being a hell-raiser and getting away with small and silly stuff was fun, like maybe dodging a police car when he was speeding or bailing out the back door of a party that was being broken up.

This wasn't silly, and it wasn't fun; but that part of him, that devious other self, was still there inside him, being called forth now to wreak a little havoc and make good on his escape. It was odd, as if those parts of yourself never really died; they just went somewhere to rest until you needed them again.

Following the plan he'd laid out in his mind earlier at Denny's, he picked up black hair dye, scissors, and a bandage for the cuts on his hand. Then he went to the greeting card aisle and found the *Peanuts* section. When he saw a birthday card of Linus and his blanket he thought it was perfect. Linus was Tamara's favorite. Lastly, he found the calling cards near the register. He would only need one, of the international variety, for calling Mexico or South

America. The cashier completed the transaction and took his cash.

Next, he went to the Dickies store, where he used more of his cash to buy a couple pairs of jeans and some plain t-shirts, one blue and one white. Nothing fancy or loud. He kept this visit quick and low-key. It helped that the girl at the register was in a deep conversation on her cellphone with her boyfriend and seemed to pay Kyle no mind. At the last second he grabbed a sports duffel that was on sale. A backpack at CVS might have been better, but again, whatever he planned on keeping with him was best kept off-camera.

His next stop was the post office. An old lady remarkably similar in looks to the librarian worked there. She took note of him but not overly so, giving him a distracted, almost contemptuous look, like an owl. He stood at the small customer kiosk near the door and filled out Tamara's greeting card as best he could, his back to the counter so he could wipe at his eyes in private. He knew what he wanted to say, but the words didn't come easy. When he was done he went to the counter and paid the extra fee for Priority Mail Express, so it would be delivered to her the next day.

He exited the post office at just before noon, and the bus stop sign told him that his ride would be arriving shortly. Now was the time to hit up the ATM, and he hoped he hadn't waited too long. It was risky, using his cash before pulling more, but his instincts told him that the minute he used that card, alerts would go off somewhere and a call would be made to the cops.

As if his fears were exorcized at that very moment, he noticed a police car coming down the street and instantly had the feeling that his time was about to run short in

Beaury. He only needed fifteen more minutes, when the bus would arrive. And the Wells Fargo up the street was only a few minutes' walk away.

The cruiser drove towards him, actually getting to within half a block before turning into the mini-mall parking lot. He noticed the logo on the door of the car: Beaury Sheriff's Department.

Shit.

He hung back near a group of trees and watched. The cruiser parked in front of the Denny's and the two sheriffs inside, one looking to be in his late-fifties and the other in his mid-thirties, got out. Their demeanor gave Kyle cause to relax, as they were laughing and joking, one of them even stopping to buy a newspaper on the way in.

He still had time, but not much. He hustled to the bank, slid in his ATM card, knowing that the camera here would certainly film him, and punched in a four hundred dollar withdrawal, cursing himself for setting that as his maximum limit back in the days when he worried about losing his card. Then... he held his breath, only exhaling when the machine began spitting out the money. They hadn't shut the account down yet. But they probably would now.

He walked nervously back to the bus stop, a wary eye on the Denny's, knowing he was being silly but waiting nonetheless for both cops to come flying out of the restaurant with syrup on their chins, already notified of what he'd done. That was impossible, he knew, but he was still very relieved when the small town of Beaury offered up a small surprise: the bus was early. Kyle joined the group of about ten people that was waiting for it, and then boarded with a smile for the driver and a request for change, which he knew wouldn't be granted.

This past summer, Janie's Girl Scout troop had gone on a field trip, and the "achievements" goal was for the girls to learn how to take public transportation. Kyle was surprised to find out how stringent the rules were regarding fees. You either had exact change or you overpaid. End of story. In Kyle's case he only had a five-dollar bill, so overpay he did, making the desired impression. The bus driver raised his eyebrows and gave his best "that's a damn shame" shake of the head. It was five dollars well spent though, another breadcrumb for the trail he was still leaving. Monterey was north. But that wasn't the direction he wanted them to think he was heading.

The 17 bus pulled away from the curb and headed south, towards Dunsmore, which was ten miles away and where he would get off. If he switched to the 38 at that point, he could continue south, with a good twelve miles across mostly farm country to the next stop in Middleton. But that wasn't the bus he was going to catch.

For now he had to wait for the flow of passengers on and off the bus to deliver him the right person. It took three stops and a few dozen folks before a Hispanic man with graying hair boarded. He wore a dirty black jacket, faded blue jeans, tan construction boots and a generic blue cap, and he shuffled wearily to his seat. He sat three rows up, and as the bus continued on its route, Kyle made his way forwards to sit with him.

The man's English was not so good, but Kyle made do with his Spanglish, just to keep the conversation going for the next twenty minutes. His name was Raul and he had hard blue eyes, like steel. He'd immigrated to America twenty-three years ago, was married with five kids, and earlier in the week he'd left his family behind in Fresno like he did every week. He shifted between construction sites in the area for his employer, a developer that had him working at mostly fill-in jobs now. Sometimes he cleaned out the construction trailers, and other times there was more exciting work, like wiring, which he had done a lot of when he was younger. Raul made the trek back home to be with his family each Saturday. It was hard, but it was worth it. His two oldest children were in junior college and expected to move on to get their degrees.

Today, though, Raul was being sent back to his company-provided room at the motel in Middleton a little early, as work was slow.

Perfect, Kyle thought.

But then the guilt of what he was doing began to weigh on Kyle. He was only pretending to care at first but now, well, if the old man got into some kind of trouble because of him, then maybe it wasn't worth it.

Logically though, how could he get into trouble? They couldn't call him an accomplice. His part in this would be innocent if Kyle pulled it off.

Raul asked Kyle some questions about himself, all of which Kyle answered fictitiously. He was down on his luck. His wife left him with his two kids. (This part actually made Kyle hesitate a bit, as he realized it might not be fiction for very long.) He had migraines and a severe skin allergy to the sun but was hoping to find work in San Diego, where his friend lived, but he'd lost his hat.

By the time they arrived in Dunsmore, they were good acquaintances, good enough for Kyle to make his proposal and for Raul to accept it with a smile. Having the rest of the day to himself, Raul told Kyle he was going to get pretty bored, but thanks to their deal he could call home to Mexico and speak with his family for a little while, just to see how things were going.

They stepped off the bus, and Raul headed off to catch the 38. Kyle had already told him that he was going to catch the 22, which would cut east a bit before taking him straight to San Diego.

The man smiled and waved goodbye, the phone card like a flag in his hand.

Kyle waved back, still feeling a little guilty, and turned away. He'd achieved what he wanted: Raul's hat.

He had no way of knowing that if left unchecked, the police would indeed track down Raul Vargas, and when they did, he would have to answer for being in the country illegally for over two decades. He would spend two nights in jail before being deported back to Sonora, without ever seeing either of his children graduate from college.

But that wouldn't happen.

Instead Raul would trip when getting off at the next stop and fall face first onto the pavement. He would lose his grip on the calling card while trying to arrest his fall, to no avail. The calling card, which had been clenched in his hand along with the dream of hearing his eighty-eight year old mother's voice, would go bouncing across the sidewalk. He would hit his head on the ground rather hard, and the world would go woozy.

Later that afternoon when his family rushed to see him at the hospital, Raul would swear to his wife that he'd seen an angel, a light gray one that hovered over him and calmed his nerves when he regained consciousness and heard the sirens coming.

"*Ay, amorcito, estas loco,*" his wife replied, her hand cupping his cheek.

"*Rosa, te hablo en serio. Te lo juro!*"

Back at the bus stop, the card would sit on the sidewalk unnoticed for two full hours before being found jammed nearly upright between the sidewalk and a hedge of grass. A small town thug by the name of Albert Granger would stumble upon it on his way to rob a liquor store just down the street.

With two strikes on his record and only one to go, Albert knew he was being stupid, but dammit, he was hungry, teetering on homelessness at this point. Life was just a pile of crap anyway, so why not? He would jam the place up, get the cash, hop on the bus and try to make his way north somewhere.

Instead, upon seeing the card, Albert figured this was some kinda luck—a calling card, just for him. He thought of the one person in the entire world who still loved him, despite all his mistakes: his mother.

It had been over a year since they'd last spoken, but he could still call her. She would be angry, but she would help. The same pride that had kept him from asking for help for years was intercepted this time by a small and gentle tug at his heart, just enough to make a difference.

Albert Granger sighed and decided he wasn't going to be robbing anybody this day. Instead, he lumbered his way down to The Home Depot workers' shed. He knew there was a payphone there, where a voice that still loved him would be found on the other end.

Just across the street, leaning against a stop sign, was The Gray Man.

He smiled.

Two birds. One stone.

* * *

Tamara managed to get Janie to calm down, insisting again that the police had simply mixed Daddy up with someone else. Seth was a tougher sell, as no matter how she tried to explain it, he couldn't understand—how could he? He was too little—and he wouldn't stop demanding to see Kyle. He finally cried himself to sleep on the couch, his long eyelashes now stuck in dried-up tears to the bags under his eyes. Tamara prayed over him, hoping that he would stay asleep for a while.

She allowed Janie to retreat to that special musical place called her iPod, which always seemed to soothe her somehow. She spent the rest of the afternoon on the couch in the den, curled up in a ball with her ear buds in, staring off blankly into the distance.

Then, Tamara finally started taking calls. She mostly made steady progress, but speaking to Kyle's mom was another matter. They had never gotten along, even on the wedding day, and her tone towards Tamara had been veiled in accusation from the outset of the call. Whatever was going on with this mad report about her son being wanted for questioning in relation to the death of some girl he worked with was—in one way, shape, or form—something for which Tamara was to blame. Kyle's mother had a voice like rubber on steel, whiny on her best day but now almost shrill in her panic. Where was Kyle? What really happened? How could Tamara not know? Rata-tat-tat.

On it went for a good five minutes until Tamara realized that she was done owing this woman any more explanations, ever, for the rest of her life. She felt bad for her, yes. Her health had swiftly declined since Kyle's dad had died, and she'd been forced to put Kyle's younger brother in an assisted living home for autistic adults. Still. Enough was enough. In one last act of restraint, Tamara made an excuse—Seth had a fictional injury from falling off the couch—before hanging the phone up so forcefully she was afraid she'd broken it.

The next call, only a few minutes after, made her wish that she had. It was a reporter from KCAL Channel 9 News, requesting an interview. Tamara hung up on him and barely had enough time to pour herself some Tejava before the phone rang again. She kept at it for a while then had to stop.

With all the calls Tamara missed three that went to voicemail. She panicked, thinking it was Kyle, but all three were from Trudy, telling Tamara to hang on, she was coming. She was in New York, scheduled to fly home to San Francisco today, but she had changed her flight to Los Angeles. Her last call said she was boarding her flight and was due in to LAX at 6:45pm. She didn't want Tamara dragging the kids to the airport in all the chaos. She would UBER to the house and be there as soon as she could.

Tamara was pissed that she'd missed the calls, but unbelievably relieved that help was on the way.

When the doorbell rang Tamara feared it was the press again, now trying to violate her space from the front porch. But when she answered the door she was startled to see Ben. In his hand he held a bag of sub-sandwiches from Pinocchio's Deli in Burbank.

"Hey, you okay?" he asked, and it was the way he said it, with his eyes as much as his words, that made her feel vulnerable. She feigned courage and pathetically even allowed a small smile to form, which caused some inner-discomfort. With her husband in this much trouble, the last thing she needed to be doing was playing the schoolgirl with the boy from work.

"Yes. I'm fine. You didn't have to—" she started to reply.

"I know. The sandwiches are for you guys, for lunch or dinner. I imagine you have family over or whatever. I didn't want to intrude, I just wanted to stop by real quick and make sure you were okay."

"Thanks, Ben. That's very kind of you."

"I'm so sorry, Tamara."

"It's okay. We don't know anything yet. It's just me and the kids right now. You wanna come in?"

"Sure."

She knew that would be the answer, but she didn't expect him to get so close to her when he came into the foyer and handed her the bag. He smelled very faintly of cologne. Her thoughts were unsettling. Inappropriate. Unlike her.

"You want some tea or a coke?" she asked politely, steering clear of any mention of any other type of beverage that might give him the wrong idea, as she walked him into the kitchen.

"No. That's okay." He put his hands on his hips and looked her in the eye, which only made her look away, as he said, "How you holding up with all this?"

Tamara shrugged and folded her arms across her chest. She felt herself nodding uncontrollably; no answer worth verbalizing was in her right now.

He prodded. "Messed up situation, huh?"

There it was.

"Yeah. You could say that."

"Have you heard from him?"

"Once. When the police were here."

"Shit. The police came already?"

"Yeah."

"No shit?"

"No shit."

He put one hand out to the kitchen island and leaned on it slightly. His brown hair, as always, was imperfect, as if he kept it that way, slightly askew with some hair gel or something. Tamara was tall, and at five foot nine she was only three inches shorter than Kyle, who was still a few inches shorter than Ben.

The thought was like a spider that crept out of her mind before vanishing quickly again into whatever hole it had come out of. Tamara remembered church and the sermon two weeks ago about struggle. The sermon topic for the entire month was "The War Within" and Tamara realized that this was what it must look like, the irrational desires in the most unpredictable of places that presented themselves and had to be dealt with.

The spider reappeared. *Yeah, and by the way, hadn't Kyle been sitting next to you at every one of those sermons, holding your hand?*

"What did he say?" Ben asked.

The question, for whatever silly reason, seemed out of bounds. The details of her conversations with her husband or the police were none of his business.

"I'd rather not talk about it," she said firmly.

He blinked and then nodded. "Yeah. Sure."

"You going to be okay taking the lead at work for a bit?"

"You really care about work stuff?" he asked, chuckling politely.

"Barely."

"Well, the Watanabe account is on hold. Lucky for us there's some sort of hurricane threat off the coast of Hawaii right now, which has grounded all flights. So they've rescheduled to Wednesday."

Tamara sighed. "Finally, a break."

"Listen. Nobody at work expects you—"

"I'll figure it out, Ben. Just tell John on Monday that I need a few days."

Ben seemed taken aback. "A few days? Wow." He looked at her funny. Was that admiration in his face?

"What?"

"You're amazing. Crazy maybe... but amazing. This is, like, a body blow most of us could hardly even begin to imagine, and you're actually worried about letting us all down on some stupid account."

Shame began to rise in her. He was right. But she wasn't amazing. She was just flat scared.

Ben took a cautious step towards her. She knew that advance. She'd seen it before. It was an approach with intent, and thankfully it was stunted by Seth's timely cry from the couch.

"Mom?"

Ben seemed startled. Of course. What man ever thinks of the kids? "Oh. Sounds like someone needs you," he said with a laugh and a smile that made her heart flutter, ever so slightly.

"Yeah." She felt herself about to cry. She blinked back the first hint of a tear and moved to end the moment, if that's what this visit really was. "Thanks so much for checking in on me, Ben. It means a lot. But I gotta get to the kids."

"Hey. No prob." He cleared his throat and began to make his way to the door.

"I'll walk you out," she said.

He protested. "No. You have your hands full. I'll let myself out. You have my number. Use it if you need it," he said. "No matter what, okay?"

"Okay," Tamara replied.

Then he was out the door and gone.

She made her way to the den, having already decided that she wouldn't mention a word of this to Trudy, even though that would normally be unthinkable. By your mid-thirties, hard core flirting by a younger guy was solid gossip material.

Except, of course, when your husband was wanted for murder.

CHAPTER 15

THE ROAD TO BEAURY was long and boring once you got past Castaic and into the open void beyond. To Napoleon, it seemed as if there was still a ton of land in California to be claimed before anyone could ever call the state overcrowded.

He and Parker talked very little, and he was thankful for that. He was still feeling drained, and this entire case was already starting to take a toll on him. Maybe this was how it happened. Maybe that fateful day when you knew it was time to hang it up wasn't a day at all, just a feeling that came over you, then lingered quietly in the background, when something you used to do was something you'd rather not do anymore. He told himself that it was just his cold giving him the blues.

It was Parker's turn with the radio, which had Napoleon praying for mercy from God on high.

Parker was of that generation that wore their caps side-ways and called their girlfriends "bitches." Napoleon was no women's libber but, well, he had a strong dislike of dogs, and to equate women with them was a negative connotation he could do without.

The current song was about the usual rap subject matter: reputation, power, sex and money. Napoleon had seen plenty of rap songs lived out in real time in the seven square miles that made up the Eastside. Rap was music that sold the lie of a glamorous death, and there was no such thing.

"There's our exit," Parker said excitedly. It was now just after 2:00 p.m., a little over two hours after they'd set off from the station house.

"Not a second too soon," Napoleon replied as he reloaded with a herbal cough drop.

The only exit to Beaury was Tree Top Road, which must've been a name given to it when there were trees around here somewhere. Now the only things visible near the road was an abandoned warehouse. A little further down they passed a Circle K, and then, like magic, a small town formed a mile and a half in the distance, made up of a mix of homes and trailer parks.

Parker turned off the radio. "So where to do we begin?"

"Where he would," Napoleon replied. "The last GPS signature came from near here. It was past one in the morning. If he was stupid, he would've looked for a hotel or motel to crash for the night. I doubt there is such a place here in lovely Beaury, but if there is, then a 1:00 a.m. check-in would certainly raise eyebrows."

Parker pulled out his cell phone and began to play with it.

"You got a signal?" Napoleon asked with a laugh.

Parker nodded. "My Cityinfo app has no hotels or motels here. I Googled it too, just to be sure. Nothing."

"Okay then. We'll still ask at the sheriff's office when we check in with them, but I'm not surprised. Who the hell would want to visit here?"

"So what next?"

"Okay, Parker, it's simple. He's a human being. He wants what we all want, but worse now, because he's on the run. He wants the basics: food, shelter and clothing. Assuming he had clothes on and assuming there was no shelter here, then—"

"—he goes for food."

"Yep. Even if he wasn't hungry, he would go for food."

"Why?"

"Aren't you listening? He's a human being. In crisis, we revert back to our original programming, like any animal, sadly. I ain't met a criminal yet who hasn't. They all do."

The words were barely out of his mouth when Napoleon realized he'd just lied. There was one who hadn't followed that pattern, wasn't there? He pushed the thought out of his mind. He was teaching the rookie the rules, not the exceptions. Joaquin had been an exception the likes of which Napoleon hoped Parker would never encounter.

"Okay. So I make the Denny's for our first stop."

Napoleon suppressed the urge to reply, *Brilliant, my dear Watson,* and instead he went with, "No? Ya think? By the looks of things, it's the only restaurant in the whole damn town."

Parker shrugged and drove to the Denny's.

It was rare when you struck gold so soon, but this wasn't Los Angeles; it was a small town that looked like it moved as fast as molasses straight out of the icebox. This being Saturday, the feeling was even worse.

Both waitresses at Denny's remembered him, and the one who actually waited on him, Jasmine, a skinny little thing with multiple piercings in her ears, seemed a bit foggy on a lot of the basic details. One would expect her to remember what he ordered and when he left, but she couldn't. She described him, but barely, as if she had amnesia—or was covering for him.

This prompted Napoleon to grill her. Hard. Did she know him? Had she met him before? Jasmine's eyes were panicked, but they had the usual look of the innocent when being wrongly accused: they got really big, but stayed focused on the accuser, no shifting up to the right or down to the left. No slouched shoulders. No words or questions repeated back to buy time. She was a dead end but not a deadhead.

Napoleon "bookmarked" the moment in his mind. It was a technique he'd begun using after a friend of his talked him into taking a psychology class at Cal State LA one year. He'd only taken the class because his "friend" was a hot redhead from the 911 call center who was playing unusually hard to get. By mid-semester he'd finally been able to get her to lower her guard, but, sadly, the class proved to be more interesting than the redhead.

"I'm… I'm sorry, but that's all I can remember. I swear, I never saw the guy before. I've had a headache all morning, and I can't seem to recall everything. He didn't stay long, though."

"You're sure he was alone, right?" asked Parker, his notepad open and his pen scribbling away as she talked.

"Yes. He maybe talked to some other guy in a hat, but, no, wait…"

"A hat?"

"Yeah. A John Deere hat, maybe? Or maybe I'm thinking of someone else who came in yesterday. I dunno." She sighed heavily. "I'm sorry."

"He looked dog-tired though, I'll tell ya that," Irene, a heavy-set waitress, chimed in.

"Yeah?" Napoleon shifted his attention to her, and as he did he could almost hear Jasmine sigh with relief.

"His hair was a mess. His shirt seemed a little dirty. He had big bags under his eyes, and he needed a shave. Still, even with all that, he was a cutie."

"Irene," Jasmine uttered under her breath.

"What? They're asking. Shit. I got nothin' to hide. I thought he was cute. So did you. You even said so when he came in. We had no idea the cops were looking for his ass."

Now it was Napoleon's turn to sigh. This was going nowhere. They'd gotten all they could out of these two.

"Ladies, please take these." Napoleon reached out and gave a business card to each of them. "Should you remember any other details you think would be helpful to our investigation, please call us immediately."

"Sure thing," Irene replied.

Napoleon noticed that Jasmine still had something on her mind. "Anything else you wanna tell us, Ms. White?"

She looked up at Napoleon kind of sheepishly. "Well… it's silly, I know… but he seemed really, really sad."

"You would be too, Jazy, if the cops were after ya," Irene piped in.

Jasmine shot Irene a look, then continued, "He seemed interested in one of the posters in the lobby too, on the way out. I do remember that."

Parker and Napoleon followed Jasmine's nod towards the lobby. From where they were standing they could see three or four small posters on a bulletin board opposite a candy machine.

"Any poster in particular?" Napoleon asked.

"I couldn't tell," Jasmine replied.

"Okay. Thanks."

In the lobby they were able to eliminate two of the posters right away. They were fairly sure that Kyle Fasano wasn't interested in either the bake sale at the Rotary Club or "Fender," the missing Jack Russell terrier that belonged to Burt and Katie Matthews and was deemed worthy of an 11x14 sheet of paper displaying six photos and a $250 reward. Napoleon wasn't sure, but $250 could most likely go a long way in Beaury. By now some of the townsfolk had probably formed a posse.

Of the two remaining posters, one was for tomorrow's gun and ammo convention at the Bentley High Gymnasium and the other was for the "Alfred Hitchcock Movie Festival" at the Beaury Public Library.

"Looks like we're going to the library," Napoleon said instantly.

Parker was, but of course, confused. "Why not the gun show? Why a film festival?"

"Well, it's neither really."

"What?"

"He's on the move. By default that means he can't be hanging around for a full day and a half for the gun show to start. Nor do I suspect that he's looking to watch any movies."

"So what's he after?"

"Follow me," Napoleon replied. As they exited the restaurant he continued, "Think, Parker. Who does Mr. Fasano work for?"

"Dynavac Industries."

"What department is he in?"

"Sales."

"Sales of what?"

Parker had to think a minute. "IT hardware."

"Exactly."

"So..."

Napoleon chuckled. "This guy lives part of his life every day in the tech world. Most everyone does now, but a guy like this, without his iPhone, cut off from the world, he's most likely gonna want one thing..."

"A computer," Parker said with a smile.

Napoleon nodded. *Light dawns on marble head.* "Every library has computers these days, even one in this Podunk town, I'll bet."

"Cool. I'll GPS it."

"Fine by me."

They walked slowly across the open asphalt to their car. To Napoleon's amazement, a lone tumbleweed nudged by a sudden gust of wind actually skirted across the edge of the parking lot.

A tumbleweed.

What was next? Vultures?

* * *

Kyle noticed the demon-woman as soon as he boarded his next bus. She was seated ten rows down the aisle and to the left. There was no missing her really. She wore the body of a woman in her mid-fifties, dressed in a white blouse and maroon sweater over a blue skirt that hung just above a pair of black flats. But her face was a garden of bone spurs that protruded slightly out of her skin at varying angles, each one circled by a little ring of blood. Like her brethren before her, she had red marble eyes that pushed back her eyelids. They burned a stare into Kyle and froze his soul.

He stopped, forcing the man behind him to bump into him and bark, "Hey!"

Kyle barely heard himself apologize as he began a measured approach to get past Bonespur. It didn't help that the line of people getting on the bus behind him was getting longer. Pretty soon he would be pushed into her. He thought of turning back, but despite the sneer she was throwing at him, Kyle sensed for some reason that she was not an imminent threat.

Watcher.

Again came that voice from inside himself, and he was learning not to ignore such revelations. It was as if he was growing a new set of instincts. Bonespur was a watcher. Her job was to follow. Nothing more.

He sidled past her cautiously, feeling her gaze as her head remained fixed straight forwards but her eyes tracked him, all the way to the corner of her eye sockets. He wondered if those eyes would just keep rotating, through her brain and to the back of her head, where they would poke out from behind her hair.

As he passed her, he heard the soft buzzing of flies, as if she were made up of them, or filled with them, or... He glanced down quickly at her and saw multiple flies on her lips.

She's breathing them.

The bus was an older model, probably a castoff from a large city where it had seen better days. The scratched aluminum siding was riddled with graffiti, tagger names or gang names, he didn't really know which. The letters always seemed like gibberish and numbers to him, as if it were a language all its own. There were assorted advertisements for condoms and television shows along the overhead runner, and the light from outside shone through the windows at muted angles, made uneven by the tinting that was peeling off the outside of the glass in certain places.

He made his way to the bench at the back of the bus, keeping Bonespur in his line of sight, before he finally sat down. As the passengers behind him scattered and took their seats, he momentarily lost sight of her, but then as the brakes on the bus disengaged and they pulled into traffic, he saw her again.

He was stunned.

She had switched to the opposite side of the aisle she'd originally been in and was now seated facing the back of the bus. Facing him. Staring.

Watching.

But why? The boy on the bike had attacked him, and so would've John Deere and his little buddy had they not been caught off guard by... the blue light. All the demons thus far had been out to kill him.

Even Caitlyn. But she hadn't been a demon. Her eyes had been black, not red. And it dawned on him as to why. These creatures were from some other place, hell no doubt. But Caitlyn had been occupied, in the midst of being persuaded: possessed.

He winced. It hurt to even think of her name. He saw her face again, in the hotel room before she finally became what she chose to become. He could still remember her pained expression of inner torture as she struggled so hard to reason with whatever it was that was changing her.

Bonespur shifted in her seat.

She's watching me for someone, for some... thing.

He couldn't help himself. He glanced at her and met her eyes again. She widened them in some sort of sickly intimidation tactic. It worked. Kyle felt his chest lock up. He couldn't breathe and... the flies. Were they multiplying? He forced his eyes away again, barely this time, but there was no shutting up his ears, the buzzing was coming on, wave after wave of sound.

He blinked. Another image of Caitlyn came to him; she was smiling at him at the bar, her blond hair tossed to one side, a bump from a tiny pimple hidden on her cheek by extra makeup revealed by the harsh light of the liquor display. He teased her about being a big college grad, and she betrayed a little bit of the girl still left in her by giggling instead of laughing. She was no innocent baby, but she was still young, still a bit of a child, still someone's daughter. What would Kyle have thought if his own baby girl, if Janie, someday right out of college had come home and confessed that she'd slept with, been used by, a married man seventeen years her senior? He shook his head.

There was no getting around it. If he failed in this task or on this mission, or plan, or whatever it was, he deserved to go to hell. How did this happen? How did he screw things up this badly?

Like bookends to the straight and narrow, Victoria and Caitlyn stood, pushing the bound pages of his life together. But they were weak bookends, lies at both ends of the truth he'd tried to make of his life, and they had now given way to the harsh weight of reality.

On some sort of autopilot, he glanced at every other person on the bus. There was only one creature to deal with, and she was a good fifteen feet away. Still staring. Not looking. Watching.

He sighed and shifted his weight, feeling anxious and alone. So this was it then. His life. A journey of sorts. No. A gauntlet. Of demons and sins. He remembered the story of Jesus in the desert for forty days. Tortured and tempted. The Son of God had prevailed.

But Kyle was the son of Frank and Georgette Fasano. The oldest of two children, he had a brother, Vinnie, two years younger, with an extra chromosome and a sleepy face, droopy eyelids and slurred speech.

And there it was: another worm turning within him. Hadn't Kyle been his hero? Hadn't Vinnie loved to see Kyle in his letterman jacket after every game? Hadn't he wanted to talk about the plays his big brother had been a part of as much as he could, in his limited capacity, yes, but still… hadn't he tried, so hard? And what did Kyle give him in return, almost every time? "Sorry, Vinnie. Big party to get to, little buddy. We'll talk tomorrow, okay?" And Vinnie always nodded his head, with those sad eyes looking very much like those of a sheepdog.

The sins were mounting.

Kyle Fasano was sure of one thing: he was no Jesus. Not by a long shot.

The tears banked across his eyelids and down his face like guilt and pain transformed to liquid form, his lips quivering with suppressed emotion and his throat burning.

He deserved hell. He did. At a wholesale price.

The buzzing stopped.

Kyle didn't have to ask how or why. He knew.

It stopped because what was watching him was very much enjoying what it was seeing.

CHAPTER 16

NAPOLEON SIGHED. THE HEAD librarian at the Beaury Public Library, Mrs. Hattie Tettle, was the exact opposite of the skinny waitress at the diner. She was talkative beyond belief and a good old-fashioned "nosey-ninny," or "*chismosa*," as his grandmother would've called her. Every cop's worst nightmare, she gave too much information about too much shit that had hardly anything to do with the questions being asked. Parker was taking notes so furiously that Napoleon feared his hand was going to cramp any minute and wouldn't that be great? Then Napoleon would have to take the notes.

"I knew he was no good, that one. He just shuffled in, looking like he'd slept in his work clothes, all charm and smiles. We had a guy like that used to work at the lumber yard for years, just all chuckles and compliments, used to bring his kids in here. Later we find out he was beating them *and* his poor wife. Can you believe that? Just horrible. I mean sometimes people can just be—"

"Mrs. Tettle, I don't mean to interrupt," Napoleon lied, "but can you describe what—"

"Oh, you're not interrupting, Officer, er, I mean, Detective. My. I don't think I've ever spoken to a detective before. And one from the city, no less! This is like in one of my Ed McBain novels. You know those, right? Have you read them?"

¡*Madre mia!* "No, ma'am," Napoleon said with a sigh, pinching the pressure points on his nose between his eye sockets for some blessed relief. "That's sorta like being a librarian and reading a book about librarians."

"Oh. Well, but there are some great books about librarians… and the library. Except that horrible Stephen King book with that story about The Library Policeman. Every year or so some poor child will read that and tell all the rest of the kids, and that's it! They're afraid to come in here. It's a shame. Though, funny enough, it *does* mean a drop in late fees on books for a while, I'll tell you that."

Parker looked at Napoleon as if suicide were swiftly becoming an option, or at the very least, a request to be transferred back to foot patrol. To his surprise, Napoleon had to suppress a laugh.

"That's fascinating, but please understand, ma'am… we're very pressed for time here and—"

"Well, of course. It's a manhunt! Like *The Fugitive*! Oh, my husband used to love that show. He's passed now. Six years ago."

Try as he might, Napoleon simply couldn't corral her. *Fuck me ten times over.* "I'm sorry to hear that, ma'am. But please, can you remember what Mr. Fasano did when he was here?"

She was a librarian. Old school. Her mind was a filing cabinet, and Napoleon had no doubt that her memories were probably arranged by the Dewey Decimal System. It took her some time to gather them up, but when she did, like everything else in their conversation so far today, they came in rapid fire.

"He walked in. Said hello. He got some magazines from the periodicals section, read for a while, and then spent some time at the computer island."

Ding! Napoleon glanced at Parker, who nodded and pursed his lips as if to say, "*Well done, Obi-Wan Kenobi.*"

"Do you remember which computer he was at?"

She blinked and pinched up her face at being asked such a silly question. "Why of course, it was number four. There are eight of them. It's the one on the far side of the island right over there, nearest the reading tables. They each have a little number on the monitor. Would you like me to show you?"

Seeing his out, Napoleon took it. "No! No, thanks. You've got the desk here to run. We'll check into it and come back with any further questions."

"Suit yourself," Mrs. Tettle replied, with no small hint of disappointment.

Napoleon and Parker made their way into the library, their shoes dragging a bit on the carpet.

"Whew!" Parker whispered softly.

"Damn. If that isn't a walking commercial for Ritalin, I don't know what is," Napoleon whispered back.

"Well, the old lady's been a widow a long time. Must get lonely."

"Yeah. Well. Ever hear of bingo?"

The computer island was a set of old computers with large monitors. As promised, each had a designated number. The library was as one would expect a library to be: quiet. Napoleon wondered if he and Parker had whispered to avoid Mrs. Tettle hearing them or because it was just part of their inner programming from childhood. He guessed it was more the latter. Like riding a bike, whispering in the library was second nature.

It appeared that Parker was going to try taking charge again. He didn't wait for Napoleon to go to the computer, but instead did so himself without asking, his assumption evidently being that he knew more about computers than the old man he had been teamed up with. Napoleon was no computer idiot, but when he saw Parker's typing speed, the way he navigated the history menus of the computer's hard drive and how he cross-referenced the computer's two different search engine histories, it was obvious that Parker knew what he was doing. He even switched to a DOS window for a minute or two, but Napoleon suspected that he was just showing off.

"So?"

"He logged into a number of places: Bank of America, Mint.com, Yahoo News. But he hardly spent any time on them. Then it gets interesting. He went to Google Maps and looked up a few addresses. No print history, so…"

"Probably just wrote them down."

"Yep. But then he went to Zillow and inputted the same addresses."

"Where at?"

"Great." Parker shook his head.

"What?"

"South of here."

"South?"

"Yeah. La Jolla and Coronado."

"He's backtracking?"

"Looks that way. But why?"

"We can ask the wife. Probably has family down that way. Or friends."

"Well, I've got a few names: Larry Klein and Timothy Reardon. He Googled them like crazy."

"Why Google someone you already know?"

"My guess?" Parker asked, surprised.

"No. I'm asking the damned computer monitor for its opinion."

"No phone. He ditched it. Probably looking for phone numbers."

Napoleon nodded. "Makes sense. These days no one remembers phone numbers. They just plug them into their contact list and speed-dial them."

"That, or he's too stressed to remember, so he comes here."

Napoleon had his own notepad open. "Larry Klein and Timothy Reardon?"

"Yep."

A good clue and a few solid leads, and Napoleon felt the stirrings of some juices inside of him, just like he used to get. It was the thrill of the hunt. They had a lead on Kyle Fasano, it seemed, and to top it off, his cold finally felt like it was subsiding a little.

"Hmm," Parker said, "that's not all"

"What else?"

"He went to Facebook too. Didn't log in as himself though, assuming he has an account."

Napoleon frowned. This was getting interesting. "What'd he do?"

"He created a bogus profile, then searched Klein and Reardon."

"Can we see what he did after that?"

"Not unless we can login to the bogus profile. We'd have to guess at the password, which could take forever. Or we can call Palo Alto."

"Palo Alto?"

"Facebook headquarters."

"Yeah, right. We'll need a subpoena for that, and it will cost us time."

"Guessing passwords will too."

Napoleon stopped to think for a bit. "I agree, but we can try a few, I guess. Passwords usually have some relation to the login name. What was it?"

Parker squinted at the screen. "Hmm. Weird. Do I have this wrong?"

"What?"

"Fasano's a white dude, but he picked a Spanish name."

Napoleon scowled. "No shit? What?"

"Joaquin. Joaquin Murrieta?"

It was as if Parker had spat in Napoleon's face or called his mother a whore. The words flew off his tongue like sprayed venom.

"What the hell did you just say?"

Parker was startled. "What? Shit. I just said the name."

"Say it again."

"Joaquin Murrieta."

All the blood in Napoleon's body flushed ice cold and his throat tightened as if a large hand were around it, choking him.

Instantly Napoleon thought of little Esmeralda in her tan dress and that puddle of blood. That huge puddle of blood. How could a child have so much blood?

"Joaquin Murrieta? You're sure?"

"You okay man?" Parker asked from a million miles away.

Napoleon felt dizzy for a second but pulled it together, intent on not losing it in front of the rookie. "Yeah. Fine. Finish the interview with the old lady. You're on your own there. I'll meet you outside at the car."

"What?"

Napoleon turned and walked swiftly out of the library. He needed fresh air, something to get his mind off that miserable murderer's face in the courtroom that day. That smile. *Watch what I do next, homie.*

Once in the parking lot, he couldn't help himself. He darted behind a row of dying hedges and puked, the whole time repeating his own personal mantra: there were no such things as coincidences. There were no such things as coincidences. There were no such things as coincidences. Which now begged a question.

How in the world did Kyle Fasano know about Joaquin Murrieta?

CHAPTER 17

THE BUS RIDE TO Monterey was going to take a good four hours. That was a long ride to be sitting fifteen feet from an agent of hell, but Kyle was managing to block her, and all the negative thoughts she stirred up in him, by saying, of all things, the Lord's Prayer. He was surprised to find that he still remembered it. Though he went to church most weekends, it was mostly for the kids and to appease Tamara.

But there was no mistaking the power of that prayer. The painful memories within him and the fear of the thing sitting so nearby subsided each time he prayed, so he did so repeatedly: "Our Father, who art in heaven, hallowed be thy name…"

Glancing up at Bonespur, he was stunned at what he saw. Her face had gone slack, and her eyes were locked in a faraway stare at the wall behind Kyle, as if she were slipping into a static state.

No. Pay attention. She's no longer…

Watching.

She can't watch while you pray. It hurts her to do so.

Kyle shifted in his seat. These thoughts disrupted his prayers, but there still seemed to be some lasting effect because Bonespur still wasn't moving.

Again, he had to stave off the idea that he was going mad. What was happening to his life? What did all of this mean? How could it be? Wasn't this all stuff you told yourself *maybe* you believed in, but then again, maybe you didn't? He still wasn't fully convinced.

That was it. His thoughts of going mad were his stubborn way of insisting, even now, after all that had happened, that maybe it still wasn't real.

A creeping unease spread to his core, because if he couldn't fully believe now, after all he'd seen, then what was it going to take to finally convince him? He didn't even want to think about that.

Bonespur's hands were folded in her lap, like a good schoolchild, but Kyle noticed one of her fingers twitch, just barely. He was going to pray again but stopped himself. If his theory were true, he had to test it. He'd only said the prayer a few times. Now he would see how long it took her to reanimate.

He took a deep breath. He was so tired, but sleep was a faraway fantasy.

Keeping his mind busy, he thought of Monterey, situated on the Central California coastline, of Cannery Row and of the restaurant at the end of the pier that served fantastic clam chowder.

He'd taken the family there on more than one occasion, mostly so the kids could check out the aquarium, but Kyle always loved it there. The sea was a darker shade of blue, almost purple in places, with jagged rocks throughout the bay that almost always played host to a basking seal or two.

It was a strange coincidence that on all those visits he'd been within miles of his first love's home and never knew it. He wondered if he'd ever walked right past Victoria on the street, or parked his car across from hers at the gas station while heading back home from vacation. Had she seen him? Had she wanted to say something to him?

He wondered if her hair was still long and brown, if it still seemed to glow with soft yellow streaks whenever she was in direct sunlight, or if her lips still curved slightly downward at the edges even when she smiled.

A heartache from lost youth stirred in him, and he remembered the very first time he made her laugh. It was as if the air around her electrified. He'd broken through those inner clouds of hers, in spite of her best efforts to the contrary. She looked at him suddenly, with such a unique and precious expression, as if the sound of her own laugh was a surprise to even her. And Kyle knew, at that very second, that she'd fallen in love with him, which was good because he'd fallen in love with her too, her laugh the final bridge they needed to cross to really meet each other.

Kyle came back to the present, to the bus, and when he did he realized he had a small smile on his face.

It disappeared as soon as he looked up and saw Bonespur staring at him again. He tried to look away, but in her eyes he saw reflected there the bitterness and regret that were the true remnants of all those sentimental memories: he'd discounted his feelings for Victoria after they'd finally had sex, even though her love for him was only growing, and then a while later he went off to the Colorado River for a family reunion just before their senior year and made out with a girl from Arizona, never telling anyone except his cousins.

When Bonespur spoke, Kyle jumped in his skin. "Made out? Oh, come now, boy. So good at lying to yourself, aren't you? What really happened? Why… you sprouted ten thumbs and couldn't keep your hands off her, could you?" Her voice was raspy and electronic, a product of one of those voice boxes that heavy smokers use near the end of their lives. "You would've gladly screwed her too if she hadn't said no. Such a looong walk back to your tent that night wasn't it? With the worst case of blue balls too. Tee-hee!"

Kyle was speechless in the face of this memory, long buried within him, that she'd somehow exhumed.

Bonespur cackled softly, lowered her chin and leered at him.

Kyle's mind slipped a little and then data flooded him again. This creature wasn't just a watcher. She was a deceiver. She and her kind destroyed people through their minds. And this one was good. She had destroyed countless lives. Over the years. No. Over a century.

Glancing around quickly at the other passengers on the bus, Kyle saw, for the third time in his life now, that the world had frozen in place, as if everyone was tucked off in some corner of the universe that was impervious to time.

Sneering, Bonespur leaned slightly forwards, as if to share a little secret between the two of them. "Come now, boy. Tell me how much you loved your dear Victoria while you were with the other girl, you randy little pig."

He wasn't crazy. Not yet anyway. But her voice? He knew at his core that her voice, which ended every sentence with a long, sucking sound, would drive him mad if he let her keep talking.

"Our Father, who art in heaven…" Kyle tried to start again.

"That trick won't fool me twice, boy. You only got me because I thought you were further along in your training. I never expected such a simple tactic. You're still so human. It will be so delightful to drink your blood soon."

"Leave me alone. I don't want to talk to you."

"Oh. I guess not, but let's go on. About that night, with your cousins? You wanted to talk about what you did, didn't you? Let's go all the way with this story, baby." And this time she managed a full laugh, deep and hearty. "What else did you do, you little pig-man?"

"Stop…"

"Why, you wanted to tell them all the details about what you did."

"Our Father, who art in heaven—"

"Shut up. I'm not finished."

"Yes, you are. I won't listen anymore."

"What? Not even about your darling Victoria?"

Kyle swallowed hard, trying to keep his composure, but Bonespur's face seemed to be bleeding more now, as if all the talking was stretching and tearing the scar tissue around all her spurs, which were glistening beneath the fluorescent lights in the bus.

"Do you know that she never loved like that again, the way she loved you? It was utterly spectacular the way you ruined her. We rejoiced, you know, my brethren and I. That's how we knew you were special, even back then. Such… a profound effect on another human being, and at such a young age. You were gifted. A true catalyst for evil."

Looking around the bus for an exit, Kyle realized it was no use; he would have to get past her to get off the bus, and he doubted she was going to let that happen.

"So she decided she lost you because she wasn't sexy enough. Kinky enough. Dirty enough. Did you know that?"

"You're a liar."

"No. Really. So in college she got a little wild. Oh my. The things she did."

"Screw you."

"Ahhh." Bonespur leaned her head back slightly and closed her eyes in a brief display of pleasure, as if his discomfort were a blown kiss.

Sitting up again, she straightened her skirt and continued. "So. Anyway. There's pretty much nothing she hasn't tried in bed now."

It were as if he'd been stabbed by her words, and now wounded he could think of nothing else to do... until something dawned on him. Each time he'd tried to pray, Bonespur had cut him off. She even rather convincingly tried to downplay what he'd pulled off earlier, when he'd stunned her. But what if...

"Our Father, who art in heaven, hallowed be thy name—"

"Shut up!"

"Thy kingdom come, thy will be done—"

"I said shut up, you dribbling piece of shit!"

Kyle looked into Bonespur's eyes again, and this time there was fear reflected in the contorted mask of her face, her eyes swimming in confusion and the blood from her spurs dribbling down her cheeks and neck. She began garbling in a cascade of unintelligible languages, as if trying to counter Kyle's prayer.

"On earth, as it is in heaven." Again he felt the blue begin to course through him, fainter this time, less a pulse and more a charge. "Please give us this day, our daily bread..."

Bonespur didn't even try to get up; instead she folded her arms backwards, like a spider, the bones and joints in her upper torso cracking. She climbed up across the bus seat, away from Kyle, until her hands hit the bus window and her bony fingers scratched at the latch to open it.

Kyle felt the simplest of guidance again, from far off. "And forgive us our trespasses..."

She glared at him. "You pig-shit little bastard, shut up, shut your filthy mouth or I'll shut it for you."

Kyle pushed on. "... as we forgive those who trespass against us."

She screamed at the word "forgive," as if he had slapped her. Kyle maintained his focus on her face, but it wasn't easy; her hands behind her were moving at such speed, but the simple logic of the latch seemed beyond her.

"I'm warning you, boy. Don't say it."

Kyle was afraid he'd forgotten the rest of the prayer, that wouldn't have been good, but then it came to him. "And lead us not into temptation…but deliver us from evil."

Shrieking, she bared fangs at him that seemed to grow instantly from her gums.

Kyle continued, "For thine is the kingdom… and the power and the glory…"

Her red eyes flared as her fingers finally loosened the latch.

"Forever and ever… Amen."

It was when she opened her mouth wide and her jaw unhinged and opened even further that Kyle knew he was in trouble. The buzzing within her erupted and flies began to pour out of her in waves, throughout the whole bus. With pure disgust Kyle realized that they were combing over his face and at the corners of his lips, trying to burrow into his mouth.

Thank God he had started the prayer when he did. There were so many flies he might never have been able to finish otherwise. They swarmed over him, as if to cocoon him in filth and germs. A few tried climbing up his nostrils.

Her voice pierced his brain. "You're lucky that I'm not allowed to chew out your eyes, boy. This time. Remember that. But maybe I'll see you again. Until then? Remember this too…"

The bus exploded in black and the image came to him: Vinnie, all grown now, only visited on his birthday and holidays, sitting alone and sad at the care home Kyle and his mother had chosen for him. Staring out at a world that didn't understand him.

Wondering why, after all this time, even his brother didn't either.

The weight of the image thrust upon Kyle by the wicked creature that had now crawled out of the bus window was crushing him. "No, no, no, no, no…"

Then it was over.

The bus, the driver, the people on board were all back in their places, undisturbed. The world outside the window began to pick up speed and Kyle collapsed sideways in his seat, drained beyond imagination, as reality was set into motion again.

The conversations of the rest of the passengers and the hum of the bus engine resumed, and Kyle knew he was safe, at least for a little while.

Then he fell into a deep sleep.

CHAPTER 18

BY THE TIME PARKER had finished in the library and made his way to the car, Napoleon had managed to get himself together. Not so much by figuring out this odd turn of events, but by simply forcing himself to set it aside for now. When something in a case didn't make sense, sometimes that was the best thing to do. But Napoleon was running out of room in his head for the things he was setting aside in this case though. There was the crime scene, the video footage and now this.

The sun hung like a stone over a distant mountain, casting partial shadows from the clouds down over the rolling plains, giving Beaury the momentary appearance of some sleepy little town in Kansas or something.

This place was the utter opposite of anywhere Napoleon ever lived, and he imagined the cops here would be different too. Time would tell.

Parker cleared his throat, opened the car door and got in while Napoleon braced himself for the questions that were sure to follow.

"You good?" Parker asked.

Here it comes. Napoleon nodded.

Instead, Parker didn't press. He simply put the key in the ignition, started the car and said, "Where to next?"

Napoleon swiftly did the calculus. At least he could still figure out Parker. The case? Not so much. But Parker?

No problem. He'd been in the library a little longer than expected before reappearing. Napoleon smiled. For the first time he sensed that the rookie had real potential. He'd had the balls to mock the captain earlier, and now he'd had the balls to dig up the dirt on his own partner.

"You Googled it, didn't you?"

"Googled what?"

"You know what."

There was silence while, Napoleon surmised, Parker weighed his answer before going with the honest route. "Yes." It was a wise choice. Napoleon hated liars. "And?"

"You said you didn't want to talk about it, man."

"So you looked it up instead?"

Parker offered up what was becoming his trademark move: he shrugged. "You never said I couldn't."

After a few seconds, Napoleon chuckled in spite of himself. Parker joined him, nervously at first, before the two men shared a genuine laugh.

Napoleon shifted his weight. "Screw it. You got any questions?"

"Nope."

"No?"

Parker scratched his chin. "Not really."

Napoleon was impressed. "Fair enough."

"I mean," Parker sighed, "what am I gonna say? Some lame shit like 'we all make mistakes'? Or 'nobody's perfect'?"

"I'd slap you if you did," Napoleon replied.

"So? Where to?"

"The Sheriff's Station. Two blocks south of Pederson Avenue."

Backing the car out of the faded parking space, Parker evidently couldn't resist putting in his two cents. "I will say one thing, if you'll let me."

"Shoot."

"It was a bullshit call by a chicken-shit DA, from what I read. But the scales will balance, man. You'll still get his ass someday."

Napoleon laughed. "Not likely. The bastard's dead."

Parker raised his eyebrows.

"You shoulda stopped Googling me and started Googling him."

Stunned, Parker shook his head. "If not for that crazy old bat coming at me again with more of her stories, I would've."

Napoleon smiled. "That makes sense."

"Okay. I admit. I'm curious now. Curiosity killed the cat, and all that."

"No. He didn't. He killed five more little girls."

The mood darkened. They drove a half-mile down the road in silence before Parker finally spoke. "Now I know why you don't want to talk about it."

The traffic in Beaury was non-existent, with the lone exception of a Lolo's Breads delivery truck that was passing through the intersection. By force of habit, Napoleon noticed the rear license plate was loose on one side. "If you were still on patrol, rookie, you could pull his ass over. That plate's about to fall clean off."

Parker glanced at the truck. "Yeah. I imagine there wouldn't be much else to do around here but harass the locals."

Napoleon cleared his throat and smirked. "Maybe you could get a free baguette to drop the ticket."

"Yeah, right," Parker replied, scratching his cheek. "There's no telling how fresh anything in that truck is."

The roads were old pavement surrounded by mostly dirt and desert foliage, and they only had to drive a while before they saw the Beaury Sheriff's Station. It was exactly what Napoleon expected: a two-car operation, no doubt with one sheriff and one deputy. Napoleon wouldn't have been the least bit surprised if each of their cruisers could be found parked in front of their respective houses on any given day, at any given time. Beaury was quiet, the pay was no doubt minimal, and boredom was probably the worst part of the job.

Today, however, having been called by Captain Bennett and informed that Napoleon and Parker were on the way, a Sheriff Conch and a Deputy Kendall were at the station waiting. Once welcomed in, Napoleon and Parker joined them in taking a seat.

Conch looked to be in his late-fifties and just a touch overweight. "You really think this asshole rolled through here?" he asked, leaning back in his chair. His desk was littered with stacks of paper. The wall behind him had a dozen or so plaques with photos of the local soccer teams the station had sponsored over the years.

Napoleon nodded. "We already spoke with two waitresses at the Denny's that identified him."

"Denny's?" Conch looked at Kendall, a slim guy who was probably in his early thirties and now looked a bit stunned. "Shit."

"You were there?" Parker asked.

Conch looked embarrassed, but, to his credit, not ashamed or the least bit defensive, he said, "Yep. About noon or so. Lunch. Didn't see him, but we didn't know to be looking for him yet. We didn't get the message from your captain or the APB on this nut until we got back."

"He was there in the morning, so I doubt you would've seen him," Napoleon said.

"Who'd you speak to? Irene?"

"Yeah. But she wasn't the one who served him."

"Who did?"

"Jasmine."

"What'd she say?"

"Not much. She could barely remember anything about him."

Conch looked perplexed. "Isn't that Jasmine White?" he asked, looking at Kendall, who nodded in reply.

Napoleon scratched his jaw, looked at Conch and waited for him to continue. After a few seconds he did.

"Jasmine's one of the smarter ones around here. Graduated three years ago. Stayed away from drugs. Class valedictorian. We figured she'd be gone by now, but her father's got lupus, bad, so she stayed."

"So you're saying…?" Parker prodded.

"I'm saying I'm surprised she couldn't be of more help to you, is all."

"You'd have expected her to remember more?"

"Unless this guy threatened her or something? Yeah. I mean, he's an out-of-towner. Right there, that makes him special."

"True. But the threat thing isn't likely."

"Why's that?"

"We think he's on the move, probably headed south now."

The old man didn't miss a beat. "South? He heads here, north of Los Angeles, only to double back?" Conch was sharper than Napoleon was first willing to give him credit for.

"Not logical, I know," Napoleon agreed.

"Worse. I'd say that dog don't hunt," Conch observed. "Especially if he crosses right back through LA, where everyone is looking for him, to get there. But he's probably pretty panicked, so I guess it makes sense. Where south?"

Napoleon sighed. "Probably the San Diego area."

Conch seemed partially skeptical. "Or more likely Mexico?"

"Maybe. It's possible."

"Well, shit. Nobody wants to go south of the border these days. Not likely anyone would follow him."

Napoleon smiled. "Not likely a white boy like Fasano with half a brain would try either. Anything past TJ and he's a dead man."

"He could still be around here though?" Kendall interjected.

"Yep," Parker replied. "We know he went to the library. We followed that lead from Denny's."

"So, you met Hattie?" Conch asked with a grin.

"Shit. Did we ever. Good God." Parker laughed.

"She's a hoot alright. I don't think I've checked out a library book in ten years." When they were all done laughing, Conch continued, "So do we think he has kin or something out this way?"

"Possible. Not likely. The… uh… kin is probably what's down south."

Conch seemed to be the decisive type; he leaned forwards and slapped his palms to his knees. "Okay then. Did you guys check out the rest of the stores near the Denny's?"

Napoleon shook his head. "The Denny's and library thing took on a life of their own, but we didn't want to go poking around town anymore until we hooked up with you guys."

"Okay. Let's head over there now."

Ten minutes later they pulled into the mini-mall parking lot behind Sheriff Conch's cruiser and joined he and Kendall in front of the CVS.

Once again Conch proved to be in command. "Well. Let's see. The post office is already closed, we can check in with them on Monday. But Kendall? You take Troutie's. Detective Parker, do you mind taking the Dickies store?"

"Not at all," Parker answered.

"Detective Villa and I will head into CVS."

They split up. They all hit pay dirt. After Conch and Napoleon interviewed the CVS staff it was apparent that Kyle Fasano had stopped in and done a little shopping. No one remembered exactly what, though one of the cashier's thought she recalled hair dye, which struck her as odd for a man. It wasn't until they asked to see the store's video tapes that things got complicated: only the store manager had a key to the security room and he, but of course, wasn't in today and wasn't answering any of his phones.

While they waited, Kendall and Parker walked in with their news. Fasano had purchased clothes and a duffel bag at the Dickies. It was no surprise to anyone that he hadn't been in the bait and tackle store.

It took an hour for the store manager to call in. Off shooting in the desert with his friends, he was on his way back now but still an hour and a half away. There was no extra key.

While they waited Napoleon munched on a bag of Doritos's and cursed his luck. Having confirmed that Fasano had been here, he couldn't just hop in the car and head off to San Diego just yet. There could be important evidence on that tape, and he didn't want to trust it to two country cops he didn't know.

When Henry the store manager arrived he was small, frail and seemed like the last guy on the planet who would be a gun enthusiast. Napoleon figured that anything bigger than the smallest pistol would knock him clean on his ass the minute he fired it. His face was pale and he couldn't stop apologizing to Conch, who let him know that spare keys were always a good idea in life, just in case, and sighed heavily at him repeatedly as he fumbled with the lock.

Once they got into the room the tapes gave up their secrets pretty readily.

"So that's our man?" Conch asked, sounding intrigued. Napoleon nodded.

The four of them watched as Fasano made his way through the store picking up hair dye and scissors first, then a greeting card, then something from the register that they couldn't make out.

"Henry!" Conch shouted.

"Yeah Sheriff?" Henry replied. He was hovering just outside the door.

"Take a look at this, will ya? What's he getting there?"

Henry stepped into the room and put on a thick pair of glasses. Even with them he had to squint at the screen from the camera over the cash registers. "Hm. Not positive. We can walk over to the registers and double check but I'm pretty sure it's a calling card."

"A calling card?" Kendall asked.

"And a greeting card," Parker chimed in.

"After looking up two men in San Diego," Conch added flatly.

"He wants the calling card to call his wife," Napoleon said firmly, "That's a gimme. We'll need to track down the receipt of that transaction and get that calling card number."

Conch nodded at Henry who then scampered off to get the information.

"You think he's taking the greeting card with him? You know, as a thanks for whoever he's going to visit?" Parker asked no one in particular.

"Possibly, yeah."

They watched as Fasano made his purchase and left the CVS.

"He turned to the right," Kendall said.

"Towards the Dickies. Which means he probably came here first," Conch added.

"What'd you find out at the Dickies?" Napoleon asked Parker.

"That the girl that works there is in a big fight with her boyfriend."

"And?"

"That she's really mad at him."

"Uh-huh. And?"

"She remembers Fasano coming in while she was on the phone with said boyfriend. Fasano made a purchase. Doesn't remember what. And then he left. End of memory."

Napoleon was going to say something but instead he just gave into the urge to sigh heavily.

"Okay. Now what?"

"We'll go with the odds and head south. But how would he get out of town?"

"No stolen car reports?" Parker asked.

"None yet," Kendall replied.

"Well. He left his own car at the crime scene. We know that."

"So he either hitched a ride with a rig—or took the bus," Conch added.

"I can swing by Addie's," Kendall said.

Parker folded his arms across his chest. "Addie's?"

"Truck stop about five miles north of here," Conch explained. "If he hitched, we may get a driver there who saw him or helped him by accident. You go there, Kendall. I'll start running down the buses."

Napoleon handed Conch his card. "My cell number is on there."

"We're running outta sunlight. We turn up anything, today or in the morning, I'll call you with it right away. You do likewise."

They all shook hands.

"Sure thing. Thanks for your help, Sheriff."

"You kidding me? This is the most action we've ever seen here."

On the walk to the car, Napoleon volunteered to drive and Parker tossed him the keys.

The temperature seemed to have dropped twenty degrees, and Parker rubbed at the back of his neck. "Whadya think?"

"I think they can handle it," Napoleon answered.

"Not chuckleheads?"

"Not at all. I get the feeling Conch would give his left arm right now to be going south with us."

Parker grunted. "Yeah. Ain't we the lucky ones."

* * *

Kyle woke up just as the bus slowed into a turn. He guessed he'd been out about three hours or so. He'd forgotten how much longer a trip took by bus. His body was so drained that he felt like he'd slept ten minutes, tops.

To his left, outside the bus windows, a rising and falling view of the Pacific Ocean greeted him, its waves breaking against the dark rocks below. The bus passed a few turnoffs and then a sign appeared announcing the distance to Carmel. He'd always wanted to golf a round at Pebble Beach, which was near Carmel, but that was a day he sensed would never come now. Ever. That was life. You shoulda, woulda and someday… just couldn't. Plain and simple.

He was so tired it took him a moment to realize that The Gray Man was sitting right next to him.

Kyle smiled weakly. "Well, well. The great leader has returned."

The Gray Man looked down at him with a perplexed expression. "You are an interesting one, that's for sure."

Kyle forced himself to sit up. "Gee, nice seeing you too."

"You're drawing on powers and forces you shouldn't even know of yet, much less be wielding. How is that?"

"What?"

"Who taught it to you?"

"What are you talking about?"

"The light. The blue light."

"Are you serious? Who *taught* it to me?"

"Yes and yes. Now answer me."

"I thought *you* were the one who taught it to me."

The Gray Man rolled his eyes and shook his head. "How could I have taught it to you when I haven't even seen you since this all began?"

Kyle was getting annoyed. "Gee. I don't know. You kinda left me on my own a bit there with that little pecker on the bike, I thought maybe you just… I dunno… sent it to me somehow, at the Denny's I guess, when those other two things came after me."

The Gray Man narrowed his eyes. "The Denny's? You went there before the library, yes?"

"Yes."

"There was a warp of some kind, a lapse in my ability to track you. So I was not privy to that moment. Tell me what happened."

"Are you kidding me? I was on my *own* then?"

The Gray Man shifted in his seat, put his hand on Kyle's forearm and squeezed it. "Evidently not, Kyle. This is important. Tell me what happened."

Kyle did, as fully and yet as briefly as he could, and afterwards The Gray Man stared out the bus window for a long time before finally asking, "The two creatures in the diner? Did you use the power on them?"

For the first time Kyle saw concern in The Gray Man's face.

Kyle nodded.

Letting go of Kyle, The Gray Man folded his arms and kicked at a spot on the floor, his eyes shifting slightly from side to side. He appeared to be thinking intently.

"Why? What's the big deal?" Kyle asked.

"The big deal is you've been noticed now. There will be unwanted attention, by forces bigger than I was anticipating."

Kyle felt a numbness settle in just behind his forehead. Perhaps relying on The Gray Man to maintain his safety had been naïve. "What forces?"

"Someone gave you the power. It isn't taught. It's given."

Kyle put his head in his hands. "This is just great." He looked up at The Gray Man. "You get me into this shit, and now you say something is what… off? Is that a good word?"

The Gray Man's eyes were piercing as his voice went firm. "Let us get one thing straight, Kyle, before any of this continues: *I* did not get you into any of this. *You* got yourself into it. I'm just here to help you try and overcome it."

Properly checked, Kyle grew quiet.

"The good news is that the power could only come to you from our side. It's something only we use."

"Who's 'we'?"

The Gray Man shook his head. "Never mind that for now. Has anyone else like me visited you?"

"No."

"How did the power manifest itself then?"

"I told you. I was at the counter, in the Denny's, those creatures were trying to scare me. I felt for sure that they were going to attack and…"

"And?"

"My hands began to glow all of a sudden. I just felt it in me."

"How did the creatures respond?"

Kyle remembered their faces clearly, especially John Deere's, which up to that point in the diner had been ferocious and intimidating. Until the light. Then? "They looked shocked, and scared."

Nodding, The Gray Man adjusted his hat. "Of course they did."

"Why?"

"The power is a direct current from a plane beyond this one. You channeled it. It can destroy them. Utterly. But it is usually not passed on, or given, until one is ready to wield it."

Despite his desire to understand what he was hearing, Kyle felt faint.

"Hey, Gray?" It was the first time Kyle had called him that, and it felt oddly reassuring.

"Yes."

"I don't feel right. I'm exhausted. And this little chat of ours isn't helping."

The Gray Man blinked. "Yes. Of course. Your body isn't meant for that much power. We have to get you someplace. You need more sleep."

"Someplace?"

"Yes. Shelter. Where you can be administered to."

"Administered to?"

The Gray Man helped Kyle stand as the bus came to a stop just outside downtown Carmel. They walked out together, the other passengers clearing a bit of a path. "Sorry. So sorry," The Gray Man said. "My friend gets very bad car sickness."

One old lady with a small piece of Samsonite luggage rudely refused to move. The Gray Man looked at her sternly and said, "He's going to throw up any second now." She moved.

Once they maneuvered out of the bus, The Gray Man helped Kyle across the street and through the parking lot beyond, then over to a small grassy area beneath a massive tree with long, reaching branches. He guided Kyle to the base of the tree and made him lie down.

"What are we doing?" Kyle murmured.

"Don't worry. No one can see us."

Kyle closed his eyes and was out almost instantly, once again falling into a deep sleep that settled all the way down into his bones. He woke once, briefly, and was amazed to see that the night sky, so full of stars, had descended down and around them, as if the universe itself were his cradle. A small orb-like fire burned a few feet from Kyle, and he saw The Gray Man talking to two other men that were bathed in light, just a few feet beyond.

They were speaking of forces at work and battles past.

Before he slipped again into the depths of sleep, he could've sworn he heard The Gray Man say Tamara's name. But that was silly.

How could she be wrapped up in all of this?

* * *

Tamara rubbed her eyes and sighed. The day had mercifully come to an end. The phone calls had continued flooding in, and each merited a glance at caller ID. But it was never Kyle. Every few minutes she checked her email on her phone. Nothing there either. He was off whatever grid there was. This scared her because it implied his guilt, and each time her mind wandered down that path it was like a stray dog: it began getting into things it shouldn't—like why she wasn't good enough to keep her husband faithful, like what it was that Caitlyn did so well that she didn't, or like how someone she thought she knew so well could betray her like this. So she called her mind back to her side and kept it on a tight leash.

Trudy's arrival from the airport was the godsend it was expected to be. When she'd first gotten there, a news van from KCOP had been partially blocking the bottom of the driveway, so Trudy called the police and had it removed for trespassing. She'd even made Tamara laugh, in spite of herself, by confronting a bold reporter who'd made her way up the driveway to the front door. Tamara had no idea a girl could moonwalk in heels, but as the reporter retreated back down the driveway in the face of Trudy's advance the only thing missing was the Michael Jackson music.

A little while later though, it was Trudy who made Tamara cry. Tamara was resting in the den, snuggled under a warm blanket, and was drifting off to sleep when she heard Janie's little voice, more innocent than usual, in the kitchen. She'd snuck out of bed somehow and was speaking softly with Trudy.

"What happened with Daddy?" she asked.

There were a few seconds of silence, and then Trudy replied: "He maybe made some bad decisions, honey, hopefully not, but it'll be okay. You just gotta help me take care of Mommy, okay?"

Tamara's tear supply seemed never-ending, and once again she found their hot sting rolling down her cheeks.

Yes. Kyle had "maybe" made some bad decisions, and because of them, Tamara needed to be taken care of now, by her friends and family. How was that fair? And why was her grief beginning to metastasize into shame? She'd done nothing wrong.

Later she heard Trudy take the biggest bullet of all: another call from Kyle's mother. She stayed on the phone with her for nearly a half-hour, consoling her, of all things, as if Kyle's mother was a dear confidant who could be trusted with all the inside information. Trudy told her that Tamara was sleeping and that nobody knew anything for sure yet, so everyone needed to stay calm, for *Kyle's* sake. Very smart.

Later that night, as the kids slept, Tamara and Trudy sipped wine on the couch in the den and watched as the moon hovered over the pool in the backyard. They talked about how crazy life was, and then they did what any reasonable adults their age did on a bad day: they watched repeats of *Seinfeld*.

When those were over, the news came on. Trudy moved to change the channel, but Tamara asked her not to. She needed an update of some kind, any kind, even if it came from the enemy.

She was astonished by this feeling, but it was true. The police, the press. She was already beginning to think of them as the enemy, to her family and also to Kyle, as if Kyle still needed to be defended somehow. This was huge for Tamara, internally, to know that deep down she still believed in him.

The story had been pushed down a few leads already, but before long a Captain Bennett of the LAPD was on the screen. He was of some girth, with peeling red cheeks and a deep voice. He rattled off the facts. Kyle was still a person of interest. They were approaching the case as a "likely" homicide. Caitlyn was finally named as the "victim," and what made it worse, far worse, was that she was the daughter of someone important: an Assistant District Attorney of Los Angeles.

She heard Trudy curse under her breath before taking another sip of her wine.

In addition, Caitlyn's mother was quite the philanthropist. A daughter from a wealthy family in Pasadena, she was an ex-Rose Parade beauty queen, headed the local chapter of the Red Cross, and both she and her husband were heavily involved with Children's Hospital of Los Angeles.

Tamara's stomach squirmed. *Shit, Kyle, you picked the wrong girl to mess up with.*

Law enforcement within the state of California as far north as San Francisco and as far south as San Diego were now involved in the "investigation" and "continuing search" for Mr. Kyle Fasano, as were authorities in Nevada and Arizona. Kyle was urged to turn himself in. Anyone with knowledge of his whereabouts was to call their local police department. If seen, he was not to be approached, as he "could be dangerous." It seemed to Tamara that the gears of some massive machine were beginning to turn, and she wasn't surprised. When a beloved child of the rich and powerful dies, things happen far more quickly than they seemed to for anyone else.

"You good?" Trudy asked, reaching across the couch to pat Tamara's knee.

"I miss him. I'm mad as hell, Trudy, but I'm worried sick about him."

Trudy put her glass of wine aside and sat closer to Tamara and hugged her. "I know, Tam-Tam. It'll work out. It will."

Tamara took comfort in her college nickname as she rested her head against Trudy's shoulder. It was from their time together on the women's volleyball team, a take on Bamm-Bamm from the *Flintstones*. Tamara was a presence at the net, and she had a mean spike that was punctuated by that little chant whenever it was successfully executed.

"Why did he do this, Trudy?"

Trudy scoffed. "Men. It's clichéd, and it's no excuse, but they screw up."

"But I thought I was making him happy. I thought we had a good life," Tamara sniffed and shook her head.

"Don't do this to yourself," Trudy replied firmly. "It's not your fault, and you damn well know it."

"But if he were happy—"

"A lot of things make up a person's happiness."

"But I—"

"You what? Built a home for him? Loved him? Gave him two beautiful babies? Worked full time just like he did?" Trudy sat upright and took Tamara by the shoulders. "We're not going to do this, okay? This is not some sappy, bullshit Lifetime special where we're going to let you blame yourself for your husband being stupid enough to risk it all to screw some little whore, okay?"

Tamara nodded.

They were silent for a minute before Tamara dealt with the last elephant in the room. "But what if he really did kill her, Trudy?"

"Jesus, Tamara." Trudy reached over and finished off her glass of wine. "If he did that, then we'll get you through that too. Somehow, someway."

"How?"

"I don't know, but we will."

Tamara was about to delve further into this when her phone buzzed.

It was a text message.

From Ben.

She ignored it.

CHAPTER 19

NAPOLEON AND PARKER HAD doubled back on the route they'd just traveled. The open spaces and dead lands of the 5 south, mixed sporadically here or there with farmlands, was a boring repeat of the same areas they'd passed while going north, but now, at least, it had given way to new areas, hilly and lush in parts, ocean side properties in others, each landscape bearing witness to the schizophrenic nature of a state that wanted to be all beach but in reality was mostly desert.

The morning sun was holding court in a pure blue sky. As they passed through Carlsbad, Napoleon found it ironic that the same sun that was tanning the pretty bodies along the coastline here was burning the necks of the field workers in the orchards off to the east in Temecula, Southern California's version of wine country. Napoleon wasn't a wine drinker, but he wondered if these pretty people could taste the sweat of the workers in the Cabernets or Pinots they so carelessly consumed.

He and Parker split the night shift on the drive down, each able to sneak in a good chunk of sleep, and Napoleon felt oddly refreshed. His body was welcoming the fact that he was feeling better, his throat was no longer hurting and his chest was beginning to clear.

"You hungry?" Parker asked, stirring in the passenger seat.

"I know you are," Napoleon replied.

"McDonald's is off the next exit."

"Yeah. Screw it. I could eat. Drive-thru?"

"Nah. I gotta crap. And I need some coffee."

Napoleon shook his head. "For a young guy, you have a really weak colon, Parker. You crap three times a day, like a baby, or what?"

Parker rubbed at the sleep in his eyes then ran a hand through his hair. "Dude. You have no idea."

"Dude? Well, it's—"

"—better than homie," Parker finished through a yawn.

"I doubt Fasano has made it this far, this fast."

"Not by bus. If he jacked a car? Different story."

Napoleon eased the car into the slow lane and took the next exit, the sight of the Golden Arches a mile off to their left with nothing but farmland as a backdrop. "I dunno. I don't see him as having any clue whatsoever how to jack, or steal or hot-wire a car."

"You leaning towards bus?"

"Yep. Or he hitched a ride with a trucker."

"His picture's gotta be almost everywhere on the news by now."

"Everywhere locally, maybe, but truckers don't always watch the news, or might get paid a little cash not to, if you know what I mean."

"Ya think?"

Napoleon smiled. "Truckers are just another shady fraternity, like bikers, like any gang. Shit. They might be the shadiest."

"Hey. I take offense to that. I got a cousin who's a trucker."

"Yeah?"

"After his second strike, he had no choice." Parker chuckled.

They pulled into the McDonald's parking lot and got out of the car.

"He got a trucking job with two strikes, huh?" Napoleon poked.

Parker shook his head. "Nope. Got his own rig. My aunt helped him. Sub-contractor now."

"Ah. So you're saying he's working cash gigs. Ten-four. Sounds like he's a regular Boy Scout."

"He's a nice young man," Parker said with a serious face, "who pays his taxes."

They laughed and went into the McDonald's. The breakfast menu being an all-day thing now made Napoleon happy. Life always seemed much simpler to Napoleon with an Egg McMuffin in one hand and a dependably perfect hash brown in the other. The coffee was good and strong. Parker, true to his word, took two sips and was off to the can.

Napoleon's cell phone rang, and he was relieved to see it was forensics. *About damn time.*

"This is Napoleon."

"Nap. Beecher here. You got a sec?"

Napoleon was immediately encouraged. He'd been hoping all along that Beecher was the one who caught the case on that end. She was a solid vet who started with the force a few years before Napoleon.

"For this case? I got all the time you need."

Beecher scoffed. "Be careful what you wish for." And it was the way she said it, like a drunken skeptic, which instantly worried Napoleon.

"Well. Shit. Let's hear it."

"You know who this girl is, don't you?"

"Assistant DA's daughter, yada yada."

"There ain't no 'yada yada' on this one. I guess this guy was gonna run for local office or something. Conspiracy theories are flying, and, well, it's ruined the plans of some very important people. This place is crawling with press too."

Napoleon was sneaking a swig of his coffee and almost spilled it on his chin. "Great."

"Yep. You really caught the case of the year this time."

"You're serious?"

"Like the clap." Beecher sighed.

"Great. Okay. Moving right along."

"My, my. The consummate professional."

"No. My partner, who just traded up from patrol, is already in the shitter, or I'd be there letting loose myself over this, trust me."

Beecher had always had a smoker's laugh, and she unleashed it now. "Well, as you can imagine, this was expedited all the way down the line. Six Flags fast. The coroner's office has the results and so do we. You ready?"

"Let's hear it."

"You sitting down?"

Napoleon rolled his eyes and jammed the rest of his hash brown into his mouth. "Quiff-fugginround."

"She was cooked."

The hash browns were a bad idea. They got stuck in his throat, but Napoleon forced them down and waited. There was no need to ask it, the words hung there like they might never land.

Beecher took the silent cue and kept rolling. "From the inside out, it appears. Like, shit, I dunno, he put her in a microwave. Her exterior—"

"Her exterior?"

"Yeah, ya know, her damned skin, and most of her muscle tissue, wasn't burned at all."

Napoleon couldn't believe what he was hearing. "So… what the hell?"

"Her internal organs, brain, heart, liver, gallbladder, spleen? Cooked black."

Napoleon took a deep breath and tried to calculate these facts against the crime scene. "But the hotel room window, it was melted, right?"

"That's where things really take a turn," Beecher mused. That old scientist's fascination that was so familiar to Napoleon now permeated her voice. "*That* was from a different heat source."

He still had a quarter of his McMuffin to go, but Napoleon was no longer hungry. Instead he downed the coffee, hoping the caffeine would wake him up, sure that he was mishearing Beecher at almost every turn. "A... different source?"

"Yep. So we got it figured this way: he cooks the girl, melts a hole in the window and chucks her out."

"Beecher. Please. You're not that stupid. Who's the 'we' that has it 'figured out'?"

There was a short silence at the other end, then: "The cap and the DA's office, mostly."

"But of course."

"I don't see it either. No microwave big enough, at least in the hotel, to do this."

"The hotel kitchen?"

"We checked. A walk-in oven is there. But—"

"—that would have cooked her outside-in."

"Exactly."

"The glass? In the hotel room? How was it heated?"

"Maybe a blowtorch. But I doubt it. There was a fluorescent-cobalt-blue-type singe around the opening. I recognized it immediately. Sulfur. It melts a bit like wax, hence the drips along the upper edges, which you could barely see because it was glass—I mean, partly because the glass had melted, and partly because it was night."

"So… then what?"

"Nap. I'm not going to lie. I have no clue. I mean, if we take this logically, step by step, it's clunky at best. I mean… he would've had to kill the girl off-site by cooking her in some microwave range of some kind, or with a microwave weapon—"

"Weapon? C'mon. This guy isn't with the CIA, Beech. Besides, we have the video. He *walked* in with her."

"I know. But, whatever, he cooks her somehow, kills her. Then he has a blowtorch, which he uses to heat the glass, super-hot—why so high on the window I have no idea. Then he chucks her out. He must've melted the sulfur onto the hole first too. It was all over her face and hair… Well, what was left of her face and hair."

Napoleon took in a deep breath and sighed. "Beech, you gotta know that this all sounds like complete horse shit."

"I know. But cut us some slack. We had to put this girl together again like Humpty Dumpty, Nap. I mean, the parking lot grit was still in her eyeballs."

Parker returned to the table, his face and hair having been wetted down.

Napoleon motioned to him. "I'm on with forensics."

Parker nodded and took a huge bite of his McMuffin.

Napoleon took a deep breath and grunted. "So, is there any other way to cook a body from the inside out?"

Parker stopped chewing.

"We're checking. Unlikely. I mean. She walked in with him, which means if there were a way to do this to her, it had to happen after she got to the room or…"

"Or what?"

"An adjacent room?"

Napoleon was incredulous. "You think he had accomplices?"

"I mean, how else?"

"Shit. The press is going to blow a huge wad over this if it gets out."

"Yeah, I know."

"We start asking the hotel guys questions about walk-in sized microwave ovens brought into the hotel, into another room... because it wasn't in the crime scene room... and about guests registered on that floor that night... because the elevator video footage doesn't show her hopping around from floor to floor. I mean, it's TMZ time."

Napoleon was impressed: Parker had taken out his notepad and was reviewing his notes from the hotel.

"Yep. And the cap wants to talk to you."

"I bet he does."

"Nap?" She sounded worried.

"Yeah?"

"Be careful on this one, *ese*."

"*¿Por qué?*"

"They're jonesing to wrap this up fast. Get an arrest. Let the DA fill in the answers later. This whole place is buzzing like a struck beehive."

"Yeah. I hear you. But, Beech... you didn't finish."

"What?"

"You shut yourself up. You suggested accomplices, now you're just moving right along."

This time there was a very long silence before she replied. "You're gonna think I'm nuts."

"Oh. Please. We're well past that point. If you were anyone else but you right now, I would think you were a certifiable drug abuser and I'd be asking for your supervisor."

"He'd tell you the same thing, albeit reluctantly. We're all tripping on this one."

Napoleon looked at Parker sitting there, concentrating so hard on his notes, and suddenly felt bad. In a few minutes Napoleon would have to inform him that his very first case out of foot patrol was one that was likely to end his career.

Cap was a rat bastard. He'd kept the two of them on this case because if the investigation went south, and odds were that it would, then he'd have his patsies to blame. One a burned-out old detective nearing the end of his career, and the other a greenhorn rookie who was just getting started. They were like lambs to the slaughter. All so the captain could cover his own ass and make his way to his pension.

Beecher forged on. "I've seen this guy on the news, this Fasano guy. I don't figure him for a Charles Manson type, but the only way this plays out is with multiple perps, like a cult, or worse…"

It didn't end. The more Beecher spoke, the more Napoleon couldn't believe what he was hearing. "A cult?"

Evidently, Parker had had enough. He put his hands out in his best Robert De Niro pose, his face a tangled mass of confusion, as if to say "Whaaaaaat?"

"Yes," Beecher finished, "I know. Don't even ask. We have no proof of anything. A body that makes no sense, a crime scene that makes less sense. I'm just guessing, and I don't like that. It's not my job. But you're asking."

Napoleon popped his jaw socket and sighed. "So spit it out."

"As far as we can tell, nothing was carved in what we had left of the body. No candles in the room. No… shit, I'll just say it. If I'm right, I have them pegged for devil worshipers."

"Oh, man. You've got to be kidding me. Why?"

"The sulfur."

"The sulfur?"

"There's another name for it, brimstone, and most of them use it in their rituals."

For the first time in a long time, Napoleon was speechless. This was all crazy, and yet Beecher was not. The facts were a mess, yes. But he was on the phone with one of the best people in forensics, who was painting some broad strokes, yes, but she was doing so with conviction in her voice. As if she knew "A" and "Z," but was at a loss as to how to fill in the rest of the alphabet.

"So you think Kyle Fasano is a devil worshipper?"

"The only thing missing is a pentagram," Beecher replied.

"Man, Beech, if this is the best you got, then I'm beyond fucked on this one."

"You said it, not me."

"You got anything else?"

"Not much. He was in the room. She was in the room. Fingerprints everywhere. The fingertips on the vic show she was desperate as hell to get out of there, though."

"How so?"

"The claw marks on the back of the hotel door."

Napoleon scoffed. "Those weren't from fingernails. Those were gouges. Deep-ass gouges."

"Exactly. And a lot of the wood of that door, from those gouges? It was under the vic's nails."

"Jesus Christ," Napoleon said.

"Quite the opposite, I think," Beecher replied glumly. "It looks like she felt she was in that room with the devil himself."

* * *

195

When Kyle awoke, it was to the kiss of cool salty air blowing in off the sea. Yawning, he realized that he felt better than he had in days. Rolling over, he looked up through the branches of a tree spread out like wings above him. His head still seemed to be a bit foggy, because he knew he should know what type of tree this was but he couldn't recall it.

He heard The Gray Man's voice. "Cypress."

Sitting up, Kyle looked over his shoulder. The Gray Man was seated casually in his suit, with his back against the trunk of the tree and looking odd without his hat, which was set on the grass next to him. His hair was white and parted neatly over his right eye.

"Good morning," Kyle said.

"And the same to you. Though it's nearly noon."

"I feel like I've slept for two days."

"Not quite. You managed a good seventeen hours, though."

"Man."

"You needed it."

"Obviously." Kyle stretched, goading his muscles and tendons awake, and rubbed his eyes. "Man. I had the weirdest dream."

The Gray Man looked over at him. "Oh?"

"Yeah. I was sleeping in the stars or something."

A slight smile crossed The Gray Man's face. "Really? Imagine that."

"Was I?"

A bigger smile this time. "You ask it like a child. I remember such days. Barely. But to answer your question, yes."

Kyle looked up at the pale blue sky, one low cloud after another drifting past the sun on the horizon, and wondered aloud, "How?"

The Gray Man nodded gently and followed Kyle's gaze out over the sea. "Normally, none of you see it, and some of you will never see it; but the difference between here and there is barely a thought… and hardly more than a dream."

Kyle blinked. "You were with people. People like you."

The Gray Man seemed impressed. "So you saw them as well?" he replied, pursing his lips and raising his eyebrows.

"Yeah. Why wouldn't I?"

"We're not meant to be seen like that."

"They were standing next to you. You were all talking about stuff, I don't remember what exactly, but I thought I heard you say my wife's name."

The smile slipped off The Gray Man's face. After reaching down to grab his hat, he began to crease the edges. "So you *heard* us too? Hmm. Amazing."

Kyle stood to stretch his back. His stomach moaned. He was hungry, but intrigued. "Why? I wasn't supposed to?"

The Gray Man stood as well, then leaned a shoulder against the tree and folded his arms, his hat still in one hand. "You are a special one, Kyle Fasano."

"What?"

"To see me is one thing, and to see my compatriots as well means your vision is already expanding. To understand our language, which has driven prophets mad at times, is quite another thing entirely."

A young couple was walking, hand in hand, down a nearby path, taking no note of Kyle or The Gray Man whatsoever. They stopped and kissed one another gently, causing a pang in Kyle's heart.

Kyle took a deep breath of sea air through his nostrils, the sleep in his eyes beginning to fade. "So what does it all mean?"

"Oh, my, young man, I wish I knew. I thought I knew. But you are one new revelation after another."

"Great. But still, you've gotta give me something here, Gray, to get my head around."

"Fine. But I think taking baby steps is the best method. The men I was with? They are like me. We do what we do. Someday you may understand the process that we are going through, but for right now, again, baby steps. We wander this earth. Others, like that woman on the bus or your diner buddies, do their thing as well. But we all have limitations, some of us more than others. We're not all-knowing or all-seeing. Only God has that much omniscience and omnipresence. And there are now forces in play."

"Forces?"

"You know which forces they are. It's just easier not to think about them, about us, or, at least, you perceive it as more fun not to."

The Gray Man put on his hat, pointed at Kyle to pick up his duffel bag and motioned for him to follow.

"Where we going?"

"To that bakery over there," The Gray Man replied, pointing across the street from a semi-busy intersection to a small shop with outdoor seating, "for some coffee. And I think I'll sneak in a piece of pie."

As they came out from beneath the shade of the tree, Kyle immediately felt what could only be described as their arrival, or their transition, back into the real world. Around them were tourists with cameras, locals walking their dogs, and kids on skateboards. It was a nice, sunny day but a few people, here or there, suddenly noticed them; by their reactions, Kyle became aware once again that he badly needed a shave and change of clothes, but more than that he realized the sight of an older gentleman in a full suit on such a warm, perfect day seemed to stand out even more.

"It's Sunday, right? They'll probably figure you for a pastor or something."

The Gray Man chuckled. "Me? A pastor? Well… if it helps us make our way to a late breakfast, so be it."

"Then what?"

"Then we'll get you into the YMCA a few blocks away, where you can have a hot shower and change into those clothes in your bag. Because if I look like a pastor to these poor people it's only because they think I'm helping a homeless man."

Kyle didn't argue. He could actually smell himself. "And then?"

"Then you take a bus to the Starbucks at Cannery Row, in Monterey. There, you will find her."

They sat down outside the bakery and were helped by the waiter, a calm silence ensuing between them. Kyle wanted his answers, but right now he was willing to wait. He watched The Gray Man out of the corner of his eye with mild fascination. He was reading the local paper word for word, and when the person next to them left behind a copy of *The New York Times*, he scooped that up and read it as well, column by column, page by page, even stopping to look at some of the car ads and coupons.

He's been here before. He used to be one of us. Human, Kyle thought. *And a lot has changed since then. A lot. What a trip.* Even more of a trip was Kyle's feeling that his thoughts were "closed" now, solely his own, and not even The Gray Man could know them anymore.

People in jeans, shorts and t-shirts—some having casual conversations, some holding ice-cream cones and others texting on cell phones—passed in front of them.

The Gray Man ordered coffee and two slices of pie, one apple and one blueberry. Kyle followed suit with the coffee but was famished; he ordered a Denver omelet with a side of pancakes.

After finishing his cup of coffee and inhaling his food, Kyle pushed his plate away and let out a long sigh to remind The Gray Man he was there.

After looking up, The Gray Man nodded. "Anyway, to go back for a second, the men I was speaking with last night had information for me, and I had information for them."

"Why? What kind of information?"

"We're each working our… respective corners, as it were. And so we help each other."

"Corners?"

The Gray Man folded the paper and put it aside. He drank down the rest of his coffee. "Yes. Think of us as sort of like…"

"Cops?" Kyle interjected.

The Gray Man moved his head from side to side as if to wiggle the definition into place, and then gave a short nod. "In a sense, yes."

Raising his eyebrows, Kyle figured there was no harm in saying it now. "I gotta be honest. I had you pegged as my guardian angel."

A broad smile came over The Gray Man's face, but he said nothing. Instead he changed the subject. "You asked about Tamara?"

"Yes."

"She was indeed part of our conversation."

"Why?"

The Gray Man motioned to the waiter for the check. "Because your use of your powers, of the blue, has changed things."

"How so?"

"The original idea was to get you through the process as covertly as possible, to not jeopardize the mission. You've dealt with some minor players thus far, but that's it."

"Minor?" Kyle thought of the boy on the bike—his feral nature, his strength—and shuddered.

"Yes. The other side talks as well, Kyle. The game is afoot and all parties are in play."

"What are you saying?"

The Gray Man looked hesitant.

A feeling of dread and panic overcame Kyle. "Tamara? You mean she's in danger? I have to—"

"Do nothing," The Gray Man said flatly, plainly and with a tone of finality.

"You can't mean that!"

"You have to focus on the mission."

"No. I can't. What are you saying here?"

The Gray Man looked Kyle dead in the eye. "I'm saying that everyone has their own demons to face, Kyle Fasano. You all do."

"Oh my God."

"You can't fight this battle for her. No one can."

It took a moment for the words to register in Kyle's mind. "Can? You mean, it's something that's going to happen?"

"Yes."

Worry washed over him, and Kyle felt his blood pressure rise. "Why?"

The Gray Man was silent.

"Gray?"

"Because word has spread. The manifestation of your powers changes everything, and now they will stop at nothing to stop you. That includes trying to find a way to get you to run back home, right into a trap. In which case you wouldn't be able to help her anyway."

Putting his face in his hands, Kyle rubbed his fingertips against his temples. Maybe The Gray Man was right, maybe Kyle couldn't help Tamara, but he had to try. "I don't care about this whole millionth thing anymore. Screw it. If I'm damned for it, so be it. I'm going home. If something happens to her, then I'd rather be dead anyways."

The air around them stood still, as if the dust particles and oxygen molecules had paused in place.

"You can't mean that," The Gray Man replied, shaking his head.

"Yes! Yes I do!"

"Nearly a million people could lose a chance at discovering their own desire for repentance, you would be dead and Tamara would be either dead or corrupted for life, ruined, crushed and heartbroken… because of what?"

Kyle felt the tears welling in his eyes. "Because…" He swallowed hard.

"Of what? Of guilt? Is it all still about *you*, Kyle?"

"No! It's not. It's because I love her. Don't you understand?" Kyle shouted. He was beyond emotional. It didn't matter though. The patrons next to them, the waiter and the street traffic were all frozen. They'd stepped outside the doors of time again, but Kyle had felt it right when it had happened this time, when those dust particles had lost their motion.

The Gray Man seemed to take measure of Kyle, and then he looked away with a nod, as if what he'd seen had confirmed his thoughts.

"I'm sorry, Gray," Kyle wiped at his eyes. "You've picked the wrong man. I can't do this."

"First off, I didn't pick you. Someone else did. And, last time I checked, He seems to know what He's doing, Kyle."

Kyle said nothing.

"You have to trust in that, Kyle. In Him. Or the whole thing falls apart. Completely. For everyone. Do you understand?"

Kyle nodded gently. But he knew in his heart he wasn't ready.

A look of sadness crossed The Gray Man's face. Then he continued. "Our meeting last night was to figure out a way to protect her going forward."

"How?" Kyle asked, feeling a sliver of hope creep into his voice.

"I'm going. I have to leave you. My job is to help you. I'm not supposed to leave your side, but I don't see how you will pull this off if your mind is only half here, half on this mission."

Kyle rubbed a hand through his hair and cleared his throat. "And?"

"So I'm going to go help with Tamara. Do you at least trust *me*, Kyle?"

Kyle looked up at The Gray Man and nodded.

"So it's settled. I'll get you into the Y. From there, it's up to you to take the bus to Monterey. Then, you'll go to the Starbucks on Cannery Row. Victoria goes there almost every morning. She owns a business on the pier, right down the street. Got it?"

Kyle nodded and looked intently at The Gray Man. "You'll protect Tamara, right? You promise me?"

The Gray Man nodded firmly.

"Then what?" Kyle asked.

The air began to move around them again, ever so slightly. "You'll figure it out. You have to, because I won't be there to help."

"Okay. But what's going to happen? I don't understand."

"You are a one. I, we, can only help you get to your final moment. We can't help you actually complete your task."

"So that's it then?"

"At the rate your powers are manifesting you might not even need me. I'll get back as soon as I can, as soon as I'm sure that Tamara's safe."

The world around them came alive again. The waiter reappeared and The Gray Man paid him, telling him to keep the change.

They left and walked the few miles to the Y in silence. The Gray Man told Kyle that a guest workout was ten dollars. "Just pay the fee."

"Fair enough. Thanks, Gray. For helping me."

"Not a problem. It's my job."

The energy around The Gray Man began to crackle.

"Any hints, for when I find Victoria?" Kyle asked.

The Gray Man thought for a moment, and then looked up. "Find a way, Kyle, to remind her that she once loved you."

Then he was gone, and Kyle felt more alone than he'd felt in his entire life.

CHAPTER 20

TAMARA HOPED GOD COULD forgive her. She knew it was all too easy to have faith when things were going well, that now, of all times, she was supposed to stand tall and lean on Him. But to be honest, it was hard to lean on someone when it felt like they'd betrayed you. She knew it was a sin to think that, but that was how she felt. He was a traitor. He'd allowed her to build a life and was now forcing her to watch it crumble.

She'd asked Trudy to watch the kids and the house so she could get away from it all for a bit and have lunch with Ben. Maybe it was irresponsible, but she didn't care anymore. She was feeling increasingly defeated by this whole mess. Talking with someone outside of her circle of friends and family seemed like a good idea. Fresh territory. Fresh perspective. That's what she told herself, though deep down she feared that she just couldn't stop talking about it. When you ran out of ears, you found new ones, even if the ears willing to listen were doing so for selfish reasons. Ben had texted her all morning until he finally convinced her. It was a beacon of hope from work, that final place of retreat. He had a few "ideas" for the Watanabe account that he wanted to go over with her.

Instead of meeting at the office first, they decided to grab a bite to eat at Lawry's. Sitting opposite one another at a corner booth with a fresh linen tablecloth, they were left mostly undisturbed, the waiter only coming over to scrape the breadcrumbs from their table into a small tray from time to time. Ben had the prime rib; Tamara barely managed to eat half of her Caesar salad. Those detectives had shown up Friday morning with all their good news—that Latin cop with his studious eyes, his partner all jock-like and intense—and when they'd left they'd taken her appetite with them.

Exactly as Tamara hoped he would, Ben was listening. That was all she needed. She noticed that he had learned his lesson, never directly prodding for information on Kyle or badmouthing him. Still, Tamara chastised herself each time Ben locked eyes with her and she didn't look away immediately. He mostly said all the right things, but finally, after she joked about why he even cared about this mess, he said something that weakened her.

"I'm not going to lie, Tamara. Because I care about you, perhaps a bit too much, and we both know it, right?"

His green eyes italicized the question. She didn't break his gaze at all this time, but held it firm. She knew better, a thousand times over, but still, she held it.

The blue polo he wore was stretched tight across his shoulders, chest and biceps. He'd gotten some sun, his tan even and glowing. He was young, but so what? Caitlyn had been young too, and that hadn't stopped Kyle, had it?

Her reply was weak and without much resolve. "That's sweet, Ben. But—"

"I know, I know," Ben said with an endearing chuckle. "I'm not trying to put you on the spot. I just wanted you to know how I felt. The timing's horrible, but I don't want you to feel so alone in all of this."

She let his assumption that his feelings for her would be comforting, now or at any time, slide. His self-confidence had always been a bit over the top. Most of the women in the office would swoon around him, and though Tamara was older and should've been a bit wiser, she did not find his extra self-assurance unattractive either. Ben seemed to know himself in a way that made you want to know him too.

Before long, they finished lunch and then crossed the street to the office. Being a Sunday, they were the only ones there. This, she imagined, was exactly as Ben had planned it. They reviewed the Watanabe plans and budget with a matched nervousness that had nothing to do with the account. A few times he invaded her personal space, leaning in close or touching her hand briefly when they passed paperwork back and forth.

It wasn't until it was time to go that he stepped towards her again, deliberately, as he had done so the day before at the house in the foyer, except this time there was no cry from Seth to interrupt them.

She knew he was tall and in good shape, but the way he enveloped her as he moved in to kiss her was a surprise. She felt tiny and safe. She tried to put one hand on his chest and the other on his bicep to slow him down, but that only made the warmth in her body spread all that much faster. He felt good, his muscles firm beneath his shirt, and when he kissed her it was with soft lips that begged for permission.

She felt shame and a touch of panic, but she kissed him back anyway, the anger of what her life had become exploding as she slid her tongue into his mouth. She lifted his shirt to feel his skin beneath it. He was hot to the touch, and soon she felt his hardness pressing against her leg.

She was wearing dark blue dress jeans and chunky heels with a white blouse. Sliding his hands down the back of her jeans, he grabbed her and picked her up before sitting her down on one of the desktops, and now, in spite of herself, she was panting for him as much as he was for her. As their breathing intensified and they groped at one another even more, she had the realization that she was going to let him do it. It was a split-second decision, but it was one she felt she was going to follow through on.

She didn't know why at first. This was only going to make things worse. She was betraying so much just by being there, much less by letting him do the things he was doing, but as he cradled the small of her back and ran his lips down her neck the answer became evident. She was betraying a lot, including her faith, but God had betrayed her too, so what was the difference? Yes.

Sometimes you can toy with your creations too much, Big Fella.

She closed her eyes and took a turn into a place of passion she hadn't been to in years. His hands held her waist as he buried his face into her chest. She sighed deeply, and it was while running her fingers through his hair that she opened her eyes and saw her fingertips: they were French manicured.

Kyle's favorite.

He'd never explained why. It just was. He loved French manicures.

And that was it. Just the thought of him broke the spell and destroyed the moment.

She couldn't do it. Kyle had done it to her, but she couldn't do it to him, and that made her loathe herself more than if she'd let Ben continue. He was trying to get her pants undone when she stopped him. Looking into those deep green eyes, which were now a mixture of frustration and defeat, she simply shook her head.

"C'mon," he urged, moving in for another kiss.

"No. Stop. I can't," she replied, putting her hand over his lips and turning her face away.

Exhaling in frustration, he dropped his head and nodded a few times.

They released their embrace, and he stepped aside as she straightened herself out and gathered her things. "I'm sorry, Ben."

He held up his hand. "Please. I'm the one who should apologize. I had no right."

The sexual tension in the room quickly subsided and was replaced with an awkward silence and an overwhelming air of embarrassment.

Tamara left without saying another word, holding it all in until a few minutes later when she was safely inside her car. She broke down and screamed, as loudly as she could. No more tears. No more sorrow. Just pure rage now.

Rage and love.

Love for Kyle.

How odd. She could contemplate betraying God, but not the man who'd held her in his arms and rocked her to sleep after Janie was born, their little baby girl, who'd been sleeping soundly and couched softly between them in the hospital bed like a little present.

That was the man Kyle truly was, and he was still alive out there, somewhere. Confused. Scared. Alone. He'd made this horrible mistake, and he would have to make amends for it. But she recalled all the good things he'd done too, in their fifteen years together, all the wonderful memories. They were almost countless.

She'd chosen to spend her life with him because he had the world's greatest laugh, a big smile, a tiny mole on his left earlobe that always made him seem boyish for some reason, and the most unbelievable ability to hit the dance floor and not care one bit that he was the worst dancer who ever lived.

When you counted the memory of the one, horrible mistake he'd made with Caitlyn against all the good memories that preceded it?

It was one in a million.

As soon as she got home, Tamara checked the mail and her heart seized. There was a Priority Mail Express Envelope with familiar writing on it. She tore it open and found a greeting card inside. Then she sat down, read it and cried.

Kyle had remembered her birthday.

Today's mishap with Ben would've never happened if she'd just gotten this sooner. It was beyond her imagination, with all the checking of texts and caller ID, that he would contact her this way, that he would send her a card.

This was not just any card either; it was a *Peanuts* card, a tradition that dated back to her twenty-second birthday, the first she'd ever shared with him. He was her "Charlie Brown," and she was his "Little Red-Haired Girl."

"Except, well, you don't have red hair," he'd said that day, so many years ago. It stuck. Every year he wrote exactly that inside the card.

This year though, he'd also written her a little note on the inside cover. She could barely read it through the tears filling her eyes, but she sniffled, focused and worked through it one line at a time.

Babe, I'm so sorry. I have no excuse for what I've done. None. I love you. I love the kids so much. I should've just been happy, but I don't know what happened. I promise you that

I've never done anything like this before. Ever. I've never even thought about it. Now I've ruined everything. One screw up, and it's all ruined. It isn't fair...

She was unable to go on. "Oh, Kyle." She put her hand over her mouth, trying to stifle her sobs so that no one inside the house would hear her. She wanted this moment to herself, even if it hurt. When she regained enough composure, she continued reading.

... but no one says it's supposed to be. I don't expect you to ever trust me again, but I hope you can still love me somehow. I never, ever wanted to hurt you.

She took a deep breath and kept going, Kyle's note now shifted in gravity.

I want you to know that I didn't kill her. Absolutely not. I mean that. I swear it on my father's soul. I don't know what did. I'm into something big now that I have to take care of. I know it sounds crazy to say "trust me," but I need you to, just one more time. I've gotta help someone. I'm not going to lie to you, ever again. Her name is Victoria. I've mentioned her in the past a few times. She was my first girlfriend in high school. I haven't seen her since then, but someone's asked me to help her. I'd tell you who but you'd think I was crazy for sure. I'm not drunk. I'm not doing drugs. I haven't had a mental breakdown. I mean all of this.

Stunned, she blinked back the tears from her eyes, her cheeks sticky with salt and smeared mascara. He closed with three words: *Pray for me.*

The three words scared her, because they were completely unlike him, the man who had to be dragged to church and rolled his eyes at most things spiritual.

She had no idea what was going on, or why, or who had asked him to go help this Victoria person, and as irrational as it was, she didn't really care. She wanted her husband back safe and sound, if not for herself then for her babies, who needed their father.

Because, if he nothing else, Kyle was a man who knew the value of having a good father.

That thought cemented it for her. She nodded and let the warm canyon breeze dry her face as it swept over Angeles Crest Highway and into the hills of La Canada.

Kyle had just sworn on his father's soul.

That was beyond huge, because Kyle would've gone to hell and back, and back again a dozen more times, if it would've given his dad a few more days on this earth.

Instead, the cancer had eaten him alive, and they'd discovered him dead in his hospital bed.

"We were only gone for the morning Dad, I had some stuff at work…" Kyle had cried at his bedside while Tamara and the nurses tried so hard to comfort him, all to no avail.

All the while Tamara couldn't stop looking at her father-in-law's face, his eyes wide with amazement and turned up to heaven, as if he'd seen the most miraculous sight.

As if he'd seen an angel of God.

She looked back down at the card in her hand, sprinkled now with a few tears, and read the words again, this time whispering them aloud. "I swear it on my father's soul."

Kyle would never use those words, ever, unless he was telling the truth.

She was sure now that Kyle hadn't killed Caitlyn.

CHAPTER 21

FOLLOWING JURISDICTIONAL PROTOCOL, NAPOLEON called San Diego Homicide when they got into town for clearance to check on two possible associates of Kyle Fasano. A Detective Bilham met them at Timothy Reardon's home and then stood off to the side as they promptly made fools of themselves.

Napoleon began to get uneasy when he saw the "Kyle, *who*?" look on Mr. Reardon's face. As the first of the two leads they'd garnered off the computer at the Beaury Library, it was not a promising start. The look was genuine too, not even close to fake and somewhere about ten miles beyond a "maybe I know the guy" look. So they stood briefly on Mr. Reardon's doorstep, Napoleon letting Parker run through most of the basic questions as it became more and more evident that this was a dead end.

An hour or so later, the San Diego sun burning bright and alone in a clear blue sky, seagulls crisscrossing overhead in a light breeze, and Bilham's car right behind them, they arrived at Larry Klein's residence.

Mr. Klein seemed to have it all: a new Porsche Panamera in the driveway of a multi-million dollar home in La Jolla to match the multi-million dollar view of the ocean below. None of this helped. His response to them was even worse.

Having recently broken his leg water-skiing, he wasn't just annoyed at being bothered, he was pissed. He knew a Kyle Dansby from back in college at Harvard but hadn't spoken to him in at least twenty years. "So, unless he went gay, married some guy and changed his damned name, I got no clue."

Napoleon sighed and bit his tongue. *What a dick.*

But he was now happy that Klein had a broken leg. It balanced the cosmic scales a little bit. If he ended up with a permanent limp? Even better.

The four of them agreed that the odds of Klein's scenario were not very high, though Parker did muse it over later, after they finished asking Klein a few more questions and Bilham had left. "Anything's possible."

"Sure," Napoleon replied. "I mean, why the hell not make Fasano a closet gay? He's already a possible devil-worshiping adulterer with a posse of friends who like to murder people with microwaves, sulfur and blowtorches."

Parker paused, and then wrinkled his brow. "Ya know, when you say it that way…"

They stopped on the sidewalk, next to the car, for an ad hoc meeting, frustrated and with tails tucked.

Napoleon cleared his throat. "That's because it's insane. The whole thing. I really expected forensics to give us more than a comic-book explanation."

"So?" Parker put his hands in his pockets and nodded. "You obviously been at this a lot longer than me, so what do you make of it?"

"Honestly?"

"Yeah."

"I have no clue. All I got is that I keep remembering the hotel footage. You kill someone; you run to the elevator. Yeah, you're scared. But you're *nervous*-scared. You're 'looking around for witnesses' scared."

"And?"

Napoleon let out a deep, cough-free sigh. "Fasano was *terrified*-scared. You could see it in his face on the tape, as if he was fleeing something."

"Besides a murder scene, you mean?"

"How do we know she was dead at that point on the tape?"

Parker was instantly confused. "Huh?"

"We have no actual proof that she was dead when he got into that elevator. We walked in, looked at all the physical evidence, and made a reasonable assumption based on what looked like a murder."

"Well, I mean... that hole was too high for her jump through. There's no way we call this a suicide, man."

"I'm not saying we do, but think, Parker. That very same physical evidence is a complete mess. The hotel room was mostly undisturbed, save for the gouges in the back of the door and the hole in the window. Those are usually clues for us, but instead they're more like damned enigmas in this case. They just don't fit. "

"Okay. I'll run with you on this for a bit. What if it was a gang rape, or devil-worshiping sacrifice, or any of that?"

"We found one condom. Gang rapes usually involve more condoms or no condoms."

"Maybe Fasano was the careful one and the other guys didn't give a shit."

"Beecher didn't say anything about semen in the girl. That would've been one of the first things she would check. Granted, the girl was splatted, and that could have made a mess of things, but still. No."

"Okay. Then the devil worshippers?"

"Maybe that plays out somehow. I don't want to be dismissive. It's early. Maybe she was into some wacked-out shit that she pulled Fasano into. Maybe vice versa. Maybe it all went wrong. No one's really dug into her history yet, and we haven't had much time to dig into his. Again, this is not a normal case. Because of the vic's family, we were sent on a manhunt before we could do any groundwork."

"Maybe Murillo or Klink, back at the squad room, could help us out," Parker suggested.

"Agreed. But we'd have to run it by the cap, because the more people we get involved… I mean, if the press gets word that we're investigating this as a possible pentagram gang rape? It's going to be off the charts."

Parker shrugged and kicked at the corner of the well-manicured lawn. "So what, then?"

"We play the odds that the devil worshipping thing is just Beecher clutching at straws."

"Is she any good?"

"At what she does? One of the best."

"Then why discount her?"

"Because she's getting rushed and pressured too, and from her call, she's feeling it."

Parker looked worried; he glanced up and down the street. "Well, shit. That's comforting."

A few cars with bicycles on racks passed by before Napoleon spoke again. "Assistant DA's daughter, evidently a hotshot of some kind to be getting this much support so fast and from so many people. The press is salivating over the whole thing. The nature of the crime—murder or suicide… sex, love and politics—that's the shit they love, and since so far this case has no firm answers, they have free rein to fill in the gaps with endless speculations."

"You're saying that we're getting pushed into a meat grinder, aren't you?" Parker asked, looking at Napoleon.

Napoleon nodded. "I don't think it's anything sinister, man, just people covering their asses, especially the cap.

This dipshit Fasano would've made things easier without the Dr. Kimble routine. But no, he goes on the run, and that really gives the press a boner. From Fasano's perspective, he's probably covering his ass in all of this too."

And there it was. Napoleon just dropped it out there like a shiny penny.

Parker lowered his gaze and squinted at him. "So. . .you really don't make Fasano for this? Seriously?"

Napoleon shook his head. "Something's not right."

"Wow." Parker raised his eyebrows. "Shit."

Even now, Napoleon was trying to train him. *How easy*, he wondered, *was the rookie susceptible to being led?* "You agree?"

Parker thought for a moment and then sighed. "Sorry, Nap. No. At least not yet."

Good job.

"I get that, Parker. That's not going to stop me from saying what I'm gonna say next."

"Which is?"

"Get off this case, man. Somehow, some way. Say you're sick. Create a family emergency. Hell, I'll kneecap you if you need me to and you can go on disability for a month. Whatever. Just get off this one. It stinks. It's a mess and it's a career killer."

Parker's face seemed to turn to stone. He blinked but said nothing.

So Napoleon did. "Look, we chase this down and Fasano isn't the guy? We lose. We chase him down and he is? A defense attorney is going to lick his chops over the so-called 'evidence' we have so far. If we have to go down the kinky sex or whole devil worshipping path and we're wrong? That Assistant DA will want our blood for ever casting his baby girl in such a light. The press will talk gang rape one day,

217

blood rituals the other. You can see the headline: 'Horny Devil Girl Gets Sacrificed.' It's a train just waiting to go off the tracks. The whole thing."

Parker whistled. "Man, Nap. When I left my station house, my sergeant, Matto—you remember him, right?"

Napoleon nodded.

"He told me I was a blessed man. He actually said that: 'blessed.' I doubt that guy has ever gone to church in his whole life. But still, he told me I was going to train with the best detective in the whole department."

"Yeah? Well, he always was a drinker."

"No, man. He meant it. And I was so excited. And here I am, on my very first case. It's a raw one, I'll admit. But here I am, and you're asking me to *quit*?"

Putting his hands on his hips, Napoleon looked Parker in the eye. "Look. I'm almost done. My career is tapped out. You understand? You're young, just getting started. From what little I've seen so far in a whole three days? You've got potential. This case ruins me, I still got my pension. But you? You'll need to get a damned job at In & Out. Trust me."

Parker smiled and shook his head. "Ya know, I haven't told you anything about me because you haven't asked. Shit, we haven't even had a beer together yet."

Nor could we, Napoleon thought, *because you don't know about that AA chip in my pocket with the VIII on it, eight years now and counting, and of having to fight "the desesperación" without the sweet help of a good scotch.* It was true. They hardly knew each other.

Parker continued. "But for the record, I served two tours in Afghanistan, in the beginning, that is, when that shit was real beyond real. My first gig? I was at Kamdesh. You wanna talk about a mess? Anyway… the one thing you learn right away is that the guys always trying to cover their own asses?"

"Yeah?"

"They're the first ones to die."

There was a moment of silence as the breeze picked up and carried some loose leaves across their feet and under an Acura parked nearby.

"If you want to survive hell," Parker added, "you gotta cover the backs of the guys who are in it with you. For some reason… I mean, it don't always work out… but most of the time, for some reason, *that's* how you survive."

Napoleon could see from Parker's eyes that he was now back in that desert, if only for a few seconds. Napoleon wanted to argue, but he knew this look, the one etched now in Parker's face. It wasn't naïve and it wasn't innocent, in any way. It was the look you earned in the street when it made you harder than you ever imagined you could be. Whether that street was made of asphalt in Boyle Heights or sand in Kamdesh, it didn't matter. "So that's it then?"

"I ain't going anywhere, partner. Fuck the politics and fuck the politicians. Let's just get Fasano."

Napoleon smiled sadly. "Okay then. Fine. But why?"

"For one, I'm still not buying that he's innocent, no matter what you say, but also… because this thing started with him, it only makes sense that it will most likely end with him too."

"Very good, Parker."

They were crawling into the car, which had become their traveling home, when Napoleon got the call from Sheriff Conch in Beaury.

"Hello?"

"Detective Villa?" Conch asked, his voice obscured by the wind wherever he was.

"Yeah. Sheriff Conch, right?"

"Yep. I got some news."

"What's that?"

"I don't know where your boy went, but I'm pretty sure he didn't go south."

Remembering the blank look they'd found on Mr. Reardon's face and the baby fit that Mr. Klein had thrown, Napoleon smirked. "Welcome to the club."

* * *

After paying the day fee at the YMCA and taking the longest, hottest shower of his life, Kyle changed into a pair of jeans and the blue t-shirt that were in his duffel bag. Then, as The Gray Man had instructed, he took the bus to Monterey and made his way to the Starbucks on the ground floor of the old Monterey Canning Company, a huge red building on Cannery Row that was across the street from Steinbeck Plaza.

It was small but cozy, with beige tile floors and the usual assortment of round tables and chairs that surrounded a large leather sofa. He'd made the short walk from the bus stop to here through a slight fog that was developing as the afternoon grew to a close.

Kyle ordered a butter croissant and a tall Pike, out of habit, and took up a chair at a table opposite the counter that had a clear view of the front door. A growing discomfort began to overtake him; he already felt like a stalker, and he hadn't even seen her yet.

And what if she saw him and recognized him? It could go either way, really. She might be happy or completely put off. His story would be that he was in town on business, but if she asked for details he was going to fumble around, he knew it, and that might creep her out. Normally he could play a lot of things cool, but this was different. This was Victoria. Playing it cool with your first love after twenty years was not an option. Not making an ass of himself was really the best he could hope for.

His stomach pushed back at his first sip of coffee, and he realized that he was beyond nervous. Just the thought of seeing her, after all this time, seemed to make this entire thing more real than any powers or demon attacks could. What was he going to say to her? What could he say to her?

He sat there for over an hour, sipping at his coffee and picking at the croissant, when she walked in.

Instantly he chastised himself for ever believing that he would be ready for the moment. He wasn't. Instead, the universe tilted to a stop, plain and simple. His breathing slowed and his mind was arrested by her presence. She was here, right in front of him, and he drank her up.

She was wearing a beige long-sleeved cotton top with the collar down and the sleeves rolled to her forearms, white dress slacks and brown heels. She was maybe fifteen feet away from where he was sitting, the third person in line, and had a confident air about her as she thumbed her smartphone.

She glanced around, thankfully missing Kyle's table entirely, and he saw that her dark chocolate-brown eyes were the same. Her hair was different, though: it used to be soft-brown with natural highlights of blond from the beach, but now it was as dark a brown as her eyes. It was styled now too, but fell to the same shoulder length it used to be.

She was still thin and had small breasts, her cleavage partially exposed, her shirt loosened a few buttons. From what little he'd read on the internet, she'd married into money. Yet she hadn't altered her body, and her face looked her age, with small crow's feet just beginning to sprout at the corners of her eyes, barely visible from the glare of the overcast sky outside, which also made her lip gloss shine. Same old Victoria; she wore very little makeup. The freckles dotting her cheeks and nose, like a net could catch your eyes and draw them to hers.

He forced himself to look away before she saw him staring and so he could catch his breath. There was no denying the ache in his heart, as real as any Shakespearean sonnet could ever describe. It was a melancholy pain, undecided between recognizing what was and what might've been, but it was accompanied by an odd relief that she was still so similar to the girl he remembered. So much had changed over the years. It seemed natural to cling to the few things that didn't.

Glancing back her way, he saw her look up, twice, at a young Latin barista with tattooed arms and a small hoop in his nose, and who was busy churning out lattes and mochas at the far end of the counter. When their eyes finally met, a mutually flirtatious smile was exchanged.

Kyle no sooner felt a twinge of jealousy than he felt it smothered by the sudden realization that this might be the very man she was planning an affair with. If he was, Kyle wondered what she was thinking. He was just a kid, barely out of college.

Yeah. Like Caitlyn. The thought shamed him instantly.

When it was her turn in line, she ordered a cappuccino with two espresso shots and made her way to the barista's counter. Again, a smile was exchanged between them, but Victoria didn't seem so confident anymore.

The two of them began to talk. When she spoke it was with the same voice he remembered, and this seemed to hurt more than anything, because Kyle realized a person's voice stayed locked in our hearts forever. This same voice had whispered so many things to him, and he'd been so damn deaf. Now, that voice was asking the barista silly questions while Victoria giggled like a schoolgirl in response to his answers.

Kyle noted the rock on the ring finger of Victoria's left hand, and this bothered him.

You should at least take off your ring.

Like I did. Another pang of guilt struck him. What was the Bible verse? "Let he without sin..."

No. He wouldn't allow himself to believe this about Victoria. She was just harmlessly flirting. But then the last patron stepped away from the counter and gave Victoria and the barista a moment to chat privately.

"You're a little late for your 3:00 p.m. caffeine boost," the barista teased.

"Yeah. We've been busy today."

"You're still missing your other half?"

"Yeah. His trip was extended."

"That sucks. I'm used to making his Americano along with your drink," he replied, smooth and easy. As if he really cared about her husband or making his Americano.

Tamara laughed softly. "Yeah. Some stupid disagreement over the exchange rate or something."

He smiled. "So how long before he gets home?"

Kyle watched his first love pause, as if she was weighing the intent of this question. Then she locked her eyes with the boy in a way that made Kyle want to squirm. *No,* Kyle thought, *you don't know what you're doing, Victoria. Trust me. You don't want to do this.*

"A few more days," she finally said.

"And the kids?"

"Visiting their aunt and cousins."

"Hmm." He smiled. "Gotta be getting pretty lonely by now. You should buy me dinner sometime."

Victoria laughed. "Oh really? *I* should buy *you* dinner?"

"Hey, I'm just a poor coffee shop boy. You're the one with the raging wine shop on the pier."

Victoria glanced behind her. There had been an odd lull in caffeine addicts thus far, but the line was beginning to form again. Their private time was about to end.

She had just enough time to make a fateful decision. Smiling shyly she said, "Ya know? Why not? We can grab some Italian from the new place down the street."

The barista smiled, his teeth pure white, his hair spiked with gel. "That sounds fantastic. When?"

"Tomorrow night should be good. You working in the morning?"

"Yep. Nine to five."

To Kyle, Victoria seemed nervously excited, and at the same time a bit reluctant, as if what she was doing had just hit her. "Okay. I'll see you tomorrow morning and we'll figure out the details."

"Cool deal."

A sudden sorrow came over Kyle. Though he would never trade Tamara for anything in the world, there was a part of him that mourned. It was his younger self, the self that didn't yet know Tamara and only knew Victoria's touch, her kiss. His seventeen-year-old self had awoken briefly, beneath the shades of the blinds in this quiet little Starbucks, and rolled over to glance across the years to have one more look at the love it had squandered, so long ago.

"See you then," Victoria said as she turned and then walked past Kyle, coming within a few feet of him. The heels of her shoes tapped on the hard floor as she went by and the spell was broken; Kyle blinked.

She belonged to someone else now. *She* was someone else now. She would never be his again, and the finality of that fact was a good thing. He wasn't the same either. He may have blown it as a dumb kid, but he'd found the love of his life already. She was miles away from him, but still, oddly, right there.

Because the heart may allow itself to wander occasionally, to look at what was or what might be, but it always returned its focus to the one it truly loved.

For Kyle, that woman would always be Tamara.

She wasn't his past or his present.

She was his now and his everything.

CHAPTER 22

TAMARA WENT INSIDE DETERMINED to check on the kids and then cry on Trudy's shoulder about Kyle's card and about what had happened with Ben, but as she closed the front door a sense of resolve overtook her. She was tired of doing nothing, of simply existing in the midst of her circumstances, nearly hopeless, because she knew that on some level it took her almost completely out of the presence of God, and she knew better than to let that happen.

As an only child and having been raised by missionary parents whose efforts over the years spanned many villages throughout Bolivia, Tamara had learned early on to be self-sufficient. She also learned the value of hard work in poor circumstances.

She was homeschooled along with the other children who were part of their church group, a lot of the faces changing over the years as various families switched missions or dropped out altogether.

Her mother was a great teacher. Tamara took her SATs at seventeen, scoring so high that Duke was more than happy to accept her application, even offering her a partial scholarship in light of her parents' limited financial resources.

Yet somehow that child, who had toiled in the fields and learned Spanish by eight, had fallen a long way down to the place she was now, where she would wait by the phone or pine over the mail. She should've known better and she was tired of *not* knowing better.

Her faith in God should have been strong enough to have handled this without her crumbling so entirely. But she'd gotten away from her faith, hadn't she? Quite a bit, as a matter of fact. The last few years it had been lukewarm at best.

Her frustrations with her husband and their marriage were part of it, yes, but working so much and missing all the time with the kids had taken a toll too.

At some point her prayers to God had become more about what she didn't have than what she did have. She allowed herself to be filled with a cavalcade of worries: that she wasn't a good mom, that she wasn't good at her job, and that she would prove all the clichés about working moms right.

"Remember, honey, the devil knows your number. And he never stops hitting redial," her mother said one day when Tamara was about thirteen. They were helping to build an irrigation system in a small town just outside of Sucre. "You worry too much about things, this or that. Don't be such a worrier. Get on with being a doer."

Tamara had mostly taken that advice to heart, but it was a long way from Sucre, Bolivia to La Canada, California, with a lot of twists and turns along the way. Somewhere, she'd just sort of dropped Jesus off on a corner and then kept on going.

No more.

After a dinner of Hamburger Helper and potato chips, Trudy had gone to bed early, exhausted from staying up so late the night before and her inner clock still being on Eastern Time from her business trip. The kids were playing Xbox together in the living room. Tamara knew what she was going to do.

She prayed. First she prayed for her children to be okay through all of this, then for her husband's safety, that the police wouldn't hurt him, then for Caitlyn's soul and for her family's comfort in their time of mourning, that the real killer would be found and, lastly, Tamara prayed for herself. She prayed for the wisdom to know how to proceed and for forgiveness for what had happened with Ben.

She sat in Kyle's recliner, a ridiculous relic that he'd begged for one football season, and let her mind rest. There were so many balls in the air, but it didn't matter.

She was dying to tell Trudy about Kyle's card but this was a bad idea. Tamara knew she couldn't wait too long to say something to the authorities or she'd be breaking the law by withholding information, and that would be putting the kids at risk, and they were her number one priority now. The last thing Janie and Seth needed was to have both of their parents end up in jail. Tamara figured she'd have a half-day, maybe a day at most, to dig.

After a half hour or so, she knew just where to begin.

After telling the kids to be quiet so Aunt Trudy could get some sleep, she crept into the garage, making her way past all the usual junk: rakes, a shovel, used clothes that hadn't been dropped off at Goodwill yet, some old furniture and the lawnmower that Kyle had used only a half-dozen times before deciding, emphatically, that they needed a gardener. She smiled at the memory.

The overhead light from the garage door opener was partially burned out, with only one working bulb casting weak shadows in all directions, her body cast like a stick person against the far wall.

Pushing her hair out of her face, she squinted up into the storage rafters overhead. Off to the right there were boxes of Christmas decorations and plastic containers of school projects that Kyle had refused to throw away, and to the left, stacks of extra kitchen tile from the remodel they'd had a few years back.

Frowning, she pushed on. They had to be in here somewhere, but it'd been years since they moved in. She was embarrassed to admit that the garage had been almost entirely neglected. There was barely enough space for one car, much less the two it was designed to hold.

There was one small window in the near corner, and she startled when something moved on the other side of it. Jumping, she let loose a small squeal. She peered at the window but the stupid garage light cast her reflection back at her, preventing her from seeing what was outside.

She'd come into the garage through the door in the house just off the hallway, and the garage door was closed, so she knew she was safe. Still, goose bumps ran up her arms and over her shoulders, her instincts insisting that she was being watched by something just on the other side of the glass.

Standing perfectly still, she contemplated the few steps it would take to get back to the light switch. If she could turn it off, then she would be able to see through the window; and yet the idea of standing in the pitch dark in the garage did not seem comforting either.

Too many horror movies, Tamara. Knock it off.

She decided to just push on.

After grabbing a ladder that was hanging from a hook on the back wall, she peered up at a high shelf stacked with boxes. She vaguely remembered the box sizes when they had moved, and since this shelf was the biggest in the garage, she suspected they would be here somewhere.

The problem was that to reach them, she'd have to place the ladder right next to the window.

She could go back and get Trudy, but that would bring complications. Telling herself to quit being silly, she took the few steps needed, opened the ladder, placed it next to the window and climbed rapidly up.

Keeping one eye on the window and the other on the shelf, she shifted a few boxes around until she saw them, labeled by name. The four white boxes stored all the stuff from their younger days: college papers, awards, diplomas and what Tamara was really after: Kyle's high school yearbooks.

The ladder shifted beneath her, and she had the searing sensation that she was being knocked over. Instead, the corner of the ladder had simply moved as she had reached out awkwardly for the box she wanted, which was labeled "Kyle."

Righting herself, she scooted the box closer to her before trying to lift it again, when something in her told her, point blank, not to look at the window again.

You might see something you don't want to see, glowing eyes perhaps, or bared teeth.

The garage was damp, with the smell of old dust and stale wood, but it was also warm and sticky, which made the chill that ran over her very unnatural.

Just get the box, get down and get out of here!

She remembered Kyle's card, or rather, something he'd written in it, "I don't know what did," when referring to Caitlyn' death. Not "who" killed her, but "what" killed her. Why would he write that? Was it just an honest slip up?

Something told her that it wasn't, but it made no sense. Anyway, maybe it was just some photographer creeping around outside trying to get press photos, or maybe it was one of the feral cats that ran rampant all over the hillsides here.

She tipped the box and looked inside, briefly debating which yearbooks to take before deciding the last two would do. They were the most she could hold in one hand and she wasn't letting go of the ladder or leaving herself defenseless to grab them all.

Moving down the steps, she felt the cold aluminum of the ladder beneath her hand. She retreated out of the garage, not looking at the window but not turning her back on it either, always keeping it in her peripheral vision.

Making it back into the hallway, she nearly slammed the door shut and locked it. She knew the living room sliding glass door was locked and the blinds were closed. The front door and kitchen door were locked as well. She'd checked them before leaving the kids.

Yearbooks in hand she checked on Trudy, who was snoring softly, safe and sound in the guest bedroom. There was no breeze moving the curtains, but Tamara checked the French doors anyway, creeping softly up to them and jiggling the handles, again not looking through the glass.

You're losing it. You really are.

Maybe she was, but better safe than sorry. Neither of the kids' rooms had exterior doors, but she checked their windows: locked.

Only then did she exhale, in one long breath, before making her way out to the dining table, where she could keep the kids in sight while she worked.

It was time to get back to being a doer.

If Tamara recalled correctly, Kyle and Victoria were in the same grade. Carefully, she opened Kyle's senior yearbook. She would find Victoria's full name, and from there Tamara could try and track her down.

Because if Kyle was headed to where this Victoria girl was?

So was Tamara.

* * *

Napoleon jammed his finger into his right ear, which was still congested from his cold. The pressure on that side every time he moved his jaw was annoying. He shifted his cell phone to his left ear, so he could better hear the sheriff.

"So what've you got?"

"Well, Kendall struck out at Addie's. No truck jockeys seen him, and we know a few who would tell us, for sure, if they'd heard of someone who had. It's a tight-knit little community up there. No one at the greasy spoon there saw him either, and the assistant manager knew who Kendall was asking about right away, due to all the news coverage on this."

"Okay." Napoleon started chewing on his lower lip, an old habit, and waited.

"So, Kendall figured he'd check a few rest stops too, further up the highway, and a turnoff down by the lake area that a few of the smaller rigs use when they pick up hookers."

"No luck in Hooker Hangout?"

"Only hard luck."

"No pun intended."

Conch chuckled and continued. "After that he bounced back and tried fishing around town, but nothing yet. I did my end around here too. We got no reports of stolen cars, no suspicious activity and no burglaries reported."

"The bus stops give us anything?"

"A lot, actually, but it just leads to more hard luck." The sheriff sounded flat, almost weary with frustration already. Napoleon smiled. Conch was getting a taste of what it was really like to be a detective: no glam, just a lot of grind.

"Well, let's hear it."

"Your boy might've taken the 82, but I doubt it."

Raising his eyebrows, Napoleon asked, "Why?"

"Well. He boarded the 17 first, which goes south to Dunsmore. The driver remembers him because he overpaid the fare and had no change. Even more notable was that Fasano didn't argue for any, which is not the experience the driver usually has. He also asked for the transfer bus from Dunsmore to get to San Diego. That would be the 22. But that driver doesn't remember anyone fitting Fasano's description, which is funny, as her load of passengers was light. The driver turned me on to someone who was on the bus that day, a guy who works at a gas station about three miles outside of Dunsmore, a little hole-in-the-wall, unofficial kinda town called Edinbow."

"Unofficial?" Napoleon asked, a little confused.

"Yeah... in the spirit of that little town outside the bayou in *Deliverance*."

"Unbelievable. In this day and age?"

"Yep. Mostly Klan and bikers. Not a place you would want to... Shit, sorry, Detective, I didn't mean *you* in particular. No offense?"

Napoleon laughed. "None taken."

Conch continued. "Anyway. I went by to visit that guy as well, just to cross my 't's as it were. The kid rides the bus six days a week, and he didn't see anyone fitting Fasano's description either, just remembered mostly old ladies and a group of stoners from town."

"Hmm."

"Hmm is right."

"So he stayed in Dunsmore, ya think?"

"I dunno."

There was silence, and then Conch spoke up. "You guys?"

"Jack shit, sadly. Both leads down here were dead too. If he headed this way, it wasn't for the people we thought."

"Well. What now?"

Napoleon rubbed the middle of his forehead with his free hand, as if to somehow massage out an answer. He had nothing. Surprise, surprise. "Sheriff, can I talk this over with my partner and call you back in a bit?"

"Sure. I'm heading back to town now. Got a dinner party for my grandson tonight. He graduated eighth grade on Friday. But I'll keep my cell on."

"Thanks, Sheriff."

"You got it."

Napoleon hung up and filled Parker in on Conch's details. Napoleon had been here before. Parker? Not so much. He was either getting antsy or had restless leg syndrome, because he couldn't stop moving.

"Well, time for the inevitable."

"What's that?" Parker asked.

"Gotta call the cap and update him."

"Shit. Good luck with that."

Napoleon nodded and got out of the car. "I'm gonna take my throttling in private, if you don't mind."

The conversation was short. The cap sounded exhausted, his voice drained. He asked a few questions and seemed to listen carefully. The bravado and bark from their last chat was gone. "Well, Nap. This is just great. We got dick. After three days."

"I shoulda called sooner, but we've been running at this guy hard."

"I know. I figured though, and really, this thing is already gobbling up six of you guys."

"Six?"

"Yep. The DA's office, the mayor's office, Jan Ready from the city council... The heat is unbearable. Even the Red Cross is in it now, trying to drag in Senator Hopkins somehow."

"Anyone tell them we do better when people leave us the hell alone?"

The captain laughed, but it was absent any humor whatsoever. "You wanna take a crack at that? Just let me know. The chief is taking bullets all over the place, but this one... I dunno. Quite frankly I was hoping you'd come up with more than your dick in your hand in sunny San Diego, Nap."

"Who's on what?"

"Klink and Murillo are doing the background on the girl. Arias and Hollywood are working the details on lover boy."

"Nothing?"

"He used his ATM in Beaury. Wells Fargo. We forwarded the info immediately to the Beaury Sheriff's office but by the time they got back to us they told us you already knew he'd been there and was on the move."

Napoleon was defensive. "Why didn't anyone notify us too?"

"Murillo texted an old number for you that we had on file. Dipshit."

"Brilliant," Napoleon said sarcastically, shaking his head. "What about the girl?"

"Well, she briefly had an S and M fetish in college, to go along with a stellar GPA—that enough for ya?"

Napoleon yawned. "You talk with Beecher?"

"Shit! Don't even bring up her name," the captain spat, "or any of her Linda-fucking-Blair theories. Just the thought of that *Exorcist* shit getting out has my hemorrhoids flaring."

"Great. How we gonna play this then?"

"Listen. If Klink or Murillo come up with something that takes us down that road, something firm and solid, mind you, then so be it. But right now, nothing. And unsubstantiated shit like that is like napalm. You know that. Her mother will come in here and rip my eyes out."

"What are Hollywood and Arias doing?"

"Oh. Nothing important. They were working on some guy carving up hookers by the Cecil Hotel. Three in the last five weeks. But who cares about them, right? Now they're working their way through Fasano's co-workers and neighbors."

Napoleon shook his head. He felt it now. His career was getting old. Ancient even. He wanted out. The thought that so little had really changed in all these years made him want to drink again. Money still talked. Reason still walked. One dead white Pasadena princess and the resources of the whole department were unleashed. Three dead hookers? Meh.

The captain's voice came at him from seemingly far away. "What's next on your end?"

"We're working on it."

"Great. I know that line. Shit. Give me something, Nap, because I guarantee you I'm already gonna kick the dog when I get home."

Napoleon froze, the captain's words ringing in his ears.

Dogs. This was the second time a dog analogy had been thrown his way. Conch had said something too, hadn't he? Yes. He had. *"South? He heads here, north of Los Angeles, only to double back?"* Then Parker had said some shit and then Conch replied, *"I'd say that dog don't hunt."*

It was the loose drawer that Napoleon had been waiting for. That's how cases turned: not on squeaky drawers, the ones that caught your attention, but on loose drawers, the ones that rattled open or refused to be shut.

Kyle Fasano was a smart man after all, wasn't he? Not in getting involved in this mess in the first place, but since then? He was consistently smart. He'd fled the hotel but hadn't taken his car. He hadn't gone home. He'd destroyed his phone to kill the GPS signal. And there was the brief time Napoleon had actually spoken to the man, on the phone at the Fasano house. Kyle was emotional, yes. That was to be expected. But his words were measured, and he'd cut the call off, probably figuring on a trace or something. Then he went to the diner... then his shopping spree at the CVS and Dickies... before the library opened.

"Shit."

"What?"

They'd been rushing too much. Sloppy.

"Nap?" The captain sounded confused, as if the call had dropped.

They shot straight over to the library and the computer and... Parker found that shit on Joaquin and...

What had Napoleon told Parker about Fasano? He was in sales, yeah, but he wasn't a complete idiot when it came to computers.

And he'd left all that information for them to find on that one computer. One computer out of eight.

Shaking his head, Napoleon muttered, "Son of a bitch."

"Excuse me?"

"Not you, Cap. Sorry. I think I got something."

"Yeah?"

"Do me a favor."

"What's that?"

"Give me some more time."

The captain laughed mockingly at him. "This guy! As if I have choice?"

"Go home and kick that dog. When you do, I hope he bites your ass."

"Yeah, right. Keep me posted."

"Sure thing." Napoleon looked up. The sun was on the decline. It wouldn't be long before the moon started to bleach its way through the sky.

He waited. The drawer was loose. It would open more, all by itself. He just had to wait for it.

You were on that bus, Fasano. You paid extra fare, didn't you? And talked bus routes with the same guy. Man. For a civilian, a domesticated man, you're smart. I don't know where you're headed yet, but I know it ain't south, and I think I'm pretty sure where I'm gonna find the answer. Because I think you're cocky too, Fasano. I think you got too far ahead of yourself, just like we have.

Napoleon walked back to the car, leaned down into the open window and smiled at Parker.

The smile seemed to knock Parker speechless. Then he composed himself. "What?"

"That dog don't hunt, Parker. But that dog leads. And he's been leading us in circles."

CHAPTER 23

A S THE SUN BEGAN to set, Kyle camped out near the Monterey pier. The barista had said that Victoria owned a wine shop that was doing well, and sure enough, there it was, Casa del Vino, just across from Bubba Gump's and sandwiched between an antique lamp store and a shop that sold handmade soaps.

He'd been brave enough to wander by the window a few times, but a display box shielded him from seeing inside. That this also shielded anyone inside from seeing him at the window gave him little comfort. Walking by it the first time he barely stopped, and the second time he nervously lingered a few minutes and read the store's awards for its wine selection.

Apparently, Victoria had become quite the wine expert. Her shop sold reds and whites from all over the world, locally from Napa, just a few hours north of here, and as far away as Venezuela, with a solid base of French and Italian wines.

Near the door of the shop hung a lacquered and framed section of the *Monterey Herald*, highlighting the shop in a feature article written the prior year called "Local Treasures." A photo of Victoria and her husband accompanied the story, and Kyle noted that he looked heavier now than he had in the internet wedding photo Kyle had seen in the library. He was tall, with sunken, weary eyes. The article made brief mention of their two children, but Kyle got fidgety, worried that Victoria might walk out of the shop at any moment and discover him, so he moved on.

Kyle doubted she'd return to the Starbucks until morning. Since he had no way of knowing what time, he'd have to get there early and just wait.

He'd cleaned up well at the YMCA. His mustache and beard were growing in nicely, and he'd decided not to shave. He hadn't had facial hair since college, so Kyle imagined that whatever pictures of him might be out there would show him clean-cut. Between this and the hat, he hoped he would be almost unrecognizable.

The change of clothes felt great and they fit nicely, for the most part, though between the stress of this ordeal and his lack of eating, he'd lost some weight already, forcing him to use his dress belt from his work outfit.

As the night came on, the light afternoon fog morphed into a dense lather, carrying with it a biting chill. Kyle immediately remembered Tully's, which was nearby and had the best clam chowder in Monterey.

The crowd on the pier was thinning, with the exception of Bubba Gump's, which still had a line out the door. He didn't want to seem conspicuous, but by now he probably was. It was time to get some food and find a bed some-where. The bed part was going to be a problem. He didn't know if any of his cards still worked, but using them to check into a hotel was obviously not an option.

At Tully's, he took a seat at the bar and ordered the clam chowder, a shrimp plate with rice and, though he was sure The Gray Man would frown upon it, a Heineken.

Once his beer arrived, he took a long swig and began thinking over his plan so far, probing it for weaknesses.

He'd ditched his old clothes in a trash bin behind the building next to the Y, along with all the stuff he bought at CVS, including the unused scissors and hair dye. Hopefully, the cops would see the security footage from the CVS and assume the opposite, figuring he'd cut his hair and dyed it.

Beyond these items the receipt would show the purchase of the calling card, and once they'd traced that, it would show calls to Mexico near Beaury. This would hopefully have the cops thinking, along with his San Diego searches on the library computer, that Kyle was making a run for the border. Whatever. He'd done his best. He could only hope it worked.

The dimly lit bar had a huge sixty-inch flat-screen television centered over the liquor display, and it showed the Sunday night football game between the 49rs and the Bears, which was just now reaching halftime.

When his chowder arrived he finished it with vigor, his teeth chewing into the crackers and chunks of clam, the creamy texture warming him with each swallow. The shrimp and rice was next, and it didn't last long. The rest of the beer was surprisingly hard to get down, as if he'd lost his taste for it, so he ordered a glass of water.

He speared the last of his shrimp as the halftime show started, but instead the NBC News broke in, reporting on a hurricane that was making landfall in Hawaii.

At first the weekend news anchor seemed a little too animated about the whole thing, but as the facts started rolling across the screen, it became more understandable. It was a Category 5 storm, with winds in excess of 180 mph, and because hurricanes were rare in Hawaii, the coastal communities were not properly prepared. Death counts were already rolling in.

The images of the storm began to flash across the screen, making Kyle freeze, the shrimp still dangling on his fork as his eyes locked onto the television. A woman a few seats down from him gasped, putting her hands to her face as other patrons began to murmur, quietly at first and then a little louder. The bartender stopped what he was doing and turned around to watch as well, a frosted beer mug stuck in one hand as his jaw went slack.

An NBC crew had gotten into a small resort town that was being crushed by the winds, rain and rising seas. Cars were being pushed around like Hot Wheels and buildings were being washed away. The reporter on the scene sounded beyond panicked, as if being in the middle of the entire situation was far beyond his pay scale and he wanted desperately to just get off-camera and get out of there.

"Oh my God!" someone exclaimed from the back of the room.

Unbeknownst to the reporter as he tried to yell over the wind and stay facing the camera, a series of bodies washed by over his right shoulder, floating like driftwood, some face down, others face up. Then a few more came, along with a hut of some kind, and then, of all things, a cow, which rolled to one side and was kicking desperately for a shore it would never see.

Evidently the cameraman tipped off the reporter to what was going on, and when he turned to face the nightmare behind him he uttered the understatement of the year. "Uh. The situation is only getting worse here, Tom."

The picture zoomed in on the raging river sweeping through the town. At first it was unclear what the cameraman was after, but then it became apparent. A wave of moans rolled through the bar as the images showed live people among all the dead bodies, bobbing up and down in the chaos, struggling for help. A man in a collared shirt grabbed frantically at some branches of a tree that had been knocked over, and then futilely at the hood of a car, before he went under. Three people clutching each other—a man, a boy and a woman—came next. Kyle imagined that they were a family, because they couldn't swim to safety this way, not like that, with only one arm chopping at the water and the other holding onto someone else.

They're going to go out together, Kyle thought.

The camera panned left as a man on a low terrace plucked someone out of the water, then it swung further left towards a hotel in the distance, where a few people were trapped in a courtyard; a tour bus dislodged from its parking spot and began slamming into a storefront, and a girl who looked to be a teenager was clinging to a newspaper stand.

But to Kyle these images were unreal, because they weren't the real images.

His eyes filled with a fluid too thick to be tears, and he had a good guess what that fluid was. He wondered if his eyes were glowing light blue right now.

At first the TV screen became blurry, and then, as if someone had slipped an old Kodak slide into the projector of his mind, an overlay image of what was really happening came into focus.

There were angels and demons everywhere.

Hundreds of them.

Kyle gasped and dropped his fork. Everything that had happened to him over the last few days should've prepared him for this moment, but it didn't. His heart stopped and his lungs clutched at whatever air was still left in them.

Mixed scenes of horror and hope unfolded before him: the man who had missed the trees and tried to grasp the top of the car earlier came up one more time, a final, desperate effort against death. But Kyle could see now that he had no chance. Some monstrosity, half-human and half-dog, had wrapped itself around the man's neck and shoulders, like a millstone, and was dragging him under for the last time.

Meanwhile the man on the low terrace, flush with victory at having saved one person, was trying to save someone else: a little boy who was clinging to a piece of patio furniture. The man reached out, but the boy was caught in a tug-of-war between an angel, glowing in white and trying to pull him towards the man, and a demon, fat and bald, who clawed at the angel and tried to push the boy away, out of reach.

The family that was fighting the water arm-in-arm was surrounded by angels ushering them through all the debris and fending off demons that kept trying to flow in and break them apart. One momentarily succeeded, knocking the boy loose, before it was attacked by an angel who flew down from the sky and struck the thing with what looked like a hammer of some kind. The boy spun off, away from the man and woman, but one of the surrounding angels pushed him hard against the current and back to the woman's grip.

There was an explosion of some kind, a white-hot light filling the camera lens for a second, and then sparks rained down on the street and water below. The camera panned up to reveal the source: a transformer on top of a utility pole had blown and was now teetering, nearly falling off into the water, the power cords still attached to it swinging menacingly over the terrified people below.

The cameraman zoomed in on the box, giving Kyle a close-up that he would have rather not seen. The culprits were four demons, two with small horns and mangled faces and two others that looked like charred circus clowns, bits of melted skin hanging off their ears and chins. They were all pushing hard to topple the box when out of nowhere came a female angel with bright eyes and a look of desperation on her face. She rushed in, threw her wings wide and used her body like a battering ram, knocking all four demons off balance. It had the desired effect; their grip on the transformer was lost, but now they all grabbed for the angel, and…

"No," Kyle pleaded in a whisper.

… the demons began to claw and bite the angel, tearing at her and chomping at her flesh and wings, dragging her down to the ground, down to…

"Oh God. No." Kyle was suffocating in the immensity of what he was seeing. A very real and visible battle between good and evil was taking place before his eyes, and it was too much.

He began to weep bitterly, his mind unable to understand reality anymore. Love and hate, just feelings before, were now real things, living embodiments of the heavenly host and the minions of hell struggling for mortal souls in the midst of this storm, as they must in the midst of everyday life. It was true then, all of it. Up to this point he'd been given glimpses at the truth, but now he was being nearly struck blind by the immensity of it.

He pushed away from the bar and stumbled towards the door, the blue fluid in his eyes dissipating a bit as his human tears diluted it. That was good. He didn't want to see anymore. No more. It was better before, when he hadn't known any better. He wanted to go back to being ignorant to it all. Just a guy who went to church a few Sundays each month. God help him, but he did.

"Hey, buddy! Your tab?" the bartender shouted, irate at first, until he saw the look on Kyle's face. "Hey man, you okay?"

Kyle wiped his arm across his eyes and turned around. "Yeah. I'm fine. What do I… Never mind, here's forty. Keep the change."

The bartender scooped up the two twenties. He was fat, with salt-and-pepper hair and a mostly pepper goatee. "You know someone there?" he asked, motioning with his thumb at the TV screen.

Kyle shook his head, then thought of The Gray Man. *I hope not.*

"Look at how huge that thing is!" yelled an old man in jeans and a blue t-shirt.

Kyle didn't want to look, but when he saw the bartender shaking his head at the screen, he couldn't help but follow his gaze. The reporter was turning things back over to the anchor in the studio, and the cameraman, in a parting shot, zoomed out as far as he could and angled the camera up, into the darkened and tumultuous sky, showing the storm's gray and black mass.

To them it was just a storm.

But Kyle saw more: in the sky were thousands of demons moving counter-clockwise, urging the storm on, opposed by thousands of angels moving clockwise, colliding with the demons and trying to slow the storm down. In a boiling sky, bodies of white and red swam in and out of the storm clouds, wrestling, grappling, struggling and battling in a fight to the death. It was the chaos and tragedy of unbridled war. Kyle swallowed hard. There was no mistaking it: on this night, in that place, evil was winning.

Kyle spun around and tried to make his way to the door but tripped on the edge of a barstool and fell to the ground instead. He felt people looking at him. He hadn't wanted to be conspicuous here in Monterey, but so much for that idea. Getting to his feet, he rushed out the door, terrified of seeing even just one more image, sure if he did his mind would snap forever.

He ran down the steps next to the pier and to the sand below. The beach was tiny, and the air on his tears only made the night, which had arrived full force, seem colder. Nearby, a lone sea lion barked in the darkness. The waves came in, spreading out thinly across the shore, one after another in a timeless march.

Kyle tried over and over to get the image of the angel who had stopped the transformer from falling out of his mind, especially her face at the end. Never in a million years did Kyle imagine that an angel could be afraid. But he understood why: it was because she knew what was next.

Humans had no real idea what hell was like.

But angels did. And that's where they had been dragging her.

A fogbank rolled in like a wall of revelation, and Kyle Fasano couldn't help himself. He cried into his hands and wished to God he hadn't seen any of it.

* * *

Having never gone to high school, Tamara was flipping page by page through the yearbook before she remembered that an old friend, anxious to share pictures of her cheerleading team one day, had shown Tamara that at the back of a yearbook there was usually an index that listed each student's name and the pages they were featured on. Her friend also explained how the index was the shorthand way of telling who was popular in high school and who wasn't, and woe to the poor kid who was only featured on the class photo page. The whole thing made Tamara happy that she'd been homeschooled.

So she wasn't surprised to see that Kyle was on five pages: 18, 120, 134, 137 and 172. She thumbed them in order, the first page showing Kyle in a nonchalant pose at a lunch table with a pretty girl who had a faint smile. The caption below the photo read: *Kyle Fasano and Victoria Duncan*. Pay dirt.

Tamara felt a small twinge of jealousy. It was silly, but it was there nonetheless. Kyle had hardly ever spoken of her, and maybe that was an early warning sign. Had he seen her since high school or since he'd gotten married? Was Caitlyn the only secret that Kyle had been keeping?

Walling off her suspicion, Tamara pushed on. The second page that featured Kyle included a photo of him along with a few other jocks, posing with some cheerleaders who'd made them banners with their names on them. None of the girls was Victoria.

The third photo was Kyle's varsity football team picture, the fourth an action shot of him playing on the field, and the final photo was his senior picture.

Only one photo of them together.

Yet, for some reason, he was now going to visit her after whatever the hell happened with Caitlyn, instead of turning himself in to the police. Was Victoria somehow involved? Did she have some piece of information that would help Kyle? It didn't make any sense. Tamara ran through options, theories and guesses in her head before it occurred to her to use the index to lookup Victoria Duncan as well.

She ranked three photos. Tamara had already seen the one of her and Kyle at lunch. The second one revealed that she was a member of the modern dance team. She had the classic dancer's body, taut and lean, and was posed off to the side of her group, her head tilted back, her ponytail falling to the middle of her back. The third photo was of her with a group of people at prom, one of whom was Kyle. This one hurt Tamara more. The two of them were smiling, Kyle hugging Victoria around the waist from behind, his chin nestled into her cheek and neck.

Prom was the one thing about high school that Tamara always envied, never having had a prom of her own to go to. Victoria was tan, in a strapless mint-green dress with a corsage on her slender wrist.

Tamara turned her attention to Kyle. His smile was so big in this photo and he seemed so happy. She'd seen his smile thousands of times, but it had never been this big or this genuine. Not even on their wedding day.

She chastised herself again for being silly. Victoria was pretty, but side by side, Tamara felt she was the prettier one. The friend who taught her about yearbooks said it was too bad Tamara had been homeschooled because she probably would've been homecoming queen. Tamara had blushed at the comment then, but now she clung to it as a shield against her mounting insecurity over this stupid girl from Kyle's high school days. Besides, Kyle had married and had a family with her, not Victoria.

"Mommy?" Janie asked from the living room.

"Yeah, baby?"

"Can I skip my bath tonight? I'm tired." She was standing next to the couch, rubbing her eyes.

Prying herself from the yearbook, Tamara stood. "Sure. Your brother needs one though. Bad."

"He's asleep," Janie mumbled.

"What?" Tamara glanced at the clock in the kitchen and was stunned to see it was almost nine. "Wow. Okay. Go to your room and get your jammies on. I'll be right in after I tuck in your brother." Janie nodded and shuffled off to her room as Tamara scooped up Seth, his arms limp and his lips pursed like a little angel's. Stopping for a second, she just looked at him. His face, his forehead and dark hair were all the same as his father's.

After she'd spent almost eleven hours in labor, he was born into the world with his little hands curled to his chest as if to ward off the cold, his fingers so close they were nearly interlaced. Since they'd kept the gender a surprise, Tamara remembered how Kyle had nearly danced around the delivery room when the doctor announced it was a boy.

Days later, Tamara's mother told her the story of how she'd stood next to Kyle as he lifted Janie up to the delivery room window to see her new baby brother. Janie was strangely sad.

Kyle asked her what was wrong, and she asked him why daddies liked having little boys so much. Janie said one of her friends told her little girls are not so special to daddies once they have a little boy.

Kyle smiled, and the way Tamara's mother explained it, he seemed totally unsurprised, as if he'd expected this. "Honey," he said to Janie, "daddies may love little boys, but their hearts always belong to their little girls." He then produced a little box from his jacket pocket and handed it to her. Janie opened it and pulled out her first necklace, a small gold chain with a solid gold heart. She hugged her father tight around the neck and squealed with joy. After that, having a little brother became a tad more tolerable.

Tamara felt her heart splitting apart again. After carrying Seth to bed, she laid him down and quietly pulled the covers over him as he stirred briefly and rolled over.

She went to tuck in Janie, but she was already out cold, just a soft mound under her comforter.

Tamara went back to the living room to fetch her iPad. The house was quiet. Peeking through the blinds she noticed that the night had cast a darkness over the patio and pool out back. The small solar path-lights barely illuminated the planters next to them. Through the window Tamara thought she saw something move near the patio table. After staring at the area for a while and seeing nothing further, she called it an illusion and blamed it on the fact that she was still feeling rattled by the whole garage incident.

She wished Trudy was awake with her, but she was still asleep, and Tamara guessed she might stay that way. She forced her focus back to the iPad and began her Google search on Victoria Duncan.

There were no hits at first, save for on Classmates.com, which might prove useful later, but only if Victoria had kept her maiden name. For now, Tamara bet she would find better information elsewhere. She struck gold near the bottom of the first page on Google: there was a link to a PDF wedding invitation and, of all things, a reception menu. The big day had been years ago, but Victoria Duncan had married Michael Brasco in Pebble Beach, CA. Tamara nodded. She now changed her search protocol to Victoria Brasco.

Her image came up immediately in an article from the *Monterey Herald*. She owned a wine shop on the boardwalk. There was another article from a fundraiser a few years back, and this one showed a picture of Victoria's husband, an international exporter. Handsome, with black hair that was slicked back straight, he looked a little bit like a shorter and heavier Pat Riley. Their two children were also in the photo, both girls, ages eight and six at the time.

Tamara looked at both articles again, this time focusing on just Victoria. Tamara felt her suspicions rising again, in spite of her best efforts. How many family vacations had she, Kyle and the kids taken to Monterey over the years? Five? Six? Had Kyle ever separated from her and the kids to sneak off and see Victoria on any of those trips? No obvious moment jumped into Tamara's mind. But what if she was forgetting something?

She sighed heavily and rubbed her eyes, the light from the iPad cocooning her in a haunting glare. The miniature grandfather clock ticked in the hallway, and with everyone else in the house now fast asleep she felt very alone. Outside, the wind chimes over the patio were brushing lightly together, spilling echoes into the air.

The rest of Tamara's research didn't take long. General listings showed the Brascos' home address in Monterey. Tamara wrote it down alongside the address for the wine shop. Zillow gave up the property value and other information, and before long Tamara could construct a simple timeline.

The Brasco's married and moved into their home almost immediately. One year later, they had their first child, and two years after that they had their second. The home had never been refinanced, and what little information she could dig up on Mr. Brasco's import and export business showed that it was privately held and fairly large.

In short, they were very well off. Tamara imagined that Victoria's wine shop was probably little more than a hobby to stave off the boredom of being a full-time, stay-at-home mom with a nanny *and* a maid.

Yawning, Tamara turned off the iPad. It was time for bed. She had a good idea where Kyle was headed now, unless they had some little chateau where they shacked up in the forest somewhere. If they were seeing each other on the side all this time then this was possible, but Tamara had a gut feeling this wasn't the case. She would find Kyle in Monterey.

In the morning she would have to find a way to tell Trudy that she needed her to watch the kids for a few days.

CHAPTER 24

THEY WERE HEADED NORTH again, and by now the 5 Freeway was beginning to feel like a carousel. Still, Napoleon had a plan. He called Sheriff Conch back and asked him if anyone could get him and Parker back into the library. It was an odd request, but once the sheriff heard why, he understood.

He told Napoleon that he was already out of town at his grandson's graduation party, and the librarian, Hattie Tettle, was the only one with the keys. Since the library was closed on Sunday's and Monday's, he could have Kendall swing by her house early in the morning to get them if that'd help. Napoleon said it would. Conch said he'd have Kendall wait for Napoleon and Parker in the library parking lot the following morning.

The funny thing was that Napoleon was starting to get paranoid. He told Conch that they felt like they'd "missed something" at the library, perhaps a book or magazine Fasano had flipped through, instead of the truth, which was that they were after those other seven internet histories on the computer island. Napoleon felt guilty about that, but better to play it safe. He didn't need Kendall trying to make a name for himself and mucking around with the computers before they got there, in the process accidentally deleting a link or piece of data or some other bullshit.

On the freeway, they passed Napoleon's apartment again. He smiled. The last time they'd been this way he'd had the oddest feeling he would never see home again. Yet there it was, zipping by as a blur at sixty miles an hour, but there nonetheless. It was a good sign that things were turning around now.

"You should get some shut-eye," Parker said, his face illuminated by the dashboard lights. The dark night sky was broken up in sections as they passed through the Lincoln Heights tunnels.

"Not likely, man."

"Yeah," Parker replied. He'd kept very quiet since Napoleon ventured his guess about the library. Napoleon knew why, and for the past hour he'd given Parker some space, but enough was enough.

"Look. I hope you're not beating yourself up over this."

Parker said nothing.

"You couldn't have known, and it still may be a dead end when we get there."

"But I should've known to at least look."

"And from now on you will."

"Great. I'm learning and all that shit."

"Yep."

"Except maybe the cost is that this asshole gets away again."

The tunnel ended and split at the 2 Freeway, which veered off to the right. They still had a little over two hours to go to Beaury.

"Yeah. Well. If we do find something, I missed it too, and we both know who's been on the job longer."

"Yeah, but you—"

"Don't say it. I had no excuse. Period."

Silence returned to the inside of the car. The radio remained off, leaving only the droning of the engine and the vibration of the road as the soundtrack to their drive.

Napoleon cleared his throat, which was still a little dry, and popped a cough drop in his mouth. The silence sucked, so he broke it. "Besides, Fasano may or may not be a panicked husband who offed his lover, but he's no psycho about to go on a killing spree."

Parker grunted, then said something Napoleon wished he hadn't. "We'd better hope not."

Damn rookies. They never knew the gravity of a jinx.

They left each other to their thoughts for the next hour, passing through Santa Clarita and Castaic, until they saw the Gorman rest stop up ahead and decided to pull off so Napoleon could take a piss.

It looked like a new facility, with map guides and shiny vending machines. A half-dozen big rig trucks were lined up in the parking lot like staggered metal walls. As they got out of the car Napoleon could smell citrus from all the nectarine farms in the area.

"You go and hit the head, I'm gonna raid those vending machines. I'm starving," Parker said, turning off the car. "You want anything?"

"Yeah. I'm hungry too. Donuts or cookies if they have 'em, and a bottled water."

"Sure thing."

It was just past nine, and the orange lighting around the facility cast the area in a Halloween-colored haze. There was only one other person around, a heavy-set trucker in a John Deere cap who was making his way to the bathroom ahead of Napoleon. What a life, trucking. Napoleon had no idea how they did it, driving all the time, cooped up in the cab all day, sleeping behind the cab all night. It was a boxed-in existence, like living in a coffin on wheels.

The inside of the bathroom glared harshly in fluorescent light, and Napoleon had to wait a few seconds for his eyes to adjust. There were four urinals and a few stalls, one of them now occupied by the trucker. Napoleon could see his workman's boots beneath the stall door. Great. He was going to have to take a piss while this guy blew his ass out. What a joy.

What he hated most about getting older was the whole enlarged prostate thing. His bladder could be full, yet it still took a good five seconds of standing around and waiting before piss came out. It wasn't fair. If anything should enlarge in a man as he got older it should be his dick, because even though you usually got to use it less, by that point in life you at least knew how to use it.

He was just going from a trickle to a stream when the trucker in the stall spoke up.

"Do you ever wonder, man?"

At first Napoleon thought he was in there on his cell phone or something, but after a few seconds of silence it was apparent that he was talking to Napoleon. Great. No one on earth lonelier than a trucker; they even wanted to chat as they crapped.

Napoleon yawned. Screw it. He'd humor the guy. "You talking to me?"

"Yeah."

"Wonder what?"

"If little Esmeralda, you know… if it felt a little good for her too?"

Napoleon's piss stream halted instantly. The room went cold as he asked himself over and over again if he'd really heard what he thought he'd just heard.

The toilet flushed, making Napoleon jump.

"You hear me, old man?"

Squinting, Napoleon zipped up his fly and turned around just as the trucker opened the stall door and walked out.

Years of being a cop taught you how to take the inventory. First, size up the individual you're facing. This guy was Caucasian, heavy set, about six foot three. Napoleon had already seen the boots, standard construction type, probably steel toed. He was wearing jeans and a white Lynyrd Skynyrd t-shirt with long sleeves that were black from the shoulder to the wrist. He had a beard and mustache covering his round chubby face and long blond hair poking out from beneath the John Deere baseball cap, which was tattered and dirty.

"I said, did you hear me?"

Besides the boots the only threatening thing Napoleon could see was a wallet chain that stretched from the man's front belt loop to his back pocket. And instead of a wallet, there could be a knife at the end of that chain. Napoleon had seen that trick a few times before.

After the inventory, you make your stand.

"I heard you. Just not sure I heard you correctly," Napoleon replied, facing the trucker full center, feeling the weight of his 9 mm on his right hip. They were about ten feet apart.

"You heard correct, man. I'm just curious, is all. I hear stories, you know, from the guy that did her, Joaquin I think's his name, and he says she liked it. She liked it a lot."

Napoleon was not used to fear, but he was way too smart to ignore, discount or dismiss it. Instead, he took hold of it by the throat. "Who the fuck are you?"

The trucker chuckled and reached up to adjust his cap. "Who gives a shit who I am?"

"Besides your momma, son? Probably no one. But you're the douche bag that started this little chit-chat."

"You still ain't answered my question."

"What question?"

"The one about the little girl, you know, that got killed. Do you think she was a horny little bitch or what?"

Napoleon smiled. This couldn't be real. He was in the car having a nightmare while Parker was driving or something. He told himself to wake up, but the trucker didn't move and the moment refused to end.

He looked the trucker in the eye, but they were dead eyes, like those of a wild animal. "I think you're barking up the wrong tree, son."

"No, old man." The trucker smiled, his teeth yellow and rotten. "You are."

"How's that?"

"You getting into things you best stay out of, with things you best not start messin' with."

Napoleon was very careful to maintain a gangster's posture: aggressive and unafraid. But on the inside his mind was going a million miles a second. *Who is this bastard? Is he protecting Fasano? Or is Fasano mixed up with the Aryan Nations, who no doubt count this fat ass as a member of their inbred little tribe? Or is he a…*

That's when Napoleon saw the chain around the man's neck, and the pentagram that hung from it.

I'll be a son of a bitch.

"Now, about our little Esmeralda…"

At some point talk is cheap. This was that point. Napoleon took three quick strides towards the man and launched both of his hands into the center of the trucker's chest. It was a standard judo move, aimed at the solar plexus and meant to stun. It knocked the trucker back a few steps into a sink, but that was all.

As the trucker sneered and righted himself, Napoleon drew his gun from its holster and simultaneously grabbed the man by the collar with one hand and jammed his gun under the trucker's chin with the other. Maybe Beecher's crazy-ass idea had been right. Maybe this was some organized shit then, some group of Satanists working with Fasano who were now out to protect him.

The trucker began to giggle like a schoolkid. "Oh man, you all jack-rabbited up, ain't you, old man? It's okay. Pull the trigger." He stopped giggling, and his face began to melt as his cheekbones elongated into the face of some horrific goat-like creature. "Cause I'm already dead, old man." And this time when he smiled it was all tooth and fang.

Napoleon recoiled in stunned disbelief, his fear now morphing into an unexpected terror. "¡*Madre mia!*"

"Oh. Mama got nothing to do with this… son." The trucker's voice had gone to gravel. "Nothin' t'all."

Napoleon stumbled backwards, almost falling, before managing to regain his balance.

The trucker let loose a belly laugh that was half bleat. "Oh, you ain't so brave now, huh, pig?"

"What do you want with me?" Napoleon asked, but his voice was barely a whisper.

The cold white tile of the bathroom walls only heightened the fluorescent glow of the room, and Napoleon could see the trucker's back in the mirror: there were large spikes sticking out of his neck and spine.

"I already told you. It's simple really: just leave this alone. Drive back home. Stay there. Die lonely. Got it?"

Napoleon shook his head and blinked three times. Still, none of it would go away.

"And just so you know, old man?" the trucker continued. "That little girl? She didn't like it. It hurt… like hell." His giggle returned, full of glee, and then, amazingly, the trucker simply stepped backwards and crawled through the mirror, to someplace else, and was gone.

Parker's voice ricocheted into the bathroom from outside. "Hey man, you still in there!"

Napoleon jumped, almost dropping his gun before he holstered it and swallowed hard. "Be right out!" It was only three words, but they left him breathless.

What's going on? What was that? Am I losing my mind now? Is this how it ends? A psych trip with three days' observation at the hospital? A medical leave? What?

He'd spent his whole life trusting his instincts and, in the end, before he left the bathroom and walked back to the car, they were what saved him.

He wanted nothing more on this earth than to splash cold water all over his face, into his eyes to wash away what he'd seen, and over his head to force himself to snap to.

But his instincts told him not to go anywhere near that mirror. To not even get close.

* * *

Kyle woke up where he'd passed out at the night before, except at some point he'd evidently collapsed onto his side. The right side of his face was numb and his nose was filled with the smell of rocks and moss.

As his eyes focused, he saw a group of sea otters rolling around on the waves some twenty-five yards away. The fog was dense and wet, and even the sand beneath his hand was damp, though he was nowhere near the tide line.

His clothes were moist and his baseball cap was tilted partially over his face. He could feel that the inside of the rim had made an indentation in his cheek. After a night in these conditions it was no surprise that he was chilled to the bone and his chest was heavy.

Despite his discomfort, the first thing to cross his mind was the images from the night before, and the dread and sorrow of the truths they'd revealed to him. It was like waking up after a bad breakup, when the day was gloomy before it ever had a chance to be anything else; except this was billions of times worse. It felt like he'd broken up with the rest of the human race.

He was seeing things now, experiencing things beyond this realm and beyond what he could explain to any other living person. People would either say he was mad or lock him up until he confessed that he was. He wished he were. He wished it would all go away. He would give anything to have one chance to go back and leave Caitlyn at the bar that night instead of taking her to that hotel. It all just turned on a dime and it'd been spinning out of control ever since.

The images of the hurricane footage came to him again and he tried pushing them away, but it was no use.

It was true then, what the Bible said: there were spirits at work around us every day, in a multitude of ways, striving for our good or plotting for our downfall. The entire story of human existence, of good versus evil, of a thin veil between this world and the next… it was true.

Every world religion discussed it in some way: a dark force juxtaposed against one of light. Why was he surprised? Did anyone really think that was a coincidence? Even his own religion was based on a leader who had to endure forty days of taunting and temptation by the devil himself, the very same devil who was there to see that those spikes were firmly nailed into that cross.

Did it really matter what name you gave him? Whether it was Beelzebub or Lucifer? The truth was that we could handle the cute concepts of guardian angels or dead loved ones coming back to help us, but the notion of a sneering monster with horns and hooved feet was dismissed as ridiculous, despite the evidence right there in our faces, throughout history; Adolf Hitler, Ted Bundy—monsters were real, and the evil they committed was no less so.

Kyle nodded. It was so obvious. He felt silly that he'd ever questioned it.

And now he was at war with that dark kingdom, drafted by the other side in spite of, or because of, his own sin.

Kyle sighed. The life he knew and had spent thirty-eight years living was over. How could it ever be the same after what he'd experienced and seen now? It couldn't, and this realization brought a depression over him so heavy that it almost forced him to sit down again.

Seagull cries echoed through the fog from somewhere out over the ocean. A sea otter was working over a clam in the distance, swimming near a small rock that was divorced from the end of a jetty. The smell of salt and seaweed filled Kyle's nostrils and, mercifully, coaxed him out of his thoughts.

Everything hurt. He'd racked his shin on a stool while trying to flee the bar. It was now joined in chorus with a dull throb in his neck and shoulders. The worst pain by far was in his back, though, which had been jammed into an unnatural position while he'd slept on the unforgiving surface of the rocks all night.

His mind kept trying to drift back to the hurricane, so he kept anchoring it in the here and now, in this situation, in what he was going to do next.

He thought of The Gray Man. Right about now Kyle could use some advice, some further explanation of what he'd seen on that TV screen. Perhaps later. All that mattered was that Tamara was safe. Right now he had to move ahead with helping Victoria.

With the fog, it was hard to gauge what time in the morning it was, but he was willing to guess it was after eight or so. He needed to get to the Starbucks to camp out for Victoria's arrival.

He was only a few blocks away, so after managing to straighten his back, he made his way to the stairs and back up to the boardwalk. Trying the public restrooms, he found them locked, so he decided his best bet for washing up was going to be the Starbucks' restroom.

After making his way to the street, he momentarily leaned on a statue of John Steinbeck. A whole town was practically dedicated to this guy, and Kyle could only remember reading one of his short stories, back in high school: *The Pearl*. According to the plaque at the base of the bust, he at least lived a full life.

Starbucks was a block up, and when he pushed his way through the door he was met with warmth and the strong aroma of freshly ground coffee beans accompanied by the hiss of a latte machine. The place was busy, but no one seemed to look up as he made a hard left to the restroom. Once inside, he washed his face. Looking into the mirror, he saw that his eyes were heavy now, with dark bags beneath them. He looked like he'd aged ten years.

While exiting the bathroom, he glanced at a newspaper stand just inside the entrance and was stunned to see a photo of a much younger man who was smiling a big bright smile. He'd been part of some tragedy, and according to the headline in bold letters at the top of the front page, he was a wanted man now, in five states.

His name?

Kyle Fasano.

CHAPTER 25

TAMARA LAY IN BED trying to convince herself that what had happened the night before hadn't really happened, but it wasn't working. Because she knew it had.

That night, as Tamara slept, she'd been awoken by a sound, soft and close. She tried to open her eyes but realized she couldn't. In a dreamy and far away place, she tried to command her senses, but only her hearing was left...

The sound grew closer, to the edge of the bed. It was like a soft hiss-whisper. Her hands were at her sides and she tried to bring them up to her chest, but they were disobedient.

Dual horrors arose in her mind. Something was in her room.

And she was completely paralyzed.

A cold snap spread across her body, up her neck and down to her feet, and she finally felt something: a sea of rolling goose bumps. But her feet, which wanted to run, and her waist, which she was begging to bend and allow her to sit up, were arrested.

The bed moved and then sunk a bit. Someone was there.

Inside she screamed, but that's where the scream stayed, in her mind alone, like a trapped echo. Her mouth wouldn't open and her vocal cords were dead. Like she would be. Soon.

Whoever was in her room had malicious intent. It emanated evil. Her mind raced. *Was it a rapist? A murderer? My God, where are the kids!? Where's Trudy?*

All her thoughts came to a complete stop when she felt a hand with very sharp nails grip her thighs and begin to spread her legs, ever so slightly.

Oh. My. God.

It was a rapist then. Some sick monster. But, oddly, she divided these perceptions so that the word "monster" was held up in her mind as the greater truth. Yes. The things lightly combing up and down her thighs weren't fingers.

They were claws.

She begged her eyes to open, her arms to rise, her legs to close. Pleaded and begged. Screamed to them. Nothing.

Then the caressing stopped and the bed began to move again, sinking on either side of her, as whatever it was sat across her chest.

She couldn't breathe now and her body shuddered in revulsion.

She had to do something, but she couldn't. It was that simple, and yet beyond comprehension. How could this be happening? As if everything going on with Kyle wasn't enough? God was now going to let her be raped too?

A moment of wishful clarity came to her: this was all a dream. Yes. That was it.

Hadn't she read about this phenomenon somewhere? It happened to most everybody, usually when you were under a lot of stress. It was the "mind/body glitch." The mind, as part of the process of preparing a person for sleep, suspended the signals to the body's nervous system briefly, right before it slid into the REM stage. But sometimes the process was interrupted and a person partially awoke, not conscious enough to restart the body but conscious enough to be aware of one's surroundings. And if this happened during the dream state? The two worlds could collide, and that's all this was: a figment of her imagination.

That had sharp buttocks that were now sliding off her chest and on to her stomach.

Jesus! This is real.

The thing grabbed her breasts and squeezed them softly, and this was worse, because it was sexual and intimate, not rough and forced, and the nails were not cutting into her but flitting over her chest and up to her neck.

Okay. Okay. Fine. If I'm going to be raped, then fine. But please, God, protect the kids, please...

Terror sprang up in her like a jack-in-the-box in her brain. *Not Janie! Please, God. No. No. No. She's still a baby. Still a little girl. Please.*

She felt a sudden exhalation of breath on her face, the sickly sweet smell of maggots on meat. Her stomach churned with nausea. Then the claws were on her breasts again, and just when she thought it couldn't get any worse, not in a million years, it spoke.

"Soft," it said, "like plums."

Her mind began to go black, and then fought back.

Was that Georgie's voice? Georgie Wilson? Who used to torture her when she was young by making fun of her breasts before they "came in," as her Aunt Leona used to say. It had to be. Tamara was a woman now, with a full chest. No one had called them "plums" in a long time. And if it was Georgie's voice, then this *was* a nightmare.

The monster chuckled softly into her ear and Tamara wanted to sob. It wasn't Georgie's voice. Just his words. Being uttered now by this creature, which was somehow turning her own mind and memories against her.

There was a sudden shift in the room, the sound of air thumping hard against the drapes, and Tamara sensed they weren't alone anymore. Someone else was there.

She felt the head of the thing that was on her snap to one side, and then the creature began to climb off her. She heard its feet hit the carpet next to the bed, on Kyle's side.

The room went silent, and whatever was happening now had little or nothing to do with her. There was no commotion, no struggle. Just silence. As if she were a fly on the wall in a room where two things were just staring at each other. Then whatever it was that had come to torment her seemed to leave, or disappear, or something. She couldn't tell. She just knew the fear in her was waning.

She felt herself coming back, coming alive, and the nerve endings in her body beginning to vaguely spark. She rushed the sensation to her eyes, wanting to see who had come to save her.

Her right eyelid fluttered open just in time for her to catch a glimpse of him, a tall glowing man in a gray suit, just as he melted through the French doors of her bedroom and back outside. The first word that came to her mind for him was "power" and she was flooded with emotions before she passed out...

Now, as she forced herself to get out of bed, the truth was as self-evident as the day before her.

A monster had come to kill her. She'd prayed for help, and God had sent someone.

There was no trying to wish it away into any dream or nightmare.

Because dreams don't allow for monsters, nor nightmares any rescuing angels.

* * *

Napoleon tried to hold his mind together, but it was like trying to hold a bag of marbles with a hole in it: shit was threatening to spill out everywhere. It was a little after eight in the morning, and fog surrounded their car on the turnoff where he and Parker had stopped the night before to get some shut-eye. They'd passed out cold, but now, as Parker snored away next to him, Napoleon was lost in thought.

How he was ever going to continue this investigation or focus on this case was beyond him. The only approach left was the oldest one in the book: one step at a time. Any wasted effort at worrying or obsessing over things was useless. If he was losing it, then he could get a psych eval and some help when this case came to a close.

If he wasn't losing it? Then his mind was the least of his worries.

He thought of his tattoo of the praying hands. Yes, that made sense. If what happened in that bathroom was real, then it was time to pray alright. Hard. He was surprised how easily, after a lifetime of using and relying on them, his skeptical, analytical and investigative instincts were being swept aside.

Like any good cop, what he saw was usually what he relied on. But Napoleon had honed his instincts too, over many cases in his career. There was no need to over-analyze what had happened. That... thing, creature, whatever the hell it was... had been there, as real as the lights, white tiles and lingering scent of piss in the bathroom. It spoke to him and he grabbed hold of it with his bare hands and... felt it. It was a physical presence that was more like a mass of vibrating atoms than it was a person of any kind, as if he grabbed ahold of a ghost.

He'd never had a panic attack before but he'd heard descriptions of them, and what he was experiencing was pretty close to one; his mouth was dry and he was short of breath, his chest felt heavy, and internally he wanted to run in every direction, all at once.

He heard the trucker's voice again: "Drive back home. Stay there. Die lonely."

Yes. That was a splendid idea. He could retire early, get eighty percent of his pension and help coach Efren's baseball team. He could watch his little nephew grow up, graduate high school, go off to college, start his own life and... mostly forget about his uncle. This was the likely scenario, if Efren's mother didn't cut Napoleon off altogether for some reason, which was always a distinct possibility.

That was her right, because no matter how hard Napoleon pretended, Efren was not his son. He would never have a son or a daughter, or much of a life at all really. That thing was right. Dying alone was most certainly going to be his end someday.

He decided against praying. What was the use? How many times had he been to a crime scene and seen the anguish of a shattered mother or brokenhearted wife, bent over the dead body of their gang-member son or husband, wailing over why their prayers had never been answered?

No. He wouldn't pray. Because guessing which ones would or wouldn't be answered was the ultimate display of human futility.

Of *desesperación*.

No. Don't. Don't think of Esperanza now too. You'll be in a bottle within the hour.

He took a deep breath and held it, trying to refocus. All he had was the job and, right now, this case. Napoleon had never walked away from a fight in his life, and he wasn't going to start now. Be it with Kyle Fasano or with that mirror creature, Napoleon was going to throw down, to the bitter end.

Because, really, he had nothing to lose.

When Parker finally awoke, they both got out of the car and pissed into the fog before heading down the road and pulling off at a small diner, where they loaded up on breakfast and coffee.

"Okay, Parker. Full night's rest. Full stomachs. Deputy Kendall is probably up now. Time to push on."

Parker only nodded weakly, his face a mask of exhaustion as they made their way back to the car and began the drive.

It wasn't long before their Caprice pulled into the parking lot of the Beaury Library. Waiting for them in his cruiser was Kendall, reading the paper as he sat in the front seat. He got out to greet them. "Mornin', fellas!" he said with an exaggerated southern accent.

"Morning," Parker replied as he got out of the car.

Napoleon's seat belt was jammed, so it took him a second longer to join them. After nodding a hello to Kendall, he looked at the library before him. He wasn't sure he wanted to go back inside after what had happened last time, and while he was in his current state. If Fasano had left any other cryptic clues about Napoleon's past, there was a real chance Napoleon was going to snap once and for all. But he had no choice. They'd overlooked something last time; he was sure of it.

Kendall rustled the keys up from his pocket. When he turned the key in the lock of the big metal double doors of the library, a loud click rattled into the air. The interior of the library was lit with muted sunlight that spilled through the windows and reflected off the used-books racks just inside the entrance.

"So what do you think you're after?" Kendall asked.

"We'll know it when we find it, deputy. Thanks for your help," Napoleon replied, implying that he and Parker would take it from here. Noted and received, Kendall stayed at the front desk, which was a relief to Napoleon. He had just as much right as Parker and Napoleon to look at the computers and be part of the investigation; it was all going down in his jurisdiction. But Kendall didn't seem to know this, which was a good thing, because the fewer people involved the better.

When they were almost to the computer island, Parker spoke softly. "So, we got seven computers we didn't get to. You good with this?"

Napoleon was irritated. "I know how to do a damned computer search."

"That's not what I meant."

"I know that too. Forget about it. I'm fine."

"Okay, then. How 'bout we take a computer at either end, then work our way to the middle?"

Napoleon nodded.

As often was the case when you were in a hurry, nothing came quickly and nothing was easy. It was as if the universe liked to be the cat and treat you like a ball of yarn.

The first four computers yielded nothing. The fifth wouldn't start and needed to be rebooted, and while it was coming back to life, the sixth computer seemed to have promise. Parker found a bunch of searched articles for the Grand Canyon, but they proved to be for somebody's school project, since they were linked back to a homework assignment website for the local junior high.

The seventh computer was Napoleon's, and he stretched his neck and shoulders as he began digging through the search history for the day Fasano had been there. After a sea of typical teenager-type searches of hot models and video game articles, there were a series of visits to a website for Khan Academy, where someone was clearly catching up on biology class. Before long though, Napoleon thought he found something.

There were searches now that were far more specific and targeted at someone named "Victoria Duncan," from general information like her age and her marriage, to more specific information like her home address.

"Finally got this one up and running again," Parker said, his fingers flying across the keyboard of the computer he'd been forced to restart.

"Fine. Finish up, but I think I've got something."

Parker stopped typing and leaned over. "Yeah? What?"

"Around the exact time Fasano was here and dicking around with that other computer, someone was on this one digging up information on some woman about his age, I think. I dunno yet. I'm working a little deeper into the Google pages to confirm a birth date, but that's an odd coincidence, don't ya think?"

"And you don't believe in coincidences?"

Napoleon chuckled wearily. "Not even on a good day."

Parker rubbed his chin, and then leaned back over his computer.

As Napoleon dug, he hit Classmates.com. Breaking out his credit card, he signed up for the service knowing that the "one month free" wasn't really free when you gave someone the right to bill you up front for the second month. He didn't care. He filled out his info and ignored his own high school—a third of his class was either dead or in jail anyway—then steered his way to the page of Victoria Duncan, who was now Victoria Brasco.

Then he searched for a Kyle Fasano.

Bingo.

She and Fasano went to the same school and graduated the same year. Seeing that it was an extra charge but not caring, he ordered the online yearbook that was available.

After a moment or two, Napoleon could only shake his head. Here it was, all they needed.

Napoleon knew he should be relieved to finally have caught a break, but instead he was pissed, especially when he went back and clicked further into the search history and saw that Fasano also searched the bus schedules from Beaury to Monterey, where "coincidentally" Brasco now lived. A round trip drive to San Diego could have been entirely avoided if they'd just been more thorough. If Parker had—

No. Don't blame him. You're the little bitch who had to go outside and puke, not the rookie.

Napoleon sighed heavily. "You got anything on a Victoria Duncan or a Victoria Brasco over there? Or anything on Monterey?"

Shaking his head, Parker looked up. "Nothing over here but searches on UTI infections, the Louisiana Purchase, training bras and different cheat codes for *Halo*."

"Then this is it. He's gone north, most likely to Monterey. Maybe he's been banging this broad too. Maybe not."

Parker walked over to him and peered at the screen. "Who the hell is she?"

Napoleon scratched his ear and began taking notes. "You'll never believe it."

"Try me."

"His high school sweetheart."

Parker laughed. "Are you shitting me?"

"Told you you'd never believe it."

The rest of the lights in the library were still off, and as a result they were enveloped in a cloud of computer screen glare that cast their faces in a blue tint. Kendall was whistling softly somewhere out in the lobby, and Napoleon noticed that Parker's face was slightly twisted in confusion. Napoleon laughed in spite of himself. "You poor bastard."

"What?"

"I've said it before. I'll say it again. Your... first... damned... case."

Parker chuckled, the glare exaggerating the weariness around his eyes. "No shit. So, why the high school skirt?"

"Like everything else in this, who knows?"

"Maybe he's a serial killer. He offs the latest love, and now he's decided to off one of the first loves?"

"Shit, Parker. That's a bit grim, even for me."

"What can I say? You're starting to wear off on me."

"Ya think?"

"So?"

Rubbing at this three-day beard, Napoleon shook his head. "Nope. I'm done guessing on this one. I only know one thing."

"What's that?"

"We're going to Monterey."

CHAPTER 26

WHEN VICTORIA CAME INTO the Starbucks at a quarter to ten she was like a walking time machine, taking Kyle back to simpler days, rooted in nostalgia.

She was more casual today, wearing a white plantation blouse over blue capri pants with white canvas shoes, and her hair was pulled back in a ponytail, revealing small blue-and-white earrings that swung back and forth as she walked.

Kyle saw her in the here and now, yes, but he could've almost sworn that he'd seen her dressed just like this once before in high school, perhaps in her locker bay the day he had starting shutting her out, or maybe before that, on one of their earliest dates. He couldn't quite place it, but right now she wasn't any "new" Victoria, she was more like *his* Victoria—and for that reason, because of the memories she brought through the door with her, it hurt more to see her this time. A lot more.

Longing welling up in his heart, he diverted his attention to the barista Victoria was here to see. His name was Sebastian. Kyle had made sure to get his name earlier, while placing his own order. Sebastian was a little over six feet, still with his piercings and styled hair, but this time Kyle noticed black eyeliner around his eyes and scruff on his face.

And Sebastian had noticed Kyle as well.

He seemed to project a negative vibe as soon as Kyle had arrived at the pickup counter. The friendly Sebastian from yesterday, who was chatty with all the customers, and especially with Victoria, had been giving Kyle sideways glances all morning.

Occasionally their eyes met, and Kyle waited for the transformation he expected, for Sebastian's face to melt away into some monstrosity looking back at him, for his perfect white teeth to turn into fangs.

Instead, Sebastian just smirked at Kyle and looked away as if dismissing him.

But now, with Victoria's arrival, another version of Sebastian appeared—that of the hunter. He saw her come in but coyly looked away, not waving at her eagerly this time, but making as if he was steaming some coffee cups clean.

As Victoria made her way through the line and ordered, Sebastian glanced repeatedly at her out of the corner of his eye, and then Kyle watched with fascination as Sebastian sped up the orders ahead of hers. Being a guy, Kyle knew exactly what Sebastian was doing: setting things up for a proper window of conversation. Opportunity didn't just happen—it was made.

Victoria, meanwhile, was nervously making her way down the length of the counter after paying the cashier, glancing coyly in Sebastian's direction, but then upon not catching his eye, looking quickly away again.

It was an awkward dance, but finally Sebastian saw her, and she saw him, and Kyle saw the specter of sin settle in between them. It was all he could do not to just stand up and scream at them to stop, but something told him this wasn't the time to make his intervention.

"Hey, you," Sebastian said softly, smiling and bobbing his chin up in Victoria's direction.

"Hey," Victoria said, smiling back and playfully tilting her head. Moving a few strands of hair from her face and pushing them behind her ear she asked, "How you doing?"

"I'm good. Better now that you're here."

"Ah." Victoria giggled. "Real smooth."

Sebastian nodded towards a second barista, a tall thin Asian kid with his cap on backwards and who up until now had been on pastry. On cue, the new barista took over drinks as Sebastian sidled off to the end of the counter.

Kyle was sitting in a leather chair opposite where he'd sat yesterday, but he was easily within earshot of the counter. Still, he had to strain to hear when Victoria and Sebastian lowered their voices.

"We still on for tonight?" Sebastian asked.

"For dinner?" Victoria said, both firmly and flirtatiously limiting his expectations.

Sebastian raised his eyebrows, and the smile turned into a grin. "Yes. Dinner."

Victoria folded her arms, but loosely. "Then, yes. I'd love to."

To Kyle it was obvious that they both knew where this was heading, even now, and that the dinner plans were just a formality, to either add a little challenge to Sebastian's usual kill strategy or some dignity to what Victoria had decided to do.

They made their plans as Kyle took mental notes. She didn't want him to pick her up at the wine shop. She'd meet him at the restaurant at six, a place called Bella Cuore. Then they exchanged an awkward, almost nervous goodbye.

Kyle held his breath the entire time, as if he were watching a pending car crash from a far off distance, and he felt himself finally exhale deeply when Victoria turned to walk away.

Except this time, as she did, she looked right at Kyle.

Sitting in his chair with one leg over the other in a nonchalant pose and his head partially down, he pretended to look at yesterday's sports page, which he'd found in the bin just inside the door, realizing the move was so cliché.

Kyle had looked a little too long, and been flat-out spotted. Clear as day.

* * *

As soon as the words came out of her mouth, Tamara knew her friend wouldn't buy any of it. She sounded too nervous, and her... dream from last night was still hanging on her like bundled rope, tripping her up with every mental step she tried to take.

"So. You want me to watch the kids while you... get away... for the night?" Trudy asked, standing with her cup of coffee cradled in one hand, steam rising from the brown mug as she looked at Tamara intensely.

"I need a break. This is all too much," Tamara replied as she stood across from her friend in the kitchen.

"A break..." Trudy let the words trail off, incomplete.

"Yes."

Tamara looked up to see Trudy still looking at her. Trudy had showered, and her hair was up in a towel. She adjusted the knot with her free hand and squinted at Tamara. "Bullshit."

"What?"

"What's going on? This is exactly what you said yesterday, to go off for lunch. Is it this Ben guy, again?" Trudy asked. "Is that really how you're going to handle all this?"

"What? God, no! It's not that at all."

"I hope not Tam-Tam. I mean, it's a little too soon for the revenge lay, don't ya think?"

"Oh my God!" Tamara put her hands on her hips. "How could you say that to me?"

Trudy shrugged. "Well, I wouldn't put it past you."

Tamara felt her jaw drop and her face flush with anger. She expected that this conversation could go a number of ways, but never *this* way. She was about to unleash a string of expletives when Trudy said, "How does it feel?"

Tamara was dumbfounded. "What?"

"How does it feel to have your best friend lie to your face?"

A silence crept in between them and sat down like a stray cat.

Trudy went to refill her coffee cup, turning her back on Tamara in the process. The ball was obviously in Tamara's court now. She swallowed hard, and again pushed thoughts of the dream from her mind. It didn't work. Her mind argued back.

If it was a dream, then why were there scratches on your breasts this morning?

Tamara felt a pressing impatience welling up inside her. Implicating Trudy with the police was the last thing she wanted; but the lie wasn't working. It was past ten and she had to get on the road, and get to Kyle, before it was too late. At the heart of her impatience was a pending sense of doom that something bad was going to happen.

"Trudy… I've gotta go. Please let me. I'm sorry. I can't tell you why."

"Bullshit. Again. You can tell me why. You just don't want to."

Tamara took a few steps forwards. "Please. It's for your own good."

Trudy spun around and folded her arms across her chest. "*Please!*" she said sarcastically, with an edge of hurt to her voice.

She was forcing Tamara's hand, and it was obvious she wasn't going to let it go.

"Trudy. Fine. I just don't want you to get in trouble and…" Tamara paused and caught her breath as her emotions began to get the best of her. The fear of this situation was being fueled by the still-burning embers of her fear from last night. She felt her lip tremble and her eyes swell with tears.

"Hey." Trudy stepped forwards and hugged her. "Tam. What's going on? Please tell me."

So Tamara did. She told Trudy about Kyle's letter, the yearbook, the internet search she'd done and where she thought Kyle was headed. She didn't bring up the thing that had visited her bed the night before though, fearing that it might shred any credibility that her story could have.

"Jesus, Tamara." Trudy sighed. "And you didn't call the police with any of this?"

"Not yet."

"Why?"

Tamara hesitated before blurting out, "Because I want a head start."

Now it was Trudy's turn to look shocked and dumbfounded. "Oh, Tamara. You can't be serious."

"I am."

"After what he's done? Seriously? Let the police handle it."

Tamara broke their hug and stepped back. "What did you say?"

A look of shame flashed across Trudy's face. "Never mind."

"No. No I won't just 'never mind'! You said 'after what he's done'… You think he's guilty, don't you?"

"I didn't say that."

"Are we still talking about lies and truth here? You want to rephrase that?"

Tears welled in Trudy's eyes now. "Fine. I said it. But I didn't mean it… Look, I didn't…"

Tamara covered her mouth, waiting for Trudy to finish.

"Tamara. It doesn't look good. That's all I'm saying."

A sense of rage came to visit Tamara's impatience. "Don't you think I know that?"

"Yes, but…"

"Yes, but what? Yes, but he's my husband? Yes, but we said our vows? Better or worse, Trudy? Isn't that what we said?"

"Yes."

"You were standing right next to me. You heard the words, right?"

"I did, yes, but—"

"No. No 'buts,' Trudy. He's had an affair. I get that. It sucks and it hurts. I don't know how I'll ever get over that. But I don't believe that he's murdered anyone and I cannot and will not abandon him, do you understand?"

Tamara was shaking now, almost uncontrollably.

Trudy rushed forwards and hugged her again, this time with such force that the rage in Tamara was pushed out. They held one another and cried together in the quiet stillness of the kitchen.

"I'm sorry," Trudy finally said. "Of course you won't abandon him. I know that. It's what makes you such a good person, and such a good friend. I'm sorry, Tam."

Tamara reached up and took the end of the towel in her friend's hair and used it to wipe at her tears. "I can't lose my best friend now, too. Right? Please, Trudy."

Trudy took Tamara by the shoulders and gave her a little shake. "Never."

"You understand then?"

"Yes, at least as much as I need to, and that's all that matters. Go ahead and go."

"The police…"

"I know nothing. No deposition would ever change that."

"I'm going to call them. I promise. I just want a—"

Trudy nodded. "A head start. I get it. Now go already. Just say goodbye to the kids first."

An hour later, Tamara exited the house and walked into the still morning air. She'd explained to the kids that she had to go and run an errand that would likely take all day. Seth and Janie had promptly burst into tears at the idea of her leaving. The only way she'd gotten them to calm down was to tell them that she was going to help Daddy.

Thank you, God.

Knowing that her children would be safe with Trudy was the final thing she needed to make the next step, even if she had no idea where it would lead.

Once in the car, she set the GPS for the address of a woman who once held her husband's heart. It was going to take just over five hours to get there. She didn't know what she was going to do when she got there, but she decided to figure it out when she arrived.

Pulling out of the driveway, she noticed the news vans; they were fewer in number now. The worst thing that had ever happened to her in her life was no longer as big a story. She made her way past them and through the side streets that took her to the freeway. She decided one more thing too: that she would call the police, namely the Hispanic detective, at some point along the journey. She fumbled around in her purse and was relieved to find that she still had his card.

Napoleon Villa.

What an odd name. He'd seemed fair the night he and his partner had come looking for Kyle, but all business too. In another life maybe he could've visited her home without offending her, and she in turn could've made fun of his name and asked him why, in a million years, his mother had named him after a French general.

But in this life he was the man after her husband and there had been a bit of deadness in his eyes that had scared her. He would hurt Kyle if he had to. There was no doubt at all in her mind about that.

She merged into the traffic on the 210 freeway and headed to the 2, which would get her to the 5. Then, she felt a chill run up her spine. She reassured herself that Kyle would be fine as long as she got there first, and, after all, she would have a good head start on them before she called the police.

She had no way of knowing the detective with the French general's name had just left the library in Beaury, CA, which meant he was already closer to her husband than she was by a good two hours.

CHAPTER 27

HIS GRANDMOTHER'S HANDS WERE both soft and worn, so that when you looked at them as she folded them in her lap, they showed her age, but when she opened them and held them out to you, to welcome you into her home or to nurse a cut, they showed her love. For Napoleon, they had always been open.

Until the day he let the pigeons loose.

He was ten years old, in his new black Vans with white trim, skittering about on the rooftop of the small three-unit apartment building that his grandmother owned and that was behind her house. She used the rooftop to grow her herbs and medicines, including marijuana, and to house her small flock of pigeons, which some of her customers from South America demanded as sacrifices in some of their healing rituals.

Having grown up in Jalisco, Mexico, on a farm, she was not at all shy about killing animals when it needed to be done. Since the bird had to be killed in the presence of the person in need of healing, and since it was a measure of last resort in most cases, his grandmother typically would go to the person's home to do it. As such, Napoleon rarely saw the practice.

But one late Saturday afternoon a family that was leaving town had come by the house and begged for her help; the mother had contracted a painful skin disease. His grandmother tried to urge a simple approach of some ginger mixed with aloe, but the family would have none of it. The sick woman was convinced she had skin cancer, and with wild eyes she pleaded for more urgent action.

Napoleon knew his grandmother well; she did not suffer fools gladly. But two of the three units had been vacant that month, one family having moved to Montebello and the other to North Hollywood. The fridge was sparsely stocked, she needed the money and the family was willing to pay well for the ritual, so she obliged their request.

She asked them to follow her to the backyard and up to the rooftop and told Napoleon to stay in the house and watch cartoons.

But that wasn't going to happen. In Napoleon's mind he had to, simply had to, see this mystical ritual that was whispered about in the neighborhood and made some call his grandmother *bruja*, witch, even though she was the most religious person that Napoleon had ever known.

His grandmother held front row at church every Sunday, rain or shine, in sickness and health, until death did its part. "Now that your grandfather is gone," she told Napoleon one day, "Jesus is my husband." And so it was.

The truth was that she considered the rituals and more superstitious elements of the Hispanic community a bit too much to take at times, including *Día de Muertos*; but her main interests were healing and helping people, and so in most cases she deferred to their beliefs, if that was what it took.

So as the sun settled over the western edge of the city, the buildings of downtown Los Angeles outlined as if traced in black chalk, Napoleon snuck up the stairs and peeked through a crack in the rooftop door as his grandmother lit incense and candles and rubbed the woman's forehead with palms and oils.

It was quiet, and the family was in a semi-circle around the woman, each seemingly in silent prayer, earnestly pleading for intercession as the woman wept in fear. His grandmother was softly singing a song as she stepped across the old, torn tar paper on the roof. The wood-framed pigeon cage was covered on all sides with chicken wire and was resting atop an old table.

The pigeons trapped within were dumb animals, but evidently not too dumb. It was as if they knew what was coming as his grandmother moved to the cage and opened it. They fluttered and scampered about inside trying to escape his grandmother's grasp, but eventually one of them was just a step too slow.

Napoleon watched in horror as his grandmother mercilessly twisted the pigeon's neck and a sharp cracked snapped through the air. The animal fell limp, and she carried it to her "potions" table, where she cut it with a knife and held the pigeon high so that its blood, thick and syrupy, drained into a small clay bowl.

Once emptied, the bird was cast aside and she began to mix various herbs, which she ground into the blood before she adding two handfuls of dirt from a bag next to the wooden stool she was seated upon. Before long she had made a paste. She spread it across the woman's back, which was covered with a large red rash with small areas of puss.

The whole time Napoleon kept looking back at the dead bird lying on the rooftop, lifeless and limp. It would never fly again, because of two hands that he knew so differently. He wondered how hands that loved so deeply and fully could also kill so easily. He didn't know it at the time, but it was a question he was going to spend much of his future career trying to answer.

Napoleon decided the other birds wouldn't suffer the same fate. They were no more special than the bird that had just died, but that wasn't the point. They were special in that Napoleon saw what was being done to them and he thought it was wrong. He was sure in his ten-year-old heart that the pigeons that were still alive were his responsibility to save now.

He snuck back down the stairs and waited until his grandmother escorted the family back out to the street, where they paid her, piled into their Chevy Van and rumbled off.

He only had a few moments before his grandmother went back into the house and found him missing, so he ran back up the stairs, across the rooftop and to the cage, where a half-dozen set of eyes looked at him eagerly, as if they somehow knew his heart and his intent.

He cast open the cage door and set them free.

They scattered like teardrops across the face of the sky and off into the distance, Napoleon watching them with a longing in his heart that he didn't understand and would never outgrow.

Then the rooftop door swung open, and he turned to find his grandmother standing there, a look of shock on her face. "Napoleon! What have you done?"

He looked at his grandmother and couldn't help himself: he began to cry, less out of fear and more out of that longing that he was feeling in his heart.

She took small steps towards him, her stern expression morphing to concern. Her heavy frame moved smoothly as she grabbed him by the arms then hugged him gently, the smell of Downy drifting into his nostrils when he pressed his face against her purple dress, his eyes cast down at her worn sandals and dark brown ankles.

"I didn't want them to die, Nana," he said.

She hushed him and rocked him gently, back and forth, the two of them like swaying statues under the dying light of the day, minutes passing until she finally spoke. "It's okay, Papi. You're too young to understand."

"Understand what?"

"What one pigeon can do, baby boy."

Napoleon stepped back, angry and confused, the feelings in him emerging and colliding. "But… you *killed* it!"

His grandmother nodded and, taking a seat on her stool, held her hands out to him, her eyes wet. "But for a good reason, child."

"What? How?" Napoleon cried, refusing to budge, holding his position beyond not only her reach but also her logic.

She sighed softly, her gray hair fluttering in the wind. With an encouraging smile on her face, she again motioned him towards her. "*Ven aqui…* Come over here… Let me explain."

When he stepped towards her it was with a resignation and a relief, an early lesson in life that you love who you love, even when you don't understand them, and that there's a surrender to it that can actually be comforting.

He fell into her arms and she scooped him up to cradle him like a baby across her legs. She looked down at his face, her dark brown eyes squinting at him as she spoke. "In this case a tiny pigeon died so that a woman might have faith. It's sad, I know, especially for the pigeon."

He blinked back his tears and looked at her intently, trying to understand.

She sniffled and continued. "But if it takes one lowly pigeon to make someone believe in a miracle, do you think it matters to God? Listen to me. There is a veil, child, between here and the next world. We must never forget that."

"A veil?" Napoleon said, not knowing the word.

His grandmother chuckled softy. "It's like a curtain, baby."

"Oh."

"God is right there, just beyond it, as are all his angels. As for that pigeon? God created it, and he can recreate it a second later, somewhere in Argentina for all we know, or New York, and the pigeon lives on. Who's to say that's not so?"

"Really?"

"And who's to say that when that woman's skin is all healed, because it's just shingles and it will be healed in time, who's to say that the 'miracle' she thinks saved her life today will not someday give her the hope to believe with right and proper faith? All because of one little pigeon."

Napoleon nodded, still not fully understanding but beyond the need to, trusting now, trusting in those soft hands as she ran her fingers through his hair. "I hope the pigeon is in heaven, Nana."

In response to this a tear escaped her eye. "Oh, child. You have such a soft heart. I envy you. Please… don't ever let this world make it hard."

Napoleon blinked.

"Hey, man! Wake up!" Parker yelled, nudging at Napoleon's shoulder.

Napoleon shifted in the car seat, groggy, his grandmother's face still fresh in his eyes as he looked around. "Okay already! I'm awake!" he barked.

"Man. You were deep down," Parker said. "I tried twice to snap you out of it. Look at this mess."

Napoleon sat up and cleared his throat. Looking out the window, he cursed. "Shit."

"Before you ask, we're on the 46. The main cut across from the 5 to the 101. GPS said it was the quickest way, but I guess that was before this happened."

In front of them were four lanes of frozen traffic that couldn't even be called "bumper-to-bumper" because it wasn't moving at all.

"It's a damned parking lot," Napoleon said.

"Yep. Overturned big rig. Took out all four lanes—the two going west and the two going east."

"We can't—"

"Re-route?" Parker sighed. "Nope. We're halfway down this road. We can double back to the damned 5 again, take it north to the 152 and cut across through Gilroy, but that puts us above Monterey when we finally get to the coast. By the time we drop back down? I doubt we'd have saved any time."

"Unbelievable."

"No kidding."

But Napoleon was also thinking of something else.

An overturned big rig.

And the trucker in the John Deere cap back at the rest stop.

And how there was no such thing as a coincidence.

When his phone rang, he jumped. "Hello?" he answered.

It was a woman's voice. "Detective Villa? This is Tamara Fasano."

This was all getting better by the minute.

CHAPTER 28

WHAT DO YOU SAY to your first love after nearly twenty years, when they've changed and you've changed and the parting between you, so long ago, wasn't a good one? Kyle was beginning to formulate the words when Victoria simply looked away and walked right past him.

A cascade of emotions ripped through him, one after the other, on a repeating loop: he was stunned, relieved and hurt. Had she really just ignored him? Hadn't she recognized him? How was that possible? He swore, when she'd looked at him, that he saw a split second of recognition cross her eyes. Was she just stunned? Shy? Unsure of what she'd seen?

Maybe she was just too full of thoughts about dinner tonight while she'd glanced at the dude sitting by the counter, who she maybe figured looked a little bit like a slightly heavier version of her high school sweetheart before dismissing it as impossible. She lived in lovely Monterey, and for all she knew Kyle still lived in LA or had moved to Alaska by now.

Still stunned, Kyle noticed that Sebastian was back on point, spinning off cappuccinos, lattes and caramel macchiatos like a maestro of caffeine. After wiping his face with a napkin, Kyle stood, threw his trash away and made his way outside for some fresh air, which was cool and stung his lungs.

He watched as Victoria crossed the street, made a left for the boardwalk and was cut off from his line of sight. For a second he thought about going after her, but was then unsure; if she had seen and recognized him, she might notice him following her, which could completely freak her out. So, instead, he turned right and made his way up the hill to a small parking lot, where he made a left into a private alleyway that was littered with cardboard boxes and trash bins.

Closing his eyes, he lowered his head and was actually about to pray for a better understanding of what to do next when he heard something near him shuffling against the wall. When he opened his eyes, there was a homeless man standing there, dressed in a heavy brown coat and dirty slacks, with pieces of his newspaper bed still stuck to one of his arms.

"Sorry. I didn't mean to disturb you," Kyle said in a startled voice.

The man said nothing. Instead, approaching Kyle cau-tiously, his eyes changed from brown to solid red orbs and he grinned, revealing tiny piranha-like teeth.

His arms were long… too long for his body… and spread wide, as if they'd once had wings and now didn't.

Kyle realized then that he was looking at a fallen angel of some kind, and as his new instincts seemed to be mul-tiplying each passing day, he wasn't the least bit surprised when something told him to be very, very careful.

Thought became reality when, in four short strides, Homeless Man covered the distance between the two of them, grabbed Kyle by the shirt and launched him into the air like a rag doll.

Kyle flew backwards and expected to land on his back, but the ground didn't reappear when he thought it would.

He'd been launched higher and more forcefully than he'd thought, his momentum allowing him to roll over smoothly so he didn't snap his spine. He was surprised when he sprang to his feet feeling little pain.

He felt strong. As if the sleep under the pier had not only recharged him but evolved him somehow. Homeless Man cocked his head to one side, his red eyes squinting in surprise, before he crouched down and stuttered forwards.

Kyle had the strange urge to cry for help, but he knew better. The Gray Man had warned him that he was on his own now.

Calling on the power within him, Kyle felt it course from his heart up to his eyes and out to his hands. The blue was there, first soft and pale, then dark as the open sea.

He put his hands together, awed as a blue orb began to form between them, but it was too late. The creature charged him with blinding speed in split-second images, as if it was traveling back and forth between this reality and another. Suddenly it was in his face, each of its spiked hands gripping Kyle's wrists and pulling them apart.

"No, poppet. Not today," it said with grim seriousness and no trace of a smile. Again it picked him up and threw him, bouncing Kyle off the alley wall and into the side of a trash bin.

This time Kyle was knocked almost senseless. Gasping for air, he looked for an escape, but a black sheet of energy was draped at both ends of the alley, cocooning them in.

"Let's see it," Homeless Man said. "Let's see the little man run."

But as it spoke, a strange war was playing itself out across Homeless Man's face; it was changing, in pulsating waves, first to an old white woman with wrinkled cheeks and deep green eyes, and then to a Middle Eastern man with short dark hair and a square jaw.

Standing up slowly, Kyle tried to figure out what to do next. He could still feel the power in him waiting to be called on again, but it was obvious that he couldn't manifest it quick enough to fight this thing. He was like a young gunslinger, unpracticed and too slow on the draw.

To buy time, he tried the Lord's Prayer again. "Our Father…" But this only made things worse.

The creature simply smiled at him and began to chatter its tiny teeth. "We know that trick, poppet. We used to say it al'a'time."

Kyle backed up to the wall opposite the trash bin and eyed the drainage pipe that ran up its length. Maybe he could get up and out of here somehow. But the thought was snuffed out like a flame in the rain when, incredibly, Homeless Man appeared in his peripheral vision crawling up the wall, his long arms having split in two so that he had four, now, to go with his two legs so that he was like a six-legged spider. The comparison was more accurate than Kyle could've imagined. Homeless Man suddenly began jumping back and forth, from one side of the alley to the other, in crisscross patterns, spreading a web made of the same dark material that was across both ends of the alley.

"Jesus…" Kyle whispered.

The creature shrieked with joy, this time with the face and voice of the old lady. "He ain't here to help you now, child. He's too busy trying to save the rest of the world." And the woman cackled, her eyes wide with madness.

Fear began to bloom in Kyle. He was in over his head this time, for real. Why in heaven was he being asked to fight a demon this strong, one that emanated evil so much that it actually caused waves of nausea in him? This thing made the boy on the bike or the woman on the bus seem like first graders in a barroom brawl.

Think. Just think.

Homeless Man finished its web and then dropped straight towards the ground, stopping and hovering six inches above the pavement.

"It's what I was promised, if I'd only give up my wings," said the face of the old Arab man. "It's much easier than flying, you know." But then his face contorted in pain and he screamed. "No. No, you can't hurt him! I won't let you."

Homeless Man's faces began to spin like images in a slot machine, blurring together as the many selves of the creature warred with each other.

Its host, Kyle thought. *The Arab man was an angel once, and the others... he let them in somehow. But now he's trying to stop them. Why?*

Homeless Man was back. "Because he's weak, that's why. Weak! Oh, you and your kind, you and your silly love of the angels!" It giggled, making a mocking face. "So strong, your little guardians. Yet your own rotten little book tells you that they are beloooooow you, human. So if *you* are so weak... what makes you think *they* can help you?"

The faces spun again until the old man resurfaced, his face teaming in desperation as he looked at Kyle intently. "Be ready, child."

Dumbfounded, it took Kyle a few seconds to realize that the old man was actually trying to help him. He stepped from the wall and called the blue to his hands again.

The old man was impeding the creature somehow, internally. It moved forwards, but in a herky-jerky motion, running and stopping, shuffling, then running again, at moments streaking towards Kyle and at others barely lumbering his way.

Looking into the creature's burning red eyes, Kyle felt himself going numb as some sort of paralysis overcame him.

The face of the old woman came cackling back. "You're gonna die now, sonny." But by appearing she had broken the numbness in Kyle, and this forced her to incur the wrath of Homeless Man, who came back with glistening teeth. Momentarily, two separate heads were visible, each on an elongated neck. The Homeless Man screamed at the old woman in a foreign language of some kind. Her face warped into desperate terror before their heads coalesced again. Homeless Man looked victorious as he once again fixed his attention on Kyle, but it was short-lived as the old man's face appeared again. "Now," he screamed to Kyle. "Now!"

Kyle launched the blue out of his fingers and it formed a solid, perfect orb between his hands. In awe, he wondered what to do with it now. Something told him to hold the orb in front of his chest and to launch it by pulling his left hand on one side of it while pushing with his right hand on the other.

With incredible velocity the orb spun true to target, striking the creature in the stomach, the spinning faces releasing a chorus of guttural screams. The shockwave nearly knocked Kyle off his feet. His right foot gave way and he almost fell on his face, but instead he used the wall to right himself.

Then, to Kyle's amazement, the creature grew, muscles bulging as it snarled at Kyle and clawed at its stomach before resuming its march towards him.

Calling again on the blue, Kyle was dismayed when all it did was light up in his hands and then sputter out. He'd used too much of it and it hadn't had time to recharge. No.

That was wrong. *He* hadn't had time to recharge. Weariness was overtaking him again.

He looked up to see the creature glaring at him with a hatred that spanned centuries and countless lives before him. Then, with reckless abandon, it pitched forwards at him, lowering its head and shoulder.

"No!" Kyle screamed.

The creature caught him square in the chest. Kyle partially deflected the blow, but it was like getting hit by a car. He skittered backwards along the wall, skin peeling off his arm when he swung it out for balance, the momentum spinning him around until he slammed hard against the brick.

He ducked as one clawed hand smashed the wall where his head had just been, shards of brick and cement cascaded over Kyle's face and down the back of his shirt.

He couldn't help himself. In a panic, he called for The Gray Man, but it was no use.

That's okay. I may die here, but Tamara will be safe. It's okay.

In pure desperation, Kyle pushed and clawed, kicked and punched at the behemoth upon him. It was like punching a bear. The creature only grunted, exhaling hot sprays of breath that reeked of hot mud.

I'm going to die. This is it. I'm—

The thought was shattered by a sensation in Kyle's chest that welled up like a balm against his terror and resignation. The blue came across him like a shield and erupted like a wave of lava over the creature. The creature's shrill cry was so loud it almost pierced Kyle's eardrums, and he scrambled backwards away from him.

"You little bastard!" it spat at him. "I will eat you one tiny bite at a time. I will butter your soul with the sorrow of those who will mourn you!"

It charged again, but it was seriously hurt now, bleeding some sort of tar from multiple wounds. Kyle dodged to one side, this time easily escaping any blows, as a clawed fist grazed the hair over his right temple.

Kyle spun around, and this time, at last, the blue came, filling his right hand, which he balled up and smashed over the creature's head.

It fell forwards, motionless for a moment before it rolled over slowly, and the slot machine faces came on again, spinning before finally stopping on the image of the old Arab man, his eyes full of relief as he looked up at Kyle. "Thank you," he said softly. "But it's my job to stop what I started."

The creature exploded in a mass of red light that enveloped the alley, the sky and the streets beyond. Blinded, Kyle grunted and fell backwards against a stack of empty cardboard boxes that collapsed and sent the rats that were nesting below them scrambling in all directions.

Then? Silence.

Looking up, Kyle saw the clouds in the sky above the alley drifting by. The ringing in his ears slowly subsided, allowing the sounds from the street beyond the alley to bleed in. Managing to get to one knee, Kyle stood up straight, his back cracking as he did. He felt as if he'd just gone twelve rounds with Joe Frazier.

If not for the old Arab man's help, he'd be dead. He was sure of it.

Leaning his face against a water pipe, he treasured the feel of its coolness.

Kyle shook his head. "God?" he asked. "Are you there?"

A car horn honked in the distance as a lone seagull wailed overhead.

That was all he got.

* * *

Just hearing the detective's voice brought Tamara to near panic.

"You better protect him! You better promise me you won't hurt him." There was conviction in her voice, but it was cracking with emotion.

"Take is easy. Tell me what's going on, Mrs. Fasano," Detective Villa replied.

"No. First you promise me that you'll keep him safe."

"I'll do my best to—"

"Screw that! You better *promise* me!"

Tamara heard hesitation in his voice before he finally blurted out, "Fine. I promise."

"He's gone to find his first girlfriend. From high school. I have no idea why. Her name is Victoria. She lives in Monterey and owns a business there, I think. He may know her home address too."

Again she listened as he hesitated, the silence on the other end of the line so long that for a second Tamara thought the call had dropped.

Finally he replied, "What gives you that idea?"

She swallowed hard. "I just got a card in the mail from him, this morning, for my birthday."

"What'd it say?"

"It doesn't matter what it said. He didn't do it, Detective Villa."

"Look, Mrs. Fasano, I don't have the time to debate his innocence right now. I understand that you think he's innocent—"

"Because he is!"

"—and that may be true, but his running away from us is not helping him. I think you know that. You're a smart woman, which is why you're calling me."

"Don't patronize me, Detective."

"I'm not, Mrs. Fasano," he replied, sounding exasperated. "To be honest, I don't have time for that shit."

She was shocked at first, and then opened her mouth to reply before he interrupted and continued.

"You want to save your husband? Fine! But we don't have the time to dance around no more. Do you know if he was having an affair with this woman too?"

"I don't know," she answered honestly. Guilt followed, and she added, "I don't think so." She realized that neither statement was a ringing endorsement for Kyle, but the time for half-answers and half-truths was just about over. So far he hadn't pried about the birthday card, which was good. If he did, she would have to tell him one more lie, and then it would be done.

"So do you know when he last contacted her?"

"No."

"Okay. What else?"

She held her breath for a second, and then she said, "I think he probably just left for there. I'm not sure, but the card was in the mailbox , Express Delivery, when I got home about two hours ago—"

"Why did you wait so long to call?" he scolded her.

"Will you let me finish?" Tamara snapped.

"Go ahead."

"I only just opened it, and then I had to search for your business card."

Silence. Her heart sunk. He had to buy it. He had to. She had to get to Monterey first, to Kyle, before they did. No matter what.

When he next spoke next it was with the overly calm and measured tone of a suspicious mind. "Okay, Mrs. Fasano. I'll tell you what. I'm going to send a cruiser over to your house right now for that card."

Shit.

"You… you can't… I'm… um… I'm not home."

"Can't we pick it up from whoever is there?"

"No. No, I have the card with me."

"Uh-huh. And where exactly are you, Mrs. Fasano?"

"Why? I mean, what does it matter? You have what you need."

There was a soft sigh at the other end of the line. "Mrs. Fasano. You're being evasive, and I think I know why."

"What?"

"You think you can help him, but you can't."

"I'm trying to help *you,* you idiot!"

He chuckled. "By what? By giving me the first name of maybe two thousand Victoria's who live in the Monterey area?"

"That's all I know."

"Fine. But you still never answered me. Where are you now, Mrs. Fasano?"

"What does it—"

"I'll send a cruiser to wherever you are to pick you up. We need that card."

It was painfully obvious that he was calling her bluff, so she lashed out. "You can't."

"Why is that?"

"Listen, Detective—"

"No, ma'am. I'm done listening. Now it's *your* turn to listen to *me.* Because now you're starting to get a little too smart for your own good; you're lying to me, which is really stupid."

"I'm not lying…"

"Really? By giving us just her first name and probably withholding her last? Tell me, Mrs. Fasano, how is it that you know this woman has a business? You'd need a full name to look that up, unless he told you that in the card too. Did he?"

She hesitated and he read her mind.

"Be careful how you answer, Mrs. Fasano. Because when we get that card, we're going to check. And if that card disappears, that card you say is with you in your car right now, the car I am going to tell you to turn around this second and drive to the police station, well, Mrs. Fasano… be careful and think about your kids here."

"Don't even go there."

"You have the only piece of solid evidence in this case right now. It needs to get to the right people," he said coolly.

Her mind began to race.

"Mrs. Fasano? Are you still there?"

"Yes. I mean… no. It doesn't say anything about her business in the card."

"So what's her last name?"

As panic began to overtake her, Tamara felt her throat clench. She clamped her mouth shut to keep from saying something she didn't want to. Then he surprised her.

"Mrs. Fasano, I'm going to help you out here, okay?"

"How?"

"Her last name is Brasco."

The word shattered her like a brick through a window. *Oh my God! They already know.*

"How do you know that?"

"Never mind. Just trust that we'll find him. What *you* need to do is simply turn around and go to Central Station on 1st Street downtown, okay? Ask for Detective Murillo or Detective Klink. Give them that card. I'm really trying to help you here. Go to the station and stay out of this."

One more lie wouldn't hurt. "I can't."

"Why?"

"Because I'm almost there."

"Where?" he sounded startled. "Monterey?" he asked firmly.

"Yes."

"That's funny," Detective Villa replied, "because so are we."

She was wrong, lies always hurt. They multiplied and came crashing down on your head in the face of the truth. She knew this. She preached it to her kids constantly. But she'd just proven that, when push comes to shove, none of us listen to our own advice.

"No," she squeaked.

"So turn your car around and go back. Now."

She looked at her GPS. She was still three hours away. She said nothing. Instead, she punched it, taking the car to 100 mph as she sped up the highway. When he spoke next it was from a million miles away. "Mrs. Fasano, you're not going to listen to me, are you?"

She bit into her lip, enraged and beyond control. "Don't forget that you promised me you wouldn't hurt him!"

"You're right, Mrs. Fasano. And I won't… if I can help it. But keep in mind that since the moment he went up into that hotel room with that girl? Your husband's been doing everything he can to hurt himself."

Tamara's heart sank, and her hands began to shake on the wheel. She was going to be too late. It was over.

All she had left was a desperate plea, which she flung at him with all the hope she had left in her heart. "Detective, please listen to me…"

"Go ahead, Mrs. Fasano."

Tears filled her eyes. "He loved his dad so much, Detective. Please. You have no idea."

Again, it sounded like she'd caught him off guard. "What?"

"His father… Detective, his father was everything to him."

"I'm sorry, Mrs. Fasano," he said, "but what does that—"

"He swore. In the card." She halted, a short sob escaping from her mouth before she was able to continue. "He swore on his father's soul that he didn't do it."

Silence again, this time longer.

"Got it," Detective Villa replied, the click as he hung up on her sounding very much like the click of a gun.

"Kyle!" she screamed, desperation scraping her voice across the glass of the windshield, the dark sky outside swallowing the road ahead of her, as if she were driving into an abyss of utter blackness.

CHAPTER 29

THE OVERTURNED BIG RIG took a mind numbing three hours to clear, and even then traffic in both directions was forced to use one lane, alternating turns with the help of one very pissed off looking California Highway Patrolman. In the meantime Napoleon stewed: the greeting card that Fasano had purchased at that CVS had been sent to his wife. The calling card just a ruse. This guy was just full of tricks and it had Napoleon a bit worried: what was next?

Once near the accident site Napoleon could see that it was a lumber spill that was going to take a lot longer to clear completely. Once past it, they took the 101 to the 68 and were now following the highway signs to the Naval School and beyond. From his GPS, Napoleon knew he had a choice coming up: either veer left and head up to the Quarry Park area where Fasano's ex-girlfriend lived, or go to the boardwalk where her wine shop was. He looked at his watch: it was just past six.

This was a tourist town, and that meant tourist hours. He Googled the wine shop and it was open until eight, seven days a week. Depending on how successful a business owner she was, Victoria Brasco could be grinding out the last hours of the day selling wine, or she could be at home right now in the hot tub while her employees closed up.

Shortly before getting to Monterey, Murillo had texted Napoleon to tell him that Monterey P.D. had been informed that Napoleon and Parker were coming, but they were short-staffed due to a carjacking gone bad that had left three dead. A Detective Medina was on call if they needed support or felt that an arrest was imminent. Remembering the delayed ATM notification from Beaury, Napoleon texted Murillo back with a hearty "thanks for getting my number right this time, jackass" and then asked him to track down the Brascos' phone numbers. It'd taken a while before Murillo texted him back with the information and a curt *"kayate guey"*, shut up dude.

But Napoleon had no intention of calling Victoria just yet. If Fasano was hiding out with his old flame the last thing they needed to do was tip them off that they were coming.

"Let's go to the wine shop first."

Parker seemed surprised. "You sure?"

"Yeah. It's closer by. We can clear it and then bounce to the house if we have to. It's about efficiency, rookie. Do I have to teach you everything?"

The Parker shrug followed. "Well… you are training me."

"Yeah, but shit, talk about a blank slate."

Parker laughed as he squinted at the road signs ahead. Napoleon noticed that for a nice town, Monterey lacked proper street lighting, especially over intersection signs.

They made their way downhill to Del Monte Ave, then merged right and drove through a tunnel to Cannery Row. Even at this hour the area was fairly busy and parking spaces were sparse. After driving a few blocks they doubled back and took a metered space in front of an abandoned dirt lot, an odd sight for such a beautiful area along the ocean.

"Too much car time, man," Parker complained as they got out and stretched.

"Ya think? We've been up and down the damn state three times in just as many days."

"And still—"

"—nothing."

"Yep. Feels like we may be getting close, though."

"True dat," Napoleon agreed, though he had a strange feeling that wasn't a good thing. They walked down the west side of the street past a few bars and restaurants, all of them advertising clam chowder. To this day, Napoleon equated eating a bowl of clam chowder with eating a bowl of hot puke. A series of collectible shops, clothing stores and nail salons greeted them next.

Before long they were at the boardwalk, the InterContinental hotel ahead and Bubba Gump's off to their right. The wine shop was across from the waiting area at Bubba Gump's. It was a perfect place to sit and wait for Mrs. Brasco to get off work.

Napoleon motioned for Parker to stop and step inside one of the stores, the Bombay Company, with him. They said nothing. Napoleon whispered for Parker to scan the crowd with him. After a few minutes, when they were absolutely sure Kyle Fasano was nowhere in sight, they headed into the wine shop.

The store was well lit, with a soft yellow glow that created a warm ambiance, and was divided neatly in half, with white wines along the left wall and reds along the right, and a mix of specialty wines and cheeses in the middle aisle.

Along the back wall was a tasting counter with a raucous crowd of wine drinkers. The girl serving them was a brunette and looked to be in her late twenties. Too young to be Victoria Brasco.

Napoleon and Parker were about to step to the counter when a thin man with a tapered mustache, long blond hair and blue eyes stopped them.

"Can I help you, gentlemen?"

Perhaps it was the way he stuck out his chin, as if he were a member of the wine aristocracy, but Napoleon decided at once that he didn't like him, so much so that he forgot to answer him, which left Parker to pick up the slack. "Yes. Is Victoria Brasco in?"

"Oh. I'm sorry. No. She stepped out."

"Hmm," Parker replied. "Do you expect her back?"

"Oh, yes. She usually comes back to make sure the store's locked up and all."

"Do you know where she went?"

The man pursed his lips and raised his eyebrows, exaggerating his distaste at being asked such a personal question about his boss. "Wellll… she went for a walk with a friend."

"A friend?" Napoleon pried.

This was the man's limit. "May I ask who you gentleman are?"

Napoleon had his badge out before the man even finished the sentence. "Detectives Villa and Parker, Los Angeles Police Department."

"Oh. My."

"Yes. We just need to contact her. It's important. Her safety could be at risk."

He was like a broken record now. "Oh. My."

Napoleon could feel his jaw tensing by the second.

Parker pushed on. "Do you know who the 'friend' was?"

"No, I'm sorry. I'm just a little shocked. She said he was an old friend that she hadn't seen in years."

The man's words felt like fists on Napoleon's chest. *Shit. Shit. Shit. We missed him. Again.* It was just before seven.

"How long ago was this?" Napoleon interjected.

"About an hour ago."

Right about when we were getting into town.

"Do you know which way they went?"

"Yes. Down the road, to the beach I think. Victoria mentioned Tully's, I think."

Napoleon grew tense. "Tully's?"

"It's a bar, about a block down on the left, by the Steinbeck statue."

Parker handed the man his card. "This is important. If they come back, you have to call me immediately, okay? The man she's with may be wanted."

"Oh. My."

He was like a damned parrot. One more time and Napoleon was going to have to hit him.

"Got it?" Napoleon asked.

"Why... yes. Of course."

When they were halfway out of the store, Parker spoke up. "How do you want to handle this? You want me to head to the beach and you take the bar?"

It made perfect sense, but something told Napoleon otherwise. "No. This bastard... there's something about him. We stick together. We take him down together."

If he disagreed, Parker did not show it. He simply stuck by Napoleon's side as he turned left and descended a set of wooden steps to the beach below. "Beach first. Bar after. Let's go with that. Besides, the beach will be easier to canvas," Napoleon added, motioning with his head to the ocean. "Less people to deal with."

"Yeah. I only see a few families, that old man with his dog and—" Parker halted his pace along with his voice.

"You see them too?" Napoleon asked, stopping alongside Parker.

"By the rocks, at the foot of that hotel?"

"Yep."

Night was falling, and from this distance they could have been anyone, but it was clear that they were a couple.

And they were arguing.

* * *

Their "dinner" together at Bella Cuore began to look more and more like a date to Kyle as it wore on. Victoria met Sebastian at the Italian restaurant right on time, at the end of the pier, a quarter-mile from the boardwalk.

When she arrived, she walked up to the restaurant with confidence and ease, seemingly at peace with the decision she was making.

Sebastian was waiting for her out front, dressed in his youthful style. He wore dark slacks and black shoes with a white shirt that was unbuttoned, revealing a leather necklace with an onyx rock on his chest. His hair was slicked back, and maybe it was the darkness or the lighting of the restaurant, but his skin was more olive in tone.

He also wore a big smile on his face, a youngster about to sink his claws into the cougar, with only the obligatory date meal in the way so she could respect herself in the morning.

It took all Kyle's strength not to walk up to them both, shove Victoria out of the way and pretty boy Sebastian into the wall. Kyle guessed that this wasn't how his "mission" worked. This was *her* choice, evidently, but at some point he would get an opportunity to intervene, he just hadn't figured out how or when yet.

He felt an uneasy pain when Victoria smiled back at Sebastian and hugged him, Sebastian's hand boldly lingering just above her butt and his thumb resting on the edge of her belt. She laughed and pushed him away gently. They were just pals on a night out. Her subsequent body language suggested to Kyle that she knew people in this town and would have to be careful.

He lost sight of them when they went into the restaurant, and was considering how he could get inside without a reservation when they reappeared and were seated in the front window, in clear sight of where he was standing. Kyle sighed. *Lucky break.*

The waiter pulled out Victoria's chair, beating Sebastian to the punch. Score one for the good guys. They laughed and talked throughout the appetizer and meal that followed, while Kyle counted the glasses of wine being served. By dessert they were on their third.

Kyle felt like a creep spying on them this way, but he knew he was just doing his job. After the alley fight, he decided he was done trying to figure out or plan any of this. He had to accept things as they happened, and this was especially true now that The Gray Man was gone.

An hour passed, during which Kyle moved from the kiosk to a bench, then over to a parked car to try and keep from attracting attention. Victoria and Sebastian finished dessert and seemed to talk softly for a moment.

Victoria lowered her chin and smiled. Sebastian chuckled, popped his eyebrows up, and then reached his hand ever so discreetly around the side of the table and closed it over Victoria's. She let it linger there for a moment, then pulled it away as the waiter brought the check.

Sebastian made a play for the check, but unless he was a rich kid doing his time at Starbucks before cashing out his trust fund, this restaurant was way beyond his means.

Victoria took the check and put her credit card into the leather folder. She seemed a little nervous now, one foot fidgeting beneath the table. She pursed her lips and shrugged sweetly, holding Sebastian's gaze just a little too long.

Kyle wondered how far this would go. The Gray Man had said that he was supposed to stop her from making the same mistake he had. So it made sense that he would have to stop them from having sex.

But only when it's obvious they're not going to turn back on their own.

Fair enough. He was okay with that; though he imagined there was no way it was going to be easy.

After they paid the check, Victoria excused herself, evidently to use the restroom, leaving Sebastian by himself at the table. Kyle expected Sebastian to pull out his cell phone and fire off an update text to his buddies about how close he was to getting some.

Instead, Sebastian just stared at a piece of cheesecake stuck to the end of his fork.

What's next, you bastard? Kyle thought.

The question seemed to travel across the plaza to the restaurant's window. Sebastian stopped what he was doing and looked outside. Kyle waited, sure that he was out of sight, but surprised nonetheless. Had he just "nudged" his thoughts at Sebastian? Like The Gray Man would always do to him?

What Kyle saw next ran a chill down his spine: Sebastian, still seated and alone, took the tip of his index finger and was slowly dipping it into the flame of the candle on the table. He flicked at it and, evidently having coated his finger in hot wax, seemed to take exquisite joy in the act. He pulled his finger back just as Victoria returned and they proceeded to leave the restaurant.

They passed a much older couple on the way out and Victoria, taking notice that the man was struggling to walk with his cane, stopped to hold the door and help guide him in, her hand briefly holding his elbow. The woman with him smiled and thanked her.

Once again, the decades between now and the time of Kyle and Victoria's romance collapsed, except this time the memory he recalled was not glazed in melancholy or loss, but instead glowed with love.

Victoria and Kyle's brother Vinnie sat on the back patio of Kyle's house each day after their homework was finished while Kyle would jabber with his buddies on the phone about fantasy baseball.

By then Vinnie's autism had taken so much, but not enough. His mind was intact just enough for Vinnie to know that he was different, too different to ever get a girl. When Kyle allowed himself to dwell on this as a young man, he would always shut out the thoughts; they were too much to bear.

Vinnie was his little brother, but Vinnie was going to trapped in that role the rest of his life. He would never assume the titles of "college graduate" or "career man," nor would he ever know what it was like to be a husband or a father. Though he loved his brother very much, Kyle could never see past the consequences of Vinnie's special needs, or see any way to help him.

But not Victoria. In her view, Vinnie was just as much a person as anybody else and his feelings were to be engaged and shared. The two of them developed quite the secret friendship, and when Kyle broke up with her, no one was more devastated than Vinnie.

"She was my gufend toooo, youknew!" Vinnie screamed at him that day, a few weeks before Kyle left for college.

Not knowing what to say, Kyle just hugged him, tears welling in both of their eyes as Kyle tried to explain that sometimes things just don't work out.

It was easy reasoning for someone who had such a blessing to squander, but to Vinnie it was beyond comprehension. He fell into a funk until the day before Kyle went to college, when Victoria called the house. Kyle assumed the call was for him, and was waving his mom off to say he wasn't home when his mother, surprised, simply said, "It's for you, Vinnie."

After he went off to college, Kyle heard about the occasional call or letter from Victoria, and how Vinnie would always glow for a day or two afterwards. In time though, the calls and letters stopped. Victoria tried. But evidently life took over and she moved on too.

Her laugh outside the restaurant pierced Kyle's thoughts and brought him back to the moment.

"No. I'm serious. My roommates are all home," Sebastian said to Victoria now that they were outside.

Kyle was happy to be able to hear them again as they walked past him in debate. The previous hour or so had been like watching a silent movie as he'd watched them through the restaurant window.

"My house?" Victoria said.

"My car's right down the street."

Victoria hesitated.

Kyle held his breath. *No. Don't do it, Vicki.*

Sebastian looked at her with puppy-dog eyes, a look he had evidently mastered. It worked. She smiled and nodded. "No. We'll take mine."

As they made their way down the street to Victoria's car, Kyle crept out from behind his hiding spot and began to follow them, taking one last look at the restaurant. A neatly dressed busboy was clearing the table, the clangs of the silverware and plates muted, the evidence of Victoria and Sebastian's dinner being wiped slowly away.

Kyle suddenly recalled the only scripture he'd ever taken the trouble to memorize: "For now we see through a glass, darkly; but then face-to-face: now I know in part; but then shall I know even as also I am known," he whispered, just beneath his breath.

The blue within him resonated in response to the words, this time much stronger than ever before, pure power, flooding his soul.

The entire world was a window of glass it seemed, and what you saw and heard from one side was not the same as what was being seen and heard on the other.

CHAPTER 30

I T WAS JUST PAST noon and for the last two hours she'd tried desperately to hold it, but she just couldn't any longer. Tamara was going to pee her pants. Her talk with the detective had pushed her nerves and emotions over the edge.

She was driving at a speed she hadn't thought her car could even reach. She was nearly doubled over at the wheel, nauseous and cramping, when she saw a small rest stop up ahead.

That can't be all that safe, but screw it. I'm not going to do Kyle any good peeing all over myself.

Braking as safely as she could, she took the turn into the rest stop still moving at about 30 mph, which jarred the car so hard that she bounced up and hit her head on the roof. She was shaking as she skidded into one of the parking spaces. It was an outright miracle that she didn't just flip her SUV.

As she got out of the car she was relieved to see a mother with her daughter, who appeared to be about nine, entering into the ladies room. She wondered where they'd come from since there were no other cars around.

Holding her thighs tight, Tamara walked in tiny steps as fast as she could across the parking lot and to the bathroom door, her bladder threatening to burst. Once inside, she took the last stall, the mother and daughter having already occupied the other two. She sat down and let go with a relief that made her head spin.

It's okay. One minute off the road. Two minutes in here. One minute back on the road. Four minutes total. It'll be okay. He'll be okay.

Finishing, she automatically reached for the toilet paper before realizing the stall was out of rolls. It didn't matter, to hell with wiping.

"Ew. What a dis-*gusting* thought!" a little voice said. Startled, Tamara was reaching down to pull up her pants when the little girl from the next stall scooted on her back across the floor and into Tamara's stall, a roll of toilet paper in her hand, her face peering up at Tamara in mock horror.

Tamara screamed and kicked her feet just as the child clutched for them. She was about to yell at her when she noticed the little girl's face begin to melt, peeling back in thin layers. "Ow, Mommy! It's happening again. Make it stop!" she screamed.

"What the hell?" Tamara yelled, yanking her pants up and launching herself into the back corner of the stall.

The girl stopped screaming and started whimpering before her mother finally answered. "It's okay, honey. It'll pass. We'll take care of this little whore, and then we can go back to where it doesn't hurt anymore."

Her voice cracked like embers on a dying fire, and Tamara was smothered in a wave of fear, the room going momentarily hazy.

No. Don't. You faint now and you die. Don't. Do. It.

She was just getting a grip when she looked down again. The mother's feet were on the other side of the stall door now, facing Tamara. She was trapped.

"When do I get to eat, Mama?" the girl said, her eyes now bulbous and draining, the sockets having mostly melted away to tiny red orbs.

"Soon enough, baby. Don't you worry."

Tamara screamed. "Help! Somebody help me!"

The mother laughed and then sighed deeply. "Why… there it is. Sweet fear. Ahhhh," she moaned. "And so soon, too."

Tamara looked down to see the little girl creeping further into the stall, sliding, no, slithering across the floor. Tamara's fear multiplied. "Help me! Somebody! Please!"

"Keep screaming. It's okay. Or why not pray, honey? See what that gets you."

More laughter, but this time it was short-lived; a sudden sizzle of energy cracked into the room. The presence Tamara felt, it was just like the night before in her bedroom, when that… thing… had attacked her.

It *was* real! If nothing else, this moment was proving that.

A brief silence followed, and then the mother's feet disappeared and a commotion broke out.

"What's happening?" Tamara moaned.

What was happening was a fight of some kind. The night before she'd been paralyzed in bed, her eyelids forced shut, but this time she was going to see, even though something in her told her not to look.

"Mom?" The little girl called out below her, and then, defying physics at a speed beyond imagination, she flipped onto her belly and scurried out of the stalls.

"You get out!" the little girl was shouting at someone. "This is the ladies room. You're not allowed in here! Get out! Get out! Get out!"

Recognizing her chance, Tamara buttoned her pants, but just as she attempted to open the stall door something slammed into it, forcing a yelp out of her as she jumped back again.

A reverberation moved through the room, rattling all the stall doors and making the floor roll in waves. A man's voice, distinct and authoritative, commanded, "Be quiet, little liar."

"Don't you speak to her that way," the mother screamed, and then she began to speak in a cacophony of languages. Tamara recognized what she thought might be Italian, German and Japanese, but Spanish she knew for sure. The woman was calling the man *Perro de Dios,* Dog of God.

Three loud booms shook the room, and something squealed in pain. Tamara couldn't take it anymore.

She flung the stall door open… and saw him.

He stood tall and was rail thin, his hue of gray both surrounding him and emanating from him in dissipating waves. Just the sight of him made Tamara drop to her knees and remember the cathedrals in Bolivia with the stone depictions of his type. He was so beautiful and so frighteningly powerful that she began trembling in his presence.

"She bows to you, and you aren't even worthy yet," the woman stuttered in complete disdain.

"Who are you to decide who is worthy?" The Gray Man replied.

Tamara couldn't believe what she was seeing; her heart was going to burst. He was an angel. As she kneeled on the floor, Tamara's body was awash in awe. It hurt to look at him, but she couldn't look away.

"I spit on you. I spit on your God!" the little girl cried, so melted away now that she was made of mostly muscle and sinew. Her hair remained in patches on her head though, like that of a badly burned doll, with only a few tufts left to brush.

"You, child, would spit on me? Aren't you the one who murdered your best friend? She was only nine."

"Shut up!" the girl shrieked. "She was prettier than me. I hated, hated, hated her!"

The Gray Man looked at her. "So what did you do? You knocked her over the head, didn't you?"

"Shut up!" the mother yelled.

Ignoring her, The Gray Man continued to focus steadily on the little girl. "Then you left her there, in the shed, and you set it on fire."

"No!" The little girl flung herself at him.

He swiped her away, knocking her effortlessly across the room and to the far wall.

Enraged, the mother launched herself at him and grappled at his chest and throat, but he held her at bay, continuing his focus on the girl.

"Come now, you hear the truth and still do not repent?"

"I'll eat you!" the little girl screamed and leaped onto one of the sinks. Her tongue slid in and out of her mouth, her eyes wide with hatred.

The Gray Man was unimpressed. "You killed her because her mother was still alive and yours wasn't, isn't that right?"

"You know nothing, God dog!" the mother clawed at him, scraping his face, forcing a wince.

At last he turned his attention to the mother. "She killed for *you,* because of *you,* the town harlot who went and found herself a good man to seduce. A man who accidentally killed you in a car crash, after a drunken drive across town."

"Mama! Tell him to stop. Tell him no, Mama. Tell him it's not true."

"You be quiet now, honey. I'll make him go away. You watch."

"And where's that man now, harlot?" The Gray Man asked as he established a tight grip on the woman's upper torso. She kicked at him in desperation.

"Oh, he thinks he's safe. He's hiding with that wife of his in the backwoods of North Carolina, limping to church and back every Sunday, because of the bad leg he got from the accident." The woman snarled, her fangs mere inches from The Gray Man's face, and continued, "As if that's going to help him. I sit next to him every night, you know, on the edge of his armchair, and I whisper in his ear. Oh, do you know how easily he forgets his prayers, God dog? How easily I can get him to touch himself and still think of the sex I gave him, all those years ago?"

Her laugh bounced wickedly across the cold porcelain floor and echoed against the stall doors. Tamara began to feel a strange pressure in her eyes.

The Gray Man took note of Tamara at last. "Child. Close your eyes. You aren't meant to see any of this."

At his command, she closed her eyes and lowered her head, oddly both overjoyed and utterly terrified by his presence.

"Woman, you tempt him to evil, and yet still he repents, time and again, struggling to forgive himself for what he did back then."

"He'll never make it. I'll see to it."

"You know. I believe you'll try," The Gray Man said, his voice lowering. "But The Father will try harder."

Crackling energy began to envelop the room, bringing a sudden, carnal fear to the woman's voice. "Charlie. Run to me! Now! Mama's going away. Quick!"

There was a rapid scampering of feet across the floor, then a lightning bolt of force shot through the room, singeing the hair on Tamara's arms. When the crackle passed, the room went still, the only sound that of Tamara's weeping.

Seconds passed, but Tamara sensed that he was still there.

Suddenly, she felt his hands cup her cheeks and his thumbs gently rest on her eyelids. Instantly the pain in her eyes was gone.

"Shhhh. No more tears, Tamara Fasano."

His voice, soft now and loving, only made her cry all the more.

"You're real. It's all real. Please. Will I forget all this?" she asked him.

"Do you want to?"

Her heart swelled as she shook her head gently. "No."

"Then you won't," he said. Then he and his touch were gone.

She opened her eyes to the cold glare of the fluorescent lights as they reflected off the mirrors. Instinctively, she forced herself to run to her car, and mostly stumbled her way there before she crawled inside, her legs like jelly. She started the car and desperately looked at the dashboard clock in disbelief. It was just past 4:00 p.m. How? How had she lost nearly four hours?

She prayed, trying to calm her nerves as she pulled back out on to the highway, the road ahead stark beneath the glare of her headlights, only the yellow strips of the dividing lines offering any proof at all that she was really moving as they sped by at a rapid-fire pace.

She would get to Kyle. She would.

CHAPTER 31

THE COLD CHILL OF the night kicked up off the ocean as Napoleon and Parker walked the length of the beach, the couple growing closer with each step.

"How you wanna do this?" Parker asked.

"If it's him, the steps up to the street are right behind him, so that's the only direction he can run without trying to get past us."

"Hard to tell for sure if it's him from this distance."

"Yeah. And two guys walking up the beach in dress shirts and ties towards them is hardly low profile."

"He probably changed his appearance too, right?" Parker asked.

"I dunno. The hair dye, beard and mustache growth, all that shit. Might be hard. But I got a plan." Napoleon moved wisely to the wet sand, which was easier to walk on.

"Yeah? Okay. Well, you share that plan whenever you're ready, but I think I'll at least be able to recognize *her*."

"Yeah? Okay. Make sure. Those internet photos, the newspaper pic, they might be outdated."

"Got it."

Fortunately, the couple was arguing so heatedly and their attentions were so riveted on each other that they didn't even notice Napoleon and Parker approaching.

The closer they got, the harder it was for Napoleon to fight the urge to just break into a bold run. The man was in a navy jacket and jeans, and looked to be about the same height as Kyle Fasano; the woman was a brunette with the same frame as Victoria Brasco, as best as he could recall.

This could be it. Finally. It was one thing to track down a professional felon, but to have a normal Joe put them through the ringer like this was getting to be embarrassing.

At ten yards Napoleon made his move, motioning Parker to the left as he stepped to the right of the couple. His plan was nothing fancy, just to walk right up with his fists clenched and say…

"Kyle Fasano?"

The man turned, not aware of how close he was to getting clocked in the face. Napoleon didn't need the bewildered, quizzical look of the man to confirm that he wasn't Fasano. His body language was neither aggressive nor flighty. He turned, irritated at being interrupted, and looked right at them. Out of the corner of his eye, Napoleon saw Parker pull up short too. The man was ten to fifteen years too old to be their guy, and that only added to the obvious; up close he looked nothing like Fasano.

"Do you mind?" the man asked while the woman he was with looked away in embarrassment.

Out of habit Napoleon scanned the woman's neck, shoulders and arms for bruises. He'd walked away from too many domestic dispute calls as a patrol officer only to have to go back again later to see the carnage that happened afterwards. Seeing she was clear of any marks, Napoleon looked to Parker to do the mop up.

"Our apologies, guys, we thought you were somebody else."

Napoleon could tell the man was about to pop off before the woman took one look at Napoleon and pulled on her companion's arm. *But of course.* She looked like money, from her Lacoste shirt to her Gucci bag. They raised them the same in all the nice neighborhoods, to beware of the darkies. Napoleon shook his head and turned on his heels, heading back down the beach.

"The bar?" Parker said aloud as he caught up with him.

"Yep. It's next on the list. Let's hope they're slow drinkers, or ordered a second round to reminisce about their first kiss or some shit."

They double-timed it back to the bar, Parker taking it in easy strides, unburdened by the extra twenty years or twenty pounds that Napoleon carried. By the time they got back to the pier, Napoleon was completely out of breath. Still, he took the salt-bleached wooden steps in twos, feeling the strain on his heart, and kept moving until he reached the front door of the bar, the word "Tully's" emblazoned on a neon sign in blue and red over the entrance.

This time they did split up, perusing the dining tables one by one, from opposite sides of the restaurant area. The place was pretty full, with only a few tables open and one stool left at the bar. They stayed within sight of one another, walking deliberately through the place, giving the hostess the impression they were just looking for someone they were supposed to meet.

When Napoleon got to the bar, he motioned for the bartender.

A stout man with a gray goatee and a round face, the bartender threw a towel over one shoulder and approached. "What can I get ya?"

Wanting to expedite the process and demand the desired attention, Napoleon flashed his badge, sparing the LAPD bit this time.

It worked. Raising his eyebrows the bartender asked, "What's up?"

"Did you see a guy in here, around six feet, dark hair, athletic? He might've been with a smallish brunette?"

Napoleon watched as the bartender scanned his memory, and then he tried to nudge him a bit more. "He would've had brown eyes and a square jaw."

The bartender shook his head slowly, and then something registered. "No. Not tonight. But there *was* a dude in here last night, jumpy as shit actually, that might've been your guy."

Parker finally joined them at the bar and Napoleon wasted no time. "Last night?"

The bartender's nod became more affirmative the more he thought about it. "Yeah. Brown eyes. Built like a baseball player."

Again with the baseball player description. Evidently it was accurate.

"That might've been him," Napoleon said. "And the girl?"

"No. He was alone."

Parker reached into his jacket pocket and pulled out his phone. He'd saved a photo of Kyle Fasano on it and he showed this to the bartender. "This look like him?"

"Holy shit! Yeah. He has a beard started now but, yeah, that's... wait a minute! Is this the guy who killed the girl in LA?"

He'd said it too loudly. The patrons at the bar stirred, some even looking over as their hushed conversations stopped.

Napoleon shot the bartender a look. "Keep it down, will ya?"

"Yeah, man. Sorry. But is it?"

Napoleon nodded.

"Shit. In here? Damn. What're the odds?"

"Not good if we don't find the girl he's with."

"Well… we get a lot of girls in here, guys. Tourists and shit."

Parker shook his head. "No. This one's a local. She owns a business nearby."

"Really? Who?"

Napoleon and Parker exchanged looks, visually agreeing that they had no choice but to clutch at straws now.

"Victoria Brasco. She owns the—"

"Wine shop," the bartender said, cutting him off. "Yeah. I know her well. She and her husband come in here from time to time. No way was she at the bar tonight. I woulda known. Five hours into my shift and no break yet."

"Okay," Napoleon said, deflated.

"One of the guys that works for her said she was with him and might stop by here," Parker added.

The bartender bunched up his face, making it redder than it normally was, his eyes flashing with confusion. "Guy? Far as I know, only Lori and Becca work for Victoria, unless she just hired him or something, which is news to me."

Napoleon felt his stomach drop. There was no rational explanation, just instinct again, but he felt that something was profoundly off. He looked at Parker and could see the rookie was feeling the same way.

"Anything you can tell us about last night?" Parker asked, breaking out his notebook.

"Like what?"

Napoleon sighed. "What was he wearing?"

"Hard to forget: jeans, a blue t-shirt and a blue hat."

In all his years, Napoleon rarely heard a witness rattle off facts in such a rapid-fire fashion. "It sounds like he made an impression. Did he get into a fight or something?"

The bartender scoffed. "Yeah. With the damn flat screen."

This time it was Parker's turn to make a face. "The what?"

"The television. Too bad Lenny's not in here tonight. He was right next to the guy when he flipped out."

"How?" Napoleon asked.

"Ya know. He musta been high or something. All I gave him was a beer. The game was on, then…" The bartender was distracted by a guy who was motioning for another drink at the other end of the bar. "Hold on, Ted. I'll be right there." Turning back to Napoleon, he rolled his eyes. "As if he needs it. Anyway, where was I?"

"The game was on. Benny was next to…" Parker prodded.

"Lenny," Napoleon interjected.

"Yeah. Lenny was next to him…"

"Oh. Yeah. So at halftime they do the news, that hurricane or whatever in Hawaii?"

Being on the Golden State road tour the last few days, Napoleon hadn't heard of any hurricanes, but he nodded anyway. "Go on."

"According to Lenny, the guy just starts freaking out over the screen, mumbling shit about angels and demons. Next thing we know he's stumbling around… tripped on a table and knocked shit all over the place, tried to bail but I called him on his tab. He paid up and then off into the night he goes, like the Phantom of the Opera or something."

Napoleon squinted and bit down on the inside of his cheek. Everything with Fasano was just getting weirder and weirder.

"Anything else?" Parker asked.

The bartender thought about it. "Nah. Nothing I can think of."

"Okay. Thanks."

"Victoria's not in any danger, is she?" the bartender pried.

"We hope not. Here's my card," Napoleon said, sliding it across the bar.

"Got it. Is it okay to tell her you guys are looking for her if she comes by?"

"Absolutely. Let us know if she does."

The bartender nodded and turned back to the bar. "Okay, Ted. Calm down, brother. I got your scotch coming, for shit's sake!"

They left the restaurant quietly and more than a little bit confused. Napoleon could feel it in Parker, and he imagined Parker could feel it in him.

"What now?" Parker said, exasperated.

"Back to the wine shop," Napoleon answered.

"I knew that," Parker said.

"Then you shouldn't have asked."

Parker chuckled and shook his head as they walked down the sidewalk. "Was your first case this jacked up?"

At that, Napoleon had to laugh, in spite of his mood. "Not even close. Double homicide. Rival gangs. Easy as a cake in an Easy-Bake oven."

"Funny. My sister and I always used to burn ours."

They chuckled and turned right on to the boardwalk. The line at Bubba Gump's had died down, and the rumbling of people within the restaurant was nearly extinguished. At the wine shop, they found the girl that was tending to the tasting bar earlier, now locking up for the night.

"Excuse me," Napoleon said.

The girl jumped back, startled. Napoleon and Parker showed their badges before she could slam the door on them. "Police. We're looking for Victoria Brasco."

She was a smart girl and looked at the badges closely. "Victoria? She's never here this late. She usually leaves at about six each day."

Napoleon nodded. "Really? The guy we spoke to earlier said she had left here about seven or so?"

Napoleon knew what was coming before she even said it.

"Guy?" the girl said. "What guy?"

Parker seemed annoyed. "What's your name?"

"Becca."

"Hi, Becca. I'm Detective Parker. This is Detective Villa. We spoke earlier to a gentleman working here, and he said she left with a guy and was headed to the beach or over to Tully's."

Becca was bemused. "Uh. Sorry, fellas, but we don't have a guy that works here. You sure he wasn't a customer or something?"

Napoleon felt his face flush red. "Well. Maybe he was. He acted like he was an employee though."

"Yeah. Sorry. No. But Victoria will be back in tomorrow at ten. Do you need her number?"

"No," Parker said. "We have it, but we haven't been able to reach her."

"Okay. Well. I'd offer to help, but I've gotta get home. My baby has whooping cough and my boyfriend is going out of his mind."

Napoleon nodded and stepped back. "That's fine. We'll try and reach her again."

"Sorry I couldn't be more help," Becca said.

"No worries," Parker said.

Becca closed and locked the door.

Napoleon turned to walk back to the car and had only taken a few steps when something on the ground caught his eye. He stooped down and picked it up. It was a business card.

Parker's business card.

And it had a hole burned right through the middle of it.

At his side immediately, Parker was stunned. "What the…"

Napoleon turned the card over a few times. Something told him to smell it, so he did, bringing it up to his nostrils for a whiff before jerking his head away.

"What?" Parker asked.

"Sulfur," Napoleon answered, his voice flat in his own ears.

"What?" Parker asked. Napoleon offered up the card and Parker snatched it from his hand and smelled it with the same reaction.

Putting his hands on his hips, Napoleon turned to the street and leaned his head back to look up at the stars before taking a deep breath and exhaling. "Man, oh man, oh man," he said.

"What does this shit mean?" Parker murmured in frustration.

Napoleon gave a short laugh, but it was absent any humor. "It means that we've fallen right down the rabbit hole, rookie."

Swallowing hard, Napoleon closed his eyes and began to run through the options before he stopped himself. It was no use. This case was beyond him. Period. He thought of the trucker at the rest stop again. *Drive back home. Stay there. Die lonely.* He thought of Beecher's devil worshipper's theory. Lastly, he thought of Kyle Fasano, that great mastermind of crime, who had managed to elude them all this time, ranting and raving about angels and demons just one night before, while he tripped and stumbled his way out of Tully's.

Parker sighed. "I don't even wanna say it…"

"What next?" Napoleon guessed.

"You got it."

Before them the night sky had finally arrived and was now in full bloom, stretched out over the sea like a shroud, its stars muted and the moon present but playing shy behind a bank of mostly invisible clouds.

Napoleon sighed. "We're going to Victoria Brasco's house."

"I knew that," Parker replied.

CHAPTER 32

KYLE FLAGGED A CAB from the front of the restaurant as soon as they left. There was no rush. He'd overheard where they were headed, Victoria's house, and he still had her address scrawled on the piece of scrap paper from the library.

When he got to the house, he quietly made his way to the front door and found it closed but unlocked. They'd obviously entered in a hurry, probably anxious to get on with things.

Kyle couldn't believe he was doing this, but he was.

He entered the house cautiously; it was completely dark inside. He could hear the sound of a woman singing and strained to identify the song before it finally came to him: "Scarborough Fair." It was playing from somewhere deep in the house, the words ushering him forwards.

Are you going to Scarborough Fair?

To his right was a living room with a couch and two chairs arranged around what looked like a glass coffee table; a massive flat screen television was mounted to the wall. His eyes hadn't completely adjusted yet so it was hard to make out the smaller details of the room, but he could see some bookshelves with large and small framed photos neatly arranged on them.

Parsley, sage, rosemary and thyme…

To his left was a formal dining room with a large wooden table and ten chairs. A bowl of fruit was centered on a round, checkered piece of linen in the middle of the table.

Remember me... to one who lives there...

He made his way further down the hall, passing a half-bathroom to his right, the mirror over the sink reflecting his movement and making him jump. Opposite the bathroom was a stairway that led upstairs. He stopped to listen.

She once was a true love of mine...

The music wasn't coming from upstairs, but instead from somewhere up ahead and to the right. He crept along, instinctively sticking to the wall on the left side of the hall.

As he got closer to the sound, he could see the kitchen to his left. It was enclosed on one side with a counter and three stools; there was an island counter in the middle with pots and pans hanging overhead. A faint light was coming from the den, opposite the kitchen.

He realized it was candlelight just as he heard their soft whispers and moans.

Tell her to make me a cambric shirt...

He peered around the corner and there they were, locked in a tangled embrace on the couch, Victoria on top. Sebastian's head was clasped in her hands as they kissed passionately. Kyle felt no jealously, only dread. What was he supposed to do now?

Parsley, sage, rosemary and thyme...

They were still dressed, but Sebastian was trying to do something about that, pulling at the buttons on Victoria's blouse.

"Ah, ah, ah..." she teased, pushing his hands away.

Unable to get to what he wanted from underneath her blouse, he instead began to softly squeeze her breasts through it, and their kissing became more feverish.

Without any seam nor needlework…

Victoria reached down between Sebastian's legs and he arched his back in pleasure.

"Do you like that?" she asked.

"Yes," Sebastian whimpered.

Then she'll be a true love of mine…

Kyle didn't know how much more of this he could take. Waiting for her at Starbucks, following her, watching her from outside the restaurant—all these things were bad enough. But to watch this? He felt uncomfortable, as if he were doing something wrong, but still had no idea what to do next. His mission so far was to find Victoria. To prevent this somehow. But when?

Ask him to find me an acre of land…

The Gray Man was gone, but Kyle decided to try to reach him. It couldn't hurt. He stilled his breath, closed his eyes to the scene before him and reached out with his mind.

"What do I do?" he whispered.

At first there was only silence. Then, clear as day, he heard him in his mind: "Remember what I told you."

Kyle gasped at the sound of The Gray Man's voice. Again, he whispered. "What? What did you tell me?"

Silence.

Parsley, sage, rosemary and thyme…

Moans of passion began to echo from the den. Kyle kept his eyes closed, trying to concentrate and hear even a whisper of The Gray Man's voice, until he heard a sudden protest.

It was Victoria. "No. I'm sorry. I can't do this."

Sebastian chose to ignore her. She pulled back from him a bit, so he gripped his fingers in her hair and pulled her back in for another kiss.

Between salt water and the sea strands…

It was brief, and then Victoria tried to pull away again. "No. I mean it. I can't."

"Whatya mean?" Sebastian whined.

"This isn't right. It isn't you. I promise. It's—"

In the moments that Kyle's eyes had been closed, Sebastian had somehow managed to undo her blouse, revealing a lacy white bra underneath. "C'mon. Don't be a tease," he complained, cupping one breast with his hand and grabbing at her butt with the other.

Victoria shifted her weight and pulled away, her right hand slapping his left hand off her bra. "Hey, I mean it!"

This was it. Kyle could see it now. Sebastian wasn't going to take no for an answer.

Then she'll be a true love of mine.

The song finished and faded softly away.

Sebastian looked at her with eyes of want and command. "I'm tired of waiting. I want it. I want *you*."

Kyle was just stepping out from his hiding place to intervene when Victoria's voice went cold, her reply curt and tinged with annoyance. "You know what? I'm tired of waiting too."

And with that, she pulled a large butcher knife from beneath the couch cushion behind Sebastian's head and stabbed him in the right side of his chest.

It was as if the entire universe had punched Kyle in the face. He froze.

Sebastian looked up at Victoria in shock and dismay, and then tried to pull away. But she closed her slender left hand around his throat, and with a strength that seemed beyond her, she viciously banged his head against the side table, twice, the sickening thud of bone on wood echoing through the house. He was still conscious, but barely.

Spinning off him, Victoria turned around, her blouse flying open and revealing her breasts in the lacy white bra, her eyes... glistening black orbs.

Kyle stood there in the hallway, unable to move, as her mouth pulled back in a sneer of contempt and her pure white teeth birthed into long fangs.

"It's about time you got here, sweetie," she said, "because I've been waiting twenty long years for this."

* * *

After breaking nearly every speed law imaginable between the tiny rest stop and Monterey, Tamara's GPS announced the arrival at her destination: Victoria Brasco's house was just up ahead, a single car parked in the driveway.

Tamara parked and got out of the car just as an unmarked sedan sped up the driveway behind her. For a second she thought of bolting for the house but... then what? The sun had just gone down. Was she going to bang on the door after dark? What if Kyle wasn't even here?

The car came to a stop, and Detective Villa jumped out. "Mrs. Fasano! Stop right there."

She did as she was told as they approached her, two figures, outlined by the light from their car's headlights.

"You can't stop me," she said.

Detective Villa disagreed. "You're trespassing."

"Did the homeowner call that in, or are you making shit up?"

Having been blasted by their headlights it was hard to see clearly, but Tamara thought Detective Villa's partner was... smiling.

"What's so funny, Detective... what was it again?"

338

"Parker, ma'am. Sorry. But this whole day has been a joke."

"When did you get here?" Detective Villa asked her.

"Just now. I was wondering if anyone is home and what to do if they are."

They were all speaking softly. Besides her car and theirs, there was a Silver Mercedes SL parked in the driveway.

"I thought I told you to drive that greeting card of yours to the station."

"Did you say that? I don't recall."

This time Detective Parker actually laughed. "Well... okay. There ya go."

"Parker," Detective Villa said curtly.

"Sorry, man. But...I mean, what in the *hell* is next?"

Tamara spoke up. "I don't know, but the three of us standing out here in the dark isn't helping anybody."

She watched as Detective Villa scanned the front of the house. It was a large, two-story, modern brick home, luxuriously landscaped with a slate porch and white fence balcony.

"Most of the lights are out, at least in the rooms you can see from here," she said.

"Yeah. You see anyone?" Detective Villa asked, then looked at her sternly. "And don't lie this time."

"No. I was just mustering the courage to go knock on the door."

Detective Parker raised his eyebrows. "And say what? 'Hi! You used to boff my husband as a teenager. How're things going?'"

"Parker," Detective Villa said, rolling his eyes.

"Yeah. That's exactly what I was going to say," Tamara retorted. "Right after I asked her if two dumb-ass detectives from LA had contacted her yet."

Detective Parker put his hands on his hips and shook his head.

"We haven't been able to reach her. But we're here now, and it looks like someone's home. You should leave," Detective Villa said, sounding weary.

"And?" Tamara asked.

"And I know you won't."

"So what, then?"

"You're going to stay right here while we go speak to Mrs. Brasco. I like you, Mrs. Fasano, but if you get out of line or interfere with this conversation, I will arrest you on the spot for interfering with a police investigation. I give you my word on that. You understand?"

Tamara looked at him in earnest, calling to mind their earlier conversation about Kyle. "Only if your word still means something. Does it, Detective?"

He looked her and nodded. "You're damned straight."

Every fiber of her body begged her not to, but she stepped out of their way and leaned against the door of her car, folding her arms in protest.

Detective Villa nodded at his partner, and they proceeded to go a few steps up the driveway just as a scream came from inside the house.

The detectives halted, and then broke for the door.

They never made it.

In stunned amazement, Tamara watched as a wall of white appeared in front of them, and the gray angel that had saved her at the rest stop stepped out from it.

Both detectives skidded to a stop, then fell backwards in shock.

Tamara's eyes filled with wonder and thanks as she looked at the calm face and confident eyes of the man before them. His very presence radiated strength and hope.

It was The Gray Angel again.

And he'd come to save her husband.

CHAPTER 33

KYLE LOOKED AT VICTORIA and was filled with horror, the shock in him melting away far too slowly as she advanced. He spoke but could barely hear himself. "No."

She crouched like a ghoul and began to creep her way towards him. "Oh, yes. You stupid man. You stupid boy!"

The blue in him pulsed, beginning to build, and still he couldn't move. *How can this be? How?*

"It took a lifetime, my love," she said in a mocking tone.

She was reading his mind, his thoughts, just like The Gray Man could.

But he was able to stop that now, to shield himself if he wanted to. He willed his mind closed.

"Oh. Don't go all quiet on me now," she said, curving her lips down into the mask of a sad little girl.

Sebastian moaned in the background, and Kyle briefly glanced his way. Blood was pooling in his shirt and on his temple.

"Victoria. Why?"

She was closer, perhaps only twenty feet away, stepping into the hallway to join him. "Do I have to explain it to you?" she sneered, using her tongue to lick her teeth. "He's a fool. Eyes all full of want. He was simply meat for pleasure."

"Victoria—"

"Sort of like what I was to *you*."

Her words pierced him. He blinked and swallowed, his throat going dry, as he began to see her more clearly. The tongue she kept licking her teeth with was long and sharp, and on each of her shoulders there was a single small spike. This couldn't be real. "Victoria—"

"Stop calling me that."

"You were never meat—"

"No, no, no. We aren't going to have *this* conversation."

"But…"

"I knew they were going to send someone for me. The Master said so. I didn't know who though, until this morning, in the coffee shop."

"You saw me?"

"Of course I saw you. What? Now you wanna know why I didn't say 'hi'?" she laughed. It was a laugh of hubris mixed with hate.

Kyle shook his head in disbelief. "I never meant to hurt you…"

She crept closer, one small step.

"Oh, please." She slammed the bottom of her fist against the wall, launching the collage of framed photos hung on it down to the hard floor below, glass shattering everywhere. "Spare me the bullshit. I've heard it before, the night you dumped me."

"No… please, listen."

"Do you want to know what all these were?" she asked, waving her right hand across the photos on the floor. "A simple construct of what I thought a happy life would be."

His eyes darted across the photos; a few were of her and her husband, others were of her kids. "It still can be."

"*Can* be?" she screamed. "It. Never. Was. No matter what I tried, I was never happy again. It was never the same with anyone else."

Adrenaline joined the blue. She was getting too close.

"Why?" he stalled, trying to plan what to do next.

Stopping her advance, she simply looked at him, cocking her head first to the right and then slowly to the left, as if she were studying a mold or germ in a petri dish. The black in her eyes shrunk into a piercing stare. "You've changed, you know."

Kyle stepped forwards from his spot in the hallway. They stood directly opposite one another on the black and white checkered tile floor, like chess pieces on a board. "How?"

"You're softer. Weaker. That girl, Caitlyn, right? She stole so much from you, even more than your wife ever did."

"How do you know?"

"About what? The girl or the wife?"

He had to keep stalling until he figured out what to do. "Both."

Sebastian stirred and saw them, a look of disbelief swimming over his face.

Victoria looked over at him and reached out her arm. Kyle couldn't believe his eyes as she levitated Sebastian. "No!" he screamed.

She smashed Sebastian, up and down, repeatedly, on the coffee table in front of the couch, his limbs flopping loosely in all directions like a rag doll's as he was knocked unconscious.

Instinctively, the blue pulsed to Kyle's hands, catching her attention immediately.

"Ahhh," Victoria sighed. She closed her hand into a fist then opened her fingers; Sebastian dropped to the floor. "Now my Romeo shows his true colors."

"Victoria, I don't want to do this…"

She mocked him. "Oh! Victoria! Tell me about your sorrows. Tell me about your fam-i-lee." She laughed. "And why… they… never… made… you… happy."

"Stop it. Don't do this."

"Tell me all your troubles, while I prepare to kill you."

He was stunned. "I'm not here to kill you."

"Ohhh? Really?" she glared, the whites of her eyes forming a thin disk around the black orbs. "How sad. I think you actually believe that, honey, but sorry. Sadly, you've been misinformed."

"What?" Kyle was confused. He thought back to what The Gray Man told him. What did he mean by "remember what I told you"? That meaning was the key to all of this; he knew it to his core. But what was it?

She sighed and gave him a pitiful look. "It's you and me to the death, my dear. That's how this works."

"No."

She suddenly stepped forwards and grabbed him by his shirt, the tips of her claws digging into his chest. "Yes."

She was pulling him close when the blue shot out of his chest and crackled. She screamed and stepped back. Knocked off balance, Kyle fell and scrambled to stand up, calling a pool of blue to each hand, and began to form an orb.

"Seriously?" she said with a sneer. "You're going to beat me with *that*?"

From seemingly out of nowhere, a spiked tail whipped from behind her, black and gleaming. It shot forwards and split the orb in half, right in his hands. Kyle charged and pushed her backwards, the blue in his hands burning into her.

Her tail shot forward again, and this time it was Kyle's turn to scream as it slashed him across his chest, gouging and tearing his skin and barely missing his throat.

So this was it. He realized with a certainty that Victoria had her mission and he had his. She was here to kill Sebastian tonight, and Kyle was here to save him. This had never been about saving Victoria from anyone else. It was about saving the boy, and maybe even saving Victoria from *herself.*

All of this cosmic chaos, and his entire mission, was balancing on the life and soul of Sebastian, lying there in the den, bleeding out quickly.

"Do you remember when you looked into my eyes and told me that you'd love me forever, Kyle? You lied, didn't you?" she said, looking at him intently. "Now… why don't you try looking me in the eyes just one more time."

Her eyes went from a glistening black, to a dull, flat and menacing black. The color of a shark's eyes. The color of death on the approach.

He let the blue flow freely from each hand, forming strands that slowly turned into whips. "Please, Victoria, don't do this," he replied.

Reaching behind her, Victoria used her right hand to carve the air.

Kyle thought he'd seen it all. He hadn't.

She sliced the very fabric of reality, through the atoms that made up the space between things, in a lazy "s," and a hole of some kind opened right there by the kitchen, a hole to another world. A cosmic wind from that world blew in hot and full of tortured screams.

Kyle was in awe. How many times had his pastor said it?

Just a veil. A very thin veil.

Between this world and the spirit world.

And Victoria had just breached it.

* * *

"Nap? Nap!" Parker was screaming, scooting back in panic from the man in front of them.

Napoleon was without words, but for Parker's sake, he tried. "Hey… it's okay. Shh. Take it easy, rookie."

As a lifelong cop, he'd learned the art of description. A vic, a perp, it made no difference; description was everything. It told a story. But what his eyes were seeing now was nearly indescribable. A man in a gray suit and wearing a gray fedora stood before them. He seemed human but evidently wasn't, or at least wasn't any form of human that Napoleon had ever seen before. And he… glowed, that was the best way to put it, in a gray aura that was a shade or two lighter than his suit. He face was chiseled, with a square jaw and firm cheekbones, and his eyes glowed in the lightest gray of all, almost white.

But there was something else about his presence; a sort of announced power, or proof of said power, that was beyond this world entirely. And it seemed to have rocked Parker to his core.

"Oh my God!" Parker screamed, falling onto his back and shielding his eyes.

There. That was it: a pretty close description of the man before them.

Good for you, rookie, Napoleon thought. *You got it.*

No more surprises. No more confusion. They were either both having the same hallucination or they were both looking at an angel. An angel of God who appeared like a man.

Napoleon thought instantly of his grandmother. "A thin veil, that's all that stands between us and the angels," she had said that fateful day with the pigeons on the rooftop.

3 4 7

Amen.

Tears filled his eyes as he struggled to one knee in the driveway of the Brasco residence and repeated aloud what he'd said that day as a child: "*Si, Abuela. Es cierto. Te creo.*" *Yes, Grandmother. I believe. It is true. I believe you.*

Then life had happened, with all its dull punches and sharp elbows, and he'd stopped believing.

Even in awe, Napoleon still tried to grab hold of some sense of order. The Gray Man seemed to be there for a reason. He stepped forwards and looked at them intently before suddenly looking back to the house.

The white wall behind him disappeared and he stood still a moment before glancing at Napoleon and, more intently it seemed, at Parker, whose fear of him seemed to pain The Gray Man somehow. Napoleon had forgotten about Mrs. Fasano entirely until The Gray Man looked lastly at her and nodded slightly, as if they'd met before.

This seemed to awaken Napoleon's sense of reason. "What's going on?" he asked.

No sooner had he asked the question, than the sound of a fight erupted from inside the house. Glass was shattering and there was yelling now.

Parker rolled over to one side and curled up, holding his hands to his face like a frightened child, obviously in some state of shock. Napoleon tried to stand up, but couldn't. The Gray Man looked at him and said firmly, "We cannot interfere."

"Kyle?" Tamara screamed as she moved towards the house.

"No," The Gray Man said. He waved his hand in her direction and she stopped cold, as if her body had betrayed her and she were helpless to push on.

"What? No. He needs our help! What are you doing?"

"Mrs. Fasano, Tamara, I know this is going to be hard for you to accept. But this is bigger than just one man; bigger than just your husband. He is fighting for so many more."

"What do you mean?" Amazingly, it was Parker again.

"Things are in motion," The Gray Man said, looking over his shoulder. "Things far beyond your jurisdiction, Detective."

The inside of the Brasco home began to erupt in color, mostly a soft blue that fluctuated and flashed like lightening.

"It's begun," The Gray Man said, his shoulders slouching in concern as he put his hands in his pockets, like a coach struggling to watch the action.

Napoleon finally stood, but made no attempt whatsoever to approach the house. This kind of noise and lightshow, especially in this neighborhood, would have his local counterparts here in no time anyway. But he noticed something else in The Gray Man's face, something he never expected to see: worry.

He saw movement behind him and realized Parker had made it to a standing position now as well.

They all were facing the large bay window at the front of the house.

"She is strong," The Gray Man said softly. "Remember, Kyle, what I told you."

Napoleon had gone from stunned to shocked; Kyle Fasano had been the center of this entire thing from the beginning? "How…?" Napoleon asked.

The Gray Man looked earnestly at Napoleon and asked. "Do you think pigeons, Detective Villa, are the only things that need saving?"

Napoleon swallowed hard against the emotions that bloomed in his chest. "¡*Dios mio!*"

The Gray Man nodded lovingly. "Yes, Napoleon. Yours and mine. Always and forever."

CHAPTER 34

A s he unleashed the whips, Kyle realized that he'd called forth a stronger level of his power; he was a little overwhelmed by the blue that was coursing from his arms and down the length of the whips.

Victoria took two steps backwards at the sight of them.

The whips were bouncing on the floor like fallen power lines. Kyle flung the one attached to his right hand out across the hall, but it was poorly aimed; it deflected off the wall nearest the den, and then bounced recklessly through the air… right towards the whip he snapped in his left hand.

At his core he suddenly realized that this was a bad thing, that if the two whips joined together it would be too much power, too much—

The whips shot down the walls and across the tiled floor in the hallway. He thought for a second he was going to get lucky, that they wouldn't intersect, but just before hitting Victoria, they crossed, forming a blue "x," and then everything exploded.

He was thrust hard and headfirst into the corner of the wall nearest the den before he ricocheted off the opposite wall and down to the floor, the power of the explosion crushing the breath out of his lungs. Stunned, dizzy, horrified, he reached out one hand to the wall and climbed up it, like a weak-legged toddler, unsure of his ability to stand.

He heard Sebastian screaming and Victoria yelling in some guttural, foreign language. She was going after him, Kyle sensed it, and he begged his eyes to correct themselves, to go from vibrating violently to fixed again so that he could get his bearings back.

The world was a screeching echo and then... not. Clarity flooded him as the blue seemed to turn inward, into him, to heal him.

To his astonishment, the explosion had not affected the hall and kitchen. But it had wounded Victoria; she was trying to get to Sebastian in the den but she was dragging one leg, which had a huge hole blown through the thigh.

Kyle half-rushed, half-stumbled towards her, the effort blurring his vision to near nothingness before he ran headlong into her. They bounced off each other momentarily before he grabbed her in a bear hug.

She turned on him instantly, clawing with her talons at his neck and shoulders like a panicked bird. Her black eyes glistening and raw...

Wait... her *black* eyes. Like Caitlyn's. The same Caitlyn who had been human enough to struggle internally back in that hotel room. Her eyes weren't red, like all the demons that had come after him, but black. She could be saved. Which meant Victoria could be saved, too.

Closing his eyes, Kyle told himself to remember what The Gray Man had said, but it was hard. His body was screaming for him to defend himself and his mind was searching for the words.

God, please, what was it? What did he say, what...

Find a way to remind her that she once loved you.

That's what The Gray Man had said. Yes. It made sense now. Sebastian. Victoria. Both. Maybe being a millionth meant that you tried to save everyone. Maybe you could. Maybe you couldn't. But you had to try.

He reached his mind back, unspooling it like fishing line, out and over a river of years, knowing he would find her; because you never really leave your first love and you never really forget them—you just simply move on, slinging the lessons that they taught you, of joy and love and vulnerability, over your shoulder, like so many fish.

When he saw her there, tucked between his memories, she was at last *his* Victoria, the one no other boy or man would *ever* know, because each of us can be only one person, at one time, to each love we have.

He saw Victoria, her hair blowing in the wind, as he lifted her up and spun her in the park, her brown Pearl Jam t-shirt with long tan sleeves soft and slippery in his hands, her eyes looking up to the sweet blue sky, a chain around her neck with a small wooden cross suspended from its length. Her lips were soft and her freckles dim under the brightness of the sun. It was the summer day that they'd picnicked in the park on Subway sandwiches and Big Gulp Slurpees, and she'd dared him.

Dared him to be silly and foolish.

Dared him to show everyone at the park how much he loved her.

For a moment Kyle felt guilty for the fullness of the memory, that it could still affect him so much, that it might be a betrayal of Tamara somehow. But no, it was okay. He was remembering Victoria as he once loved her, and even though he didn't love her anymore he could still care for her, and care what had happened to her these past years that had led her to the darkness, to her current state of being, and now, for whatever reason, back into his arms.

"Stop!" she screamed, pushing at him, writhing against the blue that was leaking out of him. "I don't want to think about all of that. It hurts!"

He held her close, an awkward hug now blossoming into a full embrace, the blood from his wounds dripping down his back, hot and sticky, as the power in him drained away. That was okay, too.

Kyle glanced over at Sebastian; he was moaning and coming around.

"Kyle! You let go of me!" The fear in her voice was pal-pable. The blue had evidently been bad enough for her, but Kyle realized that it was his *memories,* leaking out of him now, that were hurting her far worse.

He stumbled forwards, closer to the portal, tightening his grip and wincing against the pain across his chest. He was bleeding, a lot, but that didn't matter now. He was filling up with love, pure and untainted lost and regained, and he was using that love to heal whomever he could, including himself.

He'd always held Victoria close in his heart, a tiny bit of love within a nest of regret.

Now he understood. He'd been sent on this mission to deliver the only thing that could ever save Victoria: that tiny bit of love. A reminder that no love ever truly dies; it's simply left behind, like an artifact that we can dig up later to discover something about ourselves.

"Shhhh," he said into her ear. "I'm here, Victoria. I'm here."

"Let me go! Let me go!" she screamed, pulling back briefly from him to slam her fists into his chest. "You never loved me. You just used me. I was nothing to you. It was all a lie!"

The words tore into his heart. It had been a long time since Kyle had cried. Really cried. But his sadness at what she was saying was more than he could bear. "Stop it, Victoria. Please, stop. That's not true and you know it."

"I hate you. I never loved you either! I didn't!"

He held her tight, but kept moving towards the portal, not because he wanted to but because he knew he had to—in case she didn't surrender. It was just a few steps closer across the tiled floor before they might have to say goodbye forever.

Again, he called to mind the real Victoria and forced his memories into her: Victoria in her yellow bikini on the beach during their first summer together. They shared a sauce sandwich from the deli on Second Street later that same day, making a mess of their faces as they laughed at their nervousness. Just days later, after a walk in the mall, they shared their first kiss, a soft, electric thing that filled him with so much hope for life. Electric. Electric blue.

His heart and lungs began to expand in his chest, almost to the point of bursting. As they closed in on the edge of the portal Victoria reached out to either side, gripping at the edges of it, digging her claws in deep so she wouldn't budge.

"You silly, senseless idiot! Nothing you do is going to work. Nothing!"

Still crying, he pushed harder against her grip, his cheek against hers now as he let the blue emanate and envelope them. She screamed, a heinous and bitter wail filled with rage, and struggled desperately against his grip.

The memories still hadn't been enough. He had to reach her somehow, someway, for this to work. But how? Whose love could she trust, from their days together? Whose love had been the purest? One she could never, in a million years, suspect?

The answer came to him like a soft breeze on a still day.

"Victoria? Do you remember Vinnie?"

"Shut up!"

"He still asks about you," Kyle whispered with a smile.

Kyle thought of his brother now, living in a private, assisted-living community with fellow autistic adults. He had friends now. And a life all his own. And he still had his crush.

The screams coming from within the portal stopped and she stilled instantly in his arms.

When she spoke it was in the soft, timid voice of youth.

"Kyle?" she asked, sounding confused.

The cheek against his grew soft, and he turned to look at her. The black eyes were gone, their metallic sheen washed away. Looking back at him was the face he remembered. His Victoria was back, but sadly, shockingly, only for a moment.

The black exploded like ink from her pupils and Kyle felt a power from hell itself begin to flood her.

There was no time to be sad, just time to act.

He pushed forwards with all his weight and the blue around them erupted. It was the only option. The only way left to save the boy and fulfill his mission, because it was obvious now that he wasn't going to be able to save Victoria too.

Hugging her as tightly as he could, Kyle screamed in frustrated rage and pushed forwards with all his strength. Victoria's grip finally gave way, and they fell headlong into the portal—together.

Kyle Fasano had just enough time for one, final thought. A single word.

Tamara.

* * *

"No!" The Gray Man screamed, moving towards the house suddenly.

"What? What's happening?" Tamara pleaded.

The only other time she'd seen him he'd held an air of utter confidence, as if the power of faith not only filled him but sustained him. So an overwhelming panic sprang to her chest when she saw the look of utter pain and defeat that now crossed his face.

"What just happened?" she screamed, taking a few steps towards him, knowing this might not be the smartest idea, before she felt Detective Parker pulling her back by the wrist. She spun around to yell at him, but was shocked by the look of disbelief painted on his face.

They all stood in silence for a moment before The Gray Man began shaking his head. "This simply cannot be."

Tamara wanted to break free, to run into the house, to find Kyle.

"There's no use in it. He's gone," The Gray Man said, looking at her sadly, as if he'd read her mind.

"What're you talking about?" Tamara replied, her legs going weak. She looked to the house, to the door. She could make it if she ran full speed, she could... but it was no use. She sensed it. Maybe it was The Gray Man helping her to sense it, maybe it was just a wife's intuition, but the door and the house beyond it were like a void, no longer important, because Kyle wasn't there. At all.

"Oh my God," she cried, as she fell against Detective Parker and began to sob. "He's dead!"

"What?" Detective Napoleon said in shock.

"This cannot *be*!" The Gray Man screamed, the force of his voice like a shock wave, flattening the tall grass, swaying the bushes between the hill and the house, and rattling the trees beyond. His face drew back in anguish as he looked up pleadingly to the sky. "Father? Why? He repented, Father, deeply. You know this! How, Father? How has your will alone not prevented this?"

Detective Villa struggled to speak for a moment before he finally managed, "What's going on? His wife deserves to know."

The Gray Man turned to Napoleon, then to Parker, and finally to Tamara. "Mrs. Fasano, you are a woman of faith."

It was a statement, not a question. But still, Tamara answered. "Yes."

"Then you know that not all things can be explained."

She pushed off Detective Parker and wiped her eyes. "This one *has* to be. It does!"

The Gray Man sighed, and then nodded gently. "Your husband was chosen to save another soul after he forfeited his to sin. This happens every single day in your world; the saving and the sinning, the giving and the taking, the hurting and the helping. Sometimes your kind help each other. Sometimes my kind step in and help. But either way? It's about salvation. It's about the next life after this life, do you understand?"

"And?"

"He succeeded in saving the soul that was the object of his mission, that of a young man, the only person left there in that house now. But Kyle had to sacrifice himself to do so."

Tamara clenched her teeth as rage built against her pain. "No. That's not fair. I want him back. You said he repented. To God, yes, and to me too." The tears and sorrow came over her all at once. "He called me. He wrote me. He said he was sorry."

"Sometimes repentance isn't enough," Detective Villa suddenly spoke up. "Or prayer, or any of that stuff, sometimes evil just wins."

His words seemed to shock The Gray Man. "Do you honestly believe that, Villa?"

"I don't need to just believe it. I've seen it."

The Gray Man shook his head, stepped away from them and began to pace, back and forth, in short steps along the edge of the lawn, his head down. After a minute or so he stopped and, speaking to no one in particular, stated flatly, "I'm going after him."

"What?" Tamara asked incredulously. "Going where? Where is he?"

He looked at her with conviction. "There's no easy way to put this, Mrs. Fasano. I'm sorry. But your husband is in hell."

It was as if he'd slapped her across the face. Hard. She stumbled backwards, directly into Detective Parker's arms, which evidently forced him out of his silence. "What's going on here, man? This is bullshit. This is all crazy. Nap? Tell me what's going on."

Napoleon said nothing.

"I'm going after him," The Gray Man continued. "I have to. You want me to, don't you, Mrs. Fasano?"

Tamara nodded.

"But there's a problem. My kind isn't allowed there. Without a soul to shield me, they will spot me in seconds as soon as I arrive."

"And?" Parker asked.

The Gray Man squinted at them. "I have to find someone willing to go with me, do you understand, Mrs. Fasano?"

Tamara's thoughts were overwhelming. It was obvious what she could do to help save her husband, to fulfill the vows she'd made on their wedding day. No matter what. But then she thought of Janie and Seth? How in the world could she ever leave them, all alone? Kyle would never want that. How could—

"Take me."

It was Detective Villa, a look of resolve on his face.

The last strands of an eerie moonlight were now fading away behind clouds that had drifted in between the stars.

The Gray Man stepped towards Detective Villa and they stood there, eye to eye.

"You? The man who has lost his faith? You of all people are the one willing to risk going to hell?"

* * *

"Yes," Napoleon replied firmly before swallowing hard. He couldn't believe he was saying it.

Napoleon felt The Gray Man's eyes bore into his very being, pouring into every corner of his heart and mind, turning over all the boulders that were concealing his darkest thoughts.

"So much of why you suffer is due to what you hide, Villa," The Gray Man murmured. "We'll deal with that later."

Napoleon nodded. The Gray Man had evidently looked inside his mind, and had seen things. Not the least of which was Joaquin Murrieta.

"You decide with vengeance in you, Villa," The Gray Man said.

Napoleon looked away.

The Gray Man continued. "But in theory that might increase the odds of this working. Your soul can be my vehicle, and your lust for vengeance my disguise."

Napoleon felt Mrs. Fasano staring at him incredulously. "You don't even know him," she said meekly. "How can you do this? I should go."

"No. No you shouldn't, Mrs. Fasano. You have kids. They've already lost their father. Maybe forever. To lose their mother, too? No. I've been there, Mrs. Fasano. No kid should have to go through life that way."

Now it was Parker's turn. "Nap. I can't believe any of this is really happening, but if it is, ya gotta think this through," he pleaded.

A quiet fell among them, then The Gray Man turned back to Napoleon. "Do you truly realize what you're committing to?"

Napoleon nodded, then gave voice to the only concern he'd felt since first speaking up. "There's just…" He looked at Parker. "My little nephew. His name is Efren."

Parker looked stunned.

"Please look after him."

Parker nodded. "I will… until you get back."

Napoleon barely knew Parker, but so far in this case he'd shown all the right instincts and, more importantly, a good heart. "What was that you said, Parker? When we were talking about surviving in Afghanistan?"

Parker looked at Napoleon grimly. "If you want to survive hell—"

"—you gotta cover the backs of the guys who are in it with you," Napoleon finished.

Parker's face grew firm. "I got you covered on this."

"And if I don't come back?" Napoleon pressed.

"I'll still look after him," Parker said with a nod.

The determination in Parker's voice brought a peace to Napoleon's decision that helped make it final. He glanced around at everyone, locking eyes with Mrs. Fasano for a moment, and he smiled. She *was* a good wife. At least in this whole, crazy, topsy-turvy case, he'd gotten that much right. Finally, he looked back to The Gray Man.

"Are you sure?" The Gray Man asked.

"I'm sure," he said, and thinking again of Joaquin Murietta, he added, "After all, what better place to conquer your demons, right?"

The slightest, most infinitesimal smile crossed The Gray Man's lips for just a sliver of a second, and then it was gone. "He's *already* in hell, Villa. It's only the hell in *you* that now needs to be conquered."

A fear and trembling washed over Napoleon as The Gray Man approached him and put his arm around his shoulders. His body grew warm as a light from within him began to expand and spread.

It was beautiful. So beautiful.

He thought of his grandmother.

She was right; she'd always told him that—

* * *

Tamara couldn't believe her eyes. The glow around The Gray Man began to expand, enveloping him and Detective Villa.

Then they were gone and the immensity of the moment finally hit her.

"What just happened?" Tamara begged Detective Parker, who was the only one left with her, but he just shook his head.

She looked to the house and then to the sky. "Kyle? Kyle!" Her screams echoed across the lawn and down the hill.

Sirens were approaching, their wails in the distance only adding to her own now as she broke away from Detective Parker and stood before the house, determined to rush in, to see for herself that there was nothing left of her husband within.

She never made it.

A realization pierced her heart, hitting her with such an acute pain that she dropped to her knees on the lawn just before she reached the porch. She dug her fingers deep into the grass in an effort to hold it at bay.

There was no use.

Kyle was gone.

The love of her life was gone.

Just like that.

ACKNOWLEDGEMENTS

A LOT GOES INTO TEACHING and helping a writer to learn how to properly listen to the voices in his head. I'm pretty sure the process never ends. But so far, along the way, I've had some amazing people come into my life in this regard and this page is for them.

To my grade school teacher whose name is now sadly lost to me: thank you for taking the shy kid in the corner and telling him that he could write. After you came Mrs. Gilchrist at Jefferson Middle School, who taught me how to push on, Mr. Morgan McSweeney at West Torrance High, who taught me how to believe in myself, and Dr. Howard Hertz at Pasadena City College, who taught me how to tell the truth.

Thanks also to the long-standing members of my Novel Writers Group: Beverly Diehl, Bruce Bartels, Vance Gloster, Kim Townsel and Hilaree Robinson. You have all cared for me, encouraged me and sometimes critiqued the hell out of me! Also, to my beta readers: Tinky Schmidt, Amouri Burger Maryke Burger, Melissa O'Gara, Herbert Smith and Dean Baker....I couldn't possibly be more thankful to any of you.

A special nod goes out to my creative team, including editor extraordinaire Sophie Playle of Liminal Pages, Andrew and Rebecca Brown at Design for Writers and the awesome web design work of Laird Sapir at Memphis McKay.

A great big thanks and I love you to my wife Maxime, my son Anthony and my daughter Sophia. Finally, to my Dear Cousin, Diana Kobus, thanks for being my muse.

ABOUT THE AUTHOR

Tony Faggioli began writing stories in the 5th grade and continued doing so until college, when he gave up writing to pursue a very short career in politics and a much longer career in business. One day, he finally realized that neither brought him anywhere near the amount of joy as writing. Born in Pittsburgh, Pennsylvania, he was raised in Los Angeles, California and graduated from the University of Southern California. He is a happily married father of two kids, two dogs and one pretty awesome goldfish.

Website: tonyfaggioli.com

Facebook: facebook.com/tfaggioli

Twitter: twitter.com/steelertony

Books:
One In A Million (Book 1 of "The Millionth" trilogy)
A Million to One (Book 2 of "The Millionth" trilogy)
One Plus One   (Book 3 of "The Millionth" trilogy)

Coming in 2017, "The Snow Globe", a psychological thriller.

44502790R00229

Made in the USA
San Bernardino, CA
16 January 2017